JOHN EVERSON

FIVE DEATHS FOR SEVEN SONGBIRDS

This is a **FLAME TREE PRESS** book

Text copyright © 2022 John Everson

FLAME TREE PRESS
6 Melbray Mews, London, SW6 3NS, UK
flametreepress.com

US sales, distribution and warehouse:
Simon & Schuster
simonandschuster.biz

UK distribution and warehouse:
Marston Book Services Ltd
marston.co.uk

Thanks to the Flame Tree Press team, including:
Taylor Bentley, Frances Bodiam, Federica Ciaravella, Don D'Auria,
Chris Herbert, Josie Karani, Molly Rosevear, Will Rough, Mike Spender,
Cat Taylor, Maria Tissot, Nick Wells, Gillian Whitaker.

The cover is created by Flame Tree Studio with
thanks to Nik Keevil and Shutterstock.com.
The font families used are Avenir and Bembo.

Flame Tree Press is an imprint of Flame Tree Publishing Ltd

flametreepublishing.com

A copy of the CIP data for this book is available from the British Library
and the Library of Congress.

HB ISBN: 978-1-78758-628-4
PB ISBN: 978-1-78758-626-0
ebook ISBN: 978-1-78758-629-1

Printed and bound in Great Britain by Clays Ltd, Elcograf S.p.A

JOHN EVERSON

FIVE DEATHS FOR SEVEN SONGBIRDS

FLAME TREE PRESS
London & New York

PROLOGUE

Her footsteps echoed on the tile floor even though she wore gym shoes. It was that still. The corridors of the old building stood silent and empty, most of the lights turned out. Eleven o'clock at night was not a popular time for practicing, which was precisely why Gen liked to come here at this time. She had the conservatory to herself. Once in a while, she might see a light on in one of the professors' offices. Professor Von Klein, in particular, often kept late hours, and she knew from experience why. Tonight, however, his office was dark.

Gen flipped on the light in the hallway that led to the piano practice rooms and then walked down to room 342. She reserved it at this time every term for three nights a week, not that there was any competition for use. There wasn't a single note of music echoing anywhere in the building tonight. Hell, half of the students weren't even in residence yet. It was only August 21st. Lectures and classes for the new term started next week.

She turned on the overhead lights and closed the door behind her. The room was small but comfortable, kind of like a den; a black Steinway baby grand dominated the center of space, its lid raised and keys exposed. Gen shook her head. Sloppy – somebody had not closed it up earlier.

There were wooden cabinets that completely took up two walls of the room. The smaller ones held deep piles of music, some of which she was sure dated back to the eighteen hundreds after having casually explored the yellowing, sometimes handwritten staffs in the past. Floor-to-ceiling cabinets housed old brass and percussion instruments. Students also used them to hang coats in during the winter months. All of the dark wood made it feel as if you were playing in the study of an old upscale mansion.

Gen dropped her bag on the floor next to the piano bench and fished out the music she'd brought to practice – a Liszt piece that she'd be using to audition for the seasonal soloist competition next Tuesday. She set the music up on the brass-hinged wooden holder, shifted her position on the bench, and began to play. She stopped before she reached the end of the first page. Her fingers had stumbled on two sixteenth note runs. Gen lifted her hands from the keyboard with a grimace. If she did that during the audition, she was DOA.

She took a deep breath, willing herself to focus, and was about to start again when something creaked behind her. Gen swiveled on the bench to stare at the cabinets. Nothing was out of place. The doors were all closed. She got up and looked out of the narrow glass window in the door to the hall. There was nobody in sight.

Gen shrugged and returned to the bench. It was an old building. Old things creaked, she told herself. Still, when she started to play once more, she felt uneasy.

As she reached the intricate sixteenth note runs again, she could have sworn she heard another noise. She made it through the passage, but as soon as she did she lifted her fingers from the keys. The hair on the back of her neck was standing up. Why?

She practiced here all the time at this hour. Why was she spooked over a couple of creaks tonight?

Gen closed her eyes and willed the uneasiness away. The building was settling. And she needed to get some work done. Von Klein was a man of many faces. The professor appeared very friendly most of the time, but when he was behind the audition desk, he was a tyrant.

That was what she needed to be afraid of, not old joists settling. Gen started the piece once more, and was nearly through page two when she abruptly stopped playing. This time, not because she heard something, but because she didn't. She repeated the last measure, and sure enough, when she played the low E, there was silence.

Odd.

She pressed on the key, and when there was still no sound, repeated the motion harder. And harder.

Nope. The lower register E was dead. Weird. It had been fine yesterday.

She got up, walked around to the side of the piano and looked inside to see if something had fallen on the string, deadening it.

"Huh," she murmured as she stared at the pristine rows of golden strings.

There was a gap in the lower section. Someone had cut out a string. But they hadn't even bothered to remove the ends. The orphaned wire ties were still in the holes.

"What the hell," Gen said. This practice night was not going well.

It was about to get much worse.

Gen shook her head and went back to the bench. She was going to work for the next hour if it killed her. There were not many days left before the auditions.

She made it to the *pianissimo* section on page four when she heard an extended creak that came from directly behind her. Gen's fingers stopped. She turned quickly. Her heart was beating double time. That increased when she saw that one of the tall cabinet doors was open.

It had not been open two minutes ago.

As she scanned the room, the overhead lights suddenly went out. The cabinets disappeared in the sudden black. Gen turned towards the door.

Something moved in the darkness; a silhouette caught and shifted in the dim light that seeped in through the window from the hall. It looked like a person's head. She almost screamed, but then stopped herself. There was nobody in the building close enough to hear or help.

But there was definitely somebody in the practice room with her.

Somebody who apparently meant her harm.

Gen shifted her feet around to the side of the bench. She didn't know what the other person intended…but it couldn't end well for her. If she could slip behind the body of the piano, she would have a straight shot to bolt for the door. It was a long run to the front entry of the building, but she'd been on the track team back in high school. That gave her a fighting chance.

Her stomach filled with ice and her legs felt frozen, but Gen forced her body to move, to rise from the bench despite the paralyzing fear. She had to get away.

As she stood, something abruptly pinched her neck and yanked her off her feet. Gen collapsed to the bench, which rocked dangerously, teetering on the brink for just a moment before toppling completely. Her whole body spilled to the floor. The impact of her tailbone on the wood made her open her mouth to cry out. But the pinch on her neck tightened to a throttling tourniquet that choked any sound away. All that came out was a gurgle. The pressure around her throat tightened; her eyes bugged out as the force cut off her oxygen. Gen lashed out with her fists, punching in angry desperation at the air all around her. She connected with something firm. Maybe a shoulder....

The noose around her neck drew ever tighter. She stopped her attack and instead reached to the back of her neck to try to pry whatever was around her throat away. Her fingers gripped the noose; it was cold and thin. Metallic. It cut into the skin of her fingertips and she couldn't loosen it at all.

As death stars blossomed across her vision, Gen realized too late what had become of the missing piano string.

There was a blinding flash of light. And then a voice finally whispered in the returning dark.

"Live by the piano, die by the piano," it said.

CHAPTER ONE

The taxi pulled up in front of a small, but still imposing, five-story stone building. Two buildings, really. While they were interconnected on the bottom floors, the structure diverged above that into two triangular roofs that rose on opposite sides of the L-shaped structure that was bisected by a street corner. The place looked hundreds of years old. The stone facade, which might once have been white, now wrapped the structure in a rough, uneven mix of grey and black and mossy green. Dozens of narrow vertical windows rose from the street level in each half of the building.

The driver said something in Flemish, and Eve held out a twenty Euro note. She trusted he would give her correct change. He scowled slightly at the bill, and dropped a handful of gold coins into her palm. Then he quickly exited the car and pulled her two suitcases from the trunk. When she picked them up from the sidewalk, he nodded. "*Daag*," he said, and a moment later the taxi shot away from the curb.

"Goodbye," she murmured after him. "I know you know how to say it."

She knew most people in Belgium spoke at least a smattering of English, if they weren't completely fluent in English, French and Flemish. But there were always those who resented foreigners. She hoped that her reception at the Conservatory would be better. The old weathered building didn't look very welcoming. It loomed aged and tired against a grey sky.

"Not as tired as I feel," she whispered. Eve walked towards the arched wooden door on the corner. It was not even noon here yet, but she was wiped out. She'd left New York at dinnertime, and arrived in Brussels at eight in the morning. Then she'd navigated the train system to head north to Ghent, where she'd caught a taxi to the outskirts of the university. It had been a very long night.

She stopped at the door and took a breath. Then she reached out to pull on the handle and step into her new life as a student at an exclusive satellite building of the Royal Conservatory.

"Welcome to the Eyrie," a pleasant, lilting feminine voice said as Eve stepped from the humid warmth of the street into a cool, shadowed foyer. It took a moment for her eyes to adjust from the overcast but light skies outside to the dark, wooden confines of the interior of the music building. The woman stood behind a desk along the wall to her right.

"You must be Evelyn Springer," the woman said. She was tall and thin, her hair a wild tousle of brown and blonde twists.

"Yes," Eve said with a surprised smile. "But please, call me Eve."

"We've been expecting you," the woman said. "My name is Mrs. Freer. I'm the house manager and you can come to me if you have any problems during your time here. If you can just sign in, I'll get Philip to help with your bags." She pushed a black ledger to the edge of the desk and pointed at an empty line.

Eve took the proffered pen and quickly scrawled her name. "Thanks, but I can handle the bags," she said.

The woman gave a thin smile and shook her head to disagree. "That may be, but you won't want to. Your room is on the fifth floor of the East Tower, and the elevator is not working today." She picked up a phone from a holder on the wall and dialed three numbers. After a few seconds, she said something in a language Eve did not understand, and then hung up.

"He'll be down in just a minute," Mrs. Freer said. "You'll be sharing a room with Kristina Jones. She's been here a few days already, so she will be able to…show you the ropes, I think you say?" She pointed down a narrow corridor. "You'll find breakfast served in the cafeteria at six in the morning. They clean up at eight, so don't sleep in if you want food. Lunch is then from eleven to one and dinner is at six p.m. Of course, there are many places down the street and along the water to eat at if you miss a mealtime here."

Mrs. Freer pulled a large envelope from a drawer and held it out. "This is your course schedule and some helpful information about the institution. There will be an opening welcome lecture by Professor Von Klein on Monday morning in the Grand Hall. It's expected that all new and returning students attend."

A burly man with deep-set eyes and a chin like a hammer emerged then from a door behind the desk. He wore jeans and a blue-checked shirt that was half unbuttoned to show a white t-shirt beneath. Eve couldn't tell if he'd been sleeping or working. His eyes looked sullen and dark.

"There you are, Philip," Mrs. Freer said. "This is Eve Springer. She's our new pianist...from the United States. Please take her and her things up to Room 505."

The man grunted something at the house marm and swooped in on Eve's bags like a hawk. "This way," he said in a low growl. He led her down the hall away from the front desk. Eve noticed that he walked with a strange gait, as if one of his legs was longer than the other. Maybe it was just something with his shoes; he wore thick black work boots. They looked heavy, with Frankenstein's monster soles.

"I can take one," Eve argued, but he did not turn or acknowledge her offer. Instead, he led her past an elevator with a sign taped across the doors. A circle with a line through it. The universal symbol of NO.

He set one of the bags down and opened a door to a stairwell. She would soon marvel at his stamina. It only took two flights before Eve was breathing heavy and she wasn't carrying anything but herself. But Philip just kept marching upwards and around as the stairs turned like a corkscrew up and through each level.

"Wow," she gasped when they finally stepped out into a short hallway. "I sure hope the elevator isn't broken long."

That drew a gust of laughter from behind her. Eve turned and saw a girl in shorts and a pink halter top unlocking a room. "That elevator is always going out," the girl said. "That's why they stick the newbies on the highest floor. Welcome to the fifth floor of hell!"

The girl winked and ducked into her room before Eve could think of anything to say.

Philip merely grunted and set her bags down in front of a white door. An oval metal plate was screwed to the right of it with black numbers that read 505. He unlocked the door and handed the key to her. Eve realized that she had no idea if she should tip him, or if so, how much. But she fumbled in her pocket and pulled out a two Euro coin to hand to him.

"Thanks," she said.

He pocketed the coin, but Eve couldn't tell if the lines around his mouth were the wrinkles of a smile or a glare. He turned and clomped away to disappear down the stairwell.

Eve sighed and stepped into her new room.

It was a small space for two people. A counter with an oval mirror above it and two drawers below filled the wall to her right. To the left, two bunk beds had been built into the wall. In front of them, a small two-person couch faced a flatscreen TV mounted on the wall. A desk that matched the blond wood of the bunk beds stood beneath two narrow windows.

There was only one picture on the wall, but then again, there was very little unoccupied wall space. It showed a violinist playing on a beautiful classical stage. On the floor nearby, Eve saw the telltale shape of a violin case. So...she knew why her roommate was here. Just not where she was.

Eve set her suitcases down and didn't bother to unpack. She just needed to lie down. Judging from the comforter on the lower bed and the plain sheets of the bed above, she guessed that her roommate had claimed the ground floor. She didn't care at this point. Eve climbed the built-in ladder and flopped with a moan on the thin mattress.

In her mind she replayed the last twelve hours of her journey from Grand Central Station to here.

Before she reached Ghent in her memories, she was asleep.

CHAPTER TWO

"I take it you're my new roommate and not just some loony who wandered in off the street?"

The voice was female, and very British. Eve pushed her head off the pillow to sit up, eyes still blinking the fuzzy hold of sleep away. A dark-haired girl with a pert nose and welcoming smile sat at the desk across the room watching her.

"Oh, um, hello," Eve said. She felt embarrassed that someone had walked in on her sleeping. "I'm sorry, I just had to take a little nap after the trip. It's a long ride from New York City. My name is Eve."

The other girl nodded. "I hoped you were. Otherwise this could get quite awkward. I'm Kristina."

"Good to meet you!" Eve said and flipped her leg over the edge to climb down the ladder.

"I hope you don't mind that I took the bottom bunk," Kristina said when Eve reached the floor. "I don't like heights."

Eve shrugged. "No problem. Have you been here long?"

"Almost two weeks," she said. "As soon as they opened the doors, I hopped on a train. Couldn't get out of London fast enough. And it's only a couple hours from King's Cross to Brussels."

"Oh wow," Eve said. "I've always wanted to go to London."

The other girl rolled her eyes. "You can have it. Bunch of wankers there."

Eve laughed. "They're everywhere, you know."

"I suppose," Kristina said. "But I swear the lot of them around my house were intolerable." She waved at the picture on the wall. "Anyway, you can probably tell I'm here for violin. What's your instrument?"

"Piano," Eve said. "I'm working on my master's in composition."

Kristina frowned slightly.

"Is this your first year," Eve asked, "or were you here last term?"

Kristina shook her head. "Nope, I'm a noob, just like you. I think everyone on fifth floor is. They say if you survive up here the first year, you get to move downstairs."

"What's so horrible about fifth floor?"

Kristina raised an eyebrow. "These old buildings don't have a lot of insulation, you know? So, I'm told we're going to be hot for the next couple months and then cold all winter. I hope you brought blankets."

"I didn't bring much of anything," Eve said. "I figured I'd get what I needed here."

"Sounds like a shopping day trip to Brussels is in your future," Kristina said. "But first, I'd suggest dinner. The hall just opened. Are you hungry?"

Eve's stomach audibly growled at the mention of food, and she laughed. "I guess so. Let me freshen up and use the restroom. Can you just tell me where one is?"

Kristina led her down the hall to a small communal bathroom with five stalls and an open shower area. When she came out, they went straight to the stairwell.

"From what they tell me, we'll also get to know these stairs better than the elevator," Kristina said. "Although, I have to say, it *was* working just yesterday."

By the time they reached the first floor and walked through the lobby, Eve was short of breath. She'd done plenty of walking in New York, but the long halls and stairs of this building were really going to get her in shape.

Mrs. Freer was still there behind the entry desk, and smiled faintly as they walked past. "Hi, Lucie," Kristina said to her with a wave. Eve noted the first name. The house marm hadn't told her that.

Two girls and a guy were talking in the corridor as they approached. Eve caught just a sliver of their conversation before they fell silent.

"*...so much blood...*"

"...but do you think they'll catch him?"

"How do you know it was a guy..."

"They said that her neck was barely..."

A girl in dark blue shorts and faded tan sandals abruptly stopped talking as they approached, and Eve could feel all three sets of eyes follow them as they passed and entered the cafeteria.

"What was that about?" she asked. "They looked at us like we were Martians."

Kristina stuck out her tongue. "Third year snobs," she said. "You don't need to know them."

"Sounded like they were talking about a killer," Eve said.

Kristina stopped and turned toward her. "They probably were," she said. Her face grew troubled. "I might as well tell you now, because you'll hear it soon enough. Genevieve DuPont was murdered in one of the piano practice rooms in the North Tower last night. She was one of the top students, and it happened right here...so everyone is pretty much in shock. She studied with Aldo Lado in Switzerland and won a bunch of awards. Genevieve was Professor Von Klein's star pianist last year."

"So, what happened?" Eve asked.

Kristina made a face and her eyes grew large. "She was practicing alone late at night, and some crazy trapped her in the room and strangled her with a piano wire. Everyone is pretty nervous about it, right now. They haven't caught the killer, so what if he comes back?"

Eve felt a cold spot in the pit of her stomach. She had been ecstatic when she'd won admittance to the Eyrie. It was one of the more prestigious music finishing schools in Europe. There were only a few dozen students admitted each term. But now it felt like she'd walked into danger. "Geez, do you think he will?" she said.

"I don't know, but I wouldn't use the practice rooms after dark if I was you," Kristina said.

★   ★   ★

The cafeteria did not offer a smorgasbord of choices, but the food they did have smelled amazing. Eve took a plate of pork loin with some kind of brown gravy and a side of rice pilaf and followed Kristina to a table with a half dozen other students. The room was not huge, but the twenty or thirty people in it were clustered at a handful of tables in different corners of the room. Social cliques were the same in every country, Eve mused.

Before they sat, Kristina introduced two very animated girls and a guy wearing a distorted cubist art t-shirt with a German phrase she couldn't read. "This is Jean and Barbara and Sienna," Kristina said. "They're on our floor."

Eve recognized Barbara as the girl who had said the elevators never worked when she'd first arrived. Barbara smiled at her in recognition.

"Now you've met half of the people on our end of the fifth floor," Kristina laughed. "Misery loves its own company!"

"And I'm Elena and this is Erika," one of the other two girls at the table offered. "We have graduated from the fifth floor," she said with a flawless white smile.

While they wore different outfits, Eve realized that she couldn't tell the two apart. They both had shoulder-length dark hair, perfect complexions and wide expressive eyes dressed in long dark lashes. They could have been Maybelline models, if they weren't wearing sweatpants and t-shirts.

Kristina pulled out a chair for herself and another for Eve so that they could join the group.

They settled in and soon Eve learned that Elena and Erika were second-year Italian twins from the fourth floor who each played soprano saxophone, while Jean was a bearded first-year German percussionist and Barbara and Sienna were actually native Belgians who could form their own string section if they were so inclined. They played it all.

Some of the group had already been out together, exploring the old town section of Ghent, which they said boasted an old castle with a medieval torture chamber museum and some good historic and modern bars along the main waterway. "We'll take you there, maybe tomorrow," Kristina promised.

It was Sienna who broke a lull in the conversation with talk of the murder.

"Did you see Genevieve's Facebook?" she asked Kristina.

Kristina shook her head. "No," she answered. "They'd taken it down before I heard about it."

"Took what down?" Eve asked.

Barbara and Sienna gave each other looks and then focused on their dinner plates.

"Does she know about it?" Jean asked.

Kristina nodded. "I told her a little while ago."

"It was pretty creepy," he said.

"What?" Eve asked.

Kristina grimaced and said, "Somehow the killer got access to Gen's Facebook account. After he strangled her, he posted a picture of her. They say he took it while killing her."

"He had to have," Jean said. "Although I don't know how he did it while he was still strangling her. You could see her face was all red and her mouth was open like she was screaming. But the worst part was her eyes. You could just see that she was still alive, but that her light was going out."

"Can we not talk about it anymore?" one of the twins asked. Her accent reminded Eve of old spaghetti westerns. "Gen was a friend of mine."

Kristina whispered to Eve, "I'm glad I didn't see it."

Eve looked down at her plate and pushed it back. The pork had been delicious, but she found she wasn't hungry anymore.

CHAPTER THREE

The Eyrie's lecture hall turned out to be a small theater in the North Tower. Which made sense – Kristina said it doubled as the school's main concert performance space. Apparently, everyone living in the East Tower was there; the place was packed on Monday morning. It was not only the opening lecture of the semester, but rumors were that Prof. Klaus Von Klein would provide an update on Genevieve DuPont…so there wasn't a student who dared sleep in to miss it.

Eve felt a flutter in her stomach as she looked around at the throng. She was *actually* here. She was about to listen to the opening lecture at the Belgium Conservatory of Music's Eyrie, one of the most prestigious music enclaves in the world. There were negative vibes in the air because of the murder but…she couldn't get over the fact that a week ago, Eve had been in a tiny apartment in New York. Now she was halfway around the world, and about to see the world-famous Prof. Von Klein speak and officially open the semester. It was a little surreal.

The room was a buzz of student conversations when Eve and Kristina found seats; there were occasional bursts of laughter and multiple cries of "how have you been" in a variety of languages and accents from people who had not seen each other for weeks. But then, almost as if on cue, the volume of the entire room dropped to near nothing.

Eve looked up from her phone and saw why. An older man strode across the stage to the podium. He wore a grey tweed suit and looked thin but hale, his hair turning to silver but still full; his chin was hidden by a short, startlingly white beard. When he reached the microphone, he made a point of looking slowly from one side of the room to the other. When he smiled at the end of his survey, you could feel the warmth from twenty rows back.

"On behalf of the entire faculty, I would like to welcome you to the Eyrie," he began. His voice was rich and engaging, the accent faintly foreign. Eve felt a frisson of excitement. This was the moment she'd dreamed of for months.

"For those of you joining us for the first time, I cannot wait to meet you in person, and hear the music that is held in your hearts. You are the next wave of talent that will wash over us and leave us astounded and amazed. The sea is endless, but every new class brings its own unique brilliance. And for those who have been with us before…we've missed you. Welcome back. Together, we will all create things of beauty this year, songs and performances that have never existed in the past and will never grace the air exactly so again.

"Make no mistake, we will work hard, as we always do. The path to creation – worthwhile creation – is never fast or easy. You will make memories and music here that will color the rest of your lives. You will impact the lives of many others. I am proud to be a part of the process that will make that happen. What we do here? It matters. There are those who would dismiss the arts in favor of the study of commerce or medicine or other more…economical pursuits. But what we do here, what we train for, is the ultimate expression of the human spirit. The ability to transcend time and influence those who come five and ten generations later is not anything that an accounting professional, no disrespect, will ever achieve. You, here in this room, have the potential to do that. Most of you won't…but you could. And that's the promise that brings me back to this stage year after year. You are not here because you are dabblers. You are here because music is your life. And we will continue to hone the focus that you have spent years building…in the end, you will create more than music. You will transcend."

Eve felt a stir in her spine as he spoke those words. She was here to go to the next level…whatever that was. She yearned even more now for him to help guide her there.

"I have to address one thing that I know many of you are aware of. While we work here in something of a bubble to create art that will live beyond our own walk on this earth, the day-to-day politics and evils of the world still go on around us, and sometimes, enter our private walls unbidden. One of our own, Genevieve DuPont, was working this week to improve her own immense potential when someone took that away from her. From all of us. She was one of the best pianists I have ever had the pleasure to teach or...."

The professor's voice broke and he paused.

"The world is a lesser place without her music. That's all I can say. From a safety standpoint, we have asked for increased police surveillance after hours, and we are temporarily limiting the use of the music practice rooms. You all need the hours with your instruments, but after eight o'clock at night, practice will need to be confined to your rooms, or in group gatherings here in this hall. The individual practice rooms will be unavailable for late work this week, as we cannot have guards at all hours to guarantee your safety. This is not the kind of message I want to deliver on our opening week, but it is a reality of our world today. I trust you will appreciate the significance."

The exultation she'd felt just a few minutes before quickly melted away. There was crossing the world to live a dream. And then there was, as Prof. Von Klein said, reality.

He went on to talk about classes and individual instruction opportunities and more, but Eve was already looking forward to – and nervous about – her next meeting in the school. She was scheduled to have an in-person talk with the professor at eleven a.m. in his office.

"Do you have to play anything for Von Klein?" Kristina asked when Eve said how frightened she was of the introduction.

"No."

"Then what's the worry? Be yourself. You can't make a mistake with that."

"It's just that I've heard about him for years," Eve said. "I can't believe I'm actually going to *talk* to him."

Kristina snorted. "He's just a man. Don't kid yourself. His shite stinks just like anyone else's."

★   ★   ★

When eleven o'clock came, Eve was pacing just outside the professor's office. She'd climbed three flights of stairs in the North Tower (the elevator there was out too) and walked down a zigzag hallway with old wooden floors to arrive at faculty office 392. There was a tall, thin area of opaque glass next to the door. A small sign was fastened to the door that read *Professor Klaus Von Klein*. Beneath it was a sheet with a long list of fifteen-minute appointments scheduled throughout the day. At the top of the sheet, in headline-size letters, it read: *Do Not Knock. Wait Until The Door Is Open.*

Waiting put her nerves on edge. It also didn't help that now and then she heard the boom of a raised voice. She couldn't make out the words of what was being said, but it seemed like Von Klein was…yelling in there? She took a deep breath and walked down the otherwise quiet hall which apparently was the faculty wing — there were several closed doors with names on them, and another window with a list of appointments two doors down. Nobody else was walking the hall however.

When Von Klein's door finally opened, she nearly jumped. It was time, past her time, actually. Her legs grew rubbery.

A pale man in black plastic glasses, a pink and green plaid shirt and short-cropped orange hair walked out. Eve's inner voice whispered *geek!*

"Are you next?" he asked. When she nodded, he motioned her inside. "Sorry I ran over."

Eve stepped inside and pulled the door shut behind her.

The office was small, but well-appointed. An ornate wooden bookcase took up one wall, while a small spinet piano rested against the opposite. The professor sat behind a dark wood desk, with a window to the courtyard behind him.

"Evelyn Springer?" he asked.

"Yes," she said. She was too nervous to say anything else. He pointed to a wooden chair with burgundy upholstery before him. She sat.

"Your resume is excellent," he said. "And a Simonetti Scholar, as well. Most impressive. I'm anxious to hear you play."

"I am anxious to be able to," Eve said. "I've dreamed of being able to come here for years."

He smiled, a little thinly. "Well, the dream is over," he said. "Now the work begins. I've heard your audition recordings of course, but I'd like to see you play something." He gestured to the piano on the side of the room. "Would you mind?"

Eve felt her stomach clench. She had not prepared anything.

"What would you like to hear?" she asked. Her voice shook slightly.

His eyes seemed to laugh. "Whatever you enjoy playing. This is not an audition. You're in. I just want to see you at your instrument."

Eve stood and walked to the piano. It was old, but beautiful. The wood appeared to be mahogany; rich reddish brown with dark veins that was not simply square cut, but augmented with carved filigree edging and rounded sides. An ornate, classic spinet.

The keys were vaguely yellowed, but when Eve put her fingers down just to test a chord, the tone was wonderful. Rich and warm, just like the wood.

She launched into the dramatic urgent staccato opening of Ravel's 'Le Tombeau de Couperin: Toccata'. The professor listened and shook his head in appreciation for a minute or two, and then held up a hand and said, "That's enough."

Eve gulped and took her hands from the keys. She thought she'd played it well. What had he heard?

"I had no doubt that you were technically excellent, and that certainly was. But...what do you play for fun?" he asked. "What moves your soul? That's what I want to hear."

Eve put her fingers back on the keys and hesitated for a moment before she delicately began to play the song that she always played when she was alone late at night. Pat Metheny's 'Letter from Home'. A melancholy but stirring solo piece. It wasn't classical and it wasn't complex, but if you played it with the right touch, you could literally make people cry.

The professor's face warmed in recognition as soon as she began. This time, he didn't stop her, but let her play the song through all the way to the end. When she finished, pulling her fingers back from the keys as the last notes lingered in the air, he put his hands together and clapped four times.

"Well played," he said. His face beamed. "So, you're a jazz fan then?"

When she nodded, he reached into the top drawer of his desk and pulled out some sheet music. "I have an opening for a pianist in the Songbirds jazz combo. It's an extracurricular band, usually with around a dozen students, that we have sponsored as part of the Eyrie's ensembles for more than fifty years. The group plays periodically at clubs in town. Auditions start on Thursday in the North Tower at four p.m. You can apply at the main office for a slot. After what I just heard, I'd really like to see you try out."

Eve got up, took the music from his hands and gasped out a "thank you". The professor was personally inviting her to audition? She couldn't believe it…and she couldn't wait to get back to her new home and share her news with Kristina.

"Do you have any questions for me?" he asked. "We're almost out of time."

She shook her head automatically. "No, I am just looking forward to working and learning here."

He smiled faintly. "We will push you," he said. "There will be late nights."

"I'm ready," she said.

He looked unconvinced. "We will see."

Then he motioned towards the door. She mumbled thank you again and let herself out. A gaunt, dark-complexioned man was waiting just outside. "Good luck," she said as he went inside.

As she walked down the hall towards the stairs, she wondered if the guy behind her in line would be a friend, or competition this semester. It always came down to that in life, didn't it?

★   ★   ★

Eve felt a chill as she walked along a dark block. Some of the buildings had lights on behind the window coverings, but most did not. It was a brooding, cloudy night and in places she could barely see the sidewalk because of the overhang of the trees and roofs. Ghent was not like New York. There were not streetlights at every block.

She'd taken a walk after dinner to go into the old town area along the river, and now was returning home. But she hesitated when she reached blocks where there were long stretches of darkness. She couldn't shake the thought that there had been a murder at the Eyrie just a few nights before. What if that killer was wandering nearby, looking for another victim? What if she was walking through a dark block and someone jumped out and grabbed her?

It was a warm night, but she shivered at the thought. Eve scanned each small yard in front of the dark buildings, searching for evidence of someone hidden behind a bush or a pillar. In the back of her head, she heard The Cure's 'Pictures of You' playing. Why had the killer posted that on the poor girl's Facebook page?

Eve took a deep breath and started the walk down the last two blocks before the Eyrie. Ironically, they were the darkest section of her journey. After passing the first couple of buildings, where tree branches threw moving shadows against window glass that reflected the trick of the low light like grasping hands, she stepped out onto the uneven cobbled street. At least she was in the open here, and there were no cars in evidence at the moment.

The silent buildings soon passed by, and finally she reached a corner where a streetlamp illuminated the intersection. Her body relaxed a little when she stood beneath the cone of light that pushed away the shadows of the rest of the block. Eve let go of a breath she didn't know she was holding. The twin peaks of the two Eyrie building towers were just down the block now. But as she began to walk the final path that wound to the double doors, she saw something going on behind the buildings. There was a courtyard there in the rear of the Eyrie, and she could see the flicker of a myriad of tiny lights in the space between buildings.

She peered through the cover of bushes and overhanging tree

branches to get a better look at what seemed to be a hidden garden of fairy lights. Many and small. She heard voices murmuring too. Someone was speaking; a moment later a group of people responded. The sounds were too muted and faraway to make out the words.

Eve decided to walk down the side path that led to the rear of the Eyrie instead of going to the front entrance. She wanted to know what was going on. For a moment, the fears of a masked killer jumping out of the darkness left her, even though she now walked down a winding path almost completely cloaked in shadow.

And then, as she entered the back courtyard, that feeling of dread in her heart came back in a rush. Not because she was afraid that the killer was here.

But because this gathering was about the killer. Or rather, the victim.

A small table was set up on one side of the courtyard, draped in a dark sheet and topped with a large framed picture of a pretty blonde girl. A litter of things had been set in front of it, offerings maybe. Candles flickered all around the photo, with twice as many on the ground in front and to the side of the table. Many of the people standing around also held candles in their hands; the orange light of the tiny flames wavered and shone on unfamiliar faces.

Eve wished she had kept walking and not come. She had no business being here. She knew instantly what this was.

This was a candlelight vigil to celebrate the life of the dead girl, Genevieve DuPont.

As she looked around, she saw the glimmer of tears on the cheeks of many of those standing around. And then in the front of the gathering she recognized Erika and Elena, the Italian twins she'd met in the cafeteria. A girl with chestnut hair and sad eyes stood in front of them, facing the small crowd.

"There wasn't anyone like her," the girl said. "She had a beauty and a humor and a spark that truly was unique and special. I was privileged to have played with her for the past two years in the Songbirds and it was a time I'll never forget. She had a sense of melody and style like nobody I've ever played with before. No one can ever replace her. I can't begin to tell you what we've lost. But I can tell you to always remember her. And really, I don't have to. If you knew Genevieve, I know that you will never forget her. The killer took her life from us, but the power of her smile will always live on. He can never take that from us."

Eve felt a shiver go down her spine at those words. Her eyes misted up even though she had never known the dead girl.

You don't belong here, a tiny voice said in the back of her head. As the crowd raised their candles in cupped hands to protect the flames, Eve stepped backwards and out of sight, retracing her steps along the path between buildings.

The front entryway of the Eyrie did not seem as friendly and welcoming as it had earlier. It felt more like a crypt tonight. There was nobody in the lobby when she walked in. Eve hurried to the elevator, which appeared to be working today. She punched the button, took it up to the fifth floor and almost ran to her room. She bolted the door as soon as she was inside, and walked to the desk to stare out at the dark street below.

Someone had died here. Been killed. All of her dreams of coming to study at the Eyrie suddenly felt hollow and pale. Maybe she should turn right around and go home.

The chill in her heart would not thaw.

CHAPTER FOUR

"Let's hear what you've got to play for us," a voice called from the second row of the theater seats. She couldn't see the face; the lights on the stage were blinding. Everything beyond the edge of the stage was a blurred shadow.

Eve took a breath and positioned her fingers on the keys of the Steinway. This was the moment she'd been thinking of since her meeting with Prof. Von Klein. And he wasn't even here. This was a student-run audition.

She had no idea what kinds of pieces the Songbirds typically played, but she had practiced the piece that Von Klein had given her — Fats Waller's 'Honeysuckle Rose'. She wasn't sure if she should improvise, or play exactly the chart. What did they expect? She had no idea.

Eve took a breath and launched into the music. She had decided to improv on the final segment. Hopefully it would play in her favor and not against. Jazz combos were about improvisation, not playing rote music, and a jazz audition was what she was here in this room for. That was also the fundamental difference between classical study and jazz, and most pianists who were skilled at one were not keen on the other. But Eve had always enjoyed the rigor of both classical performance perfection and the luxury of calculated expression that jazz allowed. Different halves of the whole.

She did her best to wow the judges with both…her initial take on Waller was flawless, and then her improvisation (hopefully) showed both inventive flair and fluidity that other pianists might not attain. She didn't know what her competition was, but that was what she was going for.

"Not bad," the voice from out in the seats said when she finished. "We'll let you know."

Eve collected her music and stood up from the bench. "Thanks for the opportunity," she said, addressing the shadow people beyond the edge of the stage. Then she walked – with as much confidence as she could muster – to the exit door. She didn't know what they thought, but she felt confident that she'd played well. Maybe they wouldn't want the upstart American in their combo, no matter how well she played; she didn't know. But she wouldn't feel bad about what she'd done.

Instead of going back to her room, Eve walked out the main door of the Eyrie and onto the cobbled walkway to head toward the heart of Old Town. The afternoon was perfect; a faint breeze rippled the trees as she passed small grocery and tobacco and clothing shops. She stopped to admire a tall but narrow stone building with stained-glass windows and vaulting towers at each of its four corners. A church. She'd only been able to walk around town a handful of times so far, but she was amazed each time at the intricate stonework and decoration that nearly all of the buildings here displayed. The rule of thumb seemed to be, if the building was constructed more than fifty years ago, it was a work of art. Even if it served only to house a pharmacy.

While everything here felt older than New York; everything also somehow seemed fresher. The air was clean, the roads more open. The streets were a mix of cobble and asphalt, which only increased the sense of history. Now and then they were interrupted with rails for the tramlines that cut through the city. The modern steel and plastic cars felt anachronistic when they passed; the streets looked as if they should be frequented by horse and buggy, not modern vehicles.

The strains of a piano rang out from somewhere near, and when Eve reached the next street, she saw the source. A small pavilion not far from a grand old church covered an outdoor piano chained to the stone walkway. Apparently it was placed out here for anyone to simply walk up and play. She edged closer. An older Asian man in dark slacks and a blue polo shirt played Debussy's 'Claire De Lune'. A small group of people stood around the pavilion, appreciating the free concert. Eve smiled as the music drifted throughout the street, pitch perfect beauty in an unanticipated garden.

When the man finished the final melancholy strain, he stood up to instant applause from the onlookers. A faint smile colored his face and he bowed slightly before picking up a bag near the piano and walking away. After a minute, a teenaged girl in a yellow t-shirt with the emblem of a smile emoji walked towards the piano and sat down to start playing. It took Eve a moment to place it, before she realized it was Nirvana's 'Smells Like Teen Spirit'. A public piano study in opposites. But they both sounded good.

After a couple more minutes, Eve forced herself to continue on. She headed down Graslei Street along the Leie River into the heart of the old city. The sun was hot on her shoulders and the streets thronged with walkers and bicyclists enjoying the perfect day. It felt as if she were walking in a foreign postcard. But no…she was actually here. That realization hit her again and again as she looked with fresh eyes at a thousand years of history all around. Eventually, she stopped at the Het Waterhuis aan de Bierkant, which amusingly translated as the 'Waterhouse on the Beerfront'. Kristina had taken her here on her second day in Ghent, and she loved the quaint wood-plank indoor bar that overlooked a narrow walkway and the water below as much as the airy patio covered in umbrellas advertising a variety of classic Belgian breweries. Eve wasn't big on beer, but she had to admit that she'd enjoyed the fizzy, funky flavor of the blond beer with the pink elephant logo, Delirium Tremens. She ordered one, which came in a large tulip glass emblazoned with the brewery logo elephant and took a seat near the railing so that she could look down the river. A classic arched stone bridge was just a block or so down the bank. Occasionally long open boats with tourists snapping pictures of the old buildings on both sides of the bank slipped past. She shook her head at one point with a smile. It was all like a dream.

Eve sat there for nearly an hour, slowly nursing the strong beer before deciding to head back to the Eyrie. The sun was beginning to throw long shadows on the walkways, and she needed to get home and put some food in her stomach soon to soak up the beer.

★   ★   ★

"*Where* have you been?" Kristina said as soon as she stepped into their room. "I've been trying to reach you for over an hour!"

"You have?"

"I called, texted...."

Eve pulled out her phone and saw the notifications on the screen. "Oh geez, I'm sorry!" she said. "I had the volume off and honestly haven't looked at it all afternoon. What's going on?"

"You passed the audition," Kristina said, grabbing Eve's hands and shaking her arms up and down. "You're in! You're a Songbird!"

"How...."

Kristina held out an envelope. "Someone came by and dropped off a formal invitation. And they asked if you could meet with the group tonight at seven-thirty in the auditorium."

Eve looked at her phone and frowned. It was already almost seven o'clock now. She hadn't realized how long she'd been walking around.

"Crap," she said. "I need to freshen up. So much for dinner!"

"Here, eat this," Kristina said, rummaging in one of her drawers. She held out an energy bar.

"Better than nothing!" Eve said and wolfed it down. Then she grabbed her bathroom bag and headed to the showers.

★   ★   ★

There were more than a half dozen people walking around on the stage when Eve let herself in the auditorium door and started walking down the aisle to the front. One of the trumpeters put his lips to the horn and blew three fast notes as she approached the stage. Everyone stopped what they were doing and stared at her. Eve recognized the dark eyes of the Italian twins, Elena and Erika, focused on her from the back row of chairs on the stage.

It was a little unnerving. Somebody whispered something that sounded an awful lot like "dirty Americana". She hoped it was her nervous imagination.

"Hi," she said, breaking the sudden quiet. "My name's Eve. Someone left me a letter to come here tonight."

When nobody moved, she added, "I play piano."

A blond-haired guy in a blue Paris Jazz Festival t-shirt and khaki shorts stood up from next to the trumpet blower, and walked towards the stairs on the edge of the stage. She met him there.

"Hi Eve, I'm Richard. Welcome to the Songbirds." He held out a hand and she shook it. His grip was warm and firm. "Glad to have you joining us. Most of us have played together before, so it's a pretty tight-knit group. But we'll have you up to speed in no time."

He motioned towards the baby grand piano at the side of the stage. "We'll start warming up in just a few minutes. Professor Von Klein is supposed to stop by first."

"Does he lead the practices?" she asked.

The girl sitting next to Richard, who used way too much mascara, laughed out loud at that.

Richard shook his head. "No," he said. "This is a school-sanctioned, but student-run group. So, he checks in on us now and then, but we're really on our own. He's like…our spiritual leader."

A girl with long chestnut hair walked over and held out her hand. Eve recognized her instantly. It was the girl who had been speaking at the vigil the other night in the courtyard. She could hear the words of her tribute to Genevieve DuPont in her head. *"…Nobody can ever replace her…"*

"Hello," the girl said. "My name is Susie Grave. I play the bass. I was one of the ones out in the seats for your audition. You played great."

She pointed at a thin Asian guy who popped out from behind the proscenium. He wore a black eyepatch over one eye, which gave him a slightly sinister demeanor. "That's Markie, he's our drummer."

"Percussionist," he corrected, and grinned.

"Pete, Anita and Corey handle trumpets," she said, pointing to the brass section. The trio acknowledged her and then busied themselves with their instruments. Susie turned a finger to another girl with short-cropped black hair sitting near them. "And Gianna plays sax with Richard."

Gianna just stared at her and said nothing. Her eyes were as dark as her hair. Eve did not get the sense of a warm, welcoming vibe from that quarter.

"It's good to meet all of you," Eve said. "I'm looking forward to playing."

"We're waiting for a couple more to turn up, but all the charts we're going to work on are in a folder on the piano for you," Susie said. "We have already had a couple practices, so you'll need to catch up. We just added you and Dmitri on vibes and ancillary percussion tonight."

Eve walked over to the piano as Susie began to run her fingers over the heavy strings of the standup bass and Richard and Gianna blew some honking practice notes on their saxophones. Eve pulled out the bench and sat. Then she lifted the wooden lid off the keys.

And before she could stop herself, she screamed.

Right in the middle of the keyboard was a yellow canary. It was dead, its neck twisted at a crazy angle. A spot of blood hung at the tip of its beak.

The room went silent for a second, before Richard rushed over. "What's happened?" he asked.

"It's dead," she said, pointing at the broken bird.

Richard looked at the piano and frowned before looking at the rest of the band. "Uncool, Songbirds, if one of you did this."

He put a hand on her shoulder for a moment, and gripped her gently. "Everyone is still upset about losing Genevieve," he said. "She practiced with us just a few days ago."

"Wait," Eve said, a realization just dawning. "You mean, I'm replacing the girl who was murdered?" Susie's words about nobody ever replacing Genevieve came back at her again. She was *literally* here to replace her.

"Don't let it get to you. It's really sad and horrible and all…but the Songbirds have to go on."

"Apparently not this one," she murmured, looking at the dead canary.

"Hmmm, well, yes," he agreed. "Let me get rid of that for you."

He walked backstage and came back with a garbage can and a piece of newspaper. He held the lip of the can up to the edge of the keys and pushed the bird in, before wiping the ivory it had rested on with the untouched section of the newspaper. Then he threw the paper in on top of the bird.

"Good as new," he said and brushed his hands together.

Eve turned to stare at the keys but refrained from putting her fingers on them. The rest of the band went back to warming up, as she wrestled with her own private thoughts. Who would do that to an innocent bird? Who would leave such a message for her?

Richard was just returning from getting rid of the garbage can when the professor entered the theater.

"I am not hearing the profound creative notes of improvisation coming from this hall that I'd expect," he said as he walked down the center aisle.

"We were just starting to warm up," Susie said.

"I'm anxious to hear what you can do with your new voices," he said, and sat down in one of the front row seats. "How about a few bars of 'Honeysuckle Rose'? I know you used that for auditions, so everyone should have it down and be comfortable."

Susie picked up the neck of her huge acoustic bass from its stand, getting herself in position. Everyone shuffled quickly through the music on their stands and readied the piece. The horn section all straightened up and Markie quietly spoke from behind the drums. "Let's blow the lid off this." He clicked his sticks on the edge of the snare four times before launching into the rhythm.

Eve held her fingers at the ready and tried not to think about the fact that a dead bird had been lying where she needed to play just a few moments before. Or about who had put it there, a cruel reminder to her that she was replacing a 'dead songbird'.

Was it a warning? She gritted her teeth and launched into the song, refusing to let the troubling thoughts stop her.

She'd always said that music trumped all. Here was a time to prove it.

CHAPTER FIVE

"Want to come with us for a coffee?" Richard asked. Susie, Gianna and Markie stood behind him. The others were still packing up their instruments. Eve's heart beat a step faster at the invitation. They had just wrapped their third practice since she had joined the group, but she still felt like the outsider. There were a couple girls in the band that she hadn't even met yet; they seemed to keep to themselves. So far, nothing more had been said about the dead bird prank but nobody had talked to her much either. Richard was friendly, and Susie had basically said hello and goodbye. But other than that, she had come in each day, set up at the piano and followed the direction set by the bassist without chatter. Susie seemed to be the tacit leader of the group, calling the song order and giving Markie the nod to begin. Richard was clearly the most social, and genuinely seemed to like her. They had a music theory lecture class together and yesterday he'd stopped at her row in the theater and asked if he could join her. He'd then spent the next hour whispering jokes to her at the lecturing professor's expense.

But now, he clearly was trying to pull her into the existing circle. Which seemed pretty tight knit.

"There's a cappuccino place we go to a lot after rehearsals a couple blocks away, right at the start of the strip," he said. "It's called Heavy Beans. A few of us are heading over there. I think you'll like it."

Eve was exhausted and really didn't want to go out…but there was no way she was going to turn down the invitation. Maybe this was the start of something; she wanted them all to warm up to her. Not that Gianna looked like she wanted her to tag along. Richard's fellow saxophonist was staring off in a bored way to her left, with a 'can we just get out of here' kind of look on her face.

"Sure," Eve answered. "I'd love to," she lied.

"Excellent," he said. "Meet you in the East Tower lobby in ten minutes."

★   ★   ★

Eve felt alone, even though she was walking in a group of five people. The others were laughing and talking about things that had happened last semester with the jazz combo, and she couldn't share in or understand most of what they referenced. She studied the old buildings and small black wrought-iron gated gardens along the sidewalk and began to think this outing was a mistake as they traversed the dark streets. After a couple blocks, her trepidation fell away with the shadows, as they crossed an old plaza with a bronze statue and marble-enclosed fountain and got closer to the river. The low hum of conversation came from all around the open area, as people sat out enjoying the growing dusk at small cafés and bars. And then they turned a corner and she was struck by the cascade of lights down the thoroughfare. Restaurant and bar window lights. Christmas lights strung from small trees inside brick-walled patios. A bright beam came from the top of a clock tower three blocks away. "This is beautiful," Eve said.

"Isn't it?" Susie said. "I love coming here at night. It's like a fairy land."

"And...here we are," Richard announced.

A wooden sign cut in an uneven oval shape hung above the door and announced *Heavy Beans* in sunshine-accented tangerine letters over a coffee-brown backdrop. A handful of small tables were set in a row to the right of the door where people sat talking and smoking, but Richard led them past those to go inside.

The smell of rich coffee hit Eve immediately, and she breathed it in with an unconscious smile. This reminded her of the cafés of New York. The place was long and narrow, with a wall of what looked like old warehouse stone on one side. Scores of pictures hung in a dizzying mosaic of captured faces all down the wall. A long bar stretched down the other side of the room. A gelato freezer was set up closest to the door. That led to a cash register atop the long stretch of old wooden bar next to it. Chairs lined the bar from the front of the room to the back, all occupied with people talking and laughing. People also gathered in groups around the tall round tables that filled the rest of the room.

"Welcome, welcome, my Songbirds!" a voice called out as soon as they stepped inside. "It's so good to see you all again." A tall, wiry man with a chef's apron wrapped around a flamboyant electric-cherry shirt stepped out from behind the counter and walked to meet them at the door. "The music begins again, eh? Another semester?"

"We are back." Richard grinned. "It hardly seems like we were away."

"Time is like a roller coaster," the man said. "At first it's slow and creaky and it takes forever to get to where you want to go. And then you hit the top and bang, you're moving so fast you can't see what is going by around you."

"You're a philosopher," Richard said with a laugh.

The man cocked his head, looking straight at Eve. "Speaking of seeing what's around you, do we have a new girl in town?"

"We do," Richard said. "Claude, this is Eve. She's our new pianist."

The barista looked thoughtful. "Another song to learn," he said.

Claude held out his hand, and Eve accepted it in hers. His grip was surprisingly firm.

"Glad to meet you," she said.

He smiled. "Every year another and another and another. The symphony never ends, there are only new hands to play it." He pointed at the pictures on the wall. "Maybe you'll be up there one of these days?" Claude said.

"Most of the people up there were students at the Eyrie at one point," Richard explained.

"Correction," Claude said, holding up a hand. "They were not just students, they were the *best*. There are people who can play, and people who can *play*. I can tell you about the songs that every single one of them turned into their own. Oh, those nights." Claude closed his eyes and pressed his fingers to his mouth as he mimicked a kiss. "Magic," he said, reopening his eyes to their widest. "Right here on our stage, they transported us to another place. They may never become famous but for one moment, at least, they were the brightest lights in the world."

He gestured to the end of the room and Eve realized that there was a small stage in the very back, with the Heavy Beans logo hung in the center. It wasn't lit now, but she could see the stage lights that hung from the ceiling and pointed to the center of the stage.

"I'm looking forward to your first show," Claude said. "Perhaps one of you will have that one perfect moment. Excuse me now."

He hurried back across the room to help a customer at the register.

"We'll play here?" Eve asked.

Richard nodded. "Yeah, this is one of our regular gigs. Claude worships jazz and loves the Eyrie, as you can see. It's a nice, low-key spot to play in. No pressure, and free coffee."

Eve smiled. "I can feel it."

The group went to the front counter and each ordered a coffee. "Try the blueberry biscotti, it's amazing," Susie insisted, so she did. After Eve crunched one explosively sweet bite on their way to a table, she had to agree.

They all sat down along the long wall, closer to the stage than the door.

"It's too bad nobody's playing tonight," Gianna said.

"Remember that show we did here last year in March?" Markie asked, "the one where Gen decided to pull a Philip Glass and put everyone in a trance?"

Richard, Gianna and Susie all laughed and launched into their memories of what had been, apparently, a completely crazy, blow-off-steam kind of show.

"I dunno," Richard said after a bit. "I think I pulled out a solo that night that should have had me on the wall."

Gianna rolled her eyes. "If you can call the sound of two rhinos farting a memorable sax solo."

"C'mon, after Gen's left-turn into nowhere, my solo was genius. Definitely wall quality."

"You were drunk," Gianna snorted.

"I hope you have practiced a lot these past few weeks," Claude said, reappearing at their table and shaking his head at Richard. "You were *not* ready for the wall last year."

The barista pointed at an eight-by-ten of a man leaning backwards almost parallel to the stage, a saxophone jutting out in front of him. He was clearly in the midst of an intense performance. "If you can make the instrument sing like Bruno there, then I put you on the wall. That boy could make you cry and make you dance, all in the same song."

Claude pointed to the photo next to it, where a drummer was caught in mid-downbeat. You could see the sweat on his forehead and the energy in the taut muscles of his arms. "Or Paulo Orlandi there. When that cat took the skins, you knew the stage was going to move. Or...." Claude's fingers moved to the next photo, a pretty amber-haired girl leaning just enough off her piano bench to tell you that she was playing with passion. Claude looked as if he was about to say something about her, but then he simply smiled sadly and nodded at her photo before gesturing to the next picture of a dark-haired guy behind a large acoustic bass that was taller than he was.

"Even bassists can learn how to move the soul if they really practice," he said, looking pointedly at Susie. "Practice. Learn how to transcend technique to reveal passion."

His eyes roamed across the row of pictures on the wall again, before his attention returned to the table. "Is everything all right? I'm looking forward to hearing you all again." He looked at Eve. "And hearing you for the first time. A new song."

He turned away then to stop at the next table.

"Claude gets a little soap-boxy, sometimes," Richard said.

"You think that's bad, wait 'til you've got a drink or two in him," Susie said.

Eve smiled. It felt like she might have a chance at being part of this group, instead of looking in from the outside. She motioned to the photo of the girl at the piano.

"Who's that girl?" she asked. "He looked like there was a story there."

Markie shook his head. "She died last year. Right about this time, actually. I remember it was the start of the semester. She was a nice girl, Richard can tell you, but she had problems. Such a waste. Nobody likes to talk about it. I'm sure if you ask Claude though, he'll tell you. He's got a story about everyone on that wall."

CHAPTER SIX

During the first regular lecture by Prof. Von Klein, Eve sat next to a girl wearing a CBGB shirt. She didn't see anyone else she knew and the shirt was like a beacon, calling her home. She realized as she sat down that the girl was in the trumpet section of the Songbirds. One of the girls she hadn't spoken to at a rehearsal yet.

"I've seen you at Songbirds practice," Eve said.

"Yes you have," she said.

"Are you from New York?"

The girl shook her head, but her eyes sparked with sudden interest. "No, but I've always wanted to go to New York City." Her accent sounded Polish. She definitely did not sound like she came from the States.

"Where are you from?" Eve asked.

"Warsaw," the girl said. "My name is Anita."

Eve introduced herself. "I'm from New York," she said. "But I never got to go to CBGBs. They closed when I was just a kid."

At the mention of the classic New York club, Anita's face brightened. "Can you imagine to have seen Talking Heads or Blondie there back in the day?" she said. "Would have been amazing."

"I know," Eve said. "It's like, all of the music that New York became known for was just history by the time I could go out to a club. Where is the groundbreaking music now?"

"We'll only know after it's gone," Anita said.

The professor took the stage to begin his lecture then, and their conversation abruptly ceased. Although, during the talk, Eve couldn't help but sneak glances at the familiar logo on Anita's shirt. It made her strangely homesick.

When the professor finished his talk an hour later, as they were packing up to leave, Anita touched Eve on the shoulder to get her attention.

"Eve, this is my friend Nikki," she said, motioning towards a short girl behind her in a black vest and black hair with purple highlights. "There's a semester launch party tonight at Nicolai Hall, one of the university buildings near the river. Want to go with us?"

"Sure, I guess," Eve said. "What's your number? I'll text you and you can tell me where to meet up."

They traded numbers and then headed off to their next classes. Eve could barely contain her elation; first a small group of Songbirds had asked her out and now she'd finally connected with another. Maybe this being halfway around the world thing was going to work out after all.

★　★　★

Excitement gave way to nervousness by the end of the day. She had a sudden attack of insecurity; she had no idea what to wear. And Kristina couldn't go with her as moral support; her roommate had a date.

"You need to take a shot and chill the bollocks out," Kristina said. "They're just music geeks like you and me. It don't matter a bit what you wear."

It may not have mattered, but Kristina still looked through her wardrobe and helped her pick out a black sleeveless shirt with a hem of lace that sat just above the belt of her jeans and indicated her approval when Eve tried it on. Sharp but casual. It was an end-of-summer humid night, so having her shoulders free was perfect.

Anita and Nikki met her in the lobby.

"This will be a crazy kickoff," Anita warned as they walked down the uneven cobblestone sidewalks to head to the party. "They have it here every year and sometimes they are still dancing at dawn."

Eve shook her head. "I will *not* still be dancing at dawn."

Nikki raised an eyebrow, but made no comment.

The Nicolai Building was another triangular-roofed stone structure that looked like it predated the discovery of America. It was set back from the cobbled street and the girls stepped through an arched gate to follow a curving walkway of stones to reach the tall, heavy wooden door.

"I feel like we're about to enter a Viking fortress," Eve said.

Nikki shook her head. "No Vikings here. They couldn't afford the rent."

Anita laughed. "It's a weird building. They use it for classes downstairs, but there are study halls and dorm rooms upstairs. Like half of the places around this district, I think it used to be some kind of warehouse, so it's kind of funky."

"You've been here before?" Eve asked.

Anita rubbed her hand over the other girl's shoulder. "This is where Nikki and I met last year."

Eve suddenly had a suspicion that she was a third wheel here.

"They do know how to throw a party," Anita said.

Nikki only raised one well-arched eyebrow.

The Polish girl pulled the heavy door open with a groan and her last words before entering were nearly obliterated by the beat from inside. It sounded like a mix of Nine Inch Nails and Lady Gaga; edgy but threatening to turn pop. They filed inside.

Eve was impressed by the space – classic old stone recast in a modern context with the addition of steel, glass and lighting. The room stretched long in both directions, but was not deep. There was a hallway in the center that presumably led to lecture rooms, from what Anita had said. There were couches along some of the walls where people were gathered around, sitting and standing with plastic cups in hand. Colored lights had been set along the rough stone walls sending red and blue glows from floor to ceiling. The ceiling was up a couple levels; balconies on the second and third floors overlooked the party foyer. It was all open and people were everywhere, hanging over the balcony rails as they looked down through party streamers on the tight groups that thronged the first floor. A makeshift bar was at the right, and the three headed there first.

"You can't mingle without a little tingle," Anita yelled. Nikki shook her head, clearly embarrassed. Despite her edgy goth look, she was clearly the quiet one, not the wild one, of the pair.

Eve ordered a rum and Coke, while Anita started strong – vodka on the rocks. Going for the instant buzz factor. Nikki came away with a clear plastic glass that appeared to have plenty of grenadine or cranberry juice in it.

When they stepped away from the line, Anita turned and lifted her glass towards them. "Here's to a great new year," she said.

Nikki tapped her plastic to Anita and Eve's.

And then a familiar voice cut through the pounding beat.

"Eve, I didn't know you were going to be here!"

A hand grabbed her shoulder and Eve turned to find Richard standing there with a beer in hand. Gianna and Susie were right behind him. "Look who else we found," he said and held his hand out to point at Claude, who stood just behind Gianna.

"I never miss the Nicolai party," Claude said with a grin. He held out a glass and the Songbird group followed his toast. Eve sensed Nikki was fading back, ready to take Anita with her.

"It's like a Songbird party right here." Richard laughed. In minutes the entire group was chattering about professors and concerts and what they'd been doing over the break.

Eventually, they found a tall round table to anchor them; it wasn't long before the center was stacked in empty plastic glasses. More Eyrie enrollees turned up until there was a solid wall of bodies around their table in a room that had grown increasingly 'thick'. It was difficult to move and the din of hundreds of conversations threatened to overwhelm the music, which had already seemed loud when they'd first walked in. At one point, a Spanish girl named Isabella showed up, and Richard made a point of introducing her to Eve.

"This is Isabella," he said. "She's an honorary Songbird."

To Eve, Isabella looked more like a girl from *Cosmo* than a musician. She had flawless brown skin and dark, long waves of hair that slipped smoothly over her bare shoulders. Her lips were glossed and her eyes flashed with light despite being a deep brown in color. She wore a white string halter top and loose pink running shorts. The light colors popped against her skin.

"I just am thankful that Richard keeps inviting me," Isabella said.

"What does an honorary Songbird do exactly?" Eve asked. She was trying very hard to put the irritatingly unseemly ideas she suddenly had about Richard and Isabella out of her mind.

"She sings with us sometimes," Richard said. "Wait 'til you hear her. She's phenomenal."

Richard and Isabella turned away from the group and began a private conversation. At one point, the singer put her hand on his shoulder with a casual familiarity and Eve frowned. It was silly, but she found herself instantly disliking the girl. She was happy when the "honorary Songbird" excused herself and went off to join another table.

In the meantime, Anita asked Eve enough questions about New York that she actually began to feel homesick again. At one point, Nikki apparently grew bored with their conversation and disappeared into the throng to talk to someone else. When she returned a while later, she brought drinks for both Anita and Eve, and Anita absently slipped her arm around the other girl and gave her a kiss on the lips.

Yep, Eve had caught *that* vibe correctly.

"Eve, who is your favorite jazz artist?" Richard asked at one point, drawing her into an argument that was raging between him, Claude, Susie and the rest of the band gathered on his side of the table.

"Geez, I don't know." She laughed. "I mean, I love Metheny for some things, but sometimes I love to go back to the classic sixties stuff. Sometimes, I'm in the mood for Coltrane, and sometimes I'd rather put on Miles Davis. I like a lot of styles!"

"What about new artists?" Susie asked.

"Back home, I used to go out on Tuesday nights and listen to local groups," she said. "None of them had recording contracts, they were all just players. I think some of those bands were better live than any recordings."

"Nobody needs a record deal anymore anyway," Susie said. "That's the beauty of the Internet."

This time Claude leapt into the fray.

"No, you don't *need* one," he said with thick sarcasm. "You could just post your songs to Bandcamp and maybe make fifty Euros for your album that took you a year and hundreds of hours to perfect and record. Why would you want to *actually* have a company behind you with money and the connections to *actually* get your music heard by more than a hundred people? That would be silly."

"Come on, Claude," Gianna needled. "You probably still buy vinyl, too!"

"Because vinyl sounds better...."

Eve found herself drifting from the conversation. She took another sip of her drink...what was it? A Killa Vanilla, she thought Nikki had said? It had vodka, she knew that. She glanced over at the bar as she considered the drink's potency. A long line of people stood waiting to place orders at the heart of the bar, but at the corner stood Mrs. Freer and Philip. She squinted to confirm that it really was them. They were the last people she'd expect to be at a party like this and they were both staring right at her. Philip's dark eyes were set deep in that high craggy forehead, but clearly trained on her. When they realized she saw them, Mrs. Freer looked up and said something in Philip's ear. The man nodded slowly...but never took his eyes off Eve. A chill shot down her back, and Eve looked away, turning back to her group. At that moment, Richard was laughing and gesturing at something with his hands, as Gianna shook her head with a secret smile. Anita also shook her head with a rueful grin at whatever Richard was going on about. Claude looked aloof; unamused. He sipped his drink and turned away to stare in another direction.

Eve's gaze returned to the bar, but Philip and Mrs. Freer had disappeared. She took another sip of her drink and idly scanned the room. She didn't feel up to rejoining the animated conversation at the table yet. The steady pound of the bass from the speakers was lulling her. She didn't know the song but there were lots of synthesizer stabs and a very processed drum track.

Anita and Nikki had also distanced themselves slightly from the table conversation to hold a private discussion next to her. She couldn't hear most of the words, but she caught their expressions and passionate eyes. She forced herself to look away; it wasn't her business. Eve watched all of the people laughing, talking and some even dancing. She looked up and saw hands hanging over the balcony, cups lining the railing. Mrs. Freer and Philip were nowhere in sight. She turned her head to the left to see what Richard was talking about now and as she did, the blonde hair of one of the girls upstairs blurred into a golden trail that cut across the room, no matter where she turned her eyes. Eve blinked, trying to clear the strange haze away, and looked around the room again. Everything seemed amorphous, indistinct. A shifting meld of colors. The heads bobbing in the crowd dissolved even as she tried to bring them into focus.

Eve set down her drink and put her hands on the table, suddenly needing to steady herself. She didn't feel right at all. The room turned into a kaleidoscope. Fragments of heads and arms and hair and cups all cascading into an unintelligible collage.

"Eve?" Richard said.

Someone grabbed her arm.

"Eve, are you okay?" Maybe it was Anita.

All at once, her legs decided they did not want to remain upright any longer, and her knees simply unlocked.

Eve collapsed.

The floor stopped her fall. But it wasn't soft.

She saw faces bending over her but she couldn't make out who was who; they were all blurry. She saw the vibrant purple of Nikki's hair like a gauze over her face, and someone who had very, very red lips.

Her last thought was that her drink delivered on its promise.

That vanilla was killa.

CHAPTER SEVEN

"Eve, can you hear me?"

Richard leaned over her, his eyes creased in concern. She blinked and slowly his face came firmly into focus. She felt a pressure, and realized he was squeezing her hand. She also realized that she was in a bed, lying on a pillow.

"Where am I?" she whispered. Her words sounded thick.

"Your eyes got funny and then you just collapsed at the party," Richard said. "Nikki knows someone who lives here in the building, so we brought you upstairs to their room. How do you feel?"

"I don't know," Eve said. "Really weird…like, there are a lot of colors, almost like when you look through 3D glasses."

"That's a hell of a drunk," Richard said, and Eve shook her head.

"This…feels…different. Not drunk."

"Are you on any medicine?" Anita asked.

"No," Eve said. Suddenly the room swam again; cascades of cyan and indigo and orange lights swirled like a spinning wheel. "But the colors…."

Nikki looked at Richard. "Maybe someone slipped her something," she said.

"Who could have done that?" Susie said. "She was right here with us the whole night."

"Well, either she got something better than booze, or else she's a crazy lightweight," Gianna said.

"…not a lightweight…" Eve mumbled.

"She needs to sleep it off," Claude said. In the back of her mind, Eve couldn't believe even he was up here. She was making a fool of herself in front of everyone. She'd never had this kind of reaction to alcohol before. But how could she have gotten drugged? She tried to open her eyes again and see who else was here. But when she stared past the bed, it was like looking through a telescope backwards. She could make out figures and faces, but they were so distorted, she couldn't tell who they were.

"I'm going downstairs to see if the bartender has heard of any other problems tonight," Nikki said. "Maybe he's been serving something bad down there."

"Yeah, you guys don't need to all stay up here," Anita said. "Go back down and I'll sit with her for a while."

Eve heard voices murmuring but she couldn't tell what they were saying. Slowly the sounds diminished.

What is wrong with me?

She heard laughter, but it did not sound happy. It sounded mean. Like there was someone here who wanted to hurt her.

Eve struggled to open her eyes, sure that she was in mortal danger. Someone had drugged her. Someone was here right now, waiting for the moment to kill her. Probably the same person who had killed Genevieve DuPont, the last piano player for the Eyrie's Songbirds combo. The realization took hold and she felt more afraid than she'd ever been in her whole life.

Eve began to moan faintly. She could not contain it. The fear welled up inside and crashed against her emotions like a tide that would break and subsume the sand of the beach. It overwhelmed her. Her entire being drowned in terror.

She was going to die.

Right now.

Something touched her then, grabbed her shoulder.

"No!" Eve cried out. "Get away from me!"

She grabbed at the killer, intending to push him away. But instead, she found his neck. She couldn't see the face of her assailant; her eyes refused to open...but with her fingers, she gripped as tightly as she could. The killer wasn't going to do to her what he'd done to the last pianist for the Songbirds. Evelyn Springer would not go down so easily.

"*Eve!*" a familiar voice screamed.

Somehow Eve forced her eyes open to focus and realized that it was Anita bending over her.

Eve's fingers were wrapped around her new friend's neck. Anita looked terrified, her eyes bugged out, the whites of her eyes huge. Frightened.

Behind her, there was a weird flash of white light, as if the heavens had opened for just one second. Eve realized what she was doing and relaxed her grip. Her arms fell to the bed.

"I'm sorry, I'm so sorry," she whispered.

And then the blackness washed away all the light.

CHAPTER EIGHT

Anita sat back from the bed, rubbing her neck. That had honestly been scary for a moment. Whatever trip the American girl was on... she wanted no part of it.

Eve had collapsed back to the pillow. Her head lolled to the right; she appeared to have dropped immediately into sleep. Her breath came in a long, slow, steady rhythm. As Anita watched, she heard a hint of a snore.

After a bit, she texted Nikki to see if she'd learned anything. But as she sat next to the bed, the expected three dots that would show that Nikki was responding, did not appear. After a few minutes went by, she texted again. *Where are you?*

Still no answer. Her girlfriend probably had the phone in her purse and wasn't looking at it. You certainly wouldn't be able to hear it through the pound of the music downstairs.

Anita decided to take a walk back to the main floor to find her in person. Eve was doing exactly what she needed to do and Anita really didn't need to sit here and watch the girl sleep. Plus, Nikki had been gone a long time.

"I'll be right back," she whispered, and touched Eve's hair softly. Then she walked out into a small family room and out the front door. She didn't have the key, but she was only planning to be gone for a little bit, so she just left the door unlocked. Nobody was going to break in and loot the place in ten minutes.

The noise of the party echoed through the hallway. She hadn't really heard it inside the bedroom, but there was no escaping the techno beat when she moved down the hall. Anita turned right as she left the room. She thought this was the way back to the stairs. They were only on the third floor, so she could run down the stairs probably faster than waiting for the elevator.

She turned a corner, and as she did, she caught a glimpse of something black from out of the corner of her eye.

Anita paused, and then looked back at the hall she'd just left.

She saw a figure melt into the threshold of one of the apartment doors. They were all slightly inset, and she couldn't see what the person looked like. But...it *had* been a person. She was sure of that. And someone who did not want to be seen. She waited and watched, but there was no flash of light to indicate that someone had actually gone inside the apartment. No opening and closing door. Whoever it was had simply stopped upon being seen and was waiting for her to move on.

She decided that moving on was probably the best course of action.

Anita walked away from the intersection of the two hallways and each time she passed an apartment door, she glanced over her shoulder, sure that whoever had ducked out of sight before was going to follow her.

When she looked back after the fifth door, she got confirmation that she was right.

A dark figure was framed against the light from the hallway she'd just left. As she stared, it began walking towards her. With purpose.

She couldn't tell if it was a man or woman. The figure blended into the shadows thanks to a black long-sleeved shirt and dark jeans, along with black leather gloves and something equally dark pulled down to cover his or her face. It might have been nylon, because while she couldn't see features clearly, she could see the glint of eyes through the upper half above the jut of the nose.

The long sleeves and gloves were enough of a tip-off that something here was very wrong, but the face mask or hood sent Anita's stomach to her feet. Whoever was back there did not mean her any good.

She doubled her pace and looked back after she'd passed two more doors.

The figure had halved the distance between them.

Anita gasped. And began to run.

When she looked over her shoulder, she saw the figure sprinting towards her. Something silver glinted in one gloved hand.

Anita screamed. But she knew that it was not likely that anyone could hear her. The noise from the party echoed through the hall. She saw the door to the stairs and ran faster. She needed to get down to where people were. She needed to get lost in the crowd.

She slammed the door handle down and bolted through as soon as the door opened a crack. The cement stairs beyond were old, but modern. A round, grey-painted metal railing led down seven steps, hit a broad square landing, and then turned at a ninety-degree angle and went down several more.

Anita was about to reach the second landing when something hit her like a brick in the back. She fell hard. Her cheek smacked on the concrete but before the pain could register, she tried to roll away. The black figure had tackled her, and now was raising something over its head. She didn't pause to think, she kicked. Her right heel caught the creep in the midriff. But that didn't stop the attack.

The black-clad figure coughed and rolled, then came up in a crouch in front of the stairs leading down to the first level.

Shit. She wasn't going back up. But she couldn't force her way past to go down either.

Anita did the only thing she could. She grabbed the silver handle of the door to the second floor and threw it open.

"Help me!" she screamed as she fled through the door and down another hall of empty rooms. She beat her fists on a couple of the doors as she staggered past, but she knew with surety that nobody was here. This was a classroom level, and there were no classes going on tonight.

She stopped knocking and ran. When she turned a corner, one of the doors was open. She didn't even think; she ducked inside. Hopefully her stalker would keep on running, assuming that Anita had continued to the end of the hall. If not, she was going to need a weapon in short order.

Anita took in the room in a glance. There were twenty or thirty chairs set up in a three-row semicircle. A chair was positioned at the front to face the empty audience. Next to that was an instrument stand, the kind used for holding guitars and basses. It was metal, with three feet at the bottom and a half-hoop of metal at the top where the instrument rested.

She darted forward and grabbed it. If nothing else, it was something to swing.

Out of the corner of her eye, she saw a dark shape run past the classroom door. Stifling the urge to scream, Anita moved towards the wall, out of the line of sight of the doorway. There was a wooden closet there. If she could get inside....

She turned the handle on the double doors. Nothing clicked.

The doors were locked.

Shit.

There was nothing else in the room that she could hide under or behind, so she did the best she could and stood on the side of the closet, holding the instrument stand, knuckles clenched at the ready. A few seconds later she heard the creak of a hinge. Had the killer opened the door? She didn't dare stick her head out to see.

The floor creaked nearby. Anita's eyes widened and she held her breath. She couldn't afford to make a sound. Could he hear her heart beating? It sounded deafening to her.

The faint tap of a footstep came from the floor on the other side of the cabinet. Her arms tightened. She was ready to swing the guitar stand.

A black-covered head came around the edge of the cabinet. One black glove was already swinging towards her midriff.

Now Anita screamed. And swung the stand just in time, crashing into the killer's wrist hard enough that whatever was in its hand clattered to the floor.

The figure grabbed at her with its uninjured hand and Anita kicked it in the knee as hard as she could.

Pain shot through her toes. Her attacker stumbled back, then clutched at the floor to regain the weapon. Anita didn't waste a second; she bolted past the chairs and out the door.

There was bright light and the booming sounds of the party coming from the end of the hall. Anita ran as hard as she could to reach it. The balcony was just ahead. If she could get someone's attention below, she could call for help. Maybe they'd come running up the stairs, or maybe her assailant would just back off because he or she did not want to be seen by the partygoers below.

Anita now felt good about her chances. Nobody was going to attack her in plain sight of a floor full of people. She just had to get there.

The balcony railing was just a few yards ahead. Then three. Then one. Anita's hand grabbed at the silver rail just as a hand scooped around her belly and yanked her backwards.

"Hey!" she cried out. "Help!" but before anyone could have looked up, she was pulled out of view and dumped to the floor on her back.

The figure straddled her, pinned her to the ground with its thighs. With one gloved hand, the attacker slammed her head against the floor.

And again.

Anita punched at its stomach, but the figure didn't budge. She tried to use her legs to roll herself over so that she could crawl away, but instead, the black glove grabbed her by the throat again and lifted and slammed. Strangled and slammed.

Anita's eyes grew wild. She had to do something. She had to put the killer off balance.

She.

Had.

To....

With one black-gloved hand, the killer lifted something silver over its head. The thing it had dropped in the classroom. A metal rod that split from the handle into two thin steel spikes, about an inch apart.

Now that she could see it clearly, Anita recognized it instantly.

A tuning fork. Anita knew a cellist who refused to use electronic tuners and always used a tuning fork before each rehearsal to ensure that all of her strings were spot on.

There were also medical uses for tuning forks, which were used to test hearing, in particular.

At the moment, this tuning fork was about to used, not on hearing, but on sight.

The black leather glove was aiming the two points of the thing right at Anita's eyes.

She screamed and tried to roll away, but the killer's other hand stopped her chin from moving. For one split second, Anita saw the twin steel spikes coming down. Two silver rods that promised death. They bore down in a heartbeat right into the center of her sight.

And in one horrible flash of crimson stars, Anita didn't see, or scream, anymore.

CHAPTER NINE

"How do you feel?" Richard asked.

Eve shook her head and instantly moaned. It throbbed.

"I've been better." She struggled to sit up, and he reached around to support her back. When she was sitting upright, his hand didn't leave. And she didn't mind that at all. It felt good to have his touch there.

"Do you think you can walk home?" he asked. "I think the girl who lives here wants her bed back."

As he said it, Eve saw a figure loitering in the living room just outside of the small bedroom.

"Yeah," she said, and started to stand up. She wobbled on her feet a little, and Richard put his hand under her elbow, holding her up and steady. Eve smiled at how responsive he was.

"Thanks," she said. "I can do it. Just a little woozy still is all."

She took a breath and started to walk forward. Eve intended to introduce herself and thank the girl who had let her stay here, but as they walked into the other room, the girl turned away, talking in whispers to someone on her cell phone.

"Thanks," Eve called out anyway, not sure if it was heard or not. Richard opened the door for her and they stepped into the hallway. She realized it was quiet. The low murmur of many voices came from down the hall, but there was no music.

"Is the party over?" she asked.

"Yeah, you were out for about three hours," he said.

"Geez, I'm so sorry."

"I don't think it was your fault," he said. "Someone had to have put something in one of your drinks. That didn't seem like an alcohol reaction to me."

"No," she agreed. "I've never seen trails of light after drinking before! But who would have wanted to drug me?"

He shrugged. "Nikki asked the bartender if there were any other reports of people getting loopy, and he said no. Someone either was trying to get someone high and hit the wrong glass at the bar, or was just being random."

They walked out of the stairwell and into the main hall where the party had been in full swing earlier. Groups of students were standing around some of the bar rounds still, talking and finishing their last drinks. But the bar itself had been packed up and taken away.

A flash of purple darted through and around the few lingering groups from their right. Nikki. Her face looked tense.

"Have you seen Anita?" she asked Richard. She didn't even look at Eve.

He shook his head. "I thought she was keeping an eye on Eve, but she wasn't up there when I went to get her."

"I haven't seen her in a couple hours," Nikki said, "and she's not answering my texts."

"Maybe she hooked up and went home with someone," Richard joked.

Nikki's eyes flashed with sudden fury. "That's what I'm afraid of," she snapped. And then she strode away. Eve saw her talking to another group. Two of the people at that table shook their heads and Nikki moved on once more.

"I hope everything's okay," Eve said as they walked through the door and out into a perfect warm night. Richard slipped his arm around her waist as they made their way down the sidewalk away from the hall.

"I'm sure she's fine," he said. "Anita loves a party. And she's not shy either."

"Sounds like you might have had some experience," Eve said.

She couldn't quite hear his response, but it sounded like he said, "I'm not the only one."

She decided not to press the point, and just focused on not tripping down the uneven walkway. All she wanted to do was get home to her own bed.

CHAPTER TEN

"I hate Ravel," Kristina said. "I know it's a sin, but…I'm just so over it, you know?"

"I won't tell anyone if you won't tell that I hate Mahler," the girl next to her said. "What a lot of pretentious 'just because I can' composing."

"I don't think I have ever heard anyone else say that." Kristina laughed.

They were walking down the hallway to their String Theory class at Nicolai Hall. There were two other girls from the class walking just ahead of them from the other direction. They stepped into the classroom just a couple seconds before Kristina. It was just enough time that one of them screamed before Kristina was in the room.

"Oh my God!" someone cried.

Kristina stopped short and stared, aghast. She ignored the long-haired girl just to the left of her who was making strange bleating, hysterical sounds. She was a lot cooler than that.

"Bollocks," she whispered.

Sitting in the chair at the front of the room, normally occupied by Professor Curtis, was a girl in leather sandals, leather shorts and a black t-shirt with a name in glitter. Kristina didn't read the name, because her attention was locked on the girl's eyes.

Or lack thereof.

The two spots where her eyes should have been were ragged red holes, thanks to the silver tuning fork that protruded from them.

Her nose and lips and chin were shiny; streaked in heavy crimson. The glitter on her shirt was stained red, making it hard to read the B and G of CBGB.

"Holy shit," a guy said from behind her.

"Who is that?" someone else asked. And then another person

screamed. The room behind her was starting to get crowded. Two of the guys in the class walked to the front of the semicircle of chairs and looked closely at the wounds and the girl's chest.

"She's not breathing," one of them said.

"Definitely dead," the other answered.

"Bollocks," Kristina said once more, and sat down in one of the chairs. She pulled out her phone to call Mrs. Freer at the front desk.

Somebody had to do it.

★　　★　　★

Eve felt her phone vibrate during the first morning lecture. She ignored it the first time. And the second. But it kept going off. Finally, she pulled it out and clicked it on. She knew it was verboten to be reading phone messages in front of the professor, but someone was really trying to reach her. The reason was right there in a text notification on her Start screen.

KRISTINA: *There's been another murder!*

Eve clicked into her text messages and typed, *Here at the school?*

Three dots appeared almost instantly. The response came fast.

KRISTINA: *Right here in my class at Nicolai.*

Eve stiffened. She'd been there just a few hours ago.

EVE: *That's where the party was last night.*

KRISTINA: *This girl was at that party. Someone said her name was Anita.*

Eve's stomach convulsed.

EVE: *No!*

KRISTINA: *Did you know her?*

EVE: *I went to the party with her last night.*

KRISTINA: *Probably another Anita.*

Eve shook her head and typed.

EVE: *I don't think so…she was missing at the end of the night.*

Her phone buzzed again in her hand, and she saw a new note from Facebook Messenger. She didn't recognize the profile name.

BWARN: *Last night:*

Beneath the words was a thumbnail of a laughing girl holding a drink. And a link to Anita's Facebook profile. Eve clicked on it.

Anita's profile banner was a snapshot of the Ramones.

But the first post on her Wall was a photo.

It showed Anita bent over someone. Two hands were around her neck, and Anita's mouth was open, as if she were screaming. The hands looked feminine; the left one wore a ring on the fourth finger.

The photo had been posted by Anita herself, at 4:13 a.m. this morning.

Below that, she had posted a YouTube link to a song. The still image showed Robert Smith of the Cure with members of his band around him. In garish letters at the top left it read, 'Pictures of You'.

"Oh my God," Eve whispered.

She remembered what they'd said about Genevieve. There had been a picture of her being killed, and a link to the song 'Pictures of You'

This was exactly the same. Now she knew without question that the dead girl in Kristina's classroom was her friend.

But why had Anita been killed?

And why had someone IMed the post to *her*?

Her whole body shook as if it were winter.

Eve was scared.

CHAPTER ELEVEN

Eve took one sip of the martini in her hand. Then she threw the glass to the ground. It shattered, but she didn't care. She was furious. "How dare you," she screamed. "I know it was you. You did this to me."

The other girl tried to placate her. "Just chill out, Eve, it wasn't me. Why would I?"

But Eve knew better. She reached out and grabbed the other girl around the neck. And squeezed. The flesh felt soft and yet solid. Muscular. That only made her more furious. Eve tightened her hands with all of her might. She wanted to squeeze the life out of her. Make her pay.

There were gargling sounds and faint squeals. And then the body went limp. Eve dropped it to the bed. There was a tuning fork lying there on the sheets. "Never again," she whispered.

The face on the bed was purple, and the eyes looked popped. They stuck out of her head.

The girl was Anita.

★ ★ ★

Eve woke from the violent dream in a sweat. Her heart was racing. It took a moment for her to realize that she had been dreaming. She hadn't killed Anita in a drugged-out haze. Had she? Slowly, she climbed out of bed and down the ladder. Kristina was in the lower bunk, breathing deep. The room was pitch black, but Eve tiptoed her way to the desk and pulled her phone off the charger. Her screen was still on the post on Anita's profile.

She put two fingers on the screen and swiped, sizing the photo larger, so that she could see the hands again.

The silver ring on the hand looked familiar. It was blurry, but it could have had a small blue speck of sapphire in the center. She pointed the light of the phone at her own left hand. Where there was a ring on her fourth finger. One that her aunt had given her when she'd graduated high school. It had her birthstone on it. A blue splinter of sapphire.

"Oh my God," Eve whispered.

Suddenly, her app updated, and the photo disappeared. She scrolled up and down Anita's profile, and hit refresh twice, but the photo and the Cure post were both gone.

Then she went back to her IMs and looked up the message she'd received earlier. The one with Anita's picture.

There was a space where someone had messaged her. But the profile photo icon showed a broken image, and grey text to the right of it read 'removed by Facebook'.

Could she really have been that drugged out that she could have done that to Anita? Even dragged her to a classroom and put her in a chair?

No way. The idea was ridiculous.

She walked down the hall to the bathroom, and as she washed her hands, the glint of her ring caught her eye. She stared at it for a moment. Then she slipped it off, and enclosed it in a fist. When she went back to the room, she dropped it into the small wooden box with the rest of her necklaces and jewelry, and then climbed back up the ladder into bed.

It took a very long time for her to fall back to sleep.

★   ★   ★

When she came back from her shower in the morning, the house phone was ringing. All of the rooms had a wired phone that connected to the front desk of the building, though they were useless for any outgoing calls. Eve had never heard it ring before. She rubbed a towel once more through her hair, and reached out to pick up the phone. Kristina was already gone.

"Hello?" she said.

"Is this Eve?" a woman's voice said.

"Yes."

"This is Mrs. Freer. Can you come down to the front desk? There's someone here who wants to see you."

Eve frowned. Who would come looking for her at eight in the morning?

"Who is it?" she asked. But the line was already dead.

She sighed, and quickly pulled on a pair of shorts and a light t-shirt. It was going to be another warm end-of-summer day, supposedly. Then she grabbed her backpack for class and headed down the stairs. She didn't even try the elevator.

"Ah, there you are," Mrs. Freer called from the lobby. Her face betrayed no expression. "You have a visitor."

There was a man standing at the desk with her. His hair was dark and short but curled slightly on the sides. His age was starting to show in the grey and thinning on top. He wore navy pants and a light blue short-sleeved shirt that said *Polizei* just above the breast pocket.

Uh-oh. Fear iced her veins. *Why are the police here for me?*

The man held his hand out as she approached. "Miss Springer?" he said. "I'm Inspector Martino. Can we talk for a minute?" He motioned towards the sitting area just off the lobby, and led the way to two cushioned easy chairs. He pointed at one and said, "Please." It was a command though, not a request.

She sat.

Her legs were shaking.

"I'm investigating the deaths of two students here at the Eyrie," he said. "Are you aware that Anita Strindberg was found dead yesterday?"

Eve nodded.

"Are you aware of how she was murdered?"

"Yes," Eve said. "My roommate, Kristina, was actually one of the ones who walked into the classroom and found her."

He did not look surprised. "I spoke with her a little while ago."

Well, that explained why Kristina had disappeared while she'd been in the shower.

"I understand that you were friends with this girl and went with her to a party the night that she died."

Eve shrugged. "Yes, I went with her to the party. But I wouldn't say we were friends. We only just met this week."

The inspector wrote something down in a notebook. He asked her about how they had met and details about the party. "Did she get in a fight with anyone there?"

Eve shook her head. "I don't think so. She was at our table the whole night."

"Except when she was with you," he said. "I understand you were sick and had to go lie down during the party."

"Yes."

"Drunk?" he asked.

She shrugged. "Something like that."

"I understand that drugs of some kind might have been involved."

"I don't take drugs," Eve said. "Honestly, I don't. But it was strange. Like maybe someone put something in my drink."

"Tell me about it."

She described the evening, and how she'd woken up in the bed upstairs at Nicolai with Richard and Anita and others looking after her.

"Hmmm," he grunted a couple of times.

"Anita stayed with you," he said. "But she wasn't there when Richard walked you home. When did she leave?"

Eve thought for a second. "I don't know. I must have been asleep when she left the room."

"I see," he said, and continued to write in his book. "But you may have been the last person to see her alive before she was killed."

After a couple more questions, he closed the notebook. "I'm sorry to have troubled you so early in the morning," he said. "But obviously we want to know every detail of that night from those who were with her." He held out a small card. "If you remember anything else, anything at all, please call me."

"I will," she promised, and stood up with him.

"Thank you," he said.

Eve watched him walk past the front desk and nod at Mrs. Freer before exiting to the street. When she looked back at the desk, she realized that Mrs. Freer was staring at her. Her eyes were cool. Unblinking.

Eve stood up and walked quickly down the hall towards the elevator.

★   ★   ★

A short while later, Eve met up with Richard on the way to class and told him about the interrogation.

"Yeah, they talked to me too," he said. They walked together down the stairs from the lecture hall. "Not that I could tell them much."

"He asked about her staying with me and said I might be the last one to have seen her alive."

Richard looked at her and held her gaze. "That's true, you know."

"I'm scared," she said.

"Let's sit down," he suggested, and led her out of the front doors of the building to one of the benches along the tree-lined walkway outside.

When they settled on the bench, he slipped his arm around her and she didn't resist. She welcomed it, honestly.

"Did you see the picture on her Facebook?" Eve asked.

"The one where someone was grabbing her by the throat?" he asked.

"Yeah."

"I did," he said. "Super creepy, because supposedly she posted it herself...but she was dead by then."

"I went to look at it again this morning and it was gone," she said.

"I don't think Facebook has a high tolerance for snuff pictures," he said. "I'd guess that the police had it removed, honestly. It was just like the picture that appeared on Gen's wall after she was killed. Even had the same Cure video posted with it."

"What if I had something to do with it?" she whispered.

"You?" He looked at her in shock. "What are you talking about?"

She described her dream, and the fact that the picture appeared to show her hands.

"I'm sure the picture wasn't you," he said. "You were barely able to open your eyes when I was in the room. And even if it was...she wasn't strangled to death. Someone stabbed her eyes out."

Eve hung her head. "I know, but...what if...."

"Just stop," he said, and pulled her closer to him. "You may have been hopped up on some kind of weird trip, but you're not a killer any more than I am. Whoever slipped you that mickey, that's the person we should be trying to find."

"Thanks," she said, and put her arm around him in an awkward hug. "I really appreciate it."

"Can't have our newest Songbird getting upset," he said.

She pulled back from the hug then. Did he care about her, or was he just making sure the jazz combo didn't have any more personnel problems? His next question set her mind at ease again.

"Do you want to have dinner with me tonight?" he asked.

"Just us?" she asked, without thinking.

He grinned. "I'm sure there will be other people in the restaurant."

"Um, sure," she said with a smile.

"I can show you some more of Ghent," he said. "It's a great walking city at night. And I know of a great little place by the river. The fries are perfect."

"French fries?" she asked, bemused.

"Belgian fries! They take their fries seriously here. You'll see," he promised.

CHAPTER TWELVE

Richard knocked on the door to her room promptly at seven p.m. Kristina raised her eyebrows when Eve rose to open the door. "Wow, you're getting a door-to-door escort, eh?"

Eve grinned. "Yeah, but I don't think there's a sports car waiting downstairs for us."

"Exercise builds a healthy appetite. Text me if you need me to be gone after dinner."

Eve picked up a bra from the back of Kristina's desk chair and threw it at her. "What kind of girl do you think I am?"

"A girl with a healthy appetite?" Kristina laughed.

Richard's face lit up when Eve opened the door. He wore khaki shorts and leather sandals, with a green and tan patterned button-down shirt. He looked ready for a tropical cruise. She hoped she wasn't overdressed in her sleeveless black blouse and pale capris. Her fear was instantly suppressed.

"You look stunning," he said. "Let me show you off around the town."

When Eve turned to wave goodbye to Kristina, her roommate simply rolled her eyes. "Have a good time," she called as Eve pulled the door shut behind them.

Richard led them to the famous St. Michael's Bridge, an old archway across the River Leie that had a perfect view of the heart of the city. The three- and four-story buildings were set in a row along the canal, with old brick and white- or yellow-painted facings. There were orange tiled roofs and ornate window settings. And a long walkway near the water with a green railing and old-fashioned gas lamp-style light poles. "St. Michael's Church is right there," he said, pointing to a beautiful spire that stretched high in the sky. "And you can see St. Nicholas's over there. Saint Bavo's is that one." Then he pointed down the canal. "But we're heading that way, to De Graslei."

They stepped off the bridge and made their way along the cobblestone street bordering the river before arriving at an old building with a triangular roof that was crammed in the middle of several similar structures. A covered patio was cordoned off outside the building, and filled with people laughing, talking and drinking. The sumptuous smell of grilling meat wafted across the tables. Richard talked to the hostess outside, and minutes later, they were sitting in low-backed comfortable chairs beneath a square umbrella, staring out at the passersby and the buildings on the other side of the Leie.

It was breathtaking. When Eve said as much, Richard grinned. "Wait 'til you try the food."

Virtually everything seemed to come with fries, or *frites*, as the menu said, even the fancy steaks and stews and meatballs.

After making sure that she didn't mind 'spicy', Richard ordered an appetizer of Diablo prawns, and encouraged her to order the Flemish stew ("to die for," he insisted).

When the prawns came, in a sauce that screamed 'heat', she took one and gingerly bit off a tiny chunk. The flavor electrified her mouth all the way back to her ears.

"Wow," she said.

Her Delirium Tremens came in the usual tulip glass with a pink elephant, and Richard toasted her with his tall Westmalle Trappist Tripel glass. The one thing Eve had noticed in eating out here was that beer was *always* served in a glass with the correct logo of the brewery. Not like the States, where they'd pour a fancy microbrew in a pint glass that said Lite or Budweiser on the side. As she took her first sip of the golden ale, the last rays of the setting sun caught the water with a kaleidoscope of colors beneath a darkening blue sky.

"This is perfect," she said.

"Glad to be the one to show you," he said. He caught her eye, and something passed between them that made Eve's spine tingle. She said nothing, only smiled in return, and sipped the electric bubbles of her pink elephant beer.

When their main course came, Richard held up his hand.

"Okay, before you try anything...tell me what you think of the fries."

They were crescent moon shaped and golden brown. Hesitantly, she picked one up, and bit off the end. White and soft inside, and nice and crispy outside. They were good but....

"Not bad," she said. "But if you think these are the best, I clearly need to introduce you to some classic crinkly fries from New York City."

He looked crestfallen.

Eve put her hand on his wrist. "They're *good*," she said. "I'm just teasing you."

Over the course of dinner, she learned that Richard had grown up just outside of Brussels, but had nearly flunked out of college due to a preference for nights spent ingesting strong abbey ales versus knowledge.

"My sax saved me," he said.

"How's that?"

"I joined a combo, and they played out a lot. They also got pissed off when I got pissed drunk and couldn't hit my solos well. They really cracked the whip on me until I was under control. The only thing I like more than drinking is playing my sax."

"Sometimes you just need a real focus," she said.

"No, you need the *right* focus," he said. "When I got into the program up here, I knew that I had to be in the Songbirds. I gotta tell you, I practiced more that summer than I probably had in the past two years."

They talked until it was dark and the lights slowly flickered on up and down the river. When the check came, Richard insisted on picking it up. After, he led her along the river to a quiet section, and they stared out at the reflections stretched across its dark surface.

There were still a couple of small boats slipping through the water like silent arrows. After a few minutes of silence, he turned towards her with a look of intense emotion on his face. "Thanks for coming with me tonight," he said.

Eve laughed. "Thank you for an amazing evening."

"I don't want to be too forward," he said, "but I wanted to know you from the first minute I saw you walk into the Songbirds practice that day. And that's not the Tripel talking."

His face had somehow grown closer to hers, and his hands now touched both sides of her waist.

"Not forward at all," she said, and tilted her head slightly to give him a quick kiss on the lips.

When he bent down to give her a longer, warmer one, she didn't protest.

They stayed by the river for a long time as other couples and groups of tourists passed them by.

This is where I want to be forever, Eve thought as she hugged him close and guided his hand to hold her in an increasingly intimate way. As his fingers moved gently against her lower curves, she began to think about texting Kristina to take her up on her offer of leaving Eve an empty room.

But on the walk home, Richard suggested something unexpected.

"Hey, do you want to go up to Gianna's?" he asked.

That was *not* the room that Eve wanted to go to at all. The surprise must have shown on her face.

"She was having some people over tonight just to hang out and chill," he said. "She texted me while we were at dinner and said we should stop by."

"We?" Eve said. "Did she really mean me?"

"Yeah, she knew we were having dinner tonight."

Eve grappled with that a moment. Why did Gianna know Richard was out with her? She tried to push that instinctive jealous reaction away, but there was just something she didn't like about the girl. She had a sudden realization that if she didn't go, Richard would probably see her home and go to Gianna's room on his own. She wasn't proud of it, but that cinched her decision.

"Sure," she said. "I'll go if you want."

★   ★   ★

Richard knocked three times on the door to room 416, and it only took a few seconds before the lock clicked and the wooden door swung open. Eve saw a flash of dark hair and red lips.

"Hey there, join the party," Gianna said, and disappeared back into the room.

Eve followed Richard inside. The wild solo of a jazz snare assaulted them as soon as they entered, and then an offhand piano melody took over the space before a saxophone stole the center microphone. Eve recognized it instantly. 'Rhythm-A-Ning' from Thelonious Monk's classic *Criss-Cross* album from the early sixties.

The room was a revolving wash of primary colors. In one corner, a lava lamp beamed the walls with an electric shade of blue, as blobs of color hovered and shifted in the clear center. On the desk, a lampshade was draped in a red silk blouse, dimming the light and warming the room with a rich subdued ambiance. In another corner, Gianna had a tall LED lamp which oscillated slowly across the spectrum, throwing a kaleidoscope of primary colors across the white ceiling.

Her stereo sat atop a small bookshelf near the desk, and glowed with ice-blue lights as a turntable spun the anachronistic album on an anachronistic device.

There was also a haze of white smoke hanging in the air, and an earthy, pungent aroma that permeated the room. Eve recognized it, and identified the source immediately – Markie was stretched out in a beanbag chair on the floor, and handed a thin, white, rolled joint to Pete, one of the trumpet players. With his eyepatch and black silk shirt and loose silk pants, the drummer looked like some kind of pampered gangster from a seventies Kung Fu film. The twins were on the bed; they both sat crosslegged on the mattress and leaned back against a wall. Erika was smoking a joint, while Elena sipped a glass of red wine. A psychedelic poster of interlocking purple and green and gold spirals that read *Brussels Jazz Fest 2019* hung on the wall not far from their heads.

Between the poster, the sixties jazz, the warm and shifting lighting and the smoke, Eve felt as if she'd just walked into a hippie commune from fifty years ago. Corey high-fived Richard as he came in and asked both of them what they wanted to drink.

"Whatever you've got open." Richard laughed and disappeared across the room with Corey to see.

Eve felt a hand on her shoulder. "Sit down and relax," a soft, rich and Italian-accented voice said in her ear. Erika's face was just inches from her own.

"Thanks," Eve said and eased her butt onto the edge of the mattress. "You're Erika...right?" Richard had told her how to tell the twins apart, since, while they looked identical, they had very different approaches to fashion. Erika wore a low-cut shirt crisscrossed in electric yellows and purples. Across the bed, her sister eschewed color for black.

The other girl smiled. "Very good," she said. "You catch on to us fast."

She tilted her head towards Elena. "My sister and I love the same music, but we do not agree on clothes...or vices." She blew a cloud of smoke above her head, and behind her, Elena clearly overheard and only shook her head.

"How are you enjoying the Eyrie so far?" Erika asked. "You are a long way from home."

"I'm excited about the opportunities," Eve said, "but worried about the murders, you know?"

Erika frowned. "It is a strange time, to be sure. The police think that it might be someone connected with the school in some way. Maybe the girls even knew the killer. It just shows that you must be careful who you trust. Everyone here has an agenda."

"How do you mean?" Eve asked.

Erika raised an eyebrow. "Music is cutthroat, eh? Everyone wants to be the soloist and star of the show. Some people will do anything to get that. Anything at all."

"Would you do anything?" Eve asked.

Erika's expression froze for a second...and then a huge grin split her face.

A cool stem of glass suddenly slid into Eve's hand, and a solid arm slipped around her shoulder.

"Cheers," Richard said. He held out a glass of red wine, and Eve lifted the identical one he'd just pressed into her hand. Erika held her joint up in the air, as if it were a glass she was about to toast. Then she made a show of pressing it to her lips and drawing a deep toke. Richard laughed, and took a sip of his wine. Eve did the same.

"I'm so glad we could all do this tonight," he said. "It's been too long." He looked pointedly at Erika, who simply exhaled slowly.

"It's like a trip back in time," Eve said, waving at the lights and posters around them.

"Gianna's an old soul," Richard said.

"Old and bitter," Erika said quietly.

"Oh, come on now," Richard said. "She's a riot. And a realist. Plus, she'd do anything for anyone here."

"Is that so?" Erika said. She looked unconvinced.

"I'll show you," he said, and stood up from the bed. He walked across the room and drew Gianna away from a conversation she was having with Markie. He whispered in her ear, and Eve could see the girl roll her eyes. A moment later they both stood in front of the bed.

"What would you like Gianna to do for you?" he asked.

Gianna made a rude gesture with her lips and tongue. Then she feigned a curtsy, holding out the sides of an invisible dress with her hands.

Erika thought a moment. "Tell Richard that you'll let him have your solo in 'Port a Belle'."

Gianna laughed, without humor, and looked up at Richard.

"Richard knows I would do just about anything for him," Gianna said coolly. "But I won't do that."

She turned then and went back to her place by Markie. The drummer ushered her to a corner to talk about something in whispers.

"See what I mean?" Erika asked. She looked at Richard. "She's kind of a bitch." Then she looked at Eve. "Everyone here wants to be the star. Or they wouldn't have clawed their way over everyone else to be here. Always remember that."

CHAPTER THIRTEEN

This time, Eve was invited to the courtyard vigil.

"A bunch of us are going to get together at nine o'clock tonight on the back patio," Richard told her after class. "To remember Anita. Some of us will talk about the memories we had with her. You don't have to come if you don't want to. You didn't really know her."

Eve shook her head. "No, I want to," she said. "I think we would have become good friends, honestly. Should I bring anything?"

"Just a pocket of tissues," he said with a laugh.

She frowned. A vigil and tears for one of their own who'd been murdered hardly seemed a laughing matter.

"I'll see you there then," Richard said. "I've gotta get to class."

He flashed her a smile and turned quickly to head in the opposite direction she was going.

★   ★   ★

There were already a dozen people in the courtyard when Eve arrived that night. Richard wasn't among them, but Susie was; the bassist was handing out small candles to everyone who arrived. One by one, small flames flickered to life across the small crowd, casting eerie orange light on the faces of those who held them.

"Thanks for coming," Susie said, as she handed Eve a candle and offered a lighter.

"Sure," Eve said. She didn't know what else really to say and as soon as her flame was lit, Susie immediately moved on to the next couple people stepping off the path and into the courtyard.

People she didn't know or just barely recognized from class gathered around her and soon there were at least thirty people standing behind and to the side of her. She had stayed on the edge of the courtyard, so nobody was to her left, and only one person stood in front of her so she had a clear view of the table where Anita's picture was displayed in a frame. Markie and Susie and the twins and Nikki all gathered around the table. Flowers were littered near the photo. On the ground before it, people had dropped handwritten notes and signs decorated with colored markers that said things like *LOVE. NEVER FORGET. HEAVEN.*

The messages were upbeat and positive, but they dragged her heart down.

And as several of the Songbirds gathered around the table and began to talk about their remembrances of Anita, Eve began to feel more and more alone.

As Richard had said, she didn't know the girl, not really. She didn't really know *anyone* here very well yet. She was alone. And if a killer crept up on her in a hall in the school after dark and slit her throat, nobody here would have any reason to miss her much. Hell, would they even hold a vigil for her if that happened?

Eve glanced at the students around her. Their eyes were all glued to Susie, who was telling a story about a party that she threw with Anita last semester.

It didn't mean anything to Eve, and she wanted, honestly, just to leave. It wouldn't be hard. Nobody stood next to her; she could just fade back and duck down the dark path to return to the front entrance to the Eyrie. And where was Richard? He should have been here by now.

A motion caught her attention. A flicker in the bushes that she saw from the corner of her eye. Eve turned to look and her breath caught.

Eyes stared at her through the bushes.

She almost screamed, but instead put her hand over her mouth. At the front of the vigil, Susie said something and the whole crowd laughed.

Eve looked towards Susie for just a second, and when she looked back, the face was gone.

She tried to make it out through the dark spaces between the leaves of the six-foot-high bushes but all she could see were leaves rippling in the breeze.

Had she really even seen anyone there?

The rapid beat of her heart said yes, yes she had.

Maybe it was Anita's killer, lurking around to take pleasure in the pain. The thought sent a chill down her spine. What if the person who had stabbed out Anita's eyes was waiting to grab someone from the assemblage here when they streamed out and back to their rooms? If she left early…she might not make it down that short dark path and back to the front of the building.

Eve looked back and forth along the front of the hedge but saw no evidence that anyone still lurked there.

And then her attention was pulled back to the front of the courtyard by a familiar voice. Richard now stood next to Susie.

"If there is one thing that I know about Anita, it's that she loved a good time," he said. "She'd want us not to mourn for her, but to have a party to celebrate her life. So I ask all of you now to dry your eyes and think of the best time you ever had with Anita. And then remember that look she got in her eye when she was about to start singing an ABBA song just because…." He held up his phone and the familiar strains of 'Dancing Queen' began to play. Smiles spread across the assemblage. A few people laughed.

He had turned the mood around, at least for a minute. Eve smiled a little herself. She stayed to the very end of the vigil, though she looked over her shoulder every couple minutes at the bushes, wondering if she'd catch another glance at a lurker there.

She did not.

However, in the back of the crowd, before it disbanded, she did recognize a familiar scowling face. Philip stood there at the back of the students, arms crossed. Mrs. Freer was at his side, her expression blank. Eve could have sworn they were looking at her, and she quickly turned back around to stare at the vigil table. Her heart was beating fast and she didn't know why.

They were staring at the picture of Anita, not her, right? That had to be.

When it came time to leave, Eve did not hurry. She didn't want to be caught by the killer, or Philip and Mrs. Freer. She made sure she was not in the front or the end of the exiting mob.

Eve stayed safely in the middle.

CHAPTER FOURTEEN

"I can't believe you haven't gone inside yet," Richard said. "I think I did this tour the first weekend I was here."

They waited in line along the narrow winding stone barricade that led to the heart of Gravensteen Castle. It was small, at least by the way Eve thought of castles, but it stood along a main road in the center of the old town section of Ghent. Richard had taken her for a drink in a beautiful courtyard surrounded by restaurants and bars just across the street, and she'd enjoyed an abbey ale there, in an almost medieval goblet, as they relaxed in the gentle late summer breeze. It seemed natural that afterwards, they'd walk over to wander the outer yard and cool inner spaces of the castle.

"It's a must-see," Richard insisted.

After buying tour tickets and standing in line for a bit, they eventually made it inside and ascended to the battlements. To someone used to the skyscrapers of New York, the castle wasn't very tall at all, but it did give a beautiful view of the tall church spikes and orange-tiled rooftops of Ghent all around. At one point they arrived at sections of the wall that overhung the outside of the castle, and it was explained on the audio tour that the holes in the stone floor were where the castle dwellers had come to...take a dump. Eve had stifled a laugh that was tinged in disgust. Really? Come out here whether it was cold or rainy and drop your pants to poop through a hole to the ground a hundred feet below? Holy crap. No pun intended.

They reached the top of the castle soon after, and Richard shot her picture as she hung on the edge of one of the square stone turrets on the periphery. The entire city stretched out below them and Eve stared out at the horizon, enjoying the beauty of both the ancient and modern buildings of the city. Richard showed her his phone after she stepped away from the edge and it was breathtaking. The entire city was laid out behind the glow of her smile. Eve wasn't crazy about the picture of herself, but she had to admit, it was a good one. She looked unconditionally happy. And in that moment, truly, she was.

They followed the tour through several rooms, including one lower level space with the rough stone lit with a vibrant purple light. Not exactly the way it would have looked in ancient times before electricity and LED bulbs, but she had to admit, the rich cones of colored light on the ancient stone were striking.

At the end of the tour, they made the final descent into the underbelly of the structure...the section that was really what Richard had wanted her to see. On the main level, they'd seen various swords and axes and suits of iron and chain mail and other battle gear, but here...here was the torture chamber. The place where prisoners of war had been held and abused until they divulged the secrets of their masters to their enemy. When you really thought about what all of the iron chains and cuffs and spiked pieces did, it made the stomach churn.

"How would you like that as a necklace?" Richard asked, pointing at a cruel iron device that featured dozens of spikes set on the inside of an iron collar. She'd seen people wear collars with spikes sticking *out* from their necks, but not digging in.

"I guess the goths and punks have it all wrong," she said.

There were tables with glass lids protecting all sorts of torture devices; metal brands and instruments designed to hold the eyelids or mouth pried open so that...sharper things could make their point. There were jagged looped hooks that looked like dental instruments. She didn't want to think about how those had been used. There were thumbscrews. Wrist locks. Head locks. The ingenuity of human cruelty was truly frightening.

There was also a tall wooden guillotine, with its silver diagonal blade raised ten feet in the air, poised to drop and separate the victim from his or her head. A wooden bucket sat to the side, positioned to accept the deposit of the victim's head. The wood of the torture device looked like fine furniture; its finish was gorgeous and glinted in the exhibition lights. The blade shone sharp and deadly. And ready. Eve shivered looking at it. In this setting, it looked like an oddity, but the reality was…people – many people – had died beneath that blade. It was the most horrible instrument of execution. Quick. And frighteningly final.

"Hey Eve," Richard called.

He stood beside a wax dummy laid out on a long-planked surface. Rope was wrapped around the figure's ankles, while its wrists were tied and hidden behind its back. An ivory funnel protruded from the figure's mouth. What had they poured down the throat of the poor bastards who got tied up here?

"How would you like to trade places with this guy?" he asked. "Maybe I could bring this thing back to my room."

Eve's eyes widened. She shook her head slowly left to right. *Uh-uh.*

"You're sure?" he asked. "Imagine all of the Delirium Tremens I could give you that way and you wouldn't have to feel guilty at all. You wouldn't be able to say no."

Eve was not convinced. "I think it would be coming right back out of that funnel pretty fast."

"Oh no," Richard said with a wicked smile. "The real torture chamber guys knew exactly how much they could get away with before their victims choked to death. I'd make sure you could get down everything I poured into you."

Somehow, although she thought that's how he meant them, his words did not seem like comforting promises at all.

She stole a glance at his face to see if he was serious. But his eyes were already busy reading the placard description beneath a thumbscrew.

"It's kind of amazing the things they used to do to people," Richard said. "And they got away with it. Hell, it was normal. People complain these days that being in a prison with three meals a day is punishment. They have no idea."

Eve looked at the implements all around them with hooks and chains and sharp edges. "I like to think we've evolved a little bit."

Richard looked at her with a lopsided grin. "That's what you'd *like* to think, yeah. But is it true? Do you think people could still take pleasure in doling out this kind of pain? That's really the question, isn't it?"

CHAPTER FIFTEEN

"Let's pick it up again from measure 32," Susie called out.
Eve flipped the page back and readied her fingers over the keys.

Richard licked his lips and put the mouthpiece of his sax to his mouth. When he saw her looking, he raised his eyebrows and pursed his lips in the motion of a kiss.

The past two weeks had slipped by like a dream. She'd spent nearly every night since with him, either at a bar or his place, or both. It was crazy how much they'd connected. Little by little, her fears about Anita's death faded away. As did the police presence. After the murder, there seemed to be a cop in the Eyrie lobby twenty-four seven. But over the past couple days, she'd walked in and out later at night without seeing one.

As far as Eve was concerned, the nightmare was over, and the dream was in full force.

At least it was, until Susie stopped them at measure 40 because of Eve's mistake.

"Come on, people, we have our first gig of the semester tonight at Heavy Beans. Let's try to get it together."

Eve looked at Susie with widened 'I'm sorry' eyes and forced her gaze away from Richard and back to the music. Her fingers grew increasingly sure of themselves then.

★   ★   ★

The coffeehouse was more crowded than Eve had seen it before. Every table had people sitting around it, and there were a handful standing in the front of the place near the windows, talking as much with their hands as their mouths. The place was buzzing.

"Ah yes, my Songbirds," Claude called out from behind the counter. "Come in, come in! We've been waiting for you."

He came out from behind the register and offered to take one of the drums from Eve. She'd helped Markie carry things since she had nothing to bring of her own. Luckily, the café had an upright piano of its own, so she didn't need to bring an electric one.

"It's going to be a good night," he said. "It's a special night."

"Thanks," Eve said. When he lifted the canvas drum case from her shoulder, she felt the sweat sticking her shirt to her back from where the strap had been. "Why is it special?" she asked.

He looked over his shoulder at her. "This would have been my sister's twenty-third birthday."

Eve understood the charge in the words, "Would have been." Claude looked energized about the performance tonight, but those words, and the creases at the corner of his eyes, said he was hurting. And she couldn't ask him what happened. Maybe Richard would know. She made a mental note to ask him later.

There was work to be done now. The band moved quickly down the narrow aisle between the counter and the tables and began unpacking their instruments on the stage, in full view of their audience. Eve didn't have much to do — she organized her music on the piano and then tried to help Markie as he set up his small drum kit. In the end, she was superfluous and retreated to the old piano bench.

Richard finished setting his music on a small stand and then walked over to her.

"You ready for your first gig?"

"I think I can handle it," she said. "It's not like I've never played in public before."

"Remember, if you play like Chick Corea you might get your picture on the wall of fame," he teased.

Eve shook her head. "I'm fine with just getting through the show without screwing up so bad we have to restart a song."

"It's jazz, baby," he said. "We never restart. We evolve. It's all part of the extemporaneous exploration of our energies that we embark upon."

"Be careful, I might throw up in your general direction," she warned. He jumped backwards.

"Smart man," she said. However, when he began to go back to his seat near Gianna, she stopped him, motioning for him to return. "Hey," she said quietly. "What happened to Claude's sister?"

"She killed herself," he said. "But that was quite a while ago. Why do you ask?"

She told him what Claude had said, and he frowned. "Huh," Richard said. "I didn't realize that this was a special day."

Just then, Susie called for the group to get ready.

"Play like a Chick," he said with a grin, and ducked around the twins to take his chair. It was catty, but Eve couldn't help but notice that Gianna flipped her hair to the side with one hand when he was settled beside her. As if calling for his attention. Eve had asked diplomatically a few nights ago about his relationship with Gianna and he'd insisted they were just friends, though the girl seemed to always be at his side. "We just have to be in sync so we practice together a lot," he claimed.

Possessive bitch, Eve thought.

And then Susie grabbed a microphone and thanked everyone for coming and pointed at Markie to count it off. Seconds later, they were swaying to the undeniable groove of the classic 'Take Five' from Dave Brubeck. Susie had said earlier it was always good to lead with a song everyone in the audience would know, before digging into some more obscure stuff. Everyone knew 'Take Five'; it was the quintessential lounge jazz song. And it gave Pete and Corey chances to solo on trumpet.

After their first number, Claude came to the stage and picked up a microphone from in front of the horn players. He had shed the chef's apron, which had hidden some of the glare from his outfit. Eve smirked as she stared at his back. He wore a purple button-down long-sleeved silk shirt tonight with faded orange denim pants. In the small bank of lights from the ceiling that lit the stage, he veritably glowed.

"Welcome back," he said. "I'm so excited to start a new season of performances from our favorite local artists, the Songbirds of the Eyrie. Every year the faces change, but the music remains *amazing*. As some of you know, the Songbirds lost their last pianist recently, but I'm pleased to welcome a new girl to grace our keys, Eve Springer."

Claude turned and beamed at her as he applauded. The café erupted with clapping and Eve's stomach jittered. She was uncomfortable at being singled out for this attention. She felt herself blushing, but bowed from her piano bench. Claude went on to mention Susie and Markie and complimented Pete for his work on 'Take Five'.

And then they launched into an hour-long set and Eve lost herself in the give and take of the music. She loved the conversation of jazz; sometimes she was punctuating the story of Richard's saxophone and sometimes she was leading the conversation with the support of Susie's bass. Jazz was not simply playing music, it was making music. There was a script, but the memorable moments of a jazz performance were typically the extemporaneous ones.

★   ★   ★

They were midway through the first set when she noticed Claude hovering over something at the bar. She had to turn her attention back to the keys, but when she could glance to the side again, she saw him lifting a very small cake in his hands. There was a candle on it.

At the end of the song, she took a second to turn around on the bench to see whose birthday it was. It took a second, but finally her eyes spotted the cake. It was sitting on an empty table against the wall. It was right near where Eve had sat the first time she'd been to Heavy Beans. The lit candle flickered against the backdrop of the array of musician pictures. A small sign in black block letters was tented at the end of the table. It read RESERVED.

Weird, Eve thought. *Why would you take a cake with a candle out to a table before the guests had arrived?*

At that moment, Susie introduced the next song. "We play this one for Claude every time we are here, but tonight, he's asked me to dedicate this one to Vanessa because it's one of her favorites. It's one of those songs that everyone has played and yet it always sounds good. Here is our version of 'Fly Me to the Moon'."

Eve readied herself for Susie's bass intro. She was right; it was hard to go wrong with the old Sinatra classic.

They ran through it flawlessly, and Eve even got to add a few flourishes that raised a wink and a smile from Richard. There was even someone in the audience snapping pictures; she could see the white strobes of the flash, and at one point, someone crouched at the corner of the small stage with a large professional camera and a telescoping zoom lens. It was like they were rock stars or something!

Two numbers later they finished the first set to a rousing round of applause. The place was still packed with people standing near the front windows. But the table with the birthday cake remained empty. The candle had gone out, burned down to the frosting. But nobody sat at the table.

Eve looked at the area around it and realized that the table was right beneath the photo of a girl at a piano. The same photo that Claude had refused to say anything about the first time she'd been here. He'd talked about the other musicians and skipped over that one.

It suddenly dawned on her who the photo was and who the cake was for.

Claude's late sister, whose name was apparently Vanessa.

Eve frowned. That pulled at the heart just a little too hard.

★　　★　　★

"Did you see the cake?" she asked Richard as they waited in line in the break between sets. Eve had a strong craving for a strawberry gelato after seeing the frozen display case on their way in.
"No," he said. "What cake?"

She pointed over to the wall toward the empty table. But then realized that it wasn't empty any longer. And the cake was gone.

When she explained what she'd seen, Richard shrugged. "That's nice I guess," he said. "Or maybe it's creepy. I didn't realize we were playing 'Fly Me to the Moon' for a dead girl."

Eve punched him in the shoulder. "Don't be mean," she said. "It was sweet but kind of sad too."

"Not as sad as you're going to be if that gelato tin is as empty as I think it is."

She looked up and saw Claude digging hard into the strawberry to get the last bit from the pan into someone's small white shallow bowl.

"Oh no," she moaned.

"You look more like a raspberry kind of girl to me anyway," he said.

She put her lips together and gave him a different kind of raspberry in response.

★   ★   ★

Actually, the raspberry gelato was pretty good. And the second set they played was electric. Though Eve had to admit she felt a bit of jealous trepidation when Susie announced that they would have a special guest joining them to sing on the next song. She recognized Isabella, the girl she'd met at the Nicolai party, as soon as she stood up from the third row of tables and approached the stage.
Part of her hated the girl. Isabella wore a dangerously short white dress with patterned rows of sequins across the chest and hips. Slinky and stunning. After Eve provided a torchy piano introduction to 'Someone to Watch Over Me', when Isabella broke into the sultry croon of the melody, even Eve couldn't help getting chills.

She caught the flash of the camera again several times during this one. Apparently, their photo friend really liked this tune. Or at least Isabella.

When the set ended, and the applause died down, a grey-haired man with a short beard approached the stage. He wore khakis and a polo shirt. A camera hung around his neck.

She almost didn't recognize him at first, since he wasn't in his normal tweed suit. And then it clicked. Prof. Von Klein. Their photographer was the professor himself!

"Well played, Songbirds," he said. "A great opening to the semester."

He complimented Richard and Corey on particular solos. But his attention was not on the full band for long. After a moment, he turned to Isabella. "Can I talk to you a moment?"

"But of course, professor," she said softly. Her lips split into a broad smile and he took her arm as she stepped down from the short stage. As he did, Claude approached the band. He raised an eyebrow at the professor and Isabella, but said nothing about it. Instead he walked around and shook the hands of each musician, including Eve.

"I want to thank you all," he said. "You make the music that makes me want to keep doing this. What is a coffeehouse without jazz? You keep us all alive."

A few minutes later, as Eve sipped a cappuccino with Richard, Markie, Gianna and Susie, she saw Isabella and the professor sitting at a table in the corner. The professor's hands were gesturing excitedly. The vocalist listened, the faintest of smiles on her lips. Eve couldn't help but wonder what they were talking about.

"Looks like the professor has a new teacher's pet," Gianna said.

"Maybe he's just giving her tips on her vocal performance tonight," Susie said. "She was really good, I thought."

Gianna snorted. "*Vocal* performance is not the performance he is interested in."

"Meow," Richard said.

"You, of all people, know I'm right," Gianna said. She gave him a pointed look.

Richard's face feigned surprise. "It's not a crime to talk to pretty girls. I'm talking to all of you, aren't I?"

That earned him a chorus of groans.

"We all know you did more than just *talk* to Isabella," Markie said. "But maybe the professor, um, conducts a better staff than you?"

Richard bunched up a napkin and threw it at the drummer's face. Gianna frowned and took a sip of her coffee.

"Wait, you went out with Isabella?" Eve turned to ask Richard. He didn't meet her eye. He looked uncomfortable.

"Yeah, for a little while."

"Until she dumped his ass." Markie laughed.

"For the professor?" Eve asked.

Gianna waved her finger. "Nah," she said. "She's just kissing his ass because she wants the Morricone Scholarship."

It was Eve's turn to frown. "Wait, she's going for that too? I applied last week. My audition was yesterday."

"Well, the professor makes the final call on who gets it," Gianna said. "And I'm guessing from the look of it that Isabella's audition is tonight."

Eve had a sinking feeling that she might be being outmaneuvered right now. The Morricone Scholarship was a five thousand Euro scholarship awarded to students from outside of Belgium, recognizing artistic promise. It was intended to help defray the travel expenses for musicians from abroad, but it was also a coveted recognition of people who had the chops to 'go places'. If Eve could put that on her resume, it would get her in doors she could never have opened otherwise back in New York.

At that point Markie stood up with his arms crossed. He looked like an exotic pirate demanding the attention of his crew. "Have you all had enough coffee for one night?" he asked. "I say we take a walk and find something a little stronger."

"I'm in," Richard said immediately. He looked grateful for the opportunity to change the subject.

"Well as long as *you're* in." Gianna smirked. "Yeah, I'll go."

Susie looked at Eve. "What do you say?"

She really just wanted to go home. The post-show release of nervousness and tension had left her feeling like a limp dishrag. The news that Richard had had a fling with Isabella shook her confidence and left her feeling unworthy. Had he done something with Susie too? What about the twins? Or worse, his saxophone partner? She had a sudden image of Gianna and Richard drinking together and Gianna laughing at all of his jokes and putting her hands on his arm as she fluttered those sarcastic eyelashes.

Eve decided a pink elephant was in her future.

"Yeah, I'm in too," she said.

"Excellent," Richard said. "But this time I'm keeping an eye on your drinks."

When they all got up to head down the street to a bar, Eve noticed that the table with the professor and Isabella was now empty.

CHAPTER SIXTEEN

Isabella felt the faint breeze of the night air slipping across her chest in places she shouldn't have been able to. She looked down and realized that she'd not finished buttoning up.

"Nice," she murmured to herself. "Give the whole world a free show. And what the hell, after tonight, why not?"

She cinched the button and then slapped herself in the forehead. "Damnit. I left my bag in his office."

Isabella shook her head at her forgetfulness, turned around and began to walk back to the North Tower. Night birds called out to each other in faint, plaintive notes through the dark shadows of the trees, but that was the only sound. Nobody else was about. The evening smelled sweet with the cool moist air of a late summer night. It was long past midnight. After the concert, she'd agreed to go back to the professor's office for a session. There, she'd indulged him in his private office for well over an hour. She hoped that it would prove worth it in the end.

Though it was after hours, her keycard got her back into the building. The halls were dark, except for the low glow of the nightlights that were mounted at the start and end of each hallway. It was eerie to walk here at night; so different from the daytime hours when the place was a hub of activity. She was only a few steps down the main hall when she heard the front entry door click shut.

Isabella turned around, a frown on her brow. Who else would be here at this hour? The school was still restricting late-night practice sessions.

There was nobody behind her.

"Hmph," she said. Maybe the door had just been slow to latch closed behind her.

She turned the corner and walked up the steps to Prof. Von Klein's office. At one point, she thought she heard another footstep, but when she looked over her shoulder, the stairwell remained spookily empty.

"Now you're just playing games with yourself," she said. Still, the pace of her steps increased just a bit. She just wanted to find her handbag and get home. It had been a long night. With a decidedly unconventional end.

She walked past a row of dark office doors of the music faculty. Her heart sank when she saw that the opaque window of Room 392 was black. Lights out. She'd been there ten minutes ago and he had not yet packed up.

He must have left right after her.

She was sure the door would be locked, but when she tried the handle, it turned immediately.

"It's my lucky night," she murmured.

Isabella stepped inside. She assumed she'd left her bag on his desk when she'd been straightening her dress after their session. Light from the street filtered into the room and threw long shadows across the cluttered old wooden desk. In addition to a computer, the professor had stacks of papers, several pens and even a trumpet sitting there. But as she stepped closer, she did not see her purse.

Shit, she thought. *It must be in the back room.*

There was a door on one side of the professor's office that opened to a private room. Isabella had been there with the professor tonight. Few people ever were allowed there, but everybody knew about it. There was a door in the back of that room that opened onto a small theater balcony with several plush seats. The balcony overlooked the Grand Hall. The professor could often be seen sitting in one of those chairs during a rehearsal or performance, overlooking the whole theater. It was his own reserved box seat. People on stage got serious when they looked up during practices to see that one of the chairs was no longer empty. Suddenly there would be a lot less chatter and a lot more precision in the playing.

The professor stored both music and photo and lighting equipment in the room behind the balcony. It was his private studio and included a leather couch against one wall.

Sitting in the middle of that couch was her small tan handbag.

"There it is," she said and quickly walked over.

She bent to pick it up.

Two hands grabbed her arms from behind. She started for a second, but then began to smile and turn around.

"Professor, it's late—" she said.

She stopped in mid-sentence.

The hands that held her wore black leather gloves. The face was obscured by some kind of black silk hood. She opened her mouth to scream, but one of the gloved hands instantly slapped across her lips, stifling the sound.

Isabella kicked her attacker in the leg. One of her heels connected. She felt the jolt in her hip and heard the cry of anguish from her target. The black gloves dropped from her face to grab the leg. Isabella spun and ran towards the door to the professor's main office.

Her escape was short-lived.

Before she reached the doorway, the attacker dove after her and two hands closed around her left ankle. She heard a thud behind her as the black-clad body hit the floor. And then she lost her balance and fell forward, knocking her head on the doorjamb as she went down. The dark room exploded with light in her head. Isabella cried out in pain as the hands yanked her backwards by the ankle. Something wrapped around her legs and tightened. Isabella blinked away the stars and saw the dark figure crouching over her, binding her. She tried to kick it off, but her feet were already trapped; bound together.

She was not going to let herself get tied up by a maniac. No way. She might have a manicure and wear sexy dresses, but her brothers had taught her how to punch. And that's just what she did now. She aimed a smack right at the side of the assailant's face.

It connected and she felt the echo of the punch instantly seep through her fingers.

Instead of falling back, one black hand came right back at her and caught her on the chin. Isabella's head snapped back. She struck again herself, but this time, her hand connected with empty air. A hand clasped her forearm and a second later something cold wrapped fast around her wrist. The same thing happened with her other arm as she struggled to sit back up. Isabella used the grip on her arm to balance herself and came up from the floor determined to attack. She'd bite the bastard if she could get close enough.

Her attacker had other ideas. One black glove was already in the air when she finally saw what was happening. She was being expertly bound with a long black microphone wire. And as she opened her mouth to scream her anger, the business end of the cord slammed into her mouth. Ice-hot pain shot through her teeth and jaw as the small round end of a microphone buried itself in the back of her throat. She felt broken jagged edges of her teeth wash to the side of her tongue as nearby, something ripped. It was the sound of duct tape – something heard all the time at shows as people locked down wires on the floor to avoid anyone tripping onstage.

A second later, the sticky part of a wide section of tape slapped across her upper lip and fastened to the sides of her cheeks. The black gloves ripped off a section and attached another piece beneath her chin, taping the microphone in place in her mouth.

"Slut," the mouth behind the black face mask whispered. The voice was so faint, she couldn't tell if it was a man or a woman. But she could understand what it said. "You know what to do with that mouth, don't you?"

Isabella kicked and tried to roll, though with every motion the microphone ground against broken teeth and sent waves of pain through her head. She felt like she might throw up, and struggled to contain her gag reflex. She wouldn't be able to get it out of her mouth if her stomach tried to lose its contents.

The leather-clad hands lifted her legs off the ground and held on despite her thrashing. Little by little, the attacker wrapped the end of the cord around her legs, eventually binding her already tied arms to her stomach. It was one of the hundred-foot mic cords; it had lots and lots of coils. And soon, they were all wrapped around her until the end of the cord reached her neck. At one point, the hands grabbed the fingers of her right hand and pressed her thumb against something hard and cool. She recognized the touch and her suspicion was confirmed when a black glove held up her phone to check it. Her thumb had just been used to unlock the home screen of her iPhone.

Then the hands reached down beneath her shoulders, lifted her from the ground and dragged her out the back door to the professor's balcony.

She was dropped on the ground near the wooden bannister for a minute and Isabella tried to roll backwards. If she could get her head near the chair, she could lever herself up maybe....

Something flashed. And again. It blinded her and she knew immediately what it was.

A camera.

The hands yanked her upright and held her near the rail.

"Last curtain call," the voice whispered. "Live by the mic, die by the mic."

And then she was rolling over the balcony bannister and for a second, hanging in freefall.

But only for a second.

Isabella opened her mouth to scream.

And then the microphone wire around her neck caught like a noose and her weight pulled it tight, choking out all sound but the crack of her neck.

That sudden snap echoed through the empty theater as Isabella lost the ability to sing or scream forevermore.

CHAPTER SEVENTEEN

The alarm sounded like a gong. Eve forced her eyes open. The clock LED read 7:00. She had to be at her first lecture at eight. Without another thought, she slapped the snooze button. She could not face the day yet. Her head hurt. Maybe fifteen more minutes would make it better. She didn't really believe that, but it sounded good at the moment.

Instead of falling back asleep though, she lay there as the seconds clicked by, forcibly holding her eyes shut and feeling a steady throb right behind them. Her bladder was also sending alarm signals. *Just a few more minutes,* she thought. *Every second in bed will help.* But that just made her feel like she had to pee even more.

How had she ended up with a hangover again? She struggled to remember. They'd gone to an old bar around the corner from Heavy Beans and gotten a small table on the patio. The glow of a Big Ben-style tower clock loomed in the dark above them from just down the street. And a very funny waiter kept bringing them more beer. But still, she swore she'd only had three Delirium Tremens. Four at the most? But then another memory surfaced and the reason for her headache became clearer. Eve remembered one more snippet from late last night. Richard had flagged down the waiter and ordered shots of J&B for everyone. She'd protested, but the glasses came anyway, and everyone raised them up in a Songbirds toast. After that, it all grew murky. She struggled to remember. But nothing came. She couldn't even remember the walk home. She remembered that Richard had actually left before her, but what happened after...?

Finally, she could no longer struggle with the memories or deny her bladder any longer. Eve poked at the off button on her alarm and clumsily climbed down the ladder out of bed.

Blinking the sticky cobwebs away, she grabbed her robe and bathroom bag and walked, a bit unsteadily, down the hall to the communal showers. She worried as she crossed the tile that she couldn't hold it until she got to the stall. But she did. Just barely.

The subsequent shower washed away some of the sleepiness, but very little of the headache. Her mouth tasted like a shoe even after she brushed her teeth. It was not going to be a good day. She stopped in the cafeteria downstairs for a muffin before heading to the North Tower and saw a familiar shock of purple hair amid a crown of black. Nikki. She'd barely seen her since Anita had died.

"Hey," she said, as they stood next to each other at the coffee and juice machines.

Nikki looked at her with dark, unblinking eyes. She said nothing. As soon as her coffee cup was full, she grabbed a plastic lid and turned away, walking directly to the exit. Eve could almost feel the temperature in the room plummet.

Wow, Eve thought. *What crawled up your ass this morning and died?*

She grimaced, feeling the ache as she tightened the muscles in her forehead. She wasn't nauseous but…. She took a sip of orange juice and just held it for a minute in her mouth. Then swallowed. And then again.

Juice and a blueberry muffin would help even her out. She grabbed the latter in a napkin and headed towards the door. She didn't want to walk into the lecture late. Prof. Von Klein would see her. And she had no doubt that he'd put a mental checkmark next to her name.

Eve took a deep breath and walked a little faster towards the other half of the building. She was still at the base of the stairs when she heard a scream from the floor above.

What the hell?

Eve hurried up the next flight. She stepped off the landing and into the corridor that led to the lecture hall. There was a crowd of students outside the door to the hall. When she got there, people were pushing their way out of the hall and through the crowd milling outside.

Eve pushed in the opposite direction. What the heck was going on?

Richard caught her on his way out. "I don't think you want to go in there," he said. His face looked taut.

"Why not?" Eve said. "What's wrong?"

He shook his head. He was clearly struggling to find the words.

"It's Isabella," he finally said. Richard closed his eyes for a second, as if composing himself. "I can't believe it." When he opened them again, he stared at her with an intensity that made her shiver. His eyes were wild.

Eve was torn between trying to help him and finding out what had happened. Her curiosity won. She had to know. Eve pushed past two people just standing there in front of the door and then was inside the auditorium. There were a dozen or more people standing halfway down the aisle towards the stage. The reason was not immediately obvious. Eve looked ahead and saw that the stage was empty. Nobody was sitting in any of the theater seats.

Then she realized that all of the people standing in the aisle were looking up.

She followed their eyes and gasped.

Hanging from a black cord above the red velvet theater-style seats was the body of a girl. The high heels strapped to her narrow feet dangled like silver pointers above the audience. It was the corpse of Isabella. Even without Richard's words outside the hall, Eve recognized the singer instantly – she still wore the same low-cut glittery dress she had on last night at the performance. But unlike last night, when she'd been the picture of glamour, this morning, as she dangled in space above the lecture hall seats, her face was bloated, splotchy and red. A microphone was wedged in her mouth, and her eyes bulged as if she were frozen in the moment of seeing her death.

Isabella's legs were tied together with the microphone cord, and the rest of it wrapped around and around and around her body as if she were a spindle. The loops ended in one tight choker cinched at her neck. From which she hung.

It was horribly creepy how still her body was as it floated there, suspended above the seats.

"Oh my God," Eve whispered. Her legs went weak. She wanted to sit down in one of the seats along the aisle, but didn't dare. "This can't really be happening."

"Did you kill *her*, too?" a voice said from behind her. "What, was she sleeping with your boyfriend or something?"

Eve turned to find Nikki standing behind her. The ice of the morning returned. The girl looked bitter, her face accusing.

"What are you talking about?" she said.

"You strangled Anita and poked out her eyes because she was messing around with Richard," Nikki said. "Now you strangle Isabella?"

"I didn't strangle anybody," Eve shouted. Her voice echoed through the hall. The people who were looking up at the dead body all turned to look at her.

"I didn't kill Anita," Eve continued, dropping her volume to a whisper.

Nikki raised an eyebrow. "Those were your fingers around her neck in the picture," she said. "I saved it from her Facebook Wall before they took it down, and I've looked at it a thousand times since. Let me see your hands."

Eve was furious, but she held them out. She had worried about this for a while, but Richard had convinced her that there was no way, even drugged, that she could have been responsible for Anita's death.

"Where's the ring?" Nikki asked. She pointed to a pale circle around Eve's fourth finger. "I can see that you usually wear one."

Eve shrugged. "I'm not wearing it today."

"I bet it has a sapphire on it, doesn't it?" Nikki asked. "Just like in the picture. What did Isabella do to you?"

"Nothing!" Eve snapped, forcing her voice to remain low. People were still looking at them.

Someone in the back of the hall let out a stifled cry. "Oh my God, oh my God, ohmygod."

And then an authoritative voice filled the hall.

"Everybody please leave the auditorium immediately," a man demanded.

"I didn't do it," Eve said. She looked Nikki in the eye. "You have to believe me. I thought Anita was really cool, and I was looking forward to getting to know her better. I didn't do it."

Nikki looked sullen. "You put your hands around her throat. And someone caught you doing it."

Eve frowned. "That's the real question, I think. Who took that picture? Why did they take it? Why did they post it? Who knew her well enough to have her Facebook password, or access to her computer?" Eve looked pointedly at Nikki.

"The police have already accused me of that," Nikki said with a glare. "Now you are going to turn it on me too?"

"Everybody must leave the room now!" a man yelled. He began to walk down the main aisle, touching the shoulders of anyone who remained. "Out!"

"Look, can we go someplace and talk?" Eve asked.

Nikki seemed unsure for a moment. Eve could have sworn she opened her mouth to say something like "no, fuck off" but no words came out. Then Nikki shrugged and finally said, "Okay."

Eve followed the last few people out of the theater doors, and turned to the left, winding her way through the small clusters of students who all were talking outside. She looked but didn't see Richard anywhere. What she did see were a handful of policemen walking quickly towards them.

Eve stopped and stood back along the wall as they passed. She recognized the one in the lead. Inspector Martino, the cop who had interviewed her after Anita's death. His face looked pinched and serious. She wondered if he recognized her.

As soon as they passed, she said to Nikki, "Let's go before they start interviewing everyone."

Nikki agreed, and they headed back down the hall and out of the building.

"Heavy Beans?" Eve said once they were outside.

"Sure. I don't think we're going to have classes today."

They started walking towards the coffeehouse. The day looked perfect. The sky was a deep blue when it shone through the trees that lined the sidewalk; the air smelled clean, redolent with the aroma of late summer flowers. How could there be a murder on a day like this?

"Wait a minute," Nikki said.

Eve stopped. "What is it?"

"Isabella's Facebook. Are you friends with her?"

Eve shook her head. "No, I only saw her a couple times. She just came to one Songbirds practice."

"I think I am," Nikki said, and thumbed the app open on her phone. Eve watched her type I S A B on her phone. She didn't have to type the whole name before she found the full name and clicked it.

"Holy shit," Nikki said a moment later.

"What?" Eve said, and leaned over her shoulder. Then she saw what Nikki saw. "Oh my God."

The image was full screen and horrible on Nikki's phone. Isabella's face stared straight at her. A black cable wound around her neck, and her face looked petrified. Her eyes were wide and tense, her mouth plugged with a microphone, though it appeared as if she were trying to scream.

"That looks like it might have been taken just before she was thrown over the balcony," Eve said.

Nikki agreed. "The noose is already around her neck."

"Who posted it on her wall?" Eve asked.

"It says she did, at 2:40 this morning."

"I'm guessing she was dead by then," Eve said.

"I'd guess you're right."

Eve looked puzzled. "But how did the killer post the photo?"

"Who knew Isabella, Anita and Gen well enough to get into their Facebooks?" Nikki asked.

Then her eyes lit and she thumbed the feed down on her phone.

"It's there!"

"What?"

Nikki pointed. Eve shook her head in disbelief. The post just below the picture of Isabella was a link to YouTube. Posted at 2:39 this morning. It was a link to the Cure's 'Pictures of You'.

"That's fuckin' creepy," Nikki said.

"Yeah," Eve agreed. "What does it mean?"

Nikki shrugged and pointed towards their goal. Heavy Beans was just a couple buildings ahead. They walked in silence for a few more yards and then Nikki grabbed and held the door open to let Eve in.

They headed straight to the counter. Claude wasn't around; a pale, thin blonde girl was at the register. They both ordered cappuccinos. Minutes later, they were sitting near one of the front windows. The place was busy, but not jam-packed, so they could still get a good seat.

"Look," Eve said, once they'd settled, "I don't remember grabbing Anita like that picture shows. I know I was drugged up that night, and I'm sure I must have reached up while I was in the bed and she was watching me. But I didn't kill her. I could never have done that, I don't care how blitzed I was. Hell, when Richard walked me home that night, I could barely stay on my feet. There's no way I could have hurt her like that and gotten her downstairs afterwards."

Nikki frowned, but said nothing. Instead, she took a sip of her coffee, while staring hard at Eve over the rim. Then she set the cup down and crossed her hands.

"Are you sure?" she said.

"Yes," Eve said. "Please, you have to believe me. I would never have hurt her. She wanted to know more about New York and I was looking forward to showing her some of my pictures and stuff from home. I wanted to get to know her better."

"I'll bet," Nikki said. She sounded bitter.

"I'm not like that," Eve insisted. "I had no interest in her that way. Why do you even think I would?"

Nikki scowled and looked Eve straight in the eye.

"Anita had a bad habit of not always coming home," she said.

"Trust me, she would never have gone home with me," Eve said.

"What about Richard?" Nikki said. "Maybe you got angry because she did something with him."

Eve felt her throat clench slightly. Could he have been seeing Anita over the past couple weeks too? She couldn't think of when. They'd been together almost every night.

"Did she?" she asked.

Nikki looked uncertain. "I don't know. He was with Isabella last term, and now she's gone. Maybe you found out Anita was with him too. It could have happened with her."

"Seriously," Eve said, her voice raising. "I didn't do it. I didn't want to do it. I *couldn't* do it."

Nikki's face relaxed slightly. "So, who did?"

"I think that's what we have to figure out. Before we find ourselves hanging from the rafters. And a Cure song posted on our walls."

CHAPTER EIGHTEEN

"Isabella was with you the night Anita was killed, wasn't she?"

Eve took a breath before answering. Inspector Martino had called her down from her room once again. And once again, he was interviewing her in connection with a murder. This time, he seemed less friendly than the time before.

"Isabella was at our table for a little while, yes," Eve said. "There were a lot of people from the Eyrie that night at the party."

"Did you have any words with her?" the inspector asked. He stared at his notebook for a moment before looking up to meet her eyes. His gaze seemed accusatory. "A fight about boyfriends...or... scholarships perhaps?"

"Why would you think that?" Eve snapped. "Who said something about the Morricone Scholarship?"

The inspector grinned faintly. "So, there is a thread here."

Eve shook her head vehemently. "There is no thread. We were both applying for the scholarship, that's all. I didn't even know that until last night."

"So, she was killed just hours after you discovered that she was your competition."

Eve's eyes threatened to jump out of her skull. "I suppose," she said. "But I don't see how that means anything. I barely knew her and I'm sure there were lots of people applying for the scholarship."

The inspector raised an eyebrow. "There were five finalists, actually. So your chances of winning just went from twenty to twenty-five percent."

"Hardly a reason to kill anyone," Eve said.

"One would think," he said. "But one never knows."

"Who even told you we were both up for that scholarship?" Eve asked.

The inspector's face remained expressionless. "The way this works is, I ask the questions. And you answer. One-way exchange."

Eve rolled her eyes. "I get it. But obviously someone felt that they should point you at me. And I'd just like to know why. Hell, I've only been in this country for three weeks. How many axes could I really have to grind at this point?"

"That's what we need to find out," the inspector said. "Why don't you tell me why you didn't like her?"

"I didn't know her!" Eve insisted. "How could I decide I didn't like her?"

"Knowing someone is not a prerequisite to getting them out of the way."

"I don't even—" she started to say. And then stopped. Getting angry at a police inspector was not going to help her. "Look," she said. "I really liked Anita and didn't do anything to hurt her. And I didn't know Isabella and so I definitely wouldn't have done anything to hurt her either."

"What were you doing the night that Anita was killed?" he asked.

"I was at the party," she said.

"Drinking?"

"Yes."

"Did you black out that night?"

"You know what happened," she said. "Someone drugged me and I was knocked out for a while."

"So you lost consciousness for a time."

She grudgingly agreed.

"And what were you doing after the concert last night?"

"Just talking with friends."

"Drinking?" he asked.

"Sure," she said.

"Did you black out last night?" he asked.

Eve frowned. "No, I just went to bed."

"Did you sleep deeply?"

"Like a rock," she said, and then realized that sounded a bit like what he apparently wanted to hear.

"Hmmm," he said, but asked no more questions. He just wrote something in his notepad.

Finally, he looked up and met her eyes. His expression was serious.

"Everyone who was with Isabella last night is being questioned. Until we have some evidence to point us in the right direction, I'm asking everyone involved to not leave town. So...please don't go anywhere. And if you think of anything that happened last night that might help us find who is responsible...." He reached in his pocket and pulled out a card. He dropped it on the table. "Call me."

Eve picked up the card. "I will. If I think of anything."

He caught her eye and held it as he stood up.

Then the inspector turned and walked out the door of the Eyrie without another word.

Eve let out a breath and only then realized she'd been holding it.

"Who took pictures of them before they died?" she murmured to herself. "And who will be next?"

CHAPTER NINETEEN

Practice was canceled that night after classes. The police were busy, no doubt, taking fingerprints of every surface and photographs of the place from every angle. The door to the theater held a simple notice: Do Not Enter.

Police

* * *

By the following evening, however, the sign was gone. Eve had gotten a text from Susie mid-afternoon saying that the Songbirds would hold an important evening practice and urging everyone to attend no matter what plans they may have had. Eve wondered what 'important' meant.

She had dinner beforehand in the cafeteria with Kristina. Almost as soon as they sat down, Barbara and Sienna from the fifth floor turned up with plates of chicken kiev and joined them.

"Are you going to quit the Songbirds?" Barbara asked before she'd taken a bite of her chicken.

"Why would I do that?" Eve asked.

Kristina looked at her sideways. "Seems like it's a dangerous group to be associated with at the moment, don't you think? I don't really want to lose my roommate."

"I hadn't really thought of it that way," Eve admitted. "I was just thinking someone has it in for the Eyrie."

Sienna shook her head. "Someone has it in for you guys. You've had three people murdered in a month."

"But Isabella was not even really a Songbird," Eve argued. "She didn't play all of our shows and only came to one practice since I've been here."

"I think if you want to survive long enough to graduate from the fifth floor and move down to where there's actually air-conditioning... you need to focus on your Beethoven and forget about Metheny," Barbara said.

"I could never forget about Metheny," Eve said, and finally took the first bite of her meatloaf. The taste was tangy and faintly spicy, and her mouth seemed to come alive as it hit the back of her throat. "And I might not forget this meatloaf, either," she added.

"Priorities," Kristina said. "Death?" She tilted her head. "Meh. Meatloaf?" She made her eyes widen with feigned excitement. "There's the ticket. Who cares about the Reaper when you have meatloaf?"

Everyone laughed, but even as they did, Eve felt her appetite fade away. What if she really was in danger? What if she was targeted as the next victim?

★　　★　　★

Everyone filed into the theater for Songbirds practice in silence. Instead of the usual joking and chatter, the hall was quiet, except for the thuds of cases being set down and instruments being dragged across the stage and into position.

Richard walked into the hall after she had set up her music at the piano. He came immediately to her bench, set down his saxophone case and put both hands on her shoulders, gently gripping and massaging her for a second. Then, without a word, he gave her a squeeze, grabbed his instrument and went to sit down by Gianna to set up. *Always leaving you for Gianna*, a voice said in the back of Eve's head. She shrugged it away.

Susie called for everyone's attention a few moments later.

"Next Friday night, we're going to play a special benefit show at Heavy Beans," she announced. "I talked with Claude yesterday, and he was really excited about the idea. We'll have a cover charge, but also take donations. Anything we make that night will be split and sent to the families of Isabella, Anita and Genevieve. We might not raise a ton of money, but it's something we can do. It's a way for us to publicly remember them. Are you all okay with that?"

The room finally was filled with noise beyond footsteps and equipment shifts.

"Absolutely!" one of the twins exclaimed. "I'm loving this!"

"It's a great idea," Markie said. And punctuated his comment with a drum roll. Dimitiri accented the snare with a flourish on the marimba next to him.

"I'm in," Gianna said.

The rest all chimed in with similar comments and finally Susie put up a hand to silence the chatter. "Perfect," she said. "But if we want to raise money for them, we're going to have to spread the word. This needs to be a sold-out, lines-out-to-the-street kind of show. I need volunteers to make a flyer, and then I need people who will walk around town to pass them out and get them posted."

Eve volunteered to post, following Richard's lead. She didn't know where to go yet, but she could help him walk around town.

"All right then," Susie said a few minutes later, after marking down volunteers. "We've got a plan. Now we need a set. I want to play the songs that they loved the most."

Several of the band members suggested pieces, everything from old classics by Herbie Hancock and Dave Clark Five to modern songs by Jazzmeia Horn and Maria Chiara Argiró. Eve had nothing to offer since she'd barely known the girls, but was excited when a couple piano-heavy tracks were chosen.

"I'll get everyone the charts that we don't already have tomorrow," Susie promised.

After that, the vibe of the room was a little more normal, with some chatter in between songs, though it was still a little more subdued than usual. And at the end, instead of going out together, everyone seemed to go their separate ways.

"Do you want to come back to my room?" Richard asked Eve in the foyer just outside the grand hall.

"Sure," she said. "But I can't stay too late. I've got an early class."

He slipped an arm around her waist and led her down the hall towards the east wing. He had a single room on the fourth floor. After they climbed the steps it was just a couple doors to the left to reach Room 403. As soon as he opened the door and she stepped inside, Richard grabbed her and pulled her close. His lips were warm and hard. Eve had never known him to be so forceful, and surrendered to his desire without hesitation. When he finally broke the kiss, she took an audible breath. "What was that for?" she asked.

"I'm just glad you're here with me," he said. "It's been a horrible day, you know?"

She walked over to sit on the edge of the bed. He opened a small fridge and pulled out two cans of Coke before joining her. She accepted a can and took a long drink, enjoying the electric fizz as it poured down her throat. The bubbles made her eyes water.

Richard's free hand began to gently rub up and down her back. She moaned slightly as his fingers moved higher to massage her neck. The pressure of his touch felt wonderful. Then his hand moved back down and slipped under her shirt to gently follow the line of her vertebrae in a more intimate way. When his fingers traced around her ribs to touch the edge of her bra, Eve closed her eyes and enjoyed the sensation. She knew where this was going. And he was wasting no time since she'd said she wasn't staying long. Waste not, want not in the most physical sense.

"Someone told me today that you once dated Isabella," Eve said.

The motion of his fingers suddenly stilled.

"Yeah," Richard said. He sounded a bit awkward. "But that was a long time ago." His hand slipped away from her ribs to rest at her lower back. "Who told you?" he asked.

"Anita's friend, Nikki," Eve answered. "She said you might have had a thing with Anita too."

His palm left her skin completely. Richard shook his head adamantly. "I don't know why she would say that."

"But you did go out with Isabella," she said. "That must have been horrible to see her like that this morning."

"Yeah," he said. "It was like something out of a dream."

"Or a nightmare?"

He grunted but didn't answer.

"When did you stop seeing her?"

"She stopped seeing me," Richard said.

"Ah," Eve said. She put her hand on his thigh and rubbed. "Was it a bad breakup, then?"

"She was a bitch," Richard said.

Eve frowned. "I thought you liked her. When she was at the Nicolai Hall party you introduced her to me like she was a good friend and she said that you were the one who kept inviting her to sing with the Songbirds."

"I didn't want her to know how much she hurt me," he said. "And Susie always wants me to ask her because she's a good vocalist. So I do. But nobody knew what a horrible selfish diva she really was. Honestly, I'm glad she's gone."

"Wow," Eve said. She lifted her hand back from his leg. Richard's anger was palpable now. "I hope I never piss you off."

He laughed, but there was a cast of bitterness about it that made it sound uneasy.

"Don't use me to get what you want and then dump me like a sack of garbage and we won't have any issues," he said.

Eve raised an eyebrow, but didn't have anything to say to that. She sipped her soda and looked at his profile. His jaw was clenched. She had never seen him angry before now, but clearly, talking about Isabella made him furious.

"The police talked to me about the murder this morning," she said. "Did they talk to you yet?"

He shook his head. "I didn't go to classes today," he said. "I walked around down by the river. There was a message for me from that Inspector Martino when I got back, but I didn't call him yet. I went straight to practice."

"Well, I wouldn't let him see you like this when you talk to him," she said.

Richard forced a smile. "No, of course not," he said. "I figured I could let down my hair with you, though."

"You can," she said, and leaned over to kiss him. He didn't reject it...but he didn't really kiss her back.

"I'm sorry," she said. "Maybe I should go."

He wouldn't look at her. Instead, his gaze fixated on a spot on the wall just below the ceiling. "I thought seeing you tonight would help, but maybe I just need to be alone," he said.

Eve kicked herself for completely killing the mood. It was stupid to have brought up an ex just as he was trying to seduce her.

"Sure," she said. "I understand. I'll see you tomorrow."

Eve got up and walked to the door. Richard did not follow. The vibe of the room was a hundred and eighty degrees from where it had been just a few minutes ago.

"Get some sleep," she said.

The door clicked shut loudly behind her.

CHAPTER TWENTY

Heavy Beans was already packed when they got there on the night of the memorial concert.

"Damn," Markie said as they turned the corner and started down the block towards the café. There were actually people lined up on the sidewalk trying to get in.

"I guess all those flyers really worked," Richard said. "Maybe we didn't need to put up so many!"

Eve had helped Richard on three different afternoons after class over the past week, walking around in various districts of Ghent to ask bars and restaurants and other businesses to place the flyer advertising tonight's show. He hadn't said another thing about his difficult relationship with Isabella, and Eve didn't ask anything more. It seemed best to leave it alone.

"You can't bring too much attention to this one," Susie said. "This is our own."

Elena piped in then and asked in her thick accent, "What if we can't get in? There are a lot of people."

Susie smiled. "I think they'll let us in, don't worry."

The doorman, in fact, motioned everyone on the sidewalk to stand back when they arrived, and cleared enough space for them to walk the drum and horn cases in.

Eve felt the thickness in the air increase as soon as she stepped through the door. The café was humid and warm, even with the air-conditioning. Every table was full and there was a line of people standing around the back, drinking and talking and waiting for the show. A handful of people started clapping when they entered and filed between the counter and the tables to reach the stage.

Claude came out from behind the counter to greet them with his usual ebullience. He was wearing a pair of black leather pants and a white button-down silk shirt with a pattern of rain forest tree branches and exotic blue and green and yellow birds emblazoned on it. He looked like a hip, walking jungle.

"Hello, Songbirds!" he said. His teeth flashed in enthusiasm. "We are so excited for this amazing night. What can I do to help?"

"We're good," Susie answered. "We'll be set up in just a few. I'm so glad we're doing this."

He nodded. "We can't let them all in. You have done very well! Now you have to play the best you ever have. I think you will all be on the photo wall after tonight."

"It's about time," Richard said.

"You better find some solos that don't sound like rhinos farting," Gianna said. "Don't embarrass us now."

"Mind your own mouthpiece," he said. But he was grinning as he said it.

The group assembled on the stage, where Claude or someone at the café had already set up a bunch of chairs. Eve settled at the piano bench and pulled the music out of her backpack. She arranged the pages in order so that she could easily pull them off one by one throughout the concert. The rest of the band set up their own music stands and did the same, while also pulling out their instruments and tuning. Eve had to assume that the piano was in tune, so there was nothing for her to do but sit there and watch the rest. That, unfortunately, led to its own problems.

Gianna was whispering something in Richard's ear; he laughed, and then touched his saxophone partner on the shoulder.

Eve felt something bubble up inside. Seething. It was probably innocent; they had to play together all the time. They were partners there, no matter what. But Eve still felt a fire in her gut when he touched Gianna.

Jealousy?

Maybe.

Intuition?

Maybe that as well. She hoped not.

★   ★   ★

They opened with what apparently had been Gen's favorite piece, a rollicking Fats Waller ragtime piano song called 'A Handful of Keys' that kept Eve on her toes…or, rather, fingertips, for five straight minutes. She was happy to take a breath when she hit the final chord. From there, it was a mix of standards and avant garde pieces that the audience probably didn't know, but that Gen or Isabella or Anita had loved. The applause was the same either way, and it was clear that Claude knew them all. He sat on a stool behind the counter, ready to work the cash register if needed, but happy to be a member of the audience if not.

At one point, Richard stood up to take a solo and it was definitely anything but 'rhinos farting'. Eve was impressed at the fluidity and soul that he brought to it, and a part of her warmed to him even more than before. He was clearly really talented, no matter how much Gianna and others teased him.

When they finally got to the one-hour point, Susie called for a break, and asked the audience to 'pass the hat' in order to collect more money for the families of the deceased. Eve didn't have a great view from the left rear of the stage, but she could tell the hat was quickly overflowing with cash.

She bent down to retrieve her water bottle as the hat went around, but as she sat back up she saw two legs standing just behind her perch. Her eyes moved from his grey slacks past his blue and white buttoned dress shirt before realizing it was Prof. Von Klein.

"Well done on the Fats Waller song," he said. "I almost believed I was sitting in a ragtime bar in St. Louis back in the twenties or thirties."

"Thanks," she said. "I was nervous to kick off with that, but it felt really good, I have to admit. Sometimes it just clicks, you know?"

"I absolutely do," he agreed. "And I just wanted to tell you that I'm proud to have you in our program. It's horrible that we lost Genevieve, but I think you're on your way to not simply replacing her, but making your own name here. Congratulations."

Eve felt her face growing warm. She was blushing. Had he really come to the stage just to compliment her?

"You should get up and stretch before the second half," he advised. "Never just stay in place during a break. Circulate and replenish your energy."

"Thanks, I will," she said.

He tilted his head slightly and stared at her for a few seconds. Saying nothing. Eve felt naked, as if he was sizing her up for something. And then he stepped away to say something to Susie. A minute later, he had left the stage. He really had come up mainly to talk to her!

"Take my advice and steer clear of that one," a man's voice said softly from her left side.

Eve looked over and saw Claude standing near the stack of speakers. He was shaking his head. "He'll give you all the compliments in the world until you give him what he wants. And then...."

"And then, what?" Eve said.

Claude shook his head. "Just don't do it."

CHAPTER TWENTY-ONE

Gianna closed the door to Prof. Von Klein's inner sanctum, leaving him behind inside. Once she stood alone in his regular 'public' office, she took a deep breath and shook her head. The things she did to get ahead. Dirty old man. She still couldn't believe she had been lured into this situation. But once you dive into the pool, you had to keep swimming, right? Luckily, this had been a short session, since they'd had the benefit concert earlier tonight. God, she was exhausted after this day, but he always wanted just a little more. Still, even the professor had to sleep sometimes.

It had been weird to come here tonight, of all nights. This had been the first time she'd been in his office since Isabella had been killed. And they'd done it there right after Isabella's benefit concert. It had been hard to put that thought aside. At first, her gaze had kept straying to the door that led to the balcony over the theater. She had kept thinking of how Isabella had probably been tied up right here in this room before being dragged out and to the edge.

And then...*snap*.

It took effort to bring her attention back to the professor's eyes and hands.

She reached inside the loose neck of her shirt and readjusted a twisted bra strap. Gianna remembered the first time he'd invited her up here after hours. The professor had let her know that this was not something she had to do if she didn't want to. This was outside of their studies and wouldn't impact her grade at all. It was just a little extracurricular activity that he enjoyed sometimes with those female students who enjoyed it as well. Nobody would ever know.

Gianna snorted. Whenever someone said nobody would ever

know, you could pretty much guarantee that the word would get out eventually. And she didn't really believe that her participation didn't help her grade either. Was he really going to give low marks to a girl who gave these kinds of 'personal' performances for him? Whatever. She was used to giving guys what they wanted, in order to ultimately grease the rails to get what she wanted. Tit for tat. She could play the professor's game, and honestly, she didn't mind it that much.

It was funny how the game had changed though as time went on. He'd first approached her two semesters ago, and the first time she'd gone to his 'special room', they'd done almost nothing more than talk.

Now? Their sessions started later and later, to ensure that nobody else was in the building. And sometimes by the time they were done, she found herself hunting around the room just to locate her underwear.

Yeah, times had changed. The game was way dirtier. But she had surprised him a time or two, she knew that much.

The thought made her smile to herself.

Gianna let herself out of the professor's office door. The hallway was dark and shadowed, lit only by the after-hours dim lights. Because students and professors often kept late hours or started very early, the building was never allowed to be in total darkness, but someone could easily hide in the shadows and lie in wait without being seen.

That was probably exactly what had happened to Isabella, she knew. And, in fact, that little whore had probably been coming from exactly the same place that she herself had just left. She didn't kid herself; she knew she wasn't the only one the professor had private appointments with.

The thought of Isabella being killed potentially right after a session with Von Klein sank in and Gianna felt the swagger built up by her secret meeting dissolve. Anybody could be in the shadows of these halls, just waiting to pounce on her and stab her with a tuning fork.

Her pace quickened, and when she reached them she took the stairs two at a time. It had been easy to walk up here with the professor at her side. Why hadn't he walked her out, she wondered, very unnerved.

He shouldn't have asked her to come here in the first place after what had happened. He should have at least made sure she got out of the building safely.

Still, she reached into her pocket and felt the folded Euro notes there and relaxed slightly. She didn't do it for nothing.

Gianna looked behind her and saw only empty hall. She started walking again, but then stopped. She could have sworn that something had moved. Something in the corner of her vision. She turned slowly around, keeping the wall to her back and peering at the dark doorways, looking for something. Someone.

But the shadows didn't move.

Gianna forced herself to calm down and began to walk again, glancing backwards every few steps. Did she hear the echo of another footfall on the wooden floor, besides her own?

"Quit freaking yourself out, you idiot," she said half out loud.

When she reached the practice room hall, she realized that one of the night lights had burned out, leaving an area she had to cross almost pitch black. She could see the light at the end, but there were several doorways in between where she couldn't make out anything.

The stairs down to the common area so that she could return to the East Tower were just around the corner at the end of the hall. She just had to reach them without getting grabbed.

"Fuck it," she said, and took off in a sprint down the hall.

She had just about reached the end when she heard something clink from behind her.

Gianna didn't want to turn around, she wanted to keep going. But she had to know if there was someone coming out of the dark at her.

Where the hall ended in a T she turned, pressing her back to the wall to stare back down the long corridor she'd just left.

There was no fast-moving black-clad form emerging from out of the dark.

But there was something on the floor. She heard it before she saw it.

A second later it came rolling out from where she'd just been.

A drumstick.

It rolled right up to her feet. She lifted one foot and stepped on it, stopping its progress.

The hall was silent, except for her heartbeat.

Gianna slowly crouched down, keeping her eyes on the dark hall, and picked up the stick.

Maybe the vibrations of her footfalls had made it roll off from where someone had left it on a mantel or small table along the hall?

Or maybe someone had been following her. Could it have been Markie? She could picture his thin, pointed eyebrow and black eyepatch peering out at her from the shadows. She'd never completely trusted their drummer. He always seemed like he was hiding something.

Gianna looked left and right and then bolted to the stairs. She fully expected to hear footsteps pounding behind her, and a cold metal pinch at her neck. Or a stab in the back.

She reached the landing and kept running straight for the lobby. There was a man sitting at the front desk. Gianna made straight for him.

The man looked up, his hollow eyes confused. Or maybe angry.

Gianna came to a stop near the desk, and Philip, the sometimes porter, sometimes night watchman, sometimes handyman, grunted a caution.

"Slow down there," he grumbled. "You'll trip and fall and put that stick through your eye."

Gianna doubled over, putting her hands on her knees for a minute to catch her breath.

The chair creaked as Philip shifted himself from leaning left to leaning right while watching a small television screen.

"What's the matter?" he asked.

"Nothing," she said. "Nothing at all. Just running from shadows."

He shrugged. "The only shadows that can follow you are yours."

She considered that for a second and then laughed. "Yeah, I guess you're right."

After resting for a few more breaths, she straightened up and grinned at him. She felt relieved. And a little foolish. Philip did not smile back.

"Good night," she said.

He grunted as she walked away towards the elevator. Surprisingly, when she hit the button, it actually lit, and the car began creaking its way down from whatever floor it had been on.

She stepped inside when the door opened and hit the button. For a half-second she panicked when the silver panels slid closed. She was safe in here, right? She pressed the button for the third floor.

When the door didn't reopen to let some last-minute person on with her, she sighed a faint release of relief and pulled out her phone to send a text.

Is now okay? she messaged. Three dots showing that someone was answering came almost instantly.

Sure, the answer came.

Gianna stepped out into the hall. In just a few steps, she stood outside Room 403. She raised the hand without the drumstick and knocked.

CHAPTER TWENTY-TWO

Prof. Von Klein walked across the stage and immediately the low hum of voices in the theater diminished. By the time he reached the podium, you could hear the shuffle of his rubber soles on the wooden floor.

"Good morning, all," he said. "It's been a difficult week, as I'm sure you all would agree. So, I want to start this morning with some more positive news."

You could see everyone in the room come to attention at that. Eve noticed someone standing at the side of the room, stage left. He leaned against the wall, but he had an oversized camera with a large flash bulb in a reflective silver circle. It looked like something you saw reporters in black-and-white movies carrying. She wasn't sure what it meant, but something was up.

"Every year we recognize one international student who shows great potential to make an impact on modern music. In order to assist with the expense of that student leaving their home country to study with us here at the Eyrie for an extended period, we offer a five thousand Euro grant called the Morricone Scholarship. Past recipients have gone on to work with the Paris Symphony and to compose soundtracks for Steven Spielberg. This morning, I want to present this year's award to one of the most deserving students I've seen in many years."

The professor paused, and pulled an envelope out of his suit breast pocket. Then his face lit in a smile and he said, "This year, I'm happy to announce that the Morricone Scholarship is awarded to Evelyn Springer, from the United States."

Eve's heart jumped. Had he just said what she thought he'd said?

She'd wanted this so bad, but had not believed that she had a chance in hell of winning it.

"Eve, please come down and accept your award," he said.

She stood up and began to walk with shaky knees down the aisle towards the stage. Applause broke out all around her, along with a few catcall whistles.

"Go Eve," someone yelled.

When she stepped up on the stage the applause crescendoed for a moment, until the professor held up his hand.

When the crowd quieted, he held the envelope out to Eve with a smile. The photographer moved from the wall to stand right in front of them, and snapped several pictures as the professor handed her the award and then put his arm around her shoulders. She could feel his fingers gently kneading her shoulder as they stood there posing for the camera.

"Congratulations, Eve," he said, leaning into the microphone while still holding her shoulder. "We expect great things from you, and hope this helps takes away some of the financial burden of studying abroad so that you can focus strictly on your music."

Then he turned and looked directly at her while resting his hands on each of her shoulders. "Please make an appointment to come see me in my office," he said quietly, so the whole auditorium could not hear. "I'd like to talk with you about some private tutoring sessions that we could do in the evenings. I'd like to make sure you reach your full potential while you are with us at the Eyrie."

"Um, sure," Eve said.

The professor looked pleased. "Good. I'll expect to see you later this week then."

Then he motioned for her to leave the stage and she walked back to the stairs, not quite sure what had just happened.

The professor gave her five thousand Euros *and* wanted to give her private tutoring? This was like a fairy tale! She had been ecstatic when she was accepted to the Eyrie that she would actually be in the same building with Prof. Von Klein. She'd never imagined she would get individual instruction from him. He was one of the most famous composers in Europe. His 'Piano Concerto in Profondo Rosso' was one of her favorite classical pieces of the past fifty years.

Several classmates congratulated her on her way back to her seat, but Eve barely registered who said what. She was in a daze that lasted for the rest of the lecture. She opened the envelope after she sat down and read the letter congratulating her. There was a check folded inside it, which she was supposed to use to help defray her travel and lodging expenses.

Nikki caught her as she was walking out after the lecture.

"Congratulations," she said. "Looks like the professor likes you!"

"What do you mean?"

Eve backed up to the wall to get out of the way of the other students filing past.

"Last year it was Genevieve who played piano in the Songbirds and won the Morricone Scholarship. Everyone knew she was his favorite – he even gave her private lessons after hours." Nikki poked her in the arm. "Looks like you're the *it* girl this year. Hopefully you don't end up like she did."

Eve's stomach clenched. All of this had seemed like a dream a couple minutes ago. But somehow Nikki had just made it all seem like it could turn into a nightmare.

Nikki saw the discomfiture on Eve's face. "Oh, hey, I didn't mean to scare you or anything. It's seriously great. You're going to get out of here with all sorts of cred."

"If I get out of here at all," Eve said. Not for the first time, she wondered if she should just quit and go home. She desperately wanted a degree from the Eyrie, but she didn't want to end up hanging from a microphone cord.

"C'mon, don't think like that. Do you want to go out tonight and celebrate?" Nikki asked. "I hear you've got some spending money now."

"Well, I'd like to, but I'll have to see what Richard wants to do first," she said. "I think he was planning for us to go out."

Nikki shrugged. "Okay, whatever. You've got my number if you end up free. Call or text me."

"I will," Eve promised.

★   ★   ★

Richard did have plans. At Songbirds practice, he came up behind her and kissed her on the top of the head. "Well done," he leaned in and whispered in her ear. "Drinks are on me tonight, but then I think you're picking them up for the rest of the semester!"

Eve laughed and turned around. "Everyone thinks I'm rich now," she said.

"Richer than the rest of us!"

Susie called practice to order, and he kissed her again, on the lips this time.

"I'll stop by your room around eight?"

She nodded.

Richard went back to sit next to Gianna, who leaned over to ask him something. When he shook his head, Eve saw a cloud pass over Gianna's face. He said something in a low voice to her and the girl frowned. Richard's sax partner clearly wasn't happy about something.

★   ★   ★

Everyone in the Songbirds congratulated her after practice…except for Gianna. The saxophonist busied herself with her instrument and music and then went to talk with Susie in the corner. Eve had a feeling she was jealous. Had she applied for the scholarship as well, she wondered. She had no idea who else had been going for it. There were certainly more than a few people who were probably unhappy that the 'ugly American' had taken it home.

She'd never know, so it wasn't worth worrying about.

Back in her room, she looked up the history of the award and rediscovered her excitement about it all over again. The people who had won it before her had done some amazing things. The professor hadn't exaggerated. There was one who even did orchestral arrangements for a tour of the Who. She felt a pang of fear. That was a lot to live up to.

After a shower and trying on three different shirts, she settled on a light white t-shirt with a faint watercolor design over a hot pink tank. Kristina had orchestra practice tonight, so she was gone. No moral support there. Eve had to tell her reflection in the mirror that she looked great.

She sat back at the desk at quarter to eight and started watching a YouTube video of a new song from one of her friend's bands back in New York. It made her a little sad as she watched; things were amazing here, but she missed her friends. Life back home was continuing without her. Obviously.

One video led to another and then another. Before she knew it, it was almost 8:15. Still no Richard.

She frowned and thumbed open her phone.

No messages.

She went back to watching the laptop screen, and midway through the next song, her phone vibrated.

She grabbed it and saw a text notification.

RICHARD: *Eve, I'm really sorry, but I can't do it tonight. I'll make it up to you tomorrow?*

EVE: *Sure. What's going on?*

RICHARD: *I have to finish a project tonight for my Advanced Theory class. I'm really sorry.*

EVE: *No problem. See you tomorrow?*

He sent a smiley emoji with hearts for eyes.

Eve smiled at the flirtation, but she wasn't happy. Her heart felt deflated. She had really looked forward to sharing her excitement tonight with him. Now she was sitting here alone in a dorm room with nobody to talk to at all. She wasn't going to go out alone, and she didn't feel close enough to anyone else here yet to call them.

She sank back into the chair for a minute before she remembered Nikki's offer. Could she really call her this late, after she'd said no to going out? She debated with herself for a few minutes before finally texting Anita's girlfriend.

EVE: *Richard stood me up for tonight. Any chance you still want to go out?*

Her reply was almost immediate.

NIKKI: *Going stir crazy here. Meet you in the East Tower lobby in 10?*
EVE: *Deal!*

★　　★　　★

Nikki's face lit up when she saw Eve walk off the stairwell. She was leaning against the wall near the front desk, an unlit cigarette in her mouth.

"Richard's loss is my gain," Nikki said after taking the cigarette out. "You look great!"

"You look ready for the town," Eve said. "Black is definitely your color."

Nikki wore black capris and a punky black tee ripped in very calculated places. Her eyebrows were drawn strong, black slashes that extended just a little too far. But it was an evocative look; it only made her dark eyes look even darker and more alluring.

"Come on," Nikki said and pulled her towards the door. "I've been dying for a smoke."

She flipped her lighter as soon as her right foot was out the door. The ember of her cigarette reflected in her eyes as she took a long drag and then breathed out a cloud of white in the dark of night.

"I know a great little club down near the river," she said. "It's underground, but the music's great and they know how to pour a drink."

"Lead the way," Eve said.

★　　★　　★

After a few blocks they reached a strip of small businesses in what probably were old converted warehouse buildings along the water. Nikki pointed to a small neon sign on the grey stone wall of one of them. *Duisternis*, it read.

"What does it mean?" Eve asked.

"Darkness," Nikki said. "It's Dutch. It's where we celebrate the night!"

She led the way down a handful of stone steps. The pound of industrial music vibrated the door from within.

As soon as they stepped inside, Eve knew why they were here. This place was totally Nikki. Most of the people here wore black, often black leather. There were girls and guys in fishnet, and plenty of severe eye makeup that put Nikki's to shame. And tattoos and piercings. This was a total subculture hangout. She didn't recognize the music, but the beat was fast, hard and electronic.

The bar was against the wall to the right when you walked in, and they headed there immediately. A bleached blonde with a spray-painted crop top roamed the area behind the black and chrome. A chalkboard behind her listed an array of beers and drinks in different colors; each name was punctuated by skulls. While the vibe on the black-painted dance floor was decidedly biker-goth, the bar felt more upscale – this wasn't a shot and a beer haven, but a mixology station.

Nikki ordered something called a Sepulcher, an inky black drink served in a square glass with a red ice cube. "It's licorice liqueur with a cherry juice ice cube," she explained.

Eve played it more traditional, and ordered an Angel Dust, which was basically vodka over ice sprinkled with vanilla powder. She realized after a couple sips though that the ice was not simply water.... There was something more going on beneath the vanilla. A taste as rich as lilac that grew as the ice dissolved.

"I love this," she said after they'd been sitting for a while. They'd found a tall bar round with two stools against the wall opposite from the bar. It was the perfect place to relax and people-watch, as there were some couples twisting and gyrating to the music of the DJ. Eve had yet to recognize a song.

"The club, or the drinks?" Nikki asked.

Eve smiled. "Both."

Nikki held out her glass to clink against Eve's. "What we do in the Darkness stays in the Darkness," she said.

"Do you come here a lot?" Eve asked.

"No, it's 'Do you come here often?'" Nikki corrected, with a grin. "And yes, I do. Anita used to love it." Her face fell a little as she remembered the past.

"Well, I'd be happy to come back here with you, if you're ever looking for company," Eve said.

"Thanks," Nikki said and took a sip of her drink. She looked at Eve over the rim for a moment, just staring at her. And then she added, "I just might take you up on that."

"I'm glad you don't still think that I had something to do with the murders," Eve said. "I seriously couldn't do something like that."

Nikki nodded. "I know. After I thought about it, and talked more to you, I realized that. But you did get the scholarship once Isabella was out of the way."

"I would never have killed anyone to get five thousand Euros!" Eve said. She slapped her hand on the table to punctuate her statement, and Nikki put her hand on top of Eve's for a second. Her eyebrows raised in amusement.

"I was joking," she said.

"Yeah, well, the police weren't," Eve said. "That Inspector Martino seemed serious when he brought up the fact that we were both going for the same scholarship."

"They have to do that," Nikki said. "Especially since all of the deaths are here at the Eyrie. This isn't some serial killer who's roaming around town. This is someone targeted right here. And that probably means whoever it is, is also right here. It has to be someone connected with the school in some way. Or else why would they want to kill music students?"

"Maybe they hate music?"

Nikki rolled her eyes. "You'll have to do better than that."

"Maybe they hate jazz music? Everyone killed has been associated with the Songbirds."

"You'd think that would narrow the list of suspects," Nikki said.

"But what's the motive?" Eve asked. "The inspector said that I could have knocked off Genevieve to take her spot at the piano and Isabella to steal the scholarship. He didn't have an easy answer for Anita."

"I already solved that one for you," Nikki said. "You were jealous of her stealing your boyfriend."

"But she didn't," Eve said. And then she looked harder at Nikki's face, searching to see if there really was some truth there. "Did she?"

"I don't know," Nikki said. "There were some times last semester that I swear to God I almost killed her. I mean, seriously, I picked up a knife and played with it one night when I realized it was three in the morning and she was not home. Anita didn't know how to sleep alone."

Eve noticed that Nikki was not smiling at all when she said that. She had been driven to the brink, apparently.

"But you still loved her."

Nikki threw her head back and laughed. "Of course I did. How could you not? She was a free spirit and that's part of what I loved about her even though it drove me insane sometimes. But no, I don't know if she ever got it on with Richard. So don't let me make you crazy there."

A waitress came by to take drink orders. Eve felt severely out-clubbed. The girl had on black laced boots and fishnets beneath a leather mini and a lace, almost-X-rated top. She wore blue lipstick and black eyeliner and Eve could see Nikki looking the girl over with decided interest. Most likely every guy in the place did too. It didn't hurt that she had one of those low sultry voices with just a hint of gravel in it when she spoke.

In her head, Eve sighed and said, *Damn.* She would never have that kind of effect on people.

After the waitress left, and Nikki's gaze returned to her drink, Eve brought them back to the main question. "So I didn't do it," she said. "But who did?"

Nikki's eyes widened with emotion. "I don't know," she said. "Someone who wanted to get into the school but couldn't? Someone in the school who failed their Songbirds audition? Hell, maybe it's someone on the faculty. All of the girls who were killed were killed right there in the North Tower. What if they all had something on one of the professors, and so he knocked them off to keep them silent?"

Eve frowned at that.

"I can't imagine what a student would have on a professor that was so bad they'd want to kill to keep it quiet."

They were both silent for a minute, and then Eve frowned. "The night Isabella was killed, she did leave Heavy Beans with Professor Von Klein," she said. "They were sitting alone together for a while before that."

"See?" Nikki said. "It could be him. And she was even killed in that locked room behind his faculty office. I'd think that would make him the prime suspect for the police."

"Maybe it does," Eve said. "But I can't imagine he has anything to do with it. Professor Von Klein is one of the most respected people in music today. He's known all around the world in classical music circles. He's a brilliant teacher and composer."

"That doesn't mean shit," Nikki said. "The ones who make it to the top are usually the ones who are the most rotten."

Eve shook her head. "I'm sorry, I just can't believe that."

"Believe what you want, it doesn't make the truth any different. Plus... it's worth saying again, *he has a secret office behind his office*. Although it's not very secret. Everyone knows about it, because sometimes he comes out onto the balcony to see performances. But hardly anyone has ever been there."

Another round of drinks arrived. And then one more.

It was after one in the morning when they finally walked home. Neither of them was completely steady. They laughed and bumped shoulders every few yards as they weaved their way back in the dark.

"Shhh...you'll wake the neighbors," Eve said at one point.

"Fuck 'em," Nikki said. "That'll teach 'em to pass up a good time."

When they had almost reached the front entrance of the Eyrie, Nikki suddenly stopped and pointed at the dark row of windows on the third floor of the North Tower. "Look," she said. "Half the time I pass here at night, Professor Von Klein's light is on. But he's not there tonight."

Eve yawned. The warmth of the alcohol and the pound of the music had left her feeling strangely disembodied. As if she was floating through the evening. "Yeah, so what? It's the middle of the night after all."

Nikki grabbed her arm. "I have an idea."

Eve looked at her and sighed. There was a warm, comforting buzz in her head. "What's your idea?" she asked.

"I think we should go upstairs and check out Professor Von Klein's office."

Eve laughed. "You're nuts."

Nikki shook her head. "I'm not," she said. "This is the perfect time. We can go see what he really has in that secret room behind his office. Why was she anywhere near there after the concert that night? I think Von Klein took her into that room and then threw her off the balcony. But why?"

"Seriously," Eve said. "You're drunk. We need to go home." Her own words slurred a little.

Nikki pulled her by the wrist towards the main door. "I need to know. If we wait for the police to find out who it is, we will be graduates by then. Or dead. If he had something to do with Anita's death, I have to know. I'll kill him myself." Nikki sounded suddenly very sober and serious.

"How are we going to get in?" Eve said. Her lips seemed to move unnaturally slowly. "I'm sure he keeps it locked."

"No problem," Nikki said. "I have gotten into many locked doors." She turned to grin at Eve. "I *know* things!"

Eve continued to say they should turn back, but Nikki pulled her forward, up the dark stairs and around the bend. Eve's protests gradually fell away and she let the growing haze of the alcohol wash over her.

When they reached the professor's door and tried the knob, it did not budge. Nikki fished around in her purse for something to use on the lock.

"We should go," Eve said.

"Shhh. Girl's trying to work here."

Eve paced the hallway while Nikki bent over the doorknob. What if someone caught them? They'd not only be expelled, they'd probably go to jail. She couldn't imagine going to prison for breaking and entering in another country. There were stories about Americans trapped in foreign prisons....

"Got it," Nikki announced, and the door eased open. "C'mon."

She motioned for Eve to follow and stepped inside.

Eve frowned, but she wasn't going to stand alone out in the dark hall. She followed Nikki into the slightly less dark room. The faint light from the street glinted off Professor Von Klein's piano and a couple of pictures on the wall beyond. She reached for the light switch and Nikki stopped her.

"No," she said. "Don't turn on the overhead lights. Anyone on the street will know someone's up here."

"How are we going to see anything then?" Eve asked.

Almost immediately she heard the faint jingle of a chain touching metal, and a small banker's lamp on the professor's desk came on.

"Like this," Nikki said. "Close the door." She sat down on the chair behind the desk and began opening drawers and sifting through the contents within.

"What are we looking for exactly?" Eve asked.

"I don't know," Nikki said. "A blackmail note? We'll know when we find it."

Eve made a face but said nothing. This was ridiculous. Even half-drunk, she realized that they were doing a crazy, stupid thing. She couldn't believe she'd let Nikki talk her into it. But she walked around the rest of the office, opening a closet door and looking at the books tucked on the shelves inside. Jazz theory, the biography of Stravinsky. Several binders of sheet music. Nothing of interest.

"No luck here," Nikki announced, and shoved a drawer shut. "But now I know what grade I'm getting in Theory class," she said with a grin. "Time for a visit to the secret room."

She hunched over that doorknob and again, after a minute, the door creaked open.

"Were you a jewel thief in a past life?" Eve asked.

"I just don't believe in letting locked doors stop me from going where I want to go," Nikki said.

They stepped inside and this time, Nikki flipped on the wall switch. There were no windows to advertise their presence.

"Whoa," Nikki said as they took a slow look around the room. It wasn't a large space, but there was a lot of equipment inside. In the center was a tripod with an impressive looking professional grade camera atop it. The camera faced a wall where there was a retractable scene backdrop. It rolled into a stand on the floor for storage, but was currently fully set up, with rods holding it six feet off the floor from the stand. The backdrop pictured the sky, with the lower half being a thick floor of cottony clouds, and the glint of the setting sun breaking through in the upper left-hand side. Three more tripod stands were clustered around the backdrop. They held long rectangular lights.

"Looks like Professor Von Klein is a pro," Nikki said.

"Yeah," Eve agreed. "But what does he shoot here exactly?"

"There's the question." Nikki walked to the side, where there was a countertop and a couple of steel sinks. A red light hung from a wire above the area. "Check it out," she said and pointed. "Dude develops his own film here too."

"That's a lot of work," Eve said.

"Yeah, but then nobody else sees what he's been shooting." Nikki pointed at a couple of wires with clips on them that ran above the sinks just above head level. They were fastened to posts that hung down from the ceiling. "Here's where he hangs them up to develop," she said. "But where does he put them afterwards?"

There were drawers in the counter near the sinks and Nikki started opening them one by one. She found chemicals and photo paper and some other supplies...but no photos.

"Look at this," Eve said. She was crouched next to a tall rectangular steel box tucked in the corner behind some lighting umbrellas.

Nikki came up behind her. "Looks like a filing cabinet," she observed.

"Can you open it? The drawers are locked."

"Let's see!" Nikki pulled out a hair pin and started to twist it around in the keyhole. "Shit," she said after a minute.

"What's the matter?" Eve asked.

"This lock is tighter than the doors. My bobby pin just bent. I need something stronger to turn it."

"Figures," Eve said. She walked across the room to look at the developing station again, and bent down to look in a low black garbage can set nearby. It was full of papers, and she reached in to pull some out. They were bent and ripped, but Eve recognized the stage of Heavy Beans on a couple shards.

"Here are some of the pictures he took at the benefit concert," she announced.

Nikki gave up on the file cabinet and joined her. "Anything else?"

"A lot of skin," Eve said and held up a two-inch piece of ripped picture. It was impossible to tell if it was a thigh or belly or what. But it was definitely bare skin.

"Find the rest of that one."

Eve dumped the garbage over and spread out the various pieces of crumpled paper. It was a little like starting work on a jigsaw puzzle where you didn't know what the final picture was supposed to be. A lot of different photos had been ripped up and tossed in the can. But piece by piece, they began to assemble the skin.

"It's a thigh," Eve said after placing a piece. Suddenly it was clear that they were looking at a naked feminine leg bent at the knee. The woman seemed to be nude, but was posed sideways; they could see the curve of her butt, but her pubic hair was all but hidden by the angle of her stance. The next piece showed fingers cupping one breast. And the next....

"What the hell," Nikki said. "He burnt off the face?"

The piece that would have shown her neck and chin ended in brown burned edges.

"Who do you think it is?" Eve asked.

Nikki shook her head. "Someone with great skin."

"Do you think it could be Isabella?"

"I've never seen her naked," Nikki said. "But if this was her, I wish I had."

"Why would he have burned off the face?" Eve asked.

"Why would he be taking nude pictures of Isabella?"

"Good point."

"Let's see if he left us any more clues."

Together they sorted through the other shards of paper from the trash. But nothing else of interest turned up. There were several pictures that clearly were from the Songbirds' Heavy Beans concert, and a couple that appeared to be of the grounds around the Eyrie. But no other cheesecake shots.

"I'd sure like to get into that filing cabinet," Nikki said.

"I'd just like to get out of here," Eve said. She felt increasingly nervous. They had been here too long. "Let's go before someone finds us here."

"Who's going to come around at this hour?"

"The police are still supposed to be patrolling the area, aren't they?"

"Maybe," Nikki said, acting indifferent. But with her hands, she began grabbing all of the picture pieces and tossing them in the garbage. The pieces picturing the nude girl, however, she kept together and when she stood up, she slipped them into her pocket. Then she moved towards the professor's office. A minute later, she flipped off the light switch on the wall, putting them in darkness. But only for a second. She slowly eased the door open.

"All clear," she whispered, and led the way around the professor's desk to the hallway door. Nikki opened the outer door and began to poke her head out. And instantly jerked back. Her shoulder jolted Eve in the chin.

"Ouch," she complained and Nikki turned and put her hand over Eve's mouth.

"There's someone in the hall," she whispered. Then she turned back to the door and slowly eased it completely closed, carefully turning the knob so that it didn't click as the lock set.

She pushed Eve against the wall on the far side of the door. Then she pressed herself against the wall beside her. Both girls held their breath and stared at the decorative pane of glass on the side of the door. It was warped and curved so that it allowed in light, but you couldn't really see through it.

After a few seconds, a dark shadow moved closer to the glass. The figure grew larger as it approached.

Eve's eyes grew large. Was someone about to come into the office?

The glass grew completely black. A figure was standing right in front of it. The edge of a palm pressed against it right about head height. Someone was trying to peer inside. Even though the glass was distorted, could they be seen crouching next to the door?

The knob of the door turned slightly. Nikki grabbed Eve's wrist and squeezed. The knob went back and forth, clicking slightly as it met the lock.

Then it stopped.

Both girls peered hard at the shadow. They didn't dare to breathe.

After a few seconds, the glass grew slightly lighter. And then the shadow moved and disappeared completely.

Eve let out her breath and then gasped for fresh air. She sank to a crouch. Her head was spinning from both the alcohol and the scare. "Do you think he's really gone?" she finally whispered, once her breath was under control.

"I hope so," Nikki said. "I wonder if he saw the door crack open and that's why he tried to come in."

"If he did, hopefully he figured it was just a trick of the shadows," Eve said. "But if not, he may come back with a key."

Nikki agreed. "We need to split." She held up her hand when Eve grabbed for the doorknob. "Hang on. If he had to go for a key, he's got to go down three flights and get to the front lobby. Let's count to fifty and make sure he's gone."

Eve didn't want to count; she wanted to get on the other side of the door. But in her head, she started. She could see Nikki's lips silently moving as she did her own count. *One, two, three, four, five...* Eve said in her mind. Fifty was going to take way too long to reach.

Eve was thinking *forty-six, forty-seven* when Nikki took the doorknob and slowly turned it. She stared through the small crack for a second before opening it further and looking in the other direction. Eve clenched her teeth, praying that this time they could actually get out of the office and into the hallway. She didn't care if someone asked her why she was in the building this late; she just didn't want to be found in the office of one of the most respected members of the faculty in the wee hours of the morning.

"Come on," Nikki whispered, and ducked out of the door.

Eve followed. Her heart leapt with relief when Nikki pulled the door shut and the lock clicked. "Let's get out of here," Eve whispered.

Together they ran down the hall towards the stairs. They were five steps down when Nikki suddenly stopped. Eve passed her two steps before stopping herself. "What's the matter?"

"What if whoever that was comes up these stairs?"

For the first time tonight, Eve thought Nikki really looked frightened.

"Come on," Eve said, and grabbed her arm, pulling her down. "I have an idea."

They reached the second floor and instead of continuing down the steps to the main floor, Eve pulled Nikki down the hallway.

"Why are we going this way?" Nikki asked.

They turned a corner before Eve slowed down enough to answer.

"There's a stairway down that exits near the East Tower at the end of this hall," she said. "If someone went to the front desk to get a key, they'd never come back up this way."

Nikki grinned. "Nice thinking. I'll make a thief of you yet!"

They hurried down the dark stairs. At the landing, Eve slowly pushed the ground floor door open to see if anyone was about, but the main floor seemed quiet.

"We might actually be able to reach the East Tower without anyone at the front desk seeing us," Eve said.

"You spoke too soon," Nikki said.

Eve looked towards the front entrance and saw Philip leaning over the front desk, craning his head to see who was down the hall. As soon as she saw his face, Eve pulled Nikki into the stairwell leading back up to the residential area.

"Do you think he saw us?" Eve asked.

Nikki shook her head. "He saw us, but hopefully not enough to recognize us. He won't follow, but let's get upstairs."

They took the stairs two at a time. When they reached the third floor, Nikki stopped.

"Here's where I get off," she said.

"Thanks for a strange evening," Eve said with a smile.

Nikki held her arms out and after hesitating a second, Eve gave her a hug.

"Thank you," Nikki whispered. "I needed that."

And then she ducked through the door and disappeared down the hall on her way to her room.

CHAPTER TWENTY-THREE

Prof. Von Klein walked across the stage at nine a.m. as he did every day to take his place at the lectern.

But this morning, Eve felt her stomach turn to ice as he did. Could he really be responsible for Isabella and Anita and Genevieve's murders? Did he realize that someone had been in his inner sanctum last night?

Her head ached from the drinks she and Nikki had had before breaking into his office, but she knew she had not dreamed the events of early this morning. She almost wished she had. As the professor started speaking, she studied his face – those high cheekbones and piercing eyes. Could he have killed some of his students? Was he really using his back office to take nude photos at night? Was that why his office light was always on so late? And if so, why? For his own selfish benefit, or was he somehow involved in porn? Was there blackmail or some nefarious underground thing going on that led to the deaths? Or was he just trying to help someone with their photo portfolio, however risque? She had thought of the latter reason on her way from the cafeteria. He could have simply been helping someone.

But why had the head been burned off a nude photo then?

The questions gnawed at her throughout the lecture. She couldn't concentrate on anything he was talking about. But then at the very end of the session, he said something that made her heart freeze.

"That's all for today, thank you," he said. And then, "Eve Springer, I see you up there in the back. Could you come down to the stage for a moment?"

Holy shit. Did he know what she did last night? Had she been caught on a security camera? She hadn't thought about that possibility until this moment. Was there a hidden camera in his office? If he knew she'd broken in last night, her career here was finished. Part of her wanted to bolt and join the throng exiting the theater. But he knew she was there. She couldn't say she hadn't heard him call her. And in the end, if she was going to be expelled, she couldn't run. It would happen whether she walked down the aisle right now or not.

Slowly, legs shaking slightly, she rose from her chair, gathered her handbag, and began to move toward the stage. It felt like the walk to her execution. The center aisle was crowded with classmates going in the opposite direction and it took a minute to navigate down to the front. When she finally did, she had to wait. The professor had stepped down from the stage to the front aisle and was talking with another student. She wanted to use that as an excuse. "You were busy so I left and figured we could talk later." But just as she began to seriously consider that, he looked up from his conversation and made eye contact. Then he held up his forefinger, bidding her to wait one more minute.

Trapped.

Eve started thinking about how long it would take to pack up her stuff. She hadn't been here that long to accumulate much. But she also didn't have an apartment or anything to go back to in New York. All her stuff was in storage. Maybe she could try to stay in Europe for a while.

"All right then," the professor said, finally addressing her. "Thanks for staying after. Listen, I was thinking about something for the next Songbirds set. Perhaps you could consider adding in a piece I've been working on. It's a piano-heavy bebop that I think you would have a blast with. I actually started working on it after I heard you play at Heavy Beans. This would be a great vehicle for your talents, I think. And you would basically be workshopping it for me, testing how it plays for real with full arrangement. I'd like to hear how it sounds live so that I can adjust anything that's not working before I submit it to the Brussels Jazz Today! Festival. They've got an original composition section. What do you say – would you be up for it?"

"Wow, professor," Eve said. Her fears of just a moment before evaporated in a heartbeat. Instead of paralyzing fear, she felt a bizarre mix of guilt and excitement. She was undeserving of such an honor. But also anxious to see what he had written. And to think that he'd done it with her in mind? Holy crap.

"If you'd like to come up to my office, I can give you the music and see what you think? If you're interested in doing it, you would need to present it to the Songbirds for their approval. I am just an advisor, I can't tell them what to play."

His lips spread into a faint smile, and Eve almost laughed out loud. No, maybe he couldn't tell them what to play, but she couldn't imagine them saying no to a piece that Prof. Von Klein had written and asked them to perform. False modesty alert there.

"Sure," she said. "I don't have another class until one o'clock today."

"Perfect," he said. "Just give me one more minute then."

He turned away and Eve realized that a dark-haired guy with an impressive five o'clock shadow, considering it was just eleven a.m., was waiting for a word. She turned away to give them their privacy and stared at the balcony just overhead. The one that was just outside the private room behind the professor's office. The one from which Isabella had been hung, suspended over the seats where she once attended lectures.

The thought sent a shiver up her spine and she turned away.

"All set," the professor said, suddenly standing right next to her.

She nodded and followed him up the aisle and out of the theater. He made small talk and asked her how her first semester was going so far. She assured him that everything was better than she could have hoped for.

"I've been really impressed with what I've seen of you," he said as they started up the stairwell to his office. "Your technique is perfect, but more than that, you capture the spirit of the music. That's what is most important to any piece, especially with jazz. The notes on the page are only half of the equation. You must bring your soul to the audience. And then it is for them to judge whether you are true. Whether you can touch them…or not."

"Thank you, professor, that really means a lot to me. I try to let my heart move my fingers when I play. When it's really going well, I hardly even see the music."

He looked pleased. "That's as it should be. Every performance of a piece is unique. And when you consider the number of people in every ensemble, you understand that even more. So many people bringing their own nuances, their own hearts to a list of static black notes on a page. Ah, here we are."

They had arrived at his office door. He took out a key from his pants pocket. She had a moment of frisson as she watched him put the key in the lock that Nikki had picked just hours before. And then he opened the door to let them in. The office looked far more welcoming in the daylight than it had in the middle of the night.

"Please," he said, and motioned for her to take a seat. "I will play you a bit of the main theme, and see if you like it."

"I'm sure I will, professor," she said.

He put up his hand. "Say nothing until you've listened. It could be a work of utter tripe, and then what will you say?"

She grinned. As if.

"I've been working on this right here at this piano every night for the past week. Burning the midnight oil, as I think you Americans say. I put the last measures in last night at about 12:30," he said.

Eve's jaw clenched slightly at that. They had really *just* missed him last night. Or was he trying to tell her that he had been nearby when she broke into his office? She suddenly had a chill and felt uneasy again.

The professor sat down at the piano bench and arranged a series of handwritten sheets of music in front of him. "There is a great saxophone part for Richard or Gianna here," he said. "And the bass may even give Susie a challenge. But the real spotlight is right here for you."

With that, he put his hands on the keys and began.

Eve found herself smiling almost immediately. The piano theme was bold, but also imbued with a knowing humor. It referenced Bird but didn't steal. And then the counter part; it warmed the back of the spine with its bass and movement.

When he finished, and pulled his hands back dramatically from the keys, Eve clapped without even thinking.

"I love it," she said.

He swiveled around on the bench, adjusting his sports jacket as he smiled and met her eyes. "I hoped you would," he said softly. He seemed almost shy. "So, you think it is something the Songbirds would want to try?"

She almost laughed. How could they not? "I can't speak for them, of course, but I can't imagine that they won't love it as much as I do."

"I hope so," he said. "I haven't written a jazz piece in a long while."

The professor turned and gathered his music into a pile. Then he reached around to the back of the piano and brought out a stack of other music.

"I've written all of the main parts out here," he said. "You will all have room to improvise a bit, so if you come up with something that makes it even better, I'll write you all in as arrangers."

"Thank you for the opportunity," Eve said. "I can't wait to take it to the band."

His expression looked strangely hopeful. Naively so. Did he really think the Songbirds would refuse to play a Von Klein original?

"Oh, one other thing," he said as he stood up.

"Yes?"

He looked at her directly. His attention appeared serious.

"Would you mind if I took your picture?"

Eve's heart turned to ice. She had relaxed and taken the bait and now…here was the hook.

"Why?" she asked, trying not to show how on edge the question had put her.

"The Morricone Scholarship," he said. "We need to send a notice to several magazines about the award, and it's always better if you have a professional photo to go along with the press release that we send. You may not know this, but I love photography and have something of a professional studio right here. I can take your picture and have exactly what we need to send out the release this afternoon. What do you say?"

"Um, sure, I guess so," she said without thinking. A second after it came out of her mouth, she wondered if it was really a trap. This whole thing. *He just wanted to get her to come up to his office where he knew she'd been last night, so that he could take her in back and....*

"You know," she said, her mind racing, "I probably have a photo I could get you that might work. I don't need to bother you."

He shook his head and waved a hand. "It's not a bother at all," he said. "I love to do it. And then, in five or ten minutes, it is done, and you don't have to worry about anything ever again."

When he said 'ever again', Eve felt her eyes widen. She was doomed, she knew it. This was it. She'd come all the way to Europe to be murdered by the very man she had admired from afar for years.

"Follow me," he said and walked to the door to the back office. Again, he pulled a key from his pocket and unlocked it, before opening the door and gesturing for her to precede him inside.

Eve couldn't move. Her feet were rooted to the floor. *He knew that she'd been in there last night. This was just a ruse. If she let the door shut behind them....*

"Come on," he said. "It won't take but a minute."

Somehow, she moved forward instead of running away. Would he really murder her in broad daylight when students were roaming the halls right outside? She wanted to bolt back to the hall, but instead, she took four steps and found herself back in the photography room. Her mind instantly flashed back to the night before. She could see Nikki crouching by the cabinet in the corner and had to tear her gaze away from it when the professor spoke.

"I've got a whole setup here for just this kind of thing," he said as he flipped on the lights and closed the door. "It's a fun side project for me."

Eve tried to muster a smile, but had nothing to say in answer. She felt nauseous as the door put a wall between her and the corridors outside.

The professor busied himself near the camera on the tripod for a moment and then walked over to the backdrop and flipped on the umbrella studio lights on either side of the backdrop.

"You have the easy job," he said. "Just stand right there in the middle, and be yourself. We're just grabbing a headshot here, so think about something happy, give us a smile, and we'll be done in just a moment."

Eve looked into the lens of the camera. It was like a giant eye, staring her down. The lights on either side of her washed out the rest of the room. It was just her, and the camera. And the professor aiming it at her.

What if it was really a gun and when he pressed the trigger, she was done?

"Smile," he prodded. "I would like it to look like you're happy you won the scholarship."

She couldn't help but break a smile at that and the camera clicked, and then again. And again.

"Look just a hair to the left," he suggested.

She did and the clicks came again.

"I'm sorry you've joined us at such a difficult time," he said from behind the camera. "We've never had anything like this happen before. But the police promise me that they are going to keep the rest of our students safe." He stepped out from behind the lens so that she could see his face. His expression was stern. "Do you feel safe?" he asked.

She felt her thighs turn to taffy. She did *not* feel safe, particularly alone in a room with the professor.

"I'm a little worried," she admitted.

He stepped close to her and put a hand on her shoulder. "Don't be," he said. "You have nothing to worry about. I am hopeful that this whole thing is behind us now. If we're lucky, whoever did those horrible things has avenged whatever grudge they had. I am sure you would like to worry about music, not murder."

Eve nodded.

"You know," he said, "it's funny, but I shot Isabella right there where you're standing the night she was killed. I still can't believe it. But she was a headstrong girl. She must have made someone very angry. According to the police, I took her pictures less than an hour before she was thrown over the balcony. So sad. So very sad indeed."

He put the lens cap on the camera and walked over to the back door that led to the balcony. "Would you like to see the theater from above?"

he asked, gesturing to the door in the back of the studio.

Eve did not want to go to the balcony with him at that moment, but hesitantly she followed. There were a few box seats ready for patrons. The chairs on the theater main floor below were closed up and empty. But she could see the piano at the rear of the shadowed stage. "I've enjoyed seeing so many wonderful performances here," he said. "I've enjoyed watching you practice from here, though I don't believe you knew I was watching."

She shook her head. Somehow, the idea that he had watched her secretly from above did not bring her joy. In fact, it kind of creeped her out. When his hand touched her shoulder, she flinched. It occurred to her that he could push her over the edge of the balcony right now and nobody would know.

"I have to go," she blurted, and pushed back from the railing. "Thank you for taking care of the picture."

She edged past him and walked up the five steps to the door of the photography room.

"I'll give you a copy when I develop it," he called. "Don't forget your music."

The music, yes. She would have walked right out without it. And then she would have had to come back. Eve picked it up off his desk and called her thanks through the open door. But in the back of her mind, she was whispering, *Did you kill Isabella after you took her pictures? What could she have done to make you so angry? And what about Genevieve? Did you write her special music? Did she not perform it well? What if you don't like how I perform this new piece?*

Eve swallowed hard and breathed an audible sigh of relief when she stepped into the hallway beyond the professor's office. She imagined him still out there on the empty balcony, spying on the stage below.

A chill ran down her spine.

CHAPTER TWENTY-FOUR

Richard looked surprised when he answered the door. "Hi," he said. "I didn't realize you were coming over!"

A frown crossed his face, but then his expression cleared.

"Did you have other plans?" Eve asked.

"No, not at all," he said. "I'd rather study you than study books!"

"I didn't really come over here for you to study," she said.

"Oh," he said. "Well, that's disappointing. What *did* you come over for then?"

"I wanted to talk about Professor Von Klein."

"Not my *favorite* subject," he said. His brow creased. "But all right, I'll bite. What about him?"

Eve drew a breath and held it before blurting out, "Do you think he could be the killer?"

The twisted look that crossed over Richard's face would have made her laugh under another circumstance. Instead, it made her feel like he was making fun of her.

"Stop that," she said. "I'm serious."

Richard put a hand on her arm and squeezed. "You realize how ridiculous that sounds, don't you?"

She nodded, but her face remained serious.

"Okay, let's hear it. Tell me."

She related the events of the last twenty-four hours. Richard's eyebrows rose when she talked about breaking into the office, but he said nothing.

"It's just all...weird," she said. "What do you think?"

"I think you should leave the detective work to the detectives before you get kicked out of school and sent back to New York."

"But what about the photos?" she persisted. "He has his own private photo studio right there behind his office. All of the victims have had a photo taken right before they died. And the professor was at the show the night Isabella died, taking photos. Hell, they even left together."

"Everyone takes photos," Richard said. "That doesn't really mean anything."

"I suppose not," she said. "I just wish the police would get a lead on someone. I hate knowing that whoever killed those girls is still out there, probably not very far away. And probably getting ready to do it again."

Richard put his arm around her. "I know," he said. "But they are doing everything they can. You see policemen watching the school a lot. The inspector has interviewed everybody, I think. We just have to wait until they find a clue and arrest a suspect."

"I think we're all suspects at this point," Eve said.

"That's pretty much what Inspector Martino said when he talked to me."

"All of the victims have been Songbirds," Eve said. "Do you think it could be one of the Songbirds?"

Richard laughed. "Who? Do you think Markie is knocking everyone else off because they don't keep time good enough? Or Susie is killing all the other girls because she's jealous or something?"

"What about Gianna?" Eve asked. "She seems pretty dark."

"She's not like that. She's sarcastic, not psychopathic," Richard said. He looked amused. "What about me? Am I on your suspect list?"

"Maybe," she said. "But I don't know what your motive would be."

"The inspector suggested that maybe it was because I was a spurned lover."

Eve raised an eyebrow. "That's an interesting motive," she mused. "I guess I better stay in your good graces?"

"That's right." He winked. "I think you better go practice the music Von Klein gave you, too, if you're going to present it to the Songbirds tomorrow."

"I thought maybe you'd want to look at it with me tonight," she said.

Richard shook his head. "I hate to say it, but I've got to get some work done tonight. I've got a paper due tomorrow in Professor Gastaldi's class."

Eve pouted, and Richard put one finger under her chin. "I'm sorry, but tomorrow we can go out. Can you wait for me until then?"

She forced a smile. "I suppose so. And you're right, I should go practice. I guess I'll see you tomorrow then?"

He kissed her and dramatically whispered, "Tomorrow cannot come soon enough."

"Spare me." She laughed.

"I will," he said. "As long as you're good to me." Richard winked, and Eve rolled her eyes.

"Okay, killer. Whatever you say."

★   ★   ★

Eve left Richard's disappointed, but the feeling didn't last too long. She didn't like the way things had ended there but she was anxious to get at Prof. Von Klein's music, and the night was still early. She headed down the hall to the elevator. She could spend a couple hours in a practice room and get a good feel for the piece before playing it for everyone tomorrow.

There was a handwritten sign on the elevator. *Out of Order.*

"Are you freakin' kidding me?" she said out loud. She'd ridden up on the elevator less than an hour before.

Eve shook her head in disgust and made her way down a nearby stairwell. At least going down was a lot better than going up.

She walked across the lobby and back up a different flight of stairs to reach the practice room floor. It was mostly quiet, but she could hear the strains of a trumpet leaking through the walls of a room a couple doors down from the piano room she'd chosen.

It was good to not be alone in this building at night.

She set up at the piano and started to sight read the professor's music. It called for some solid skills; he had to have spent more than a week writing this. The shit was complex! But it sounded good. She found herself smiling in parts, which were almost musical in-jokes as they referenced old time jazz riffs that aficionados would recognize instantly. At the same time, there was an original consistent theme that the professor built upon, which was really catchy.

"They're going to love this," she told the empty room.

She played it through several times, and then moved into working on a classical piece that she was studying for Prof. Margheriti's class. She stopped periodically to take notes; she was supposed to be breaking down the structure and explaining why the counterpoint themes developed a sense of anticipation in the listener.

It was after eleven when she finally decided to call it a night. She hadn't intended on staying this long. But as it turned out, she was destined to stay even later. As she was packing up the sheet music, her phone rang.

"Now what?" she murmured, and quickly grabbed and thumbed it on to answer without looking at the number.

"Eve?" a male voice said. "Is it too late to call?"

"Richard?" she asked.

"No, it's Billy," the voice said. "Who's Richard, and…um…wow, how quickly we forget!"

"Oh my God, Billy." Her lips slipped into a smile of surprise, finally recognizing the voice of the bassist from the last ensemble she'd been in back in New York. As soon as she recognized his voice, she felt a pang of homesickness.

"I just got off work," he said. "It's only five here, but I know it's later at night by you. It this okay?"

"Sure," she said. "I was just wrapping up practicing actually, so it's perfect."

They talked for almost a half hour, and Eve found herself trading stories and relaxing in a way she hadn't in weeks. There was nothing like hearing from an old friend to even out all of the stress and emotions that you'd been bottling up inside.

"I miss you, buddy," she said as they closed.

"Maybe. But maybe you miss Richard more now?"

"Jealous?" she said. "You had your chance and you didn't take it."

"And I'll forever regret it," he said. "Go get some sleep and dream about those of us you've left behind in your meteoric rise to the top of the world's so-serious-nobody-cares-about-it music scene."

Eve laughed, before they finally said goodnight and ended the call. After she slipped the phone in her pocket, she grabbed her purse and sheet music and walked to the practice room door. As she turned, a movement caught her eye. A shadow near the door in the hall.

Eve paused. Was it just a trick of the light? She held a breath and leaned close to the doorway to peer out into the hall.

She saw nobody.

Her heart was pounding now, but she went ahead and flipped the light switch to off. She waited a moment until her eyes adjusted, and then stepped into the hall, looking quickly right and left, ready to run.

There was nobody there. Just a long, dimly lit, old wooden-floored hallway.

She let out a breath and shook her head. Spooking herself.

Eve walked towards the stairs, but then, instead of going down them, she went left. She was curious. It was just a short walk to the faculty offices.

She looked down the hall when she reached it, and her suspicion was confirmed. There was light coming out of the bottom of one of the doors. And she had a bet that she knew whose it was.

Eve moved quietly down the hall, conscious of not letting her shoes slap the floor. The last thing she wanted was for that door to open because she made noise in the hall.

The light was Prof. Von Klein's office. Just as she'd known it would be. She paused just outside; she could hear voices from within.

The faint low rumble of a male voice. And a higher pitch that answered. She couldn't make out the words. Eve moved closer to the door, edging near the glass. She wouldn't be able to tell who was in there, but maybe she could make out figures through the block glass and see if the two were near.

Just as she decided that one of the shadows distorted in the glass was a person, the tall shadow began to move. Towards the door!

Eve backpedaled. She considered dashing down the hall, but there was no way she could make it to the corner before whoever was in there came out and saw her.

The metal click of the doorknob sounded, and Eve did the only thing she could think of. She backed into the entry to a nearby maintenance room. The doorway was inset by a foot, and if whoever was leaving Prof. Von Klein's office went the other direction, they'd never see her.

Eve imagined herself as thin as paper and held her breath. She leaned her head forward just an inch to watch the office. A female hand held the inner doorknob. Eve could see a bare arm, but the rest of the girl remained half inside, still talking apparently.

And then finally, she came all the way out, and closed the door behind her.

Eve struggled to see if she could recognize who it was. The professor was presumably staying inside a while. Developing the pictures they'd just taken?

The girl looked just for a second in her direction, scanning the hall, and then turned and began to walk quickly towards the stairs.

It was one of the twins, Elena or Erika. Based on the electric green and orange and purple interwoven circles of the short summer dress that she wore, Eve guessed it was Erika. She always seemed to wear the brighter outfits, while Elena seemed to always be in black. Elena also often wore a choker, and the girl who had just left Prof. Von Klein's office had nothing around her neck.

Why was she up here so late? Eve thought again. She quickly tiptoed past the professor's door and began to follow. Maybe she could find a way to 'accidentally' run into her and ask her what she was up to tonight.

Erika moved down the hall ahead, but Eve held back. She didn't want the other girl to turn around and see her. Not yet. Maybe when they reached the elevators or the main lobby. She didn't want Erika to know that she'd seen her at the professor's office.

It struck her that Erika had to use the East elevators the way she was

walking, so instead of directly pacing behind her, Eve ducked down
another hall so that she could 'bump into her' coming from a different
direction – in front of Erika instead of behind her. She could catch her
at the elevator and easily just tell the truth if Erika asked why she was
here. She had been practicing.

Eve moved quickly down the corridor, half running so that she
could 'go around the block' via the hallways and still catch the other girl
before she went downstairs.

At the end of the final hall that would connect with Erika's path, she
stopped and hugged the wall. She peeked carefully around the corner.

It was dark and empty. Erika was not there.

Damn it.

But then she looked in the other direction. And her mouth dropped
in frustration. There was the girl's colorful back, walking away. Erika
had already passed her. Her detour had taken longer than she counted
on. She'd wanted to be ahead of the girl. Eve sighed and began to
follow. But as she did, she saw someone else ahead. A dark shape that
slipped out of an alcove and turned the corner just a few seconds after
Erika passed.

Eve frowned. She quickened her pace. Maybe it was just a cop who
was walking the building. It had been too dark to see from the other end
of the hall. But she was sure that someone had turned the corner ahead
right after Erika.

Halfway down the hall, Eve broke into a run.

As she rounded a corner, she could see Erika waiting at one of the
elevator doors. There didn't look to be anybody else around.

Eve stopped, wondering if she'd been seeing things. She scanned the
hall behind and ahead of her. And then the elevator opened, and Erika
stepped in.

As she did, a figure emerged from one of the nearby doorways and
stepped inside the elevator with Erika just as the doors were closing. Eve
ran towards the elevator.

"Erika, wait!" she called.

But the elevator door creaked shut.

She reached it and instantly punched the call button, hoping that it might reopen the door if she had gotten there fast enough.

It didn't.

Instead, unseen gears hummed into motion, and took Erika – and the black-clad figure – out of reach.

CHAPTER TWENTY-FIVE

The hall was dark when Erika stepped out of Prof. Von Klein's office. She had not meant to stay that long, but the professor had been a lot of fun tonight. He was totally different than what he seemed like on the teaching stage. There he was so tight-laced and 'respectable'. She would never have guessed the kinky side of him. Hell, she would never have guessed that she would be willing to play along. The things he made her do! She knew she wasn't the only one, but that was okay. She was enjoying herself. And being one of the professor's 'pets' was certainly not going to hurt her career here at the Eyrie. She knew it had opened doors last year for Genevieve, and she hoped that it would end up playing well for her.

She was anxious now, however, just to get home and get in the shower. Her skin glinted even in the low hallway light from oil. She'd used one of the professor's towels to wipe it off, but she still felt greasy all over. Her panties were literally glued to her ass. She wished she hadn't even bothered to put them back on.

Erika hurried down the hall, heading to the elevator as fast as she could. She shifted from one foot to the next after she pressed the down button on the wall next to the elevator bank. She really wanted to move.

She didn't notice the dark-clad figure moving in the shadows behind her until after she'd stepped into the elevator and hit the button. She bent down to look at the sheen of her calves, and there was suddenly a shadow on them. Just as she noticed that someone had gotten in the elevator after her, she swore she heard her name called from out in the hall.

Erika looked up as the doors began to close. The newcomer was completely clad in black. Her heart skipped. She slowly straightened up, noting the black shoes and pants and long-sleeved shirt of the person in front of her. She could only see the back of the person, who did not turn around. She couldn't even tell if it was a girl or a guy – the head was covered in a black winter pullover hat. Which was scary all by itself because it was still at least sixty degrees outside tonight. Summer was slipping away into a fall memory, but it wasn't completely gone yet.

The head remained motionless as the elevator creaked its slow descent. Erika realized she was holding her breath as she stared at the back of the head. She wanted to say something…but she was afraid to encourage the head to turn around. What if this was the killer?

Hoy shit, she could be locked in an elevator with the same psycho who murdered Gen and Anita and Isabella!

Erika's throat went bone-dry. Her fingers clenched white on the grips of her purse. She inched a step backwards. Not that there was anywhere to run.

Please don't turn around. Please don't look at me.

Her heart beat like a jackhammer in her chest. Could it be heard in the elevator?

The head tilted slightly towards the buttons that controlled the floors. *Oh God. What if he or she pushed the button to stop the elevator between floors?* She'd be trapped here. Completely at the mercy of the figure in black.

Erika backed up another step.

Please don't turn around.

Her hand found the brass guide rail on the wall and she squeezed it. She prayed for the door to open.

Open, open, open, she begged.

The elevator stopped.

Erika's entire body stiffened like a spring pushed tight. She was ready to lunge if the person made any move in her direction.

The face turned towards her then, and she saw that it was obscured by sunglasses and a face mask that covered its nose and mouth. She still couldn't tell if it was a woman or man. All she could see really were the upper cheeks and a strip of forehead.

The head nodded as the elevator doors spread open. As soon as they did, the figure stepped out and moved away to the lobby.

Erika heaved out a huge sigh and collapsed against the back wall of the elevator. "Oh my God," she whispered. She had an overpowering need to go to the bathroom. She could feel the sweat under her armpits. A drop trickled down her backbone as well.

"That was insane," she told herself.

The elevator doors began to close.

"Oh no you don't," she said, and leapt forward to put her hand between them so that it would stop closing. She was not getting stuck in there again.

Erika barely slowed as she passed the elevator bank that led to the residential floors. It had an out-of-order sign on it once again. Naturally. She turned the knob on the stairwell and resigned herself to three flights of stairs. Her legs were 'well-oiled' for the exercise, she thought. She took a breath and began the climb.

A minute later, the door silently slipped back open. A figure stepped through and its black-gloved hand eased the handle closed so that it did not make a sound.

One by one, the figure then climbed the steps, always remaining just a flight below the girl above.

CHAPTER TWENTY-SIX

Eve stood at the elevator door where Erika had been just a minute before. She punched the button quickly several times, but the elevator gears were already in motion and the car was descending. She didn't know what to do. Should she wait for the elevator to come back up? What if the killer was stabbing Erika one floor below her right now? What if the elevator was stopped mid-floor to allow the luxury of the poor girl's torture?

She couldn't wait for another car to come. Eve ran to the stairs and took them two at a time down to the main floor lobby. Then she ran across to the front desk where Mrs. Freer was stationed. She slapped a hand on the counter to get the woman's attention as she gasped for breath.

Mrs. Freer shifted in the chair and reached up to pull out her earbuds. Then she grabbed the remote and pressed pause before turning fully to look at Eve.

"Did you just see someone come off the elevators?" Eve asked. "A girl in a short dress and someone else, all in black?"

The house marm looked vaguely amused. Her mouth puckered. "Didn't see anyone," she said. "Maybe try calling whoever you're looking for instead of chasing them?"

"Are you sure?" Eve pressed. "It's important – the girl could be in danger. They would have just come down."

Mrs. Freer raised her eyebrows and turned behind to a small row of television monitors.

"I'd have seen them right here," she said. Her body language made it clear that she felt Eve was bothering her unnecessarily. "Hold on."

She bent down and rummaged for something before coming up with a remote. Then she aimed it at the small black-and-white screens and hit a button. The screens flickered, with white lines taking over the middle of them. She was rewinding the feed of the security cams.

A few seconds later, her expression changed, as suddenly there were people on one of the screens. Mrs. Freer thumbed another button and the fast flickering motion stopped. Together they watched Erika standing in the back of an elevator. A dark figure stood in front of her, but the face was too close to the door to be seen.

When the elevator opened, the unidentified figure stepped out and shuffled towards the front desk, one hand against its thigh. Eve noticed something strange about the way it walked, just as the black figure moved out of camera range. Was it limping?

They watched until Erika shoved her hand in the opening, almost missing her chance to exit. And then the elevator feed was once again still, and empty.

"Looks like she is just fine," Mrs. Freer said.

"Hmm," Eve said, thinking of the video. The shadow person had gotten out first. And Erika was not lying in a pool of blood in the elevator. Maybe it *was* all right.

The house marm shoved the earbuds back in her head and turned back to whatever she was watching on the screen. It looked like something set in Italy; Eve recognized the Colosseum as two cars careened around a street corner chasing each other.

The heavy chair creaked as Mrs. Freer turned her back on Eve without another word and settled in.

Eve stepped away from the desk and headed towards the stairs to her room. The evidence said Erika seemingly was safe, but she couldn't help but still feel uneasy.

CHAPTER TWENTY-SEVEN

The hall was silent when Erika exited the stairwell. The communal bathroom also appeared empty when she passed. Just as well; she really didn't want to be seen right now. People would wonder why her skin was so shiny and where she was coming from at this hour looking like that. She didn't need the looks and talk. She didn't want to hear it from her sister either. Hopefully Elena was out for the night. She'd had a date with Corey, so....

She keyed open the door to her room and tiptoed inside. A quick glance in the dark showed that Elena's pillow and comforter remained in place from the morning. She hadn't been to bed yet. Erika relaxed in relief. Her sister was gettin' some tonight and that was good for her; that meant Elena couldn't throw stones at Erika's extracurricular activities.

She flipped the desk light on and began to strip, first pulling the colorful sundress over her head, and then releasing the clasps on her bra. She was going to have to throw in some extra laundry detergent on these, she mused, looking at the darkened spots where the oil had been absorbed into the material. Hopefully it would come out. Oh well.

Erika slipped a finger beneath her g-string panties and slid them off, to toss in the pile with the other clothes. She smiled faintly. Von Klein loved those. She bought pairs just for her nights with him now. Then she reached into her wardrobe and pulled out a thin pink satin robe. She hesitated a moment before putting it on; she didn't want to get any residual oil on that too. But she couldn't very well walk down the hallway naked. Or could she? There wasn't anyone else about. Erika's face set in a devilish smile and she picked up her shampoo bottle. She flipped the inner metal lock bar the wrong way so that it lodged the door open, and then stepped out nude into the dimly lit hall. Still nobody around.

Erika walked quickly to the door of the bathroom. Her heart beat a little faster. She was brave but not shamelessly brazen.

She flipped on the lights and went to the shower area to hang up her robe on the hook just outside. There were eight nozzles inside the large tiled rectangular area. A lip of tile formed a barrier to keep the water from flooding the rest of the bathroom, forcing the water to dissipate down the drains set every few feet in the floor around the room.

Erika used the commode, and then returned to the showers to turn the water on.

★   ★   ★

In the hallway outside, a dark figure moved slowly along the wall. It stopped at Erika's room, carefully pushed the door open, slipped inside and then let it settle back to rest on the metal latch that kept the door from closing all the way. Inside, the figure stepped around the beds, studying the pictures hung on the wall. Something caught its attention on the floor and one hand reached down to lift up Erika's discarded pink panties by the hip string, studying them intently, before dropping them again.

One black-gloved hand reached out to the desk. It flipped the metal clasps on her instrument case, and then lifted the lid. A beautiful silver soprano saxophone was inside. Except for the wider bell where the sound released, it could have been a fat flute or a metal clarinet based on its petite shape. The uninitiated would never have thought the instrument was a saxophone; there was no J shape to the long metal curve of the mouth as there was with a tenor or alto sax.

The black glove clenched the center of the instrument tight and lifted it from the case. A faint smile creased the edges of the face, still hidden beneath a black mask. Then the figure turned and moved out of the room, instrument still in hand. A moment later, Erika's door gently closed again.

Black leather shoes with heavy rubber soles stepped silently down the hallway carpet, following the path of the bare feet that had touched there just minutes before. They paused at the threshold of the bathroom. The sound of water splashing off tile echoed from within. The shoes moved into the bathroom entryway, but stopped at a taupe-colored door just inside. One leather-gloved hand reached out and turned the silver knob of the side door to open it. There was a light switch just inside. With a flip, the room was illuminated by one bare-bulb light fixture above, and the glove pulled the door shut.

The room was small, but there were shelves of hardware from floor to ceiling. Next to the door was a supply of bath towels, and the black glove temporarily set down Erika's soprano saxophone on a pale green one. Beyond the towels were things that a maintenance crew would keep on hand for quick fixes without having to leave the floor. Toilet plungers, curved segments of silver and plastic pipe. Wrenches, gloves, and an assortment of power tools.

The black glove picked up a large hammer and tested the heft, swinging it back and forth in the air as if bringing it down hard on a wall.

Or someone's head.

Then it picked up a hacksaw and turned it back and forth, considering. Apparently finding that mode of execution wanting, it replaced the saw on the shelf and touched the top of a large red-painted metal cylinder that sat in the corner on the floor. A tube extended from the top with a silver nozzle at its end. The glove twisted the small spokes of the nozzle and a faint hiss of air emanated from the end of the tube. The black-masked face nodded understanding then, and twisted the nozzle back to off.

The hand then lingered on the shelf just above, where there were several types of tape – electrical, duct and masking – as well as a roll of rubber-coated twine. Again, the head nodded, but didn't take anything from the shelf. Instead, the black glove reached down and pulled a pair of rubber boots from the bottom shelf. There were several pairs of different sizes, but the medium pair seemed right. Moments later, both black shoes were encased in rubber. Then one hand picked up the rubber twine, while the other retrieved the soprano saxophone from the shelf near the door.

The shower was still running as the boots clunked faintly on the tile outside of the maintenance closet. Erika didn't hear; she was rinsing the shampoo from her long black hair. After her fingers ran cleanly through the long wet strands, she rubbed them across her chest and belly, ensuring that all of the oiliness was gone. Then she slid one hand between her legs and up and down her inner thighs.

She closed her eyes with a faint smile of pleasure. She'd been a bad girl tonight, for sure. But it felt luxurious to stand and soap and preen beneath the hot spray in the middle of the night afterwards. She slid both hands up her thighs and tilted her head back to let her face catch the shower spray.

Something slid around her neck and she choked. *What the hell!* She grabbed for her throat and felt a smooth thin cord or wire encircling it. She tried to pry it away but the pressure only tightened. That's when she finally turned enough to see the black figure standing right behind her.

Erika opened her mouth to scream, but a black-gloved hand slipped over her lips. The hand dragged her backwards, away from the spray of the shower. She slapped and punched at her captor but that just made the grip around her neck constrict until she was gasping and choking. A voice whispered in her ear, "Stop struggling, or I will strangle you. That would be a shame."

She dropped her arms to her sides and the pressure against her airway loosened. Erika gulped for air.

"Why?" she gasped.

"I know you give private photo shoots," the voice said. "You gave one tonight, isn't that right?"

"I don't know what you're talking about," Erika said. In her mind, she panicked. Who else could possibly know that but Prof. Von Klein?

The result was a hard yank of the noose around her neck.

"Okay," she tried to say, but it came out as a wheezing gurgle of air. The pressure eased again.

"I'd like to get a picture here, now," the voice whispered. "I have a camera ready."

The figure reached one hand into a front pocket and pulled out a cell phone with a pink case studded in rhinestones. It pushed one finger in a swipe to bring up the camera app. Then, with one hand still holding her by the rope, it pushed a button and the phone flashed, illuminating Erika's red, wet face and wide eyes.

For a second, she thought the person behind the mask might be a woman, given the phone. And then recognition set in.

"Hey, that's *my* cell phone," Erika gasped.

The head held it up to one black lens of its sunglasses.

"I'm going to release you now," the voice said. "But don't even think of running or screaming. I will kill you if you do. Understood?"

She nodded quickly.

The pressure on her throat suddenly eased. The glove tugged and it slipped off her neck completely.

"Strike a pose."

Erika shook her head and clasped her hands protectively over her chest. Tears mixed with the water from the shower.

"Do it," the voice demanded. It came out as a sharp whisper. Erika still could not tell if it was a woman or man behind the black mask and sunglasses.

"Put your leg out for me, and your hand on your hip. I know you know how to do that."

Erika's heart beat even harder. The voice was demanding that she pose just as she had for the professor an hour ago. Could it *be* the professor?

"Please," she cried. "Just let me go."

"Show me," the voice whispered. "Let me see it now."

Erika shook her head. "No," she said, her lips shaking as tears streamed faster and harder from her eyes. "Go fuck yourself."

The phone flashed.

One gloved hand reached out and pinched the meat of her thigh, attempting to force her leg out in a pose.

"I said 'No!'" Erika shouted, which only made the glove yank harder. The force unbalanced her and she fell to one knee as her foot slipped on the wet tile.

That seemed to make her attacker furious. The figure threw itself against her, and tackled her all the way to the tile. Erika punched out with one hand, but a glove only grabbed it and shoved it hard to the tile. She kicked out with her feet, trying to roll away, but the legs of the person on top of her only scissored against her thighs and pinned her in place. Erika used the only weapon she had left.

She bit the arm that locked her down as hard as she could. The figure gave out a sharp cry. And then both hands grabbed Erika around the neck and squeezed. She tried to scream but barely any sound came out. She could feel her face heating up.

Erika threw her body back and forth, trying to break free, but her captor hung on fast. And then lifted her by the neck and slammed her head on the tile. And again.

And again.

Erika's vision blurred and turned red. There were white points of light in front of the black mask in front of her. She could feel something warm running out of the back of her head on the cold floor.

"Be still," the voice whispered. The direction was unnecessary; she found she had no more ability to fight. In a daze, Erika felt her wrists pulled together. Bound together.

The black mask and sunglasses loomed over her face. And then the black glove dangled a silver instrument in front of her eyes.

"You used to play this with your mouth, but your real talent for it might be elsewhere."

Erika didn't understand at first.

And then something cold touched the inside of her thigh. A cold kiss of metal slid between her 'other' lips.

"I think you'll be a natural at this," her captor whispered. "Slut."

The cold turned to a jab of pain. As if the gynecologist had pushed in the speculum a little too hard, and too far.

Usually it only hurt for a second. This was excruciating.

Erika opened her mouth to scream, but the glove covered it. She tried to bite, but the saxophone stabbed inside her. It was like a jackhammer. Push, pound, jam. Something ripped and she could feel the warmth of blood trickling out from inside. The rough edges of the instrument shredded her tender inner flesh as it was pounded, centimeter by centimeter, into her vagina.

"Save your breath," the voice whispered. "You'll need a whole different way to blow."

Erika couldn't save her breath…she couldn't breathe at all. Something was wrapped around her mouth and nose and she was smothering. She tried to roll over, but the glove only slammed her head once more to the tile. She lost track of everything then for a second or two.

The next thing she knew, the glove was back. Only this time, there was a steel canister throbbing and humming next to her head. And a tube. Something peeled away from her lips for a second, just long enough for the tube to be slipped into her mouth. She felt it going down her throat, and her gag reflex kicked in.

"Oh no," the voice said, and the sound of duct tape filled the bathroom. The tube was sealed inside her throat with the tape, which was wound around and around her head. Just before she passed out, Erika heard one final whisper.

"Let me help you give that saxophone a blow."

CHAPTER TWENTY-EIGHT

Eve unlocked the door to her room and stepped inside. She pulled it closed behind her carefully so as not to wake her roommate, and then tiptoed over to the desk and set her purse on it. The room was dark, but she could make out enough of the tightly drawn blanket in the lower bunk to realize that Kristina wasn't home.

She hoped that Erika had made it to her room safely. The memory of the dark figure that had gotten in and out of the elevator with her still bugged Eve. She couldn't shake it. What if the guy had forced his way into her room? What if he walked ahead of her only because he knew where she was going?

Eve pulled the shirt over her head to get ready for bed. Then she peeled off the rest of her clothes and left them in a pile near her desk. She'd sort them in the morning. She retrieved a nightshirt from the top drawer of her bureau and slipped it on before grabbing her toiletries bag and heading to the bathroom to brush her teeth and take off her makeup.

The light in the hallway made her blink after she'd gotten used to the darkness of her room. Eve squinted faintly at her reflection in the mirror as she pulled out a makeup remover pad and sponged her face. Then she splashed herself with some warm water from the tap and used one of the bath towels stacked up nearby to dry off.

She was brushing her teeth when the feeling of uneasiness reached a zenith.

Could she really just go to bed without knowing that Erika was safe? She looked up with the toothbrush still in her mouth. Wide brown eyes stared back at her with a look that said, *Can you? Can you really?*

She closed her eyes so they couldn't accuse her of anything. Then she spit out the foam of toothpaste and rinsed her mouth.

When she looked up again, those brown eyes were wider and the pale lips beneath them were pursed.

"All right, all right," Eve told her reflection. "I'll just check on her."

Eve turned the water off and dropped her toothbrush back in her bag. She walked back to her room and opened the door, dropping the bag on the floor just inside. Then she went to the stairwell and quickly walked down two flights. She knew that Erika was in 320 – she'd been there a few nights ago when they hosted a post-practice get-together.

She exited the stairwell and stopped to look down the hall to make sure nobody was around before she continued. There was a faint moaning whistle coming from somewhere down the hall, but it sounded far away. Eve felt naked, wearing only her nightshirt. She hadn't intended on going wandering when she'd left her room. But...it was the middle of the night on an all-girls section of the floor. She shouldn't cause any scandal if anyone saw her here.

Eve walked down the hall past 316 and before stopping at 320. She raised her fist to knock. What if she woke Erika up and made her angry? Could she be asleep already? Or what if the killer was inside? She hadn't thought of what she'd do if she actually discovered that her fears were true.

It was a little late now to back out and just return to her room. She was standing in front of the door. Eve took a breath and gently knocked.

She realized after a few seconds that she was holding her breath as she waited for the door to open.

Nothing happened.

Eve frowned, and then raised her fist to knock again, a little harder this time.

She waited. As she did, she once more noticed the odd keening sound coming from down the hall. She looked in the direction it came from, but saw nothing but carpet and closed residential doors.

Her heart was beating faster now. Why wasn't Erika answering? She should have gotten back to her room before Eve reached hers. Unless something had happened.

She knocked a third time. Harder.

Maybe she was still getting ready for bed. She could be in the shower.

Eve's lips drew tight. What should she do? She couldn't go back upstairs and go to sleep now. She stepped back from the door and hesitated. Then she shrugged and walked towards the bathroom. Did going after someone in the bath constitute stalking? What would she say if Erika was there and asked her what she was doing on the floor?

"The truth," she whispered to herself. "It's all you've got."

The odd noise grew louder as she drew near the entrance to the third-floor communal bath. It was almost like someone was blowing into a horn without quite staying on key. It oscillated, but not in a musical way. It made the hair on the back of her neck rise.

Eve entered the bath. The maintenance door on the left was open; maybe that's where the sound was coming from? But who would be working on the bathroom at this hour? She stepped further inside, increasingly hesitant in case there was a maintenance man there. When she finally walked into the wide room with sinks and mirrors along one wall and toilet stalls on the other, she stopped fast, as if she'd just hit a wall.

Her eyes tried to register what she saw.

She'd found Erika.

And she'd found the source of the horrible sound. It emanated from the bloody silver soprano saxophone shoved between the Songbird's naked legs.

The girl lay on her back, nude, on the tile. Her abdomen looked distended; as if a balloon had inflated inside her. Streaks of blood crisscrossed her breasts and belly, but it was her face that Eve stared at, not fully understanding at first what she was seeing.

Duct tape wrapped around and around Erika's mouth and nose, leaving only her eyes visible. They bugged out in pure, frozen terror. Locked in that single final moment of pain and fear. A tube ran from a metal cylinder, under the tape and into the girl's mouth. Eve suddenly understood why the saxophone sounded so disturbing.

"Erika!" Eve cried out and broke free of her paralysis to run across the tile and kneel at the girl's side. With her fingernails she pried the edges of the duct tape away from Erika's cheeks and quickly yanked it up without worrying about hurting the girl's skin. She didn't know if there was anything left of Erika to hurt. Eve lifted the girl's head so that she could unravel the tape. It peeled back with a wet snapping sound and then the airhose popped free of Erika's lips.

The crying moan of the saxophone quieted.

Eve worked the rest of the tape off Erika's nose and mouth. But those frozen eyes did not change.

"Erika," she called, trying to wake her with words. Then she pressed her ear to the girl's bare chest.

There was no heartbeat.

"No!" she screamed. "No, no, no." Eve sat back on her haunches and realized that her calves were sticky with Erika's blood.

If she was honest with herself, she'd known the girl was dead as soon as she'd entered the bathroom. She shouldn't have touched the tape. Maybe there were fingerprints that she'd just messed up.

"What's going on?" a sleepy voice said from behind her.

Eve turned to see a blonde girl with ice blue eyes staring at her in confusion. Eve's body momentarily blocked the sleepy girl's view of Erika, but when she shifted, the newcomer drew in an audible breath. "Oh my God," she said. "What did you do to her?"

"I didn't do anything," Eve insisted, and stood up. She realized her white nightshirt was sodden at the bottom with Erika's blood and she still held a piece of duct tape in her hand. She dropped it.

"I found her like this," she said and stepped towards the blonde girl.

"Police!" the girl yelled, her eyes bugging as she backed away from Eve. "*Politie!*"

She turned and ran from the bathroom. Eve started to follow but stopped. There were more voices now in the hallway. She could hear the girl frantically telling whoever was out there what she'd just seen in a machine gun torrent of frightened Dutch.

Eve felt like throwing up.

Instead, she sat back down on the tile next to Erika to cry. There was no use in leaving the scene.

After a few moments, she turned around and found the switch on the air compressor, and flipped it off. The steady hum behind her died away, leaving the room in silence. She could hear voices talking excitedly somewhere down the hall but Eve didn't get up.

She sat in Erika's blood to wait for the police.

CHAPTER TWENTY-NINE

"Everyone back to your rooms and lock your doors," Mrs. Freer demanded. She walked up and down the hall outside the bathroom, calling for attention and order as the voices of hysterical girls rose and fell.

"The police will be here any minute; let's all get out of their way. Come on," she insisted. "If you didn't see the murder, I want you back in your beds. Genie, Louise, Myla – to your rooms, now."

The house marm's voice cut through all of the other voices, and little by little, the din outside of the bathroom diminished.

Mrs. Freer had already been in to talk to Eve. When Eve had explained what happened, the other woman's eyes had narrowed slightly. She'd looked down at the bloody body, and then stared hard at Eve's bloodstained nightshirt. Eve had the feeling that the dorm manager didn't believe her. And just as that thought crossed her mind, Mrs. Freer said something that made Eve more afraid than ever.

"All of this started right when you arrived here, you know that?" Mrs. Freer shook her head. "Stay here until the police come. I'm sure they will have plenty of questions."

Eve wished that she had never left New York City. She settled into a haze of sadness and depression and the voices outside all merged into an aural blur. And then she heard something that made her start.

"Richard, what are you doing on this floor?" Mrs. Freer said out in the hall. "Get back to your room this instant."

Eve pushed herself off the cold floor and walked to the door of the bathroom. She looked down the hall to see Mrs. Freer's back and a dozen other girls beyond her. The door to the stairwell was just closing. Had it been her Richard? And why was he up here?

Eve felt her throat constrict with a lump of emotion.

"Miss Springer," a voice said from the hallway behind her. "You seem to always be in the wrong place at the right time."

Eve turned and found Inspector Martino standing behind her with his arms crossed. The unforgiving face of Mrs. Freer loomed nearby.

The inspector turned to the house marm and asked, "This is the girl who was watching the elevator security tapes and then followed the girl upstairs?"

Mrs. Freer gave a short nod.

"Interesting," the inspector said. "Thank you. Please try to clear the floor and get the girls back to their rooms." He turned from Mrs. Freer to look at Eve.

"Show me," he said to her.

Eve led the way back into the bathroom. The inspector walked around the body and knelt at her right shoulder to peer into her eyes.

"She saw her death," he said. With his forefingers, he drew the eyelids closed. "Death by gunshot or car crash or falling from a high place...you see a different look in the eyes. Surprise mostly. This girl had plenty of time to see her death coming. I hate to see that. I think it's more humane to be surprised. To not have time to think about it."

He turned to look at Eve. "Tell me, did you want her to die?" His voice was emotionless.

Eve shook her head adamantly. "No, of course not," she said. "I told you, I saw someone all in black following her, so I came to her floor to see if she was all right."

Inspector Martino looked unconvinced. "You watched the security tape from the elevator. But the person who exited did not go after her. Whoever it was, left the car first and walked in the opposite direction. You, however, followed her."

Eve couldn't believe the implication of that. First Mrs. Freer, and now the inspector? Did they really believe that she could have been responsible?

"I followed her because I was worried about her," she said. Her voice rose an octave as she spoke. "Mrs. Freer didn't care that there was someone covered in black in the elevator with her, and I couldn't go to sleep without knowing she was all right. I am here because I cared."

Inspector Martino raised an eyebrow. "You are not dressed for a psychosexual impaling, I will grant you that." Then he stared pointedly at her chest. Eve realized her nipples were clearly visible through the thin cotton of her nightshirt. "Or...maybe you are. I'll leave that to the psychiatrists."

"Inspector, you have to believe me," she protested, but he raised a hand.

"I only have to believe the evidence. We'll take a statement at the station. But I suspect you'll want to get out of that shirt first."

She nodded.

"Let me take a picture, so we have it in the file."

He pulled out his cell phone and aimed it at her.

Eve crossed her hands across her chest. "No, please don't," she said.

"You don't want to go down to the station like that for the professional photographer, do you?" he asked.

"No."

"Then stand still," he demanded.

The flash went off three times, and then he pointed the phone lower to focus on the bloodstains at the base of her shirt. It flashed twice more as Eve swallowed hard. How had she gone from getting ready for bed to being a suspect in a murder investigation?

She looked back at the floor and suddenly didn't feel sorry for herself at all. She couldn't imagine being sexually impaled with an instrument. And then suffocated as her body played her own funeral dirge. God.

"Can I go change?" Eve asked.

"As long as you come right back," he said. "And bring your nightshirt with you. Unless you'd like to take it off here."

He reached out to the towel stack and offered her one.

Eve shook her head. "I'll come back. Where else am I going to go?"

"If I was you, back to New York City," he answered pointedly.

★   ★   ★

Eve felt the eyes of Mrs. Freer and the inspector on her back as she walked to the stairs. The voices of the handful of students still gathered along the wall of the hallway silenced as she passed. The blood-wet cotton of her nightshirt kept sticking and clinging to her calves. Eve had never wanted to be back home in New York as much as she did in that moment.

She was halfway between floors on the stairwell when it occurred to her that the killer could still be here. Could be above or behind her on the stairs, actually. Waiting.

Eve stopped for a second to listen.

All she could hear was the hum of the ventilation system. White noise.

"If the killer wants to take me out, I won't have to go down to the station," she said to herself. *"Maybe that would be easier."*

With the bravery of fatalistic resignation, she continued the climb. Something clattered on the stairs below her, but Eve did not quicken her step. She finished climbing the last five stairs, and only looked behind her when she opened the door to her floor.

There was nobody on the steps below.

Eve stepped into the hall and headed back to her room to get a change of clothes and her shampoo. Before she left this building, she was going to wash Erika's blood off herself if it killed her. She glanced behind her at the thought. It very well might.

Kristina still wasn't home and she was happy for that, actually. She didn't feel like explaining the events of the past hour again. Eve gathered her things quickly and went to the shower. Nobody was in the bathroom when she reached it, though she heard a door slam shut somewhere in the hall outside. She wasn't the only one up on the floor right now. She imagined news of the murder was spreading throughout the building.

Her face wrinkled with disgust as she lifted the bloody bottom of her nightshirt over her shoulders. She let it fall in a rumpled heap on the pale grey tile at her feet. Her legs were smeared with crimson marks. The image of Erika, with her eyes wide, naked legs smeared with blood, and her instrument sticking grotesquely out of her, immediately came to mind. Eve forced herself to look away from the bloody nightshirt.

She stepped into the shower and turned on the spray. The sooner she washed the blood, and this memory away, the better.

Eve rubbed soap up and down her legs quickly, both because she hated touching the blood and because she was anxious to clean the blood of her bandmate from her. She also really wanted to finish and get out of the shower. She kept stealing glances at the open area of the bathroom, confirming again and again that no one dressed all in black had wandered in after her.

The tile outside remained empty.

★ ★ ★

Eve quickly toweled herself dry and dressed. She brushed her hair quickly in the mirror, took out her cell phone and texted Richard. *Are you around?* she wrote.

She waited a few seconds for the telltale three dots that showed he was responding.

But they didn't come.

Eve frowned and gingerly picked up the bloody nightshirt with one hand. Then she walked back to her room to drop off her shampoo. When she stepped back into the hall, closed and locked her door, she checked her texts again.

Still nothing.

She didn't want to wake him up if he was sleeping but…she also did not want to go to a police station in a foreign country without someone knowing. And Mrs. Freer had talked to a Richard in the hall just a half hour ago. It had to be him, didn't it? Eve thumbed his contact info and hit call.

The phone rang and rang, until Richard's familiar, languid voice announced that "I am so sorry but I'm afraid I'm otherwise involved right now, and something is preventing me from clicking the answer button. Please leave a message and I'll hit you back as soon as I possibly can."

She grimaced, but left him a message asking him to call, no matter how late it was.

Then she walked to the stairwell. She stared at the door for a moment before opening it. There could be a killer waiting for her a few steps below.

But more likely, what was waiting for her was a hellacious visit to the Ghent Police Department. She took a deep breath and stepped through the door and walked slowly down the stairs to rejoin Inspector Martino.

He and Mrs. Freer stood near the bathroom, right where she'd left them. But another figure was there as well. A tall, thick-shouldered man in a blue-checked shirt. He turned and met her eyes for a moment. Philip. She thought his standard scowl turned to a faint knowing smile. And then he looked away and began to walk towards the stairwell on the other side of the hall.

The hair on Eve's neck rose.

She realized he was limping.

CHAPTER THIRTY

"Was there a lot of blood?" Markie asked. "Do you think she suffered a lot?"

"Yes and yes," Eve said quietly. "There was blood all over the floor around her head and her legs and her face looked...I can't even describe it. Like, scared beyond belief. The way the saxophone was inside her, and the air hose taped in her throat...I think it might have taken a long time for her to die." She wiped tears from the corners of her eyes. "I'm sorry, but it was awful."

Richard reached over and put a hand on hers to squeeze. They were sitting at a table at Heavy Beans, talking about the events of the night before. Susie, Gianna, Pete, Corey, Markie and even Dmitri all had come tonight. Only Erika's sister Elena was absent. Nobody wanted to say it, but they all were wondering if this was the end of the Songbirds. They could live without Isabella as their occasional vocalist, but could they really audition at this point for people to fill the empty slots of Erika and Anita? And should they? Susie said Elena would probably quit school and go back home. How could she stay in the same building where her twin sister was brutally murdered? And...what about the ones remaining? Who was next? Why were the Songbirds targeted?

"Did anyone check her Facebook this morning?" Markie asked.

"I did," Pete said. "It was just like all the others."

"Really?" Gianna asked. "I looked a couple hours ago, and there was nothing there."

"It was removed," Pete said. He thumbed on his phone and pulled up his Photo app. "I took screenshots though because I figured it would be. This time there was a gallery. Here."

He held the phone out and Gianna took it. Her face grew just a little pale as she stared. She said nothing, but handed the phone over to Corey, who took one look, shook his head, and handed it to Susie.

When the phone reached Eve, her stomach contracted. All of the horror of last night came flooding back as she saw a picture of Erika's face and chest. The girl was obviously nude in the bathroom, though the image didn't quite extend low enough to show her nipples. It focused more on her eyes, which were clearly terrified. Mascara ran in tear trails down her cheeks. Eve thumbed the screen to see the next photo and that…showed everything. Her body glistened, still wet from the shower, and her mouth looked as if she were gritting her teeth. The next photo showed her hands modestly covering her breasts, clearly refusing the photographer's intent. Eve realized that Erika had been standing in basically the same spot where, just minutes later, Eve had sat down in her blood.

The final photo showed a mascara-wearing Robert Smith. There was a YouTube 'play' button in the middle of it and the words *Pictures of You by the Cure* beneath it.

Eve shivered, and held the phone out to Richard without a word.

Claude walked over to the table at that moment with a tray of brown ceramic mugs. They all had the image of a bean on the side with the name of the shop emblazoned in an arc over it. Faint wisps of steam rose from them when he reached their table.

"Here we are, Songbirds," he said. One by one he passed out cappuccinos and americanos and black coffees to whoever had ordered them. When he finished, his smile disappeared and he looked at them all seriously. "I am guessing I know why you all are together here," he said. "I heard about Erika and I just wanted to let you know that I'm really sorry. She was an excellent musician."

Richard suggested quietly, "You should add her to the wall of fame."

Claude looked faintly surprised. "Yes, maybe so!"

If Eve had to guess, she didn't think he would. Despite his words, his face didn't look like he embraced the idea. Claude only posted photos of performances that blew him away.

"Eve was just telling us about what she saw last night," Richard said, patting her on the arm. "She was the one who found Erika."

Claude looked surprised. "Indeed?" he said. "That must have been quite distressing for you."

Eve squeezed her eyes shut for a second, as if to blot out the memory. "It was," she agreed. "Absolutely horrible. And I was at the police department giving them a statement until three in the morning."

"Did they tell you anything? Do they have any leads yet?" Pete asked.

Eve shook her head. "They told me not to leave town. Maybe I'm their prime suspect, I don't know."

"You said you saw her leaving Professor Von Klein's office and then saw the killer start to follow her," Gianna said. "But what were you doing at the professor's office at that time of night anyway?"

"You sound like the inspector," Eve said. "I was using a practice room."

Gianna raised one eyebrow. "Sure, but...the practice rooms aren't in the faculty hall. Did the professor, maybe...invite you to stop by after hours for one of his late night 'photo' sessions?"

Eve's eyes widened. Did they know about the professor's after hours activities? "What are you talking about?" she asked.

Richard laughed. "Well, he did have you over for an introductory session. Did you agree to do some after-dark shots too?"

"I did not," Eve said and slapped his shoulder. "You should know I wouldn't do that."

"Too pure?" Gianna asked sweetly.

Eve glared at her but didn't answer.

"I warned you about the professor," Claude said. "He is very talented, but you don't want to become one of *his* girls."

"Look," Eve said, "I was leaving the practice room late, and I decided to look down the faculty hall to see if anyone was still around. There was a light on, so I walked down to see who it was, and that's when I saw Erika leaving the professor's office."

"Did the killer start stalking her right away?" Claude asked. He had dropped all pretense of being a server and now was leaning one hand on the table. He had fully joined their conversation.

"No," Eve said. "She was a little ways down the hall when I saw this dark figure slip out from a doorway and start trailing her. I tried to catch her at the elevator, but was too slow. The two of them had gotten in and the door was closing."

"How did you end up finding her in the bathroom later?" Gianna asked. "She's not on your floor. You're up on five with the rest of the newbies!"

Eve related her visit to the front desk and the elevator videotapes.

"What did he look like?" Richard asked.

She shrugged. "I don't even know if it was a *he*. Black shoes, black pants, black gloves, a black mask over the face, and sunglasses. And maybe a slight limp, I'm not sure."

"Could you at least tell the hair color?" Claude asked. "That could help the police maybe?"

"Nope. There was like a hat over the head. Really, you could just see a little skin between the sunglasses and the mask, but that was it."

"Was there an Adam's apple?" Susie asked. "That's a good indicator."

"I don't know," Eve said. "I never got that close."

Claude reached out to pat her shoulder. His eyes showed his concern. "That's probably for the best, for you at least."

"Is it?" Gianna asked. "If she had gotten closer, maybe she would have seen something that could actually help catch the bastard, before anyone else gets slaughtered. She was basically an eyewitness, yet she's completely useless."

"I know," Eve said with a frown. Tears were welling up again in her eyes. "I wanted to make sure she was all right, that's why I went to her floor. I didn't know if that was the killer in the elevator or not."

"Because people walk around in black hats and masks and gloves in our building all the time, right?" Gianna said with a heavy bite of sarcasm. Eve didn't know why the girl hated her.

"I hate to ask this," Claude said, "but what are you going to do about the Songbirds?"

"That's what we were just talking about," Susie said.

"I would hate to see the music die," Claude said. "Maybe you should audition more male replacements this term."

Susie wadded up a napkin and threw it at him. "Nice," she said. "Very thoughtful of you."

Claude made a face. "Just being practical," he said. "The killer doesn't seem interested in guys in the band, and that would keep the Songbirds going – and safer – until this is over."

"You mean, after Susie and Eve and I are bludgeoned to death with a tuba or something," Gianna asked.

Claude held both hands up. "I'm sorry, I didn't mean to be insensitive."

"I still just keep wondering about whether this all has something to do with the professor," Eve said. "I mean, why was the killer basically just waiting outside of his office to pick Erika off? Why was Isabella hung from the balcony behind his office?"

Claude shook his head. "Mark my words," he said. "Stay away from his office. Do not let the professor use you for his own perverted reasons thinking that you'll get ahead at the Eyrie. If you don't want to be the next girl hanging, maybe from a piano wire, do not get involved with Professor Von Klein."

CHAPTER THIRTY-ONE

Her cell phone rang when she stepped back into her dorm room. Eve answered the call, and as soon as she said hello, a familiar voice blurted, "Please tell me you didn't break into the professor's office again last night!"

Eve laughed for the first time all day. It was Nikki.

"No, I didn't," she said.

"I heard about what happened," Nikki said. "You didn't tell the police we were in his office, did you?"

"No, I'm not a complete moron," Eve said. "Don't worry. But I'd still like to see what's in his locked drawers."

"So what exactly happened?" Nikki asked. "How did you end up finding her?"

Eve gave her a quick synopsis of the night. When she finished, Nikki said one word that stretched out for fifteen or twenty seconds: "Daaaaaaaaaammmmmn."

"If I was you, I wouldn't go anyplace near that office again," Nikki said. "How are you holding up? That is a Class A disaster of a night."

"I'm okay, just really tired," she answered. "I hope that Kristina sleeps here tonight. I don't think I want to sleep alone just yet."

"You can come to my place if you want," Nikki offered. "Just to sleep," she added. "I promise I won't put the moves on you!"

Eve laughed. "I'm not worried," she said. "I'd just like to sleep in my own bed if I can, you know?"

"I hear you. Just let me know if you decide you want to come over. We could make popcorn and watch a movie or something."

"Thanks," Eve said. "I'll let you know. If not, maybe we can do something tomorrow."

They talked for a couple more minutes and then Eve said goodbye and collapsed into her desk chair. It had been good to talk with Nikki, but after reliving last night multiple times in conversations today, she was emotionally wiped out.

Her phone vibrated on the desk. She picked it up and frowned. The caller ID said Klaus Von Klein.

She picked it up and hesitantly said, "Hello?"

"Miss Springer, I'm so glad I caught you," he said. "This is Professor Von Klein. I was wondering if you were not busy this evening, if you might be able to stop by my office?"

Eve's heart clenched. The professor's office was the last place she wanted to go.

The professor seemed to sense her hesitation. "I have made some changes to the piece I gave you for the Songbirds to consider," he said. "I was hoping to go over them with you and see what you think. It shouldn't take too long, but I'm anxious for you to hear."

"Um, sure," Eve heard herself say. She didn't have an excuse to say no. And it was still early enough that there were probably other people still in the North Tower. "I'll be there in a few minutes."

"Excellent," he said. "I'll see you soon then."

When he hung up, Eve realized her heart was beating faster. Why had she said yes?

She thought about calling Nikki back, but instead decided to call Richard and tell him so at least someone would know where she was going. Maybe he'd go over with her.

Eve clicked his name in her recent calls list and dialed. Normally he picked up within a couple rings. But not this time. She let it go until his voicemail greeting answered, and then thumbed it off. He might not have heard the ring; she'd left him with most of the group at Heavy Beans. The exhaustion from the events of last night had hit her and she'd excused herself. Richard had kissed her goodbye, but had not walked her home – he had just ordered another latte.

She thumbed her Messages app and sent him a text.

EVE: *Prof. Von Klein called me and said he has new music to show me. So, I'm walking over to his office now. Thought you'd want to know.*

She waited for a minute for some kind of response, but none came. After a bit, she sighed and stood up, shoving the phone in her pocket.

"Let's see what the good professor has done," she said, and walked out the door.

The North Tower was quiet tonight. After another Eyrie murder, that was no surprise. Everyone was probably afraid to leave their rooms after dark. Eve looked at the empty hallway on the faculty floor and mentally slapped herself. Why had she even said yes? She could have said she was busy and could come by after class tomorrow.

But, she had to admit, she was curious. What had the professor done to the piece that made him so anxious to have someone hear it...literally the day after one of his students was killed? The musician in her wanted to know.

His office door was closed, but she could see the light from inside emanating from the crack at the floor. She knocked, and almost instantly heard the professor's voice bid her to "come in."

"How are you tonight?" he said when she stepped inside.

"I'm okay," she said.

"I've been thinking about you all day," he said. "Last night must have been very trying for you. Such a horrible thing."

She nodded. "I would never have imagined that someone could be so cruel."

The professor's face was impassive. "You must try to forget, and focus on the now. I feel horrible for Erika. About Erika. She was one of us. A prized student of the Eyrie. A Songbird. It breaks my heart that we could not protect her from whatever force is preying upon our school right now. They are talking about possibly closing the whole building because of this."

Eve's eyes widened. "Really? I hadn't heard."

He shook his head. "Just a conversation at this point. But we can't continue to put the lives of our students – the future of music – in jeopardy if the police cannot start finding some leads. I hope it doesn't come to that. I guess, in a way, that's why I wanted you to come here tonight. Who knows what tomorrow or the next day will bring for the Eyrie? But this afternoon, I sat down and made changes to the piece I gave you that, I think, make the second section more pointed. May I play it for you?"

"Of course," Eve said, and the professor picked up a stack of sheet music on his desk and walked over to the small piano.

Before he sat, he motioned to a chair near his desk. "Please, sit down," he said. "Be comfortable."

Eve sat, and without further introduction, the professor began to play. She closed her eyes as the notes filled the room. There was a wonderful repetitive six-note theme at the outset that repeated and evolved as the song went on, and she loved how he had structured a kaleidoscope of anxious harmonies and alternate melodies around it, but in the end, it all came back to that one riff. It offered an immense playground for the saxophones and trumpets to build on and punctuate.

He was about a third of the way into the song when she realized what he had done. Up to now, it had been a building, but always upbeat song, slowly growing in rhythm and intensity. But then, right at the end of the first third, the piece now took a dip. It slipped into a minor key version of the main theme, and the tempo slowed. A new tertiary theme emerged, one that evoked an immense sadness. If Eve had to describe it, she would have called it…a longing. For a few moments, she thought to herself that this…was no longer jazz. This was a funeral procession. But then, just as she felt that it had gone to a place that evoked sadness just a little too perfectly, the professor worked in a question. A half-hook of the original melody. And then a new response, one that said that maybe, there was hope.

The third act of the piece now had both themes represented, one counterpointing the other, until, with a perfectly phrased build, the sadness was driven back to just a dim echo, and the theme of the song that Eve loved won the stage. But in this new rendition, the final repetition of the theme was like a victory. It made her chest exult and her mouth split into an unconscious grin. When the professor played the final notes, she instantly raised her hands and began to clap.

"Bravo," Eve said with a huge grin. "I love it."

The professor twisted his body and slid a leg around the bench so that he faced her. "Do you?" he asked. "Do you really?"

She nodded quickly, and a smile lit his face.

"Good. I added that new theme for Erika. It's the sadness of loss – of inescapable and unpredictable tragedy – overcome by the knowledge that we who remain must go on. And raise tribute to those whose light had shone before, albeit too briefly."

Eve struggled to keep her composure. She wanted to laugh and cry at the same time. What he described was exactly the way the music had impacted her.

"It's perfect," she said. "It was good before, but now…it has something true to say. And I heard the truth in it before you explained what you meant. I love it."

The professor beamed. "I can't bring her back," he said. "But I can pay her tribute."

"It's good, really," she said. "I hope that the Songbirds get the chance to play it."

His face turned serious. "I do too. It is time for this horror to end. We can't live in fear forever. We have to stop this." He held her gaze, with eyes unblinking. "Did you see anything last night that might help the police find the killer?"

Eve shook her head. "I wish I had. I feel terrible today, because all I can say is that someone with black gloves and a black mask and hat followed her into the elevator. There was nothing I saw that gives a clue about who it was. I wish so badly that there was. I wish the person had had a lock of blonde hair sticking out of the hat, or a scar across the little bit of face that I could see. But there was nothing."

"Try to remember," he urged.

She gave a short laugh. "Trust me, I have. I did at two a.m. this morning at the police station, and at eight a.m. this morning when I had breakfast and after school today when I met the rest of the Songbirds for coffee. There is nothing in my head except the shadow of a horrible killer."

The professor's eyebrows wrinkled with concern. "I understand. I am sorry to give you any more stress."

"Don't be," she said. "I feel like a failure. I was there. I was a witness. And I can help basically...not at all."

"I have something that perhaps will lift your spirits a little," the professor said, and rose from the bench. He walked to his desk and opened the top drawer to remove several papers. He leafed through them and selected one. Then he reached out to hand it to Eve.

"Your photo that we took the other day," he said. "I already submitted it for the scholarship publicity but...I think it turned out really well."

He watched her as she looked it over. Waiting for her response.

Eve looked at the photo, noting the strong line of her nose and the smooth curves of her cheeks. Her eyes were perfect in this pose, dark and maybe hinting at mystery...or the exoticness of unknown music. And her lips were not quite pouty, but perhaps poised to say something evocative.

"It's a good shot," she admitted.

"I'd like to take some more, if you'll let me," the professor said. "You're a good model. And one of my hobbies, outside of music, as you've seen, is photography. I've had several of the girls in the Songbirds model for me over the years. They've always enjoyed it."

"Did Erika?" Eve asked. As soon as the words were out of her mouth, she gulped. She couldn't believe she'd said it.

The energy in the professor's face faded. He suddenly looked grey.

"Yes," he said. "I'm afraid she did. So did Isabella. They were two of my best models and so when they were killed...a part of me died also."

"Maybe it was a message," Eve said.

"I can't imagine what it was trying to say, if so," the professor said. "Don't take pictures? What kind of message is that? They were beautiful girls, and we made some beautiful photos. I'd love to do the same with you, if you are willing."

Eve bit her lip. The last thing she wanted to do was go into the professor's secret studio and porno gallery. But she also didn't want to offend him. Certainly not now.

"I don't think I can even think of such a thing right now," she said. "But thank you for asking me. I'm flattered, truly I am."

"I understand," he said. "This is a strange time. But I hope you'll reconsider when things go back to normal. I think we could make some amazing art together."

Eve gave a hesitant smile.

"In the meantime," he added, "I hope you'll present the new version of my piece to the Songbirds. I'm anxious to hear what they say. I'd love to see you perform it in Erika's honor."

"I'd love to do that," Eve said, and rose from the chair.

"I'll see you in class tomorrow. And, perhaps, tomorrow night at practice, if I'm in my office." He gestured behind him at the door that she knew led to the balcony overlooking their practice space. It was a little unnerving that he spied on them all the time as they played. Up here, quiet and unnoticed. But always watching.

"Yes," she said. Her voice trembled slightly. "I'll see you tomorrow."

★ ★ ★

Eve stepped into the hallway and pressed her back against the wall. She took a breath and closed her eyes. That had been...creepy. But she thought she had excused herself without harm. The professor was clearly both a talented musician...and a lech. The new additions to the piece though...they were sublime. She was anxious to introduce it to the group tomorrow. Though...she'd like to do it without thinking that he was sitting up on the balcony, invisibly spying on them. She was anxious to play the new theme herself.

Eve walked towards the stairwell but then gave a mental shrug and stopped. Why not? She was here, after all, and there was a piano a few yards away. She turned and walked down to the practice room hallway. It wasn't that late.

She took the first practice room with a piano, flipped on the light, and closed the door behind her. Then she set her purse on the floor, arranged the music on the black wooden sheet music holder above the keys, and began to play.

The fears and stress instantly faded away as Eve concentrated on the music, noting the places where the new version diverged from the original. When she hit the middle section where 'Erika's Theme' took over, she felt her eyes mist up. The notes were melancholy, and she had too much understanding of what they meant. This was going to be hard to play in concert, she realized.

When she finished, she removed her fingers from the keys and took a breath. That had affected her more than she'd imagined.

She wondered what Richard would think of it. There was a great space for a saxophone solo if he could steal the spotlight from Gianna. Then it occurred to her that she hadn't looked at her phone since she'd left her room. Had he answered?

Eve pulled it out and saw the text notification on her home screen. He'd answered her just a few minutes ago. But all he'd said was, *Okay. See you tomorrow.*

Nice. Apparently he wasn't too concerned about her being in the music building. She started to type a reply and then frowned. Why bother? He clearly hadn't taken any time away from whatever he was doing for her.

She slipped the phone in her pocket and went back to the music. If she was going to play it for the rest of the Songbirds, she wanted to do it justice. So a little practice was in order.

Eve ran through the song a half dozen times, and then slipped into a couple of her old favorites. When she finished a Metheny song, she felt a buzz from her phone and pulled it out. Just a Facebook notification. But she realized it was after 10:30 p.m. Time to go home.

She was picking up her purse when she caught the shadow of someone walking past the glass pane next to the door. Her stomach turned to ice.

Stop, she told herself. It could have been anybody who had come over to practice. Eve rolled up the music slowly, all the while staring at the dim light from the hall. She did not see anyone loitering outside. Had she really even seen anyone at all, or had it been a trick of the light when she'd moved her head?

Now she wondered if she was just scaring herself. Slowly, she moved to the door and pressed her face to the narrow glass pane next to it, struggling to see as far down the hallway in either direction as she could.

She couldn't see much. But what she saw was empty.

Eve took a deep breath and twisted the doorknob. She pulled it open and stuck her head out into the hall. She could hear her pulse pounding.

There was nobody there. She did not see any lights emanating from any of the other practice rooms either. The practice hall was truly deserted.

She started to walk in the direction of the main staircase.

Idiot, she said to herself. *Keep that shit up and you'll give yourself a heart attack.*

Her heartbeat had just about returned to normal when a figure suddenly stepped into the entrance to the hall. Just ten yards away.

The figure was backlit, a dark silhouette of someone with legs slightly spread apart and hands on hips. She couldn't make out anything about the face but darkness, though it seemed like she saw the rims of glasses.

Eve stopped walking.

"Who's there?" she asked. Her voice trembled audibly.

The person took one slow step in her direction, but did not answer.

Eve took a step backwards.

The figure took two more steps towards her, and lifted its hands in front of its chest. It looked as if it was stretching out and tightening a rope between its fingers.

Eve turned and ran in the other direction. When she reached the end of the hall, she went right without thinking. The slap of her footsteps echoed through the empty space. As did the heavier plod of the steps growing closer behind her. She was just a few yards down the passageway when she realized that the only way out of this hall was to go through the theater. This passage hit a dead end, but there was an access stairwell down that led to backstage.

Shit! The last place she wanted to go right now was the theater.

But she didn't have any choice. If she turned around, her pursuer would be able to grab her easily.

Eve forced her feet to go faster. She needed to get to that stairwell door with enough time to open it.

The hallway emergency light was dead, which meant the last third of the hall was black as night.

Which side was the door on? She'd only used it a couple times when she'd left Songbirds rehearsals to come up here to practice.

Eve was pretty sure it was on the left and began to edge in that direction. If she was wrong, she was going to waste a couple precious seconds. Seconds that she didn't have. She could hear the footfalls pacing her.

At the end of the hall she reached out to grab a door handle. She prayed it wasn't the storage closet.

When she yanked the door open, Eve almost yelled in relief. It wasn't the closet. There were stairs just beyond the door and an emergency light at the bottom of them, which gave her just enough light to dash down them two steps at a time, pausing only for a second when she reached the bottom to look behind her. A dark figure was already moving down the stairs.

Shit.

Eve turned and threaded her way around the debris of hundreds of past performances. Boxes filled with speaker wire and old lights. A metal lighting rig that had been stashed along the back wall for future repair. A clothing rack filled with performance costumes.

She headed towards the side stage entryway. If she could reach the front of the stage, it was a quick leap to the main aisle and then straight up the incline to the exit doors.

Eve could see the amber light from the exit signs in the auditorium just as a hand punched hard at her shoulder from behind. Instead of dashing onto the main stage, Eve stumbled and fell through the entryway.

Her hands hit the wooden floor with a hard smack that nearly stunned her. The shock jolted all the way up to her shoulder, but she had to keep moving. Eve knew better than to stop and take stock. There was no time. She hoped she hadn't broken her wrist, but she used it anyway, flipping her body to roll towards the back of the stage as the figure passed her and came to a halt just a couple yards beyond.

Eve drew herself up into a crouch as the dark figure walked towards her. Just before it reached her, she launched herself. A hand grabbed at her shirt, but she was able to pull free. She aimed for the front lip of the stage. The emergency exit signs gave just enough light to see where it ended, though she could only barely make out the shadows of the seats beyond.

She slowed before reaching the edge so that she could judge her jump. Just as she steeled herself to go, something hit her in the back of the head. Hard. She collapsed at the edge of the stage. She didn't lose consciousness, but her vision was filled with stars. Eve felt nearly paralyzed. Her whole body lit with fire. Somehow she rolled to her left and saw what had hit her. A microphone stand. The base had probably caught her.

Black boots planted themselves a foot away from her eyes. And then two gloved hands reached down and grabbed her beneath the armpits. Her body rose from the floor; she was being dragged backstage once more.

Eve tried to escape, but the pain in her head made it difficult to focus. She was struggling to stay conscious when she was dropped again to the ground, this time backstage. The jolt to her head was excruciating, but it also helped; it shocked her back to life.

The figure walked over to an old piano and lifted the lid to expose the keys. Then it played a C and a G. And then a B flat. Eve tried to move, and found that she could make a fist and move her arm. She wasn't broken.

Then the figure played something that made her freeze again.

The main theme from the professor's new piece for the Songbirds. Only a handful of notes, but there was no mistake.

Eve's eyes widened. What did it mean?

The lid of the piano suddenly crashed closed, and the figure toppled the piano bench. It fell on its side, and two black-gloved hands grabbed one of the bench legs while a black boot stepped on the other leg to pin the bench to the floor.

The top leg separated from the bench with a dry snap.

The killer held the broken leg out, studying it. And then smacked it against one hand like a police baton as it advanced again in her direction.

Eve realized that she was about to be bludgeoned to death with a piano leg.

No way, she said to herself. *Not me.* She tensed both of her legs, and with one hand pressed against the floor. Testing. She had to be ready because she would only have one shot at this.

The black boots halted two feet away from her. Eve could see the black glasses and black mask – the same things the killer had worn in the elevator with Erika. Then she wondered if she was going to be beaten to death with the leg, or impaled with it, as Erika had been with her instrument.

No way, she said again and readied herself.

The piano leg raised in the air, poised to land with its heavy square part against her skull. The killer would be ready and expecting her to roll away.

Instead, Eve launched herself straight towards the boots. She threw her entire weight at her attacker's shins. The gambit worked. The figure in black toppled backwards, surprised, and Eve completed her roll with a leap to her feet.

Her head throbbed with a pain that made her unsteady and nauseous, but she forced herself to keep moving. She staggered left, away from the figure getting back on its feet just two yards away. It stumbled after her in pursuit.

Eve looked for something, anything she could use to keep the killer at bay. There was junk all around them, but nothing that she could really use as a weapon. She walked two more steps towards the stage entryway. There was a row of black metal music stands lined up there.

She reached out and grabbed one by its black pipe center. As she did, she saw the arms of the killer in motion, swinging the piano leg at her like a bat. On reflex, she reacted and swung the music stand in the direction of the killer. The leg slammed into the stand with a clang. The force drove her backwards, but not down.

Eve backed away from the figure as it readied to swing at her again. This time, when the bat came, she ducked to the right and at the same time, swung her own makeshift weapon. The bent metal tongs on the end of the stand – metal fingers meant to prop up music – raked across the killer's shoulder and back, catching in its shirt. In a flash, she saw black material rip along the left shoulder blade and the white of bare flesh beneath. White that almost instantly went red. She'd scored first blood. That was something.

The figure uttered a high-pitched cry of pain and twisted, grabbing at its wounded back with one hand.

Eve used the moment to move. She ran to the edge of the stage and launched herself across the orchestra pit to land in the main aisle. The pain that jagged through her head when her feet hit the aisle almost made her collapse. But she refused to topple or slow. Eve kept going, dashing up the main aisle on pure adrenaline to punch through the entry doors.

This time she didn't look behind her, but kept running in a desperate sprint down the long hall until she reached the main lobby, and saw Mrs. Freer sitting at the front desk.

"Call the police," she demanded breathlessly. "The killer is in the theater!"

CHAPTER THIRTY-TWO

"Wherever you go, the killer seems to be there," Inspector Martino said. "But yet, you still say you can't tell us anything that will help the investigation."

"There was nothing to see," Eve said. "Gloves, boots, a mask, a hat...everything was covered. I can tell you that whoever it is, they're taller than me by at least six inches. And now has a cut on their back."

Martino nodded. "That may prove to be the only bit of evidence we have. The music stand is already on its way back to the station for DNA testing."

Eve's head was throbbing and she reached up to massage her temples.

They were sitting in the chairs in the lobby of the Eyrie. After Eve had shown them the music stand that had cracked her in the back of the head, they had come here and called for paramedics.

"The ambulance is here now, Inspector," a voice said from behind them.

"Thank you," he said. He turned back to her. "Let's make sure you don't have a concussion. I can't afford to lose my only witness at this point."

Eve forced a smile. "As you just said, I can't tell you anything useful, so I don't think it would be much of a loss."

"I'd like to talk to you tomorrow regardless," he said. "Maybe you'll remember something more."

Two paramedics walked up at that point, dressed in heavy coats and boots. "Are you able to walk?" one of them asked.

Eve shook her head, instantly regretted it and stopped. "Sure," she said. She stood up and looked at the inspector. "Until tomorrow then."

The paramedics flanked her, gently holding her arms as they walked out of the front door of the Eyrie to the ambulance waiting outside. There were at least a dozen students all standing around in small groups watching, wondering, no doubt, what had happened to her. She didn't recognize anyone.

★   ★   ★

Eve lay on a cot in the back of the ambulance with one of the paramedics sitting beside her. The flashing lights in the dark with the gentle rumble of the ambulance made it hard for her to stay awake. Maybe it was the trauma, but the lights of the street outside turned into nothing but a colorful blur. When they reached the emergency room, she walked as if in a dream. At one point, they asked her name and she hesitated a moment before answering.

A man in a white coat with jet-black hair and ice-blue eyes examined her. He reminded her of a young professor she'd once had a crush on. His mouth was speaking words, but she realized that she wasn't paying attention.

"...I don't think it's serious, but you are zoning in and out I've noticed," he said in perfect English, but with a decidedly Dutch accent. "Definitely a concussion. I want to do a CT scan and keep an eye on you for a couple hours before we send you home. Okay?"

"Sure," she said. "What do I need to do?"

He shook his head. "Nothing at all. Just lie back and enjoy the ride. I'll have one of the techs come get you in a few minutes."

When he left the room, Eve drifted into an uneasy sleep. Soon she was locked in a horrible dream, chased by not one, but three pursuers wearing all black. She ran through the North Tower corridors, but ultimately, they ganged up and cornered her in one of the music practice rooms. One held a tuning fork, and one a piano bench leg. The other twisted piano wire between its black-gloved hands.

"You can't escape this time," they all said in unison. It was like a 3D audio echo.

"But who are you?" Eve asked.

They all reached forward to rip at her shirt, and she fought back, punching and clawing at each of them as she felt the buttons of her blouse popping and heard the rip of shredding material. Hands grabbed at her bra and that was instantly gone too. But as she felt the cool air and cold gloves touching her naked skin, she was able to reach up and snatch at the mask and glasses of one of her captors. When they came off, she recognized the face and gasped.

"Professor?" she said.

Then she grabbed at another one and instantly knew the sarcastic mouth beneath. "Gianna?"

She was grabbing for the third when her bed began to move and she was jarred back awake.

"This won't take long, miss," a dark-skinned man in light green scrubs told her. He pushed the bed out of the room and as they passed the doorway, Eve realized that there was a police officer standing next to the door.

They were keeping watch on her.

CHAPTER THIRTY-THREE

"Does this hurt?" Richard was gently running his fingers through the hair on the back of her head.

Eve made a face. "Just a little when you touch that goose egg. But don't stop. It feels good to have you do that."

She'd spent half the night in the E.R., but ultimately was cleared to go home with the diagnosis of "you're extremely lucky." The doctor had discharged her with a prescription for a painkiller and anti-inflammatories and the admonition to take it easy for a couple days.

Eve had stayed home from classes and spent most of the day in bed. Richard had come over and taken her to dinner at a quiet, low-key café by the river. At first, she'd insisted she wasn't hungry, but once the bowl of Belgian fries came, she found she couldn't stop eating. They'd walked hand-in-hand along the river afterwards, as the sun set and its golden rays turned a vibrant orange and red on the horizon.

Eventually, they'd gone back to his place. For the first time in days, Kristina was actually home for the evening studying for a theory class, and Richard and Eve wanted to spend time together alone.

"You've had a helluva week," he said.

"Yeah, this isn't exactly what I had in mind when I decided to study abroad." She smiled. "But at least I got to meet you."

"If I'm your highlight of Belgium, you need to get out more." He laughed.

"I don't think so," she said. "At the moment, I'd like to stay in more."

She propped herself up on one elbow to look over his face. Richard's hair was thick and slightly curly, but he kept it short. His nose was strong, aquiline. His eyes were shadowed but looked tender in the low light from his desk lamp. He'd trimmed his goatee, so that the hair on his chin was just barely there. She had to smile; his eyebrows were actually thicker than his beard. Eve bent down to kiss his lips. One of her favorite parts of him. Maybe it was from always playing the sax, but they felt thick and warm but still soft.

Richard slipped his arms around her and pulled her tight as their kiss deepened. When she drew back finally, her face was flushed and her lips felt hot.

"Well, if that's a taste of what you mean by 'staying in', I'm all for it," he said with a grin.

Eve laughed. "That's a hint," she said. With one hand, she reached down and began to unbutton his shirt. It was one of his wilder ones with a pattern of emerald leaves and tropical birds.

"What's good for the gander is also good for the goose," he said when she ran her fingers through the thick dark hair on his chest.

Richard reached up to grab her t-shirt and began to tug at both shoulders. She lifted her arms so he could slip it over her head. Then he ran a finger beneath the edge of her bra and traced her skin on the inside of the cup.

Soon they were kissing harder, and when his fingers fumbled, she reached back and helped him remove the bra. Soon, she shimmied out of her shorts.

Richard was a gentle lover, and took his time with her. Almost too much time. After a while, Eve pressed him to the bed and took him inside herself with a faster rhythm than he had set. He protested at one point, concerned about her concussion.

"Don't worry about my head," she begged, and pressed herself into him as hard as she could. He felt so good, she wanted their skin to not just touch, but join.

When they were both spent, Richard lay on his back next to her, their shoulders touching. It was just close enough. Her entire body was damp and she didn't want to embrace any more. But it was perfect, pleasantly warm just to have that faint contact. Eve luxuriated in the afterglow. There may have been someone trying to kill her twenty-four hours ago, but right now…she had rarely felt happier and more secure.

"I need to get something to drink," he said when his breathing slowed. He turned his head to look at her on the pillow, and their noses touched. "You wore me out. Do you want water or soda or something?"

"Sure," she said. "A Coke would be great, but water's fine too."

Richard pushed himself to sit on the edge of the bed and stretched both arms into the air.

Eve saw a dark line across his left shoulder blade. She reached out to touch him and he jerked away slightly when she ran her finger across the scab. It was thin and rough and extended three or four inches from the top of the bone to the soft flesh nearby. There were two more red marks next to it. "What's this from?" she asked.

"Oh, I was carrying something yesterday and got scratched."

"It looks deep," she said. "Does it hurt much?"

He shook his head. "It's fine. Bled some and ruined my shirt though."

Richard stood up and grabbed a pair of sweatpants and a t-shirt from a pile across the room. Then he grabbed his wallet from the pocket of his jeans and flashed her a grin. "I'm going to the soda machine. Be right back. Don't let any black-gloved maniacs in while I'm gone."

"No, I won't," Eve said with false humor. Her heart was beating fast again, and not because of their exertions. She remembered that moment on stage last night when she'd swung the music stand and the prongs at the top had hit her attacker in the left side of the back...enough that the shirt ripped and blood welled up.

All of her good feelings of seconds before blew away, replaced by an icy pit in her stomach. She'd told Richard where she was going last night. Could it have been him in the black mask and boots? But why? She couldn't believe that Richard – sweet, gentle Richard – could possibly be the killer. And then she remembered that Mrs. Freer had told a 'Richard' to go back to his room the night when she had been sitting with Erika's body. What had he been doing on the third floor at that hour? Unless he was the one who had just brutally murdered Erika? Didn't they say the killer always returns to the scene of the crime?

Eve slipped out of bed and walked over to his wardrobe. She put her hand on the knob to pull it open. Would she find a black outfit hanging inside? With black boots? Gloves? A ski hat?

She gulped and pulled the door open. The wooden closet was jammed inside with shirts on hangers. Lots of colorful shirts, as was Richard's style. There was a shelf above the shirts where he'd stashed belts and a folded stack of jeans.

Her breath caught when she saw the reflection from a bit of dark plastic tucked in back.

Was that a pair of black shades? She was reaching in to pick them up, when she heard the dorm room lock click and the door begin to creak open.

Shit! Eve yanked her arm back and quickly pressed the double doors closed, but as she did, she caught a glimpse of something black hanging between the kaleidoscope of colors in the closet. Then the wood of the doors met and she had to step back before he saw her. She realized too late that the doors didn't close all the way; there was a small lip on the inner door...and she'd closed the one that should be shut last, first. *Crap.*

"I got you a Coke," Richard said from the entryway.

She couldn't fix the doors; she just prayed they stayed closed. Eve turned to face his desk and put her hands on the back of the chair just as he walked into view.

"There's a nice view," he said, looking up and down her bare body. "What are you doing up?"

"Just wanted to stretch," she said.

"I'd love to have you stretch in here every night."

Would you now? she thought. *Then where were you last night?*

He sat on the bed and held out the soda can. Eve took it from his hand, but didn't join him on the mattress.

"Sit," he said, and patted the sheets next to him. Then he popped the tab on his can and took a sip.

Eve shook her head. "I think I'm going to head home," she said. "Sleep in my own bed."

Richard didn't allow her to stay away. He grabbed her forearm and pulled her down to sit on the mattress.

"Don't be silly," he said. "You haven't spent the night here in a week. I want you next to me all night."

Eve waged an internal war with herself as she sipped the Coke. Her eyes welled up with tears from the first blast of the carbonation. Or... maybe fear. She wasn't sure which. She brushed them away and tried to muster a smile.

"I've got an early class tomorrow," she said.

"What time do you want me to set the alarm for?"

"Seven a.m.," she said absently.

Was she being ridiculous? Why would Richard want to kill the members of the Songbirds? The jazz combo was his *life*! When she said it like that, she felt ridiculous for even thinking so.

Richard leaned back to his headboard to set the alarm and then sat back up. "All set," he said. "What do you say we get some sleep? You wore me out!"

Eve still hesitated, but Richard took the can from her fist and set it on the nightstand.

"C'mon," he insisted. And kissed her softly. When she looked into his eyes, she felt like an idiot. He loved her, you could see it. He'd never hurt her. Would he?

Richard pulled her back to the pillow and stroked her hair. After a while, she felt her tensions ease, and she began to drift towards sleep. Richard rolled over, and the motion made her open her eyes. His back was to her, and the scratch on his shoulder stared back at her. Nausea suddenly gripped her, and Eve couldn't close her eyes. She stared at the scab and replayed the moment last night when she'd hit her attacker with the music stand over and over in her brain.

As Richard's breathing grew deeper and turned to a light snore, Eve lay wide awake next to him, unable to close her eyes.

CHAPTER THIRTY-FOUR

"Time to rise and shine!"

Richard's voice was quiet but demanding in her ear.

Eve struggled to open her eyes; they felt glued shut. When had she finally fallen asleep? It had seemed like she'd been listening to the creaks and rattles of the old building all night.

"C'mon," he said. "You're going to be late. I hit snooze a couple of times because you were so deep."

She looked at the clock and saw that it read 7:15. "Crap," she said, and sat up quickly. She slid her legs over his and got out of the bed snatching her clothes from the floor. She pulled on her underwear as Richard reached out from the bed and stroked her bare back. When he tried to pull her back for a kiss, she pushed him away.

"Not this morning," she said. "I've got just enough time for a walk through the shower. I can't be late."

"How about this afternoon?" he said. "Or tonight? I liked sleeping next to you."

"Hmmm," she said, and patted his shoulder. "We'll see..."

He stretched his arms in the air while still keeping his head cradled in the pillow. Richard looked like the cat who'd eaten the canary. She bent over to give him an obligatory kiss.

"We can talk about it later," she said, and then darted for the door.

As it shut behind her, she realized she'd never fixed his wardrobe door. She'd intended to look in it again if he had gotten up and gone to the bathroom during the night and then close it properly.

"Damnit," she said under her breath. Hopefully when he noticed it, he'd assume that *he* was the one who hadn't completely shut the doors.

All of her fears of the night before came rushing back as Eve ran up the stairs to the fifth floor to return to her room for shampoo and a change of clothes.

★   ★   ★

She pushed open the theater door at 8:03 a.m., and Professor Von Klein was already at the podium speaking. Shit. He'd notice that she'd walked in late. He always noticed when students came in late, and frequently commented on it.

This morning, thankfully, he did not seem as if he was going to call her out, however. His face looked very serious, and she slipped into a seat and tried to pick up on the thread he was discussing.

"...as you are well aware. And so now I'd like to give our dean, Professor Hilton, the microphone to speak directly with you about the situation."

Von Klein stepped back from the podium and a tall man in a pale blue jacket got up from the front row of the theater and walked up the steps to the podium.

"Good morning," he began. "I'm glad to see you all, but I wish it was under different circumstances. As Professor Von Klein said, the administration has been in constant communication with the Belgian police. Since the very first murder, our faculty and administration have also been in daily internal discussions about how to deal with the issue. While our passion is music, at the end of the day our most important mission is to keep our students safe. We have tried to add security cameras and more night guards over the past month, but this has clearly not stopped the monster who is preying upon our students. The police have suggested additional ways that we could lock down the building to make it safer for all of you, but even those actions won't guarantee that the killer cannot strike again. In my mind, the solutions that have been proposed only serve to make our student body bait in a trap to catch the killer. I cannot in my conscience put any of you at further risk in this regard. The past month has truly been the most horrible days of my life, and I cannot imagine what it has been like for you to walk these halls in fear rather than in excitement for the new music that you are creating. This is not the environment we want to foster, and yet, we are currently powerless to stop it."

He paused a minute, looking out at the crowded theater seats.

"After much discussion, we have reached a unanimous conclusion about our course of action. It is with a very heavy heart that I must announce that we will be closing the Eyrie for the rest of the semester."

The whole room gasped as one. And then erupted into a flurry of voices.

Prof. Hilton put up both hands and leaned in to speak into the mic. "Quiet, please," he said. And then in Dutch, "*Wees stil alsjeblieft!*"

Slowly the room quieted.

"Listen now," he said. "We will reopen. But for now, we think the best thing that we can do for everyone is to shut our doors and give the police more time to track down who is responsible for these murders. While we are closed, we will also renovate our security systems and protocols, so that you all will be safer when we return. We know that you will need to make travel arrangements and that may take some time for you to get plane flights or other accommodations, so we will keep the building open through the weekend. But classes for the rest of the week are hereby canceled and on Monday the Eyrie will be completely closed until the new year. I recognize how disruptive this will be for all of you, and I hope that you understand and support our decision. Please watch your email for additional information and updates. Thank you, and be safe. I look forward to hearing the beauty you will create next term. But you can't create if you aren't alive. For now, we must separate. Adieu."

Eve sat in her seat, stunned, as students filed out of the aisle next to her. Was this the end, then? She'd dreamed of coming here to study for so long, and now that she was here, the entire institution implodes? She didn't know if she could realistically go home for three months and then come back again. The reality was, she might go home, get involved in other programs and pursuits, and choose not to come back. If they didn't catch the killer, would anyone come back? This could really be the end, not a hiatus, for the Eyrie. And they had to know that. The gravity of the situation weighed on her heavier than ever.

She had sat in someone's blood, and now was fighting with the idea that her boyfriend might be a murderer. Might be the one who tried to kill her! Yet...she'd still slept next to him and she still wanted to finish the school year here. It may have been irresponsible and foolish...but Eve had never considered throwing in the towel.

A hand rested on her shoulder. She looked up to see the sad smile of Prof. Von Klein.

"I'd really hoped to hear the Songbirds play 'Lost in the Labyrinth'," he said. "Now, who knows if it will ever be performed? It may truly become lost."

She mustered a small smile. "It's a great piece, professor. And I really like the new parts for Erika. With or without the Songbirds, it will be played."

He patted her shoulder then, and withdrew his hand. "I do hope our paths cross once again," he said. "Hopefully next term."

The uncertainty welled up in her then. "I hope so too."

His mouth pursed as if he was going to say something, but then thought better of it. He reached down to squeeze her shoulder once more. "My door will always be open for you, Miss Springer. Be safe."

Then he walked up the aisle and out of the theater without looking back.

CHAPTER THIRTY-FIVE

"Did you hear the news?" Kristina said as Eve walked into their dorm. "They're closing the Eyrie for the rest of the semester."

Eve nodded. Her roommate wasn't wasting any time; Kristina's suitcase was already open on the bed with a pile of clothes around it.

"What are you going to do?" Kristina asked. "Will you go straight back to New York, or stay on the continent a bit?"

"I'm honestly not sure," Eve said. She'd been thinking about her options the entire walk back from the theater. She *could* leave here and tour Europe for a couple weeks, since she was here already. If for some reason she didn't come back next term, she knew she'd kick herself for missing the opportunity.

"You're welcome to come stay with me in London for a few days if you like," Kristina said. "I'm catching the train back tonight."

"Thanks," Eve said. "I might do that. I'm not sure what I'll do yet, but I don't think I'm going to decide by tonight."

Kristina grinned. "There's a concert I wanted to see tomorrow night at the Royal Albert Hall. I wasn't going to go, but when they announced the closing this morning, I got online and found a ticket. So...I'm heading home immediately! I'll leave you my address if you want to follow. Just don't make it tomorrow night because I only bought one ticket."

Eve laughed. "No problem. I won't crash your concert."

Her phone buzzed and Eve picked it up from the desk. It was a text from Susie to the Songbirds group.

SUSIE: *Hi gang. Crushing news today. But I'd still like us to get together for practice this evening unless you all are going home. Would love to play with you at least one more time. Let me know.*

The answers poured in even as Eve watched.

RICHARD: *I'm there.*

GIANNA: *See you at six.*

MARKIE: *I would be honored to keep the beat one more time.*

She dove in herself.

EVE: *I'll come. I'll even bring an update to the piece Von Klein wrote and wanted us to play. Might be the only time we get to run through it. I'll make copies.*

PETE: *Not going anywhere else.*

DMITRI: *Sorry gang, I'm already at the airport. Play well!*

COREY: *Sounds good.*

And then came a surprise.

ELENA: *I would be honored.*

Wow. Eve had not expected that last answer. She was surprised that Elena was even still in Ghent. It would be nice to see her once more… but also potentially uncomfortable. After all, she was the one who had found Elena's sister. And failed to save Erika when she'd had an inkling that she was in danger. She had mixed thoughts about seeing Elena. But it would be good to have the group together one last time. Those who were left.

Then Kristina pulled her away from her phone to ask her about one of the posters they'd bought together at a local art shop.

"Do you want to keep this? I feel like you might have liked it even more than me."

It was an art print that showed a long-necked bird sketched in yellow amid a kaleidoscope of rainbows.

"I do love it," Eve admitted. "Are you sure?"

Kristina's face lit. "I want you to have it. You can put it on your wall back in New York and think of that weird Brit bird you lived with for a few weeks on the other side of the world. We made a good nest here for a bit, yeah?"

"We did," Eve agreed and moments later, the two girls were hugging. Eve felt the tears welling up and realized that the next forty-eight hours were going to be an emotional roller coaster.

★   ★   ★

It was almost five p.m. when Eve helped Kristina down to the lobby with her bags. She had a cab coming and would be back in London in time for a late dinner. They hugged again in the lobby and said their goodbyes.

"I want to see you play on stage," Eve told her. "I want to hear you solo. I *will* hear you solo."

Kristina laughed. "Come visit me," she offered. "There are so many things I'd love to show you in London. I might even play at a local pub while you're there."

"It's a deal," Eve promised.

And then the cab door closed and Kristina was whisked down the old street into the evening.

Eve walked slowly back inside. It felt like the world was shutting down. Still, she had things to do before the Eyrie disappeared behind her. The first was to make copies of Von Klein's music. She went back up to her room to retrieve it, and then took it down to the front desk. There was a copier in the back office, and she knew that Mrs. Freer sometimes would help students with copies for a small fee.

★   ★   ★

"What's the point?" the house marm asked, when she presented the music at the front desk. "In a couple days nobody will be here to care about music thanks to the murderer. I've never heard of anything like this."

"I know," Eve said. "But the Songbirds are still going to play together another night or two until we all are gone."

Mrs. Freer snorted. "The Songbirds. This is their fault that the entire school has to close. All of the murders have been related to them. What did they do to bring this on us all?"

Eve was shocked that the jazz group could actually be blamed for the situation.

"It's not our fault some maniac decided to make us a target."

"I don't see why they couldn't just disband the group instead of sending us all away for weeks," Mrs. Freer said. "Some of us have families to feed after all. But they said they didn't dare risk the killer coming after the rest of you even if the group stopped. Or going after some of the other students. So here we are. God knows whether we'll even be able to reopen once they close."

She grabbed the music from Eve and abruptly turned and walked through the door into a back room.

Wow, Eve thought. *That wasn't at all the reaction I would have expected.*

Mrs. Freer returned a few minutes later with a stack of criss-crossed sheaves of paper. "Here you are," she said. "That will be four Euros."

Eve reached into her purse and pulled out a couple coins.

"Play well," Mrs. Freer said. "You'll be providing the funeral. Next week, these halls will be like the grave without any more music to lighten the air."

"The music will return, I know it," Eve said.

Mrs. Freer raised an eyebrow. "I hope you're right, girl. I'd like it all to go back to the way it was before you arrived."

Eve shook her head. There was the accusation again. "I have nothing to do with this," she insisted.

The house marm did not comment but her face suggested she wasn't completely convinced.

★   ★   ★

Markie was playing a drum solo when she walked into the theater. When he came off the last snap on the snare, Susie began to finger a low bass line and worked her way through a sinuous funk groove. Markie picked up the beat and backed her up. Eve couldn't help but smile and feel her spirits lift as she walked down the aisle towards them. Richard and Gianna were on the stage already as well, unpacking their instruments and setting up their music stands. Pete and Corey entered behind her, just as she reached the stage.

Susie stopped playing when Eve stepped onto the stage. But she wasn't stopping because of Eve. Markie stopped playing as well, and Gianna got up and walked to the edge of the stage. Pete stopped where he was on the steps.

Elena had entered the back door wearing a short black dress and black choker. The casual observer might have guessed that she had just come from Isabella's funeral. But the Songbirds knew better. It was almost a uniform with her. They all watched her as she made her way down the aisle. It was the first time any of them had seen her since her sister was killed.

"We are so glad you could come," Susie finally said.

"Yeah," Gianna said. For once her caustic tongue seemed at a loss for words.

Elena smiled sadly. "I thought that maybe playing some music would help. I'm going home for good on Saturday. There were some arrangements I had to make here."

"Then let's make this a goodbye concert," Pete said. He still stood on the stairs.

"Yeah," Corey agreed. "Let's raise the roof!"

"I'm up for it," Elena said. "This has been the worst week of my life. I want to play again. I need to."

Pete and Corey and Elena all took their places on stage as Eve began to arrange her music on the piano. Susie caught her eye and held out a hand.

"You've got something new for us from on high?" Susie asked.

Eve held up the stack of photocopies. "Yep," she said. She looked at Elena, not sure how she would take what she was about to say. "And there's a theme that he wrote specifically for Erika."

Elena didn't say anything, but her lips widened in a faint sad smile.

"Let's take a look," Susie said, and Eve walked around, passing the pages out to the group. When she reached Elena, she paused as she handed over the music. "He gave you a good solo," she said. It sounded stupid to her after she said it, but Elena took the music.

"I can't wait to play it."

"Let's warm up first," Susie said. "How about a little 'Sweet Georgia Brown'? I'm feeling classic today."

Markie counted off and Susie and Eve began. Seconds later and the entire group was adding their textures to the old bayou-flavored standard. When it was finished, everyone had a smile on their faces, including Elena, and Susie took them through the first three songs of their last Heavy Beans set.

"You've still got it, Songbirds," Susie said when they finished. "Feel up to trying something new?"

"Anxious to," Richard said. "Let's hear what the professor has cooked up."

Everyone pulled the music out and arranged the first couple pages. When they were set, Markie called out the tempo and then said, "One, two, three, and...."

Eve led off and marveled as the saxophones and trumpets took their lead lines. She knew the melodies, but hearing everyone together was like the difference between a one-dimensional and a three-dimensional picture. What she had played last night was just a pale blueprint to the energized and yet still sometimes now melancholy song. When they finished, she turned around on her piano bench to look at Elena. The dark-haired soprano sax player's face looked serious, but she caught Eve's eye and gave one solemn nod. It was good.

Eve looked up then, half-expecting to see the professor lurking on the balcony behind his office. But the upper reaches of the theater were dark and appeared empty.

"That was solid," Susie said. "I wish we could spend some time with it. I bet it would sound great in a club. Could be a set closer."

"What if we played it at Heavy Beans tomorrow?" Richard asked.

"We're not booked there this weekend," Susie said.

His expression suggested otherwise. "Yeah, but I was in there this afternoon and told Claude we were rehearsing one last time tonight before everyone headed out. He suggested we do a last performance there, if enough of us would still be in town. What do you all think?"

"I can do it," Markie said.

One by one, the rest chimed in. Everyone had planned to go home over the weekend, so Friday night was free.

Even Elena voiced assent. "I was going to pack mine and Erika's things tomorrow, so I could use something to look forward to tomorrow night."

Richard looked pleased. "It's a deal then. I'll let Claude know we're in right now. Maybe he can put a sign up tonight in the window."

He pulled out his phone and walked backstage while dialing. Susie threw out some ideas for the set list, and Gianna and Markie offered songs as well. By the time Richard was back, they had already pulled together a potential list of what they'd be playing.

"It's all set," Richard announced as he took his chair again. "Tomorrow at seven p.m."

"We'd better run through the professor's song a couple more times then if we're going to play it to an audience," Susie said. She looked at Eve. "You should let the professor know. I bet he'll want to come out."

"I'll email him," she promised.

They spent the next hour practicing the new song, and running through a couple of their other more recent set pieces before calling it a night.

★ ★ ★

"Can I walk you home?" Richard asked, falling into step beside her on the way down the hall from the theater.

"Who said I'm going home?" she asked. In actuality, she had planned to go back to her room, but no matter how much she told herself it was ridiculous, she was uneasy to be alone right now with Richard. At least until she saw the contents of his wardrobe. There had been sunglasses and some kind of black shirt in there. And he had a cut on his back right where she had hit the killer. It wasn't enough to make a case...but she was still nervous. And what if he was the killer, and he realized that she had been in his wardrobe and left it open?

"Touché!" he said. "Do you have another date?"

Eve laughed. "Not a date, but Nikki invited me over," she lied.

"She did, huh?" He looked puzzled for a moment. "Do you have time to come back to my room for a little while first?" he pressed. His face looked anxious. As if he really needed to convince her. That only made Eve want to go less.

"No," she said. "In fact, I'm heading straight to her place right now."

Another lie, but she just had this feeling that she needed to shake him.

"All right then," he said, reaching out to hold her arm, stopping her in the hall as the rest of the band continued to walk. "Text me if you get free early!"

"Will do," she promised. He bent to kiss her, and she forced herself to return the gesture. Her fears were ridiculous, she insisted. His lips met hers, soft and gentle and warm.

"Have a good night," he said and broke the kiss.

"You too," she said, and watched as he walked away.

She pulled out her phone then and texted Nikki. Maybe it *would* be a good idea to stop by her place tonight. Eve needed a friend more than ever right now.

EVE: *Do you mind if I stop by tonight?*

NIKKI: *Sure! But could you make it after 10? I'm going to be busy for a while after dinner.*

EVE: *No problem. I'll see you later.*

The third floor was already quiet when Eve arrived at Nikki's room at 10:15. Her friend answered the door in a purple nightshirt. The familiar patchwork, red-haired character of Sally from *The Nightmare Before Christmas* dominated the shirt, a gothic haunted house behind her. Nikki's hair looked tousled, as if she'd already been asleep. Eve could see the bed was unmade.

"Oh geez, I'm sorry," Eve said. "I didn't mean to wake you up." She started to back away from the door. "Go back to sleep and we can talk tomorrow."

Nikki reached out and grabbed Eve by the arm. "You're not going anywhere," she said, even as she stifled a yawn. "I was just lying in bed reading. Come on in."

Nikki closed the door behind them and walked back into the main part of the room. "Do you want some water? Or wine? I've got a bottle open from earlier that I need to finish off."

"Sure, wine is good," Eve said.

Nikki poured them each a glass and left the bottle on her desk. She handed one to Eve and then sat down cross-legged on the bed. With her free hand she patted the black sheets next to her. "Sit down," she said. "And tell me what's the matter."

Eve hesitated. It felt weird to get into another girl's bed. Especially a girl that she knew...liked girls. But it would be just as weird to stand there next to the bed while Nikki was sitting. She eased herself onto the edge of the mattress and took a sip of the wine before speaking. It was a heavy red, and the smoky acidic taste bit her throat as it went down. The warmth instantly made her feel better somehow.

"So what's the deal?" Nikki prompted.

Eve slipped her shoes off and twisted her body to face Nikki. She drew her feet up and tucked her feet to her butt. "It's about Richard," she said.

Nikki cocked her head. "What about him? Did he do something to hurt you?"

"I'm not sure," Eve said.

Nikki's brows creased. She looked at Eve expectantly. "Then?"

"I think Richard might be the killer."

Nikki snorted. A drop of her wine dripped over the edge of her glass to land like a blot of blood on her calf. Still laughing a little, she ran a fingertip over her skin and then brought the finger to her lips to lick it clean.

"You realize how absolutely ridiculous that sounds, don't you?"

Eve's face fell. She knew it sounded crazy, she did. But she couldn't shake the feeling of uneasiness.

Nikki stopped laughing then as she saw Eve's expression. She touched Eve's shoulder. "Okay, you're not just pulling my leg. You really think this."

Eve nodded.

"At least there was a pervy reason that maybe Professor Von Klein could have had something to do with it. Why on earth would you think Richard could have done it? The Songbirds are his life. Why would he do anything to hurt them?"

Eve shrugged. "I know it sounds insane, and I don't know why he would. I only know what I saw." She took a breath. "You know that the killer almost got me backstage."

"But why do you suddenly think that was Richard?"

"I got away because I hit whoever it was with a music stand. And it cut through their shirt. I actually saw blood well up where the stand hit. Those metal things on the end that hold the music can be sharp. They hit like a pair of scissors."

"Yeah, so?" Nikki said.

"Last night when I was with Richard, I saw that he had a big cut on his shoulder. The same shoulder as the killer."

Nikki's lips pursed. "Did you ask him where he got it?"

"Yeah, he said he was carrying something heavy over his shoulder and got a scratch. He even said it ruined his shirt."

"And you don't believe him?" Nikki asked.

"Why would Richard have been carrying *anything*?" Eve said. "The only thing I've ever seen him lift is his saxophone case."

Nikki laughed. "Maybe he's got a new job working at the docks."

Eve shook her head. "I don't think so. And here's the other thing I realized. When Isabella and Erika were killed, Richard was missing. He either didn't answer my texts, or said he was busy. I don't know where he was when Anita was killed, because I was out cold half the night."

"Not exactly strong circumstantial evidence," Nikki said. She slipped forward on the bed and hopped to the floor to retrieve the bottle. She refilled both of their glasses and then slipped back onto the mattress, resting her back against the wall and stretching her feet out to the edge.

"Maybe not, but it's odd. Usually he's trying to get me to come over and sleep at his place, but on those nights...he was too busy to talk to me."

"Hmmm," Nikki said. "Well, maybe he just had classwork to do."

"I also saw that he has a pair of black shades in his wardrobe, and a black shirt."

Nikki stifled a laugh, holding a hand to her lips to keep from spitting the wine out. When she got herself under control, she swallowed, and with a smile asked, "Do you know how many people in this world have black shades?"

"I know it sounds ridiculous," Eve said. "But when have you ever seen him wear sunglasses? Or a black shirt for that matter? All of his shirts are obnoxious. Like the stuff tourists wear on vacation in the islands."

"That doesn't mean that he can't own a black shirt or shades without being the killer," Nikki said.

"I know, I know," Eve said. "It all sounds stupid. But I just have this feeling. Something's not right. When I touched that scratch on his shoulder, it was everything I could do not to run out of his room. What if it is him? The inspector has said that it's somebody who's close to the Songbirds. Somebody who knows us. God, Nikki, I've never been this scared in my life."

Her eyes were instantly wet. Eve reached to wipe a tear from her cheek and as she did, Nikki sat up and took her glass. She set both of them on the end table next to the bed and gave Eve a huge hug.

"Come here," Nikki whispered, and pulled Eve's face to rest on her chest. Eve was acutely conscious that Nikki was not wearing a bra, but at that moment, she also decided she didn't care. She needed the hug. She needed someone to love her and tell her it was all going to be okay. And that was exactly what Nikki did.

"I know you're scared," Nikki said. "But it's all going to be fine. In a couple days, you'll be back home, far away from this place. And hopefully the police will finally catch the killer so that we can all sleep better. Don't you think I want to know who took my Anita from me?"

Eve rubbed damp eyes against the soft warmth of Nikki. "I know," she said, finally lifting her head to look Nikki in the eye. "I'm sorry for being a baby. You should be the one crying."

Nikki brushed a tear from Eve's face. "Trust me, I've done my share."

"I'm so sorry," Eve said.

Nikki shook her head. "I can't bring her back by crying. God knows I could have strangled her myself sometimes, but…I have to tell you, I don't think Richard did it. I would already be out of this room and on my way to kill him if I thought for a minute that it was him. Have you talked to the inspector about your suspicions?"

"No," Eve said. "I would never do that to him unless I was one hundred percent sure. And like you said, all of these things can be explained away. I just feel…something's not right."

Nikki retrieved their glasses. "Have another drink," she said as Eve took the glass. "You'll feel better in the morning."

"You mean I'll have a headache," Eve said.

Nikki shrugged. "A headache is better than thinking your boyfriend is a murderer, isn't it?"

"I suppose so."

"Do you think you'll come back here when they reopen the school?" Nikki asked.

Eve made a face. "I don't know. I hope so. I dreamed of coming here for so long. I just don't know what will happen in the next few months while we wait to see if they can reopen."

"I hope you will," Nikki said. "I'll be here. I'd hate to think that I'd never see you again."

"You could always visit me in New York," Eve said.

Nikki closed her eyes a moment. "Anita would have wanted me to do that," she said. "She wanted to go there so bad. I would love to go see it for her and pretend that she was seeing the city through my eyes."

"I'd show you all the things I know she wanted to see," Eve promised.

"I'd like that," Nikki said. "I just don't know that I could afford to do it."

"You could stay with me, and you wouldn't have to worry about hotels," Eve said. "Assuming I can find a place to stay myself when I get back."

Nikki slipped out of the bed once more and retrieved the wine bottle. This time, she emptied the last of it into Eve's glass.

"Drink up, and then let's get some sleep," she said. "It's late."

Eve looked at her phone and realized it was after midnight. "Oh geez," she said. "I didn't mean to keep you up so long. She took a long sip of the wine and realized that her whole body was warm. The wine had caught up with her.

She set the glass on the nightstand and stood up. "I'd better go home," she said. "Thanks for listening to my craziness. I have to admit, I do feel better."

Nikki caught her by the wrist.

"You're not going anywhere. Kristina's gone. You're scared. I don't think you should go back to that room tonight. Stay here with me."

Eve opened her mouth to say no but her words caught. She didn't know what to say, really. She didn't want to go back to that empty bunk bed. She didn't dare call Richard for comfort.

"I didn't bring my pajamas or my toothbrush or anything," she said awkwardly.

Nikki laughed. "The wine will keep your mouth clean. You can wear one of my nightshirts. Please, stay here with me tonight. I'd really feel better if you did."

"Well, I...."

"Look, I won't grab your boobs or anything, so don't worry about it," Nikki said with a wicked grin. "We'll just have a sleepover, like kids do. And if the killer tries to break in, well, the two of us together have a much better chance. Trust me, I'll kick his ass if Richard breaks in here."

"I thought you said it couldn't be Richard?" Eve said.

Nikki got out of bed and pulled a long pink shirt out of a drawer in the base of the bed. She tossed it to Eve.

"It can't be," she said. "Now put this on and let's get some sleep, okay?"

Eve grinned. "I'll put it on in the bathroom."

"Why, because you're afraid to get naked in front of a goth dyke?" Nikki taunted.

"No, because I really need to pee."

"Touché." Nikki laughed. She walked over to her desk and pulled a key from the top drawer. "Here, take this. You'll need it if you have to go during the night. It was Anita's."

Those last three words hurt Nikki to say, Eve could tell. She realized how much Nikki had to still be hurting. Here she was being suspicious of her boyfriend and accusing him of being a murderer...when Nikki had lost her girlfriend forever. She couldn't accuse her of anything ever again.

"Come on, I'll go with you," Nikki said.

They left the room and walked down the hall together. When Eve stepped into the bathroom and saw those too-familiar tiles, she froze.

She hadn't thought of it until she was two steps into the room but... this was where she had found Erika.

The killer had been right *here* just a couple nights ago.

She had been here too...and had left covered in a dead girl's blood.

Nikki must have sensed that she was having an issue; she grabbed Eve by the hand and pulled her past the utility closet and into the room.

"Do your business and let's get some sleep," she said. Nikki pushed her gently towards a stall and then walked to one herself.

Eve took the one next to Nikki. She didn't want to be more than a couple of feet away from her right now. She didn't want to spend a second that she didn't have to in this room. She could see Nikki's bare feet on the tile just below the metal stall divider. She could hear when her water hit the water of the toilet next door. Hearing that sound of life gave her strength. She 'did her business' as Nikki had said, and pulled on the toilet paper roll as the commode next door flushed and the door to Nikki's stall slammed shut. She was done already.

For a second Eve panicked and wiped herself as fast as she could. She didn't want to be left behind. But when she hurriedly bolted through the metal door back into the open room, Nikki was just standing there waiting for her. Nikki's face was soft and caring, unguarded – unlike her usual sarcastic sneer. "Ready for bed?" she asked.

Eve nodded, and followed her new roommate back to the room.

She still felt a little odd sleeping there. But Nikki's bed was comforting, despite the fact that she slept on black sheets. Eve sank into the pillow and realized just how tired she truly was.

"You don't kick, do you?" Nikki asked, as she pulled the comforter up over them.

"I don't think so," Eve said. "But I guess you'll find out if I do. Thanks for letting me stay here."

"Thank you," Nikki said. "It feels good to have you here."

Eve rolled on her side, facing away from Nikki. After a minute, Nikki's arm slipped across her shoulder. Her arm lay across Eve's breast; her fingers draped loosely across her belly.

She could have flinched and gently shifted her off. But instead, Eve took a breath and relaxed in the embrace of her friend.

They both needed a night of comfort.

In seconds, she was deep in sleep.

CHAPTER THIRTY-SIX

Heavy Beans was packed on Friday night. Eve walked over from the Eyrie to the café with Markie and Susie. Richard had texted her earlier and promised to meet them all there, as he had an errand to run. That was a relief in a way. She didn't have to worry about him stopping by her room while she was alone to pick her up.

"At last you are here." Claude's voice cut above the din as they stepped through the door. "My Songbirds, come, come! One last farewell before winter, yes?"

The barista wore a bright pink shirt beneath his coffee-stained white apron tonight. He moved through the crowd and swiftly took Susie's arm in his own to escort them to the stage.

"I was so excited when Richard said you would all play for us once more this term before...I can't even say it. So horrible. But...in a few weeks, we will all be back to normal, won't we?"

"Let's hope so," Susie said.

"Do you want coffees, tea, something else?" he asked. "On the house. I am so happy you are spending one of your last nights here with us. All of us are." He gestured to the audience as he spoke.

"Does that mean we'll all get our pictures on the wall?" Richard said walking up behind them.

Claude laughed. "You are relentless. But I suspect this will be an amazing night. So, you never know...perhaps!" After he wrote their drink orders down on a small notepad, he disappeared back behind the bar. Seconds later, the familiar sound of the coffee grinder filled the café.

The rest of the Songbirds slowly gathered over the next five minutes. Susie and Gianna both gave Elena a hug when she reached the stage, and the girl shook her head. "Stop it," she said. "I've cried enough for one day, don't get me started again." She set her instrument case on the ground near her chair.

Eve realized they had all stopped and were just standing there staring at the poor girl when Elena looked up from the ground and waved them off. "Let's make some music for my sister tonight," she said. Her voice broke slightly as she said it.

As the horn players warmed up, Eve looked out into the crowd and saw the familiar faces of many, including Nikki. The goth girl's purple highlights shone bright in the reflection of the stage lights, just two tables back.

Also in the room, still standing near the front windows, was Prof. Von Klein. Eve wasn't sure why it surprised her, but she was a little shocked to see Mrs. Freer and Philip standing together in the back as well. The two of them looked sour. As she watched, they threaded their way through the crowd to a long table near the right side of the stage which still had two open seats.

And then Claude was back on the stage with them, his eyes bright with excitement. "When you're ready, I will introduce you, okay?" he said.

"I think we're ready now," Susie said.

Claude spread his arms wide. "Well then, let's begin!" He turned to the audience with his face beaming with obvious excitement.

"Ladies and gentlemen, this is a special night and I thank you for coming. We're here because of bad things. Terrible, unspeakable things. But music, maybe even more than medicine, truly has the capacity to heal. The Songbirds are here to honor those we have lost. Please sit back, and enjoy the set our Songbirds have put together for us. I know it will be spectacular."

He stepped off the stage then as the audience clapped. Markie counted out a rhythm before coming in on the beat with a snare fill. Susie joined him with a shuffling bass before Eve rounded it out with a piano riff in E.

In seconds, the whole band was jamming on a tight groove. Eve glanced to her left and saw Susie grinning at Markie. Richard and Gianna stood up and traded solos, each of them swaying back and forth as they punctuated the bass and piano with color. Even Elena looked happy as they played. They had all lost themselves in the music. It was the therapy they all needed. Claude was right. Nothing could cure the blues like jazz.

The audience was clearly picking up on the energy as well. Feet were tapping the floor and shoulders shifted back and forth at each table. If the bodies weren't moving, the heads were nodding. Everyone in the café let go. Many of them were students, some were faculty. All of them knew that this was the last time the Songbirds would play here for who knew how long. With that in the back of everyone's minds, nobody held back. They let the music take over their limbs and wash away inhibitions. It was a sonic catharsis that was palpable.

Finally, as the Songbirds reached the end of their first set, Susie stepped up to a microphone. "This is our last song before the break, and it's a special one for us." She motioned to Prof. Von Klein and asked him to stand up.

"You all know Professor Von Klein. He's known the world over for both his original compositions and his reinvention arrangements of classics. He has mentored some of the top classical and jazz instrumentalists in modern music, and we are privileged to have worked with him over the past few weeks this fall. We all look forward to returning to the Eyrie next year and continuing our studies under his tutelage. But right now, I have something special to say goodbye to him with. It's a new song that he wrote this week. It means a lot to all of us, because he wrote it with the Songbirds in mind. In particular, he added a new theme to it just the other day commemorating Erika, the last member of our combo who was taken from us so horribly. We dedicate this to Genevieve DuPont, Anita Strindberg, Isabella Neri and Erika Bolkan, our beautiful Songbirds whose lives were cut short so cruelly. And to Prof. Von Klein for creating such beauty for us to play."

Eve looked in the direction of the bar as Susie talked and saw Claude standing there with his arms folded. Out of everyone in the place, his face looked the most serious. When Susie said Prof. Von Klein's name, he scowled.

He did not like the professor at all and made no bones about it. He'd warned Eve away from him in the past, and she'd noticed that he made it a point to never be near the stage when the professor was there. He disapproved of the most famous member of the faculty at the Eyrie. What did he know about the professor's secret room of photography, she wondered. He'd warned her not to take pictures there. Why?

It was not something she could continue to consider at that moment. Susie gestured to the professor, who received a round of applause as the bassist returned to her instrument and gestured for Markie to start them off. Seconds later, Eve launched into the music the professor had just given her yesterday. It took all of her attention, because the beginning was highly dependent on piano. He'd written it to put her in the spotlight. That thought made her both warm and a little queasy at the same time.

When the soprano sax solo section came, Eve tried to watch Elena. She wondered how the poor girl could play this, knowing that it had been written for Erika. But Elena ran through it flawlessly. She stood and closed her eyes as she ran her fingers up and down the silver keys of her instrument. Eve marveled at her strength. The wound was too recent.

At the song's end, Elena had the final note. She took it with a quiet flair, raising her instrument up and then lowering her hands and head as she let the sound trail away.

The room hung on the silence for a second…and then exploded in thunderous applause that went on and on. Susie gestured to the professor at his table in the crowd. He stood and bowed, and then gestured back at the Songbirds, deflecting the applause back to the performers.

Finally, the adulation died out and Susie announced that they would be back in fifteen minutes to play their second set.

"So that went over well," Richard said. Eve looked up to see him standing at her arm. "Looks like the professor has a hit on his hands."

She shrugged. "Maybe, if anyone ever plays it again."

"Are you kidding?" he said. "He's a big shot. He'll have bands all over the place picking this one up after he puts it in the competition. Not only is it a Von Klein composition, it has a great backstory. Everyone will want to try it out. But nobody will remember that we played it live first." He took her arm and pulled her to the side of the stage. "C'mon, let me buy you a cappuccino."

"They're free," she said. "Claude's treat." Her skin crawled just a little when he touched her. She couldn't shake the memory of the cut on his shoulder. And the black shades in his wardrobe.

"Even better." He grinned. "I'll get you two."

★　★　★

The second set went just as well as the first, though the audience had thinned by the time they finished. Claude came on stage and thanked the band profusely, calling it one of the best performances Heavy Beans had seen in years. Richard raised his hand at that, as if he were in class. But Claude only looked at him and shook his head, cutting off the request he knew was coming. Susie and Gianna both stifled laughter at the silent exchange, though nobody in the audience would have understood the joke.

Nikki waited by the side of the stage when Eve finished gathering her music and stood up from the piano.

"Hey," Eve said. "I'm glad you could come."

"Wouldn't have missed it," Nikki said. "How are you doing tonight? No regrets from last night?"

"No. Not at all. Thanks for not putting the moves on me though."

Nikki rolled her eyes. "As if. You think you're my type?"

"I don't know if I should be offended at that or not."

"That's up to you," Nikki said. "But maybe this will help you decide. I'd like it if you spent the next couple nights with me before you go home. I just think we'd both feel safer. I don't know about you, but I have hated sleeping alone in that room these past weeks. Last night was the best night of sleep I've had in ages."

Eve was torn. "That's nice of you to offer but...."

"Oh come on. Are you saying you didn't sleep well?"

"No, I did," Eve said.

Nikki leaned forward and whispered, "And you're not going to sleep with Richard, right?"

Eve shook her head.

"Then stay with me this weekend. It will be like a long sleepover. There are no guarantees we'll ever see each other again. What if the school never reopens the Eyrie?"

"You're going to come to New York, so we will see each other," Eve said.

"Hope so. But—"

"Are you still talking about my solo?" Richard asked, walking up behind them. He put a hand on each girl's shoulder. "It was amazing, I know."

Both Eve and Nikki groaned and turned to face him.

"Are you both going to go over to the Waterhuis for a drink?" he asked. "The band is all going. We need something a little stronger than caffeine tonight."

Eve looked at Nikki, who gave a slight nod.

"Sure, just for one beer though," Eve answered.

"Only one? It's Friday night," Richard said. "And we've just played the performance of our lives."

"Okay, maybe two."

"Perfect," he said. "We'll take over the place."

He grabbed Eve by the hand and pulled her towards the front of the café. She looked behind her at Nikki with a look of panic on her face. Nikki shook her head, and silently moved her lips to say, "I'm coming." She started to follow them, and Eve relaxed a little, turning her head back to watch where they were going as Richard threaded their way through tables. Suddenly he stopped, and Eve almost crashed into him.

"Crap," he said. "I almost forgot my sax. Hang on."

He turned and hurried back to the stage just as Eve's 'new roommate' reached her. "Never fear, Nikki's here," she said quietly. "I won't let the big bad man drop a piano on you."

"You're making fun of me." Eve frowned. "I thought you took

me seriously."

"I know you're afraid it's him," Nikki said. "But I just don't think it is. If I did, I wouldn't be joining you for drinks, I'd be clawing his eyes out in the alley."

"I just can't shake it," Eve said.

Nikki opened her purse and unzipped an inner pocket. Then she pulled out a key.

"Here," she said. "It's my spare. If we get separated or something, whatever happens, you come back to my room tonight, okay?"

Eve nodded. "You win."

Richard rejoined them as Eve slipped the key into her front pocket. "We're all going to meet over there, because Susie and Gianna want to take their instruments back to the Eyrie. I'm thirsty and lazy."

"You're a guy," Nikki said.

"And proud of it," he answered.

Markie, Pete and Corey met them at the door and the group walked over together. It was a perfect fall night; the air was crisp but still warm as the breeze riffled dried leaves that scattered with faint scratching sounds across the sidewalk. The sky was a deep black that hosted a rich tapestry of stars, faint wisps of cloud and the moon rising to their left. There were no streetlights along the small street, but most of the old brick and stone houses had small lanterns near their front doors that twinkled with the glow of golden light through the trees and shrubs that bordered the walk.

Eve felt an overwhelming ache in her chest. She did not want to leave Ghent. She was afraid to stay, but she didn't want to leave.

Nikki seemed to read her mind. Her hand slipped into Eve's briefly and gave a squeeze of reassurance before dropping away.

★　　★　　★

The Waterhuis was packed when they arrived. No surprise; you could hear the crowd noise a block away.

"Let's see if anyone inside is nearly done," Markie suggested.

"No way we're getting a table inside," Pete said, but they walked past the patio umbrellas advertising Gulden Draak and the pink elephants of Delirium Tremens that topped all of the metal tables along the river and filed into the rustic plank building interior. Every bench inside was jammed with people laughing and talking. The place wasn't huge; the outside patio alongside the river had twice as many tables.

"What about that one?" Corey suggested, pointing to the left corner near the window. The people sitting around it had clearly been there awhile…the glasses were stacked three deep in the middle.

Markie instantly walked over, never afraid of being forward. He came back a moment later smiling.

"Good call. They're getting the check now…it's ours!"

They struggled to stay out of the way for a few minutes until the table cleared, and then finally claimed it when the group rose, waved and disappeared out the door.

Even with the wait for the table, they were already most of the way through their first round when Susie, Gianna and Elena finally peeked through the door. Susie's face lit when she saw the guys sitting in front of the window. A second later, they slipped into the open seats and joined the party. Susie and Elena sat down on the bench next to Eve and Nikki. Gianna slipped in on the other side next to Richard. The choice wasn't lost on Eve. Even with her fear that he was the killer, a pang of jealousy still grabbed her heart. Gianna never seemed to be far from Richard's side.

"It's about time you lot finally got your asses here," Richard said. "I think the latecomers get the next round, right?"

"Richard is just a cheapskate who doesn't want to have to cover everyone," Corey laughed.

"That's okay," Susie said. "I'm buying next round regardless of Richard. I want to thank everyone for all that you've done these past few weeks. And I want you all to promise that you're coming back when school reopens. We are *not* done."

Pete and Markie raised their pints. "We are not done!" they echoed.

"We have more beer to drink," Richard said, lifting a Westmalle

Tripel glass half full of amber beer after theirs.

Susie shook her head. "That's not what I meant at all."

He smiled. "I know what you meant. And I know we're all going to play the professor's *pièce de la résistance* come January together again. It's just going to be fuckin' frigid when we come here afterwards to celebrate."

Their waiter was a burly, bearded man with ice-blue eyes and waves of chestnut hair that touched his shoulders. With his red and brown square-patterned shirt rolled up to his biceps, Eve thought he would have looked at home in the woods. When he came to take their orders, she tilted back the last of her Delirium Tremens beer to finish it. Nikki's expression said she disapproved, but Eve defended herself. "Look, it may be the last time I have one of these for a long, long time."

Susie ordered some kind of Trappist Monk ale with strawberries in it, while Gianna went light and got a Jupiter. Eve thought of it as the Belgian equivalent of Miller, though it had a lot more body and taste. When the waiter turned to her and pointed at her empty tulip-shaped Delirium Tremens glass, she simply said, "Yes."

"I was going to order you a Killa Vanilla," Richard threatened.

"Over my dead body," Eve retorted. And then she thought about what she said and who she said it to, and got a shiver.

"So, what is everyone going to do for the next couple months?" Markie asked.

"Sleep late," Gianna said.

"I'll be binge-watching everything I've missed since August." Corey laughed.

"The funeral for Erika is Monday in Tortolla," Elena said. "So, I'll be there."

That put a damper on the conversation for a while. Everyone focused on their glasses. Eventually, a new thread began, and soon they were all laughing again. Despite her pledge to have one beer, Eve had four...and with the 8.5 percent alcohol content, when they finally all pitched in to pay the tab and stood, Nikki had to prop her up.

"You're going to be shit tomorrow," Nikki said with a smirk.

"Tomorrow is another day," Eve said and smiled. Crookedly. Together, they navigated through the now mostly empty tables of the Waterhuis. The head bartender had already announced last call. Richard made fun of her for staggering, but didn't attempt to take over from Nikki's guiding arm. Gianna leaned up and whispered something in his ear at one point as they all gathered at the exit to the patio, and Richard laughed.

Bitch, Eve thought. She'd never liked Gianna, and she liked her less every time she saw her talking to Richard. But then another voice in her head reminded her of why she shouldn't care. *Let her have him*, it said. *He'll probably stuff her saxophone down her throat.*

But what if she was wrong?

The rest of the walk home, through shadowed streets and dark, cobbled crossways, was a blur for Eve. Nikki held her hand, and clenched when Eve was listing too badly. When they arrived at Nikki's room and her friend let go of her to take out her key, Eve leaned against the wall with a smile.

"Thank you for taking care of me," Eve mumbled.

"It's the least I could do," Nikki said. And then she put her arm around Eve's waist and pulled her into the room to undress her for bed.

CHAPTER THIRTY-SEVEN

When Eve finally woke up, the bright sun of noontime was already streaming through the window. The space next to her in the bed was empty and the room beyond was equally vacant. Nikki was gone.

Eve grimaced at the ache in her temples, and hugged the pillow tighter. She had a vague recollection of Nikki holding her close like that during the night. It had been warm and welcome in the hidden hours. For a moment she questioned herself, but then shook her head. That was a painful mistake. But she had no feelings other than friendship for Nikki. The girl had been bitter and surly to her after Anita's death but she was glad that had finally changed. She didn't know what she'd have done without her these past couple weeks.

She slowly pushed the covers off and rolled to the edge of the bed. This day was going to suck. She had to get moving though. She needed to go pack up her room and get everything ready to ship home. She had decided ultimately to leave Europe and return home. And her flight to New York was tomorrow morning. She hadn't come here with a lot of things, since she'd had to carry everything on a plane. But she'd already amassed enough extra stuff since arriving that she would need to box some things up and ship them.

Eve found her clothes in a heap at the foot of the bed, and discovered her phone sitting on the nightstand. There was a text from Nikki on the home screen. She thumbed it on.

NIKKI: *Hey Lush! I had to run some errands while the sun is still out and you didn't look like you were getting up anytime soon. See you tonight?*

She answered quickly.

EVE: *You bet. I'm finally up and going back to my room to pack.*

There was also a text from Richard.

RICHARD: *Figured you were best sent straight to bed last night, but I hope we can get together today before you leave! Text me back!*

She didn't answer that one. Instead, she slowly got dressed and headed back upstairs. Her stomach was rumbling, but strangely, she didn't feel at all like eating.

It was going to be a long day.

★   ★   ★

She'd lived there for the past two months, but with Kristina and her violin picture and other things gone, the room felt strange. The lower bunk was stripped to the mattress, and the walls seemed bare. Eve hadn't put much up; Kristina had been the decorator.

Still, it took her a long time to pack. She was moving slower than usual. Kristina had left her a box of snack bars, and she nibbled through two of them as she got out her suitcases and pulled her clothes out of the wardrobe and drawers. She took a break after filling one suitcase and boxing up some of the souvenirs she'd bought in her first weeks here to take a sack of dirty clothes down to the laundry. She poured herself into an uncomfortable plastic chair and wedged her feet against the wall as the clothes ran through their cycle behind her. As the hour ticked by she zoned out, closing her eyes and thinking of everything that had happened the since she'd arrived in Belgium. When the washing machine buzzed that it was complete, it startled her so much that she nearly fell out of the chair.

While the clothes tossed in the dryer, she wandered back to the cafeteria to get an energy drink. She needed a boost.

It was weird walking through the lower hall and then the main floor and not running into anyone. The place had all but emptied on Thursday and Friday. Anyone semi-local or in the adjoining European countries had done as Kristina had and packed and gone immediately. As she walked into the café, there was one guy with dark hair and a denim jacket sitting at a table by himself. There was nobody behind the counter; only the vending machines were available for use right now. It felt cold...and lonely. The denim guy caught her eye and held it, unblinking, from across the room. The intensity of his stare was unnerving. His eyes seemed oddly bright, the dark eyebrows above them sinister.

A chill ran down her back and Eve broke from his stare. She turned, put her coins in, reached down to grab her can from the dispenser quickly and exited the room without talking to its sole occupant. She didn't know him and didn't want to. He gave her the creeps. What if he was the killer, just sitting there waiting for the building to empty before murdering again?

When she walked back into the laundry room, Eve realized how alone she really was. Denim guy was just about the only person she'd seen all day. The Eyrie was no longer a home.

The whir of her dryer was the only sound in the basement laundry and as she sipped her drink, Eve suddenly got a chill. She looked over the row of white, silent machines between her and the door.

She thought back to her fears in the cafeteria. What if the killer was still here, in the all-but-empty building? If someone came through that door right now, she could never get past them. And nobody would hear her scream. She knew Richard was still here today. If he was the killer, as she feared...well, he knew she was still here too.

A cold pit was growing in Eve's stomach as she watched the door. She could see the grey and white hallway wall beyond, the sterile harsh light of fluorescent fixtures lighting it with long shadows.

If Richard walked in that doorway right now without a mask...she might scream.

As soon as the buzz announced that her laundry was dry, Eve stuffed it into her laundry bag and all but ran for the door. Normally she'd fold it here but...not today.

She moved quickly through the silent hall and took the stairs back up to the lobby two at a time. When she stepped back out into the hallway near the front desk and saw Mrs. Freer sitting there a few yards away, reading a magazine, she took a deep breath. And relaxed a little. Panic Level 8 decreased back to a 3. She leaned back against the hallway wall, swallowed, and listened as the beating of her heart quieted. Finally, she pushed away and went to the stairs leading back up to the fifth floor. She had to get this laundry folded before it was impossibly wrinkled.

★   ★   ★

Eve ignored another text from Richard asking if she wanted to go to dinner, and instead decided to duck into the downtown river area to grab a last bite by herself. Ironically, she ended up eating at Mosquito Coast, one of the places that Richard had taken her, on Hoogpoort Street just a few blocks away from the river. It was an exotic café with rough timber ceilings and wide yellow hanging lights decked out in 'safari deco'. The heads of a zebra and other exotic animals were mounted to the walls, and giraffe-skin footrests and brown leather couches filled the lounge area.

She ordered a Monk's Café Flemish Sour Ale at the bar and a Ghent beef stew, figuring it might be her last time to have the traditional dish. The place was nearly full; the only reason she was able to sit at the bar was because she was alone. She sat at the left end, and to her right, two burly guys were gesticulating and going on about a soccer match that must have just ended. She didn't know anything about the teams, but she got the gist. Machismo in Europe was no different than machismo in the States. Guys always had a favorite team and passionately argued in their defense.

She sipped her sour and watched the bartender – a dark-haired girl with skin-tight jeans and a black t-shirt – moving back and forth along the bar, laughing and pouring. The girl seemed to know a lot of the people; either that, or she was just insanely sociable. She was actively taking part in the chatter of three different groups. The conversation all around her was thick, and not just from those groups huddled around tables. Even the people sitting in the big decadent leather chairs out front on the 'safari'-like throw rug were talking animatedly with those nearby; she didn't hear individual conversations, but together, the various groups made a din that almost drowned out the beat of the dance club music that was playing through the speakers overhead.

Despite all of that going on around her, when Eve's stew arrived and she took her first bite, she realized she could not have felt more alone. She had not known anyone when she had arrived in Belgium, weeks ago…and she had felt less isolated then than she did now.

Eve tried to focus on the rich savory taste of the stew and the tart flavor of the sour and the warm homey feeling of the room. This was her last night in Europe. And she had had amazing experiences here. She had enjoyed the nights at Mosquito Coast when Richard had been by her side, quietly rubbing her neck and back as they sipped their drinks on a leather sofa.

Back when she was not so afraid of him that she wouldn't answer innocuous texts.

She turned down a dessert menu, but ordered another sour before thinking about heading back. What a way to spend your last night in Ghent.

Alone and afraid.

Eventually, Eve paid the tab, and slowly walked through the front lounge, past the 'homey' bookcases with their fake rhino horns and old-fashioned globes and leather chairs and back out to the street. She followed a couple who leaned a little too close to each other every few steps back to the main drag, and then cut away from them to walk down the dark side streets back to the Eyrie. The air was chilled with the bite of fall, and she shivered as she picked up her pace. Night had fallen, and it was not a welcoming blanket.

She was crossing an empty intersection when she realized that she was just a couple blocks away from the Stadshal public square where she'd listened to people playing the outdoor piano not so long ago. The faint notes of something classical hung in the air; someone was playing it now. Eve decided to take a brief detour and walked down the street to see who was performing. It would be a nice way to cap her last night in Belgium.

The song ended just as the piano came in view. A teenaged boy stood up from the bench after finishing a Beethoven sonata. A handful of people loitering along the edges of the square clapped, and then one by one, the pianist and bystanders all disappeared in different directions away from the square. An older woman passed her on the sidewalk and then Eve realized she was now alone.

The piano now stood vacant, its top looking somehow forlorn as it reflected the light of a streetlamp. Eve could see people walking in front of St. Nicholas church just across the way, but otherwise, the entire block was deserted. She shrugged. Why not? She'd wanted to do it last time she was here.

She approached the piano and pulled the bench out; the legs made a scratching sound as they dragged across the rough pavement. It was dark on the periphery of the canopy that sheltered the instrument, but she could see the lights of bars and restaurants and the church in the distance. Part of her worried that it was too late to be playing, but…there was nobody around. And someone else had just finished. She decided to play something quiet. An old favorite. Pat Metheny's 'Letter from Home'.

As soon as the first notes echoed through the night, her heart warmed. The song calmed her every time she played it. Gentle, hopeful, a little melancholy. She played and forgot about where she was for a moment. The music drew her in. She took a deep breath just before the finale, and then kept her foot on the sustain pedal to let the last note linger. It brought a smile to her face.

But as the sound trailed into silence, the hair stood up on the back of her neck.

She was alone in the heart of old town. The song did not seem to have attracted an audience, but she had the creepy feeling that someone was watching her.

All of that good feeling from the music drained away as she craned her head right and left, suddenly very uneasy, looking to see if she could spot the source that had triggered her sixth sense. There appeared to be nobody on the street to her right or on the path to St. Nicholas at her left. Slowly she turned around on the bench to look behind her.

A shadow caught her eye and her heart stopped.

There was a face out there in the dark space where the streetlights didn't reach. Someone standing near a bush. A man. Tall and thick, stocky. His face was shadowed but long. His eyes were pits that glinted just enough in the dark to tell it was a face. Something made her think of Philip. As she peered into the night, trying to see closer, the face abruptly turned away as if not wanting to be seen, and took the arm of someone she hadn't noticed standing nearby. The two disappeared down a path that wound around a hedge.

Had the man limped as he turned? Just slightly?

Eve stood up from the bench and tried to catch sight of the man again, but he didn't reappear. After a minute, she took a breath and walked quickly back the way she'd come.

It was just someone enjoying the song, she tried to tell herself.

But that didn't stop her heart from pounding. She all but ran the final shadowed blocks back to the Eyrie.

★　　★　　★

There were not many lights on in the building when she turned down the sidewalk and approached the main doors.

It was all but over. A Saturday night, and nobody home.

No more concerts for Claude and Heavy Beans, she thought.

Eve pulled open the main door and walked immediately to the front desk before going up. She'd never asked Mrs. Freer if she could leave her packed boxes in the school mailroom to be shipped. She realized before she got there that the high-backed chair was empty. She stood at the counter for a while, wondering if Philip or Mrs. Freer were just through the door in the back office. But there was no bell to ring, and nobody came out. She watched the hallways of the school on the black and white TVs behind the chair. Long angles of shadow faded from burnt-out bright in the foreground to shadow and darkness on the far end.

She looked at each screen, trying to identify which hallway the cameras were in. But it really didn't matter. Nothing was moving in any of them.

Empty.

Just like this front desk. Maybe they were gone because it had been them, Philip and Mrs. Freer, spying on her in the public square.

The thought made her shiver. Why would they be watching her and not say hello? Eve vowed to call down to the desk later and headed back up the steps to her room. Suddenly she didn't want to be face-to-face with Philip or Mrs. Freer, if one of them happened to turn up.

CHAPTER THIRTY-EIGHT

Richard opened his wardrobe and reached deep in the back around his usual attire to pull a dark shirt off the hanger. No island prints for him tonight. He couldn't afford to be recognized where he was going. He slipped it over his head and then reached back in to the top shelf. There was a new pair of black nylons tucked behind a stack of shirts. He looked secretly pleased as he pulled them out, and shoved them deep in his pocket. Then he grabbed a pair of black shades and slipped them on.

Incognito was the name of the game.

He thumbed on his phone and checked his messages. After a moment, he frowned. Eve was still ignoring him. The last message he'd sent her a couple hours ago remained unanswered. He shrugged. He'd deal with her later. For now, he had another fish to fry.

He'd already packed a bag for this evening's 'catch'. He picked it up off the desk and slung it over his shoulder. Richard was halfway to the door when he paused, and looked back.

The saxophone case was still sitting next to the desk. He had no intention of playing it, but it occurred to him that if he was seen and recognized somehow…it would offer a good excuse for why he was going over to the North Tower.

He went back to pick it up. *What the hell*, he thought. After he was finished with her, maybe he'd play a late night saxophone solo just for laughs. One last song before they kicked everyone out on Monday.

Richard stepped out of his room and pulled the door tight behind him. He didn't even consider trying the elevator. Instead, he walked to the far stairwell and descended the steps two at a time. When he reached the ground floor, he took the hallway by the cafeteria to slip out the back door and avoid walking past the front desk.

The night was chilly.

Richard stood still for a minute, breathing in the cold night air. He was a little winded from coming down the stairs so fast. There were no lights out here around the back patio; it was as if he was all alone in the world. He couldn't stay here to enjoy it though. He felt the goosebumps rising on his arms.

There was a solid breeze blowing tonight. The leaves rustled in the dark trees overhead, broken ghosts of a summer past. Richard dug out a hat from his pocket and pulled it over his head. He wasn't going to be outside long, but it was another prop to make sure he wasn't recognized. Then he slipped on his gloves and began to walk around the North Tower to reach the main entrance. Everything else was locked.

His nervousness at sneaking around in full view quickly abated. Nobody seemed to be around. Richard smiled. This was going exactly according to plan. He walked up the path and pulled the old wooden door open to step inside.

As the door clicked shut behind him, it was as if he'd entered another world. The crackling of the leaves in the wind disappeared instantly.

The atrium was silent. He stood there for a few seconds, just listening. You could almost hear the air move.

Eerie.

Richard walked across the large open area until he came to the steps leading up to the third floor. With one hand on the rail, he began to walk up the stairs to Room 354. He considered how the evening might play out.

She would not be expecting the surprise he had in store for her.

Not at all.

CHAPTER THIRTY-NINE

Eve was out of breath when she reached her room, and almost didn't notice that something was amiss. She should have seen the gap, but when she reached out to put her key in the door, the door moved. It swung inward.

The door had not been closed.

But...she knew she had closed it behind her when she left. Hadn't she? She never propped it open, like some of the girls did. And Kristina, the only other person with a key, was long gone. The hall around her was silent. Eerily so. Normally there were doors half open, and the sounds of televisions and stereos and muffled conversations. But right now, there was no sound at all.

Eve took a step back from the door.

And then another. She realized she was holding her breath and forced herself to carefully breathe out. There was no way she was going into that room by herself. What if the killer was in there waiting for her? She pictured a figure dressed all in black, a hood and mask obscuring its face, standing behind the door right now, a long silver blade held ready in its gloved hand. What if, even now, she was being watched through the crack in the door? The hair on the back of her neck stood straight up for the second time in an hour.

As she realized that someone could be watching her, waiting for their moment to strike, she decided not to give them any opportunity.

Eve sprinted for the stairwell at the end of the hallway. She slammed through the door and took the stairs down two at a time to reach Nikki's floor. She passed the fourth floor and kept on going to the third.

She barreled through that door into the hallway beyond and kept going straight to the room where she'd spent the last couple nights. She knocked quickly when she reached it, looking back over her shoulder at the stairwell. What if the killer was behind her? What if the door opened again and a figure in black faced her here in the hallway…where nobody else was present to see or help?

Nikki wasn't answering.

Eve realized she still had the key in her pocket that Nikki had given her. She pulled it out and shoved it into the door. It didn't go in at first; her hand was shaking. She looked frantically at the door to the stairs. Still closed.

Then she focused, slowly steadied her hand and used the key to open the door. Eve pushed her way inside and quickly slammed and locked the door behind her.

"Nikki?" she called out, though she knew just by the silence that the room was empty. Even if someone was sleeping, there was always a 'feeling' that someone else was there. She found the wall switch and threw it, lighting the overhead ceiling lamp as well as a lamp on the desk across the room.

The desk and the nearby bed were both empty.

Now what? She didn't dare go back out in the hall.

Eve pulled out her phone and texted Nikki.

EVE: *Hey, where are you right now?*

The telltale three dots of a pending answer…did not appear.

Shit. She didn't want to just sit here all night waiting. And she didn't dare text Richard, because part of her still suspected him. She knew several of the other Songbirds had already left for home today.

Eve frowned, set her phone down on the desk and leaned back in the chair. That's when she noticed the torn plain white envelope lying at the foot of Nikki's bed. The front part, where the address would go, simply said 'Open Me' in black pen. There were three underlines beneath the words.

She reached over and picked up the envelope. It wasn't her business…but 'Open Me' was a strange way to address a letter. A folded piece of loose-leaf paper fell to the floor as she lifted the envelope. Eve scooped it up and turned it to see the writing before propriety suggested to her that she should not read what it said.

She read it anyway.

There were only two lines on the paper, written in the same heavy black ink as the envelope.

★   ★   ★

Meet me in Practice Room 354 at 9 p.m.
I have a picture I think you'll want to see. Don't be late. Running out of time.

★   ★   ★

Beneath the short note was a slanted signature that was a little difficult to read…but not so scrawled that Eve was left with much doubt.

Richard.

Her heart froze as her mind created scenes of Nikki being stabbed and strangled and tortured in Practice Room 354. She saw the cut on Richard's shoulder in her mind once again and knew with certainty that his injury was a cut she had made. He'd been wearing a black mask, but Eve saw the music stand slamming into the black-clad shoulder and the shock of red that followed.

The killer was Richard. And Nikki had gone to meet him.

Nikki was doomed.

Eve needed help. She looked at her phone contacts again and saw Gianna's name. She thought Gianna was still in town but… Gianna? There was something between her and Richard, and she didn't believe that it was simply a love of the saxophone.

She dialed the number anyway. A few seconds later, she heard Gianna's voice.

"Look, either I'm busy, or I just don't feel like talking to you right now. Leave me a message and I'll probably get back to you. Probably."

Eve almost hung up, but then blurted out, "Hey Gianna, if you care about Richard at all call me back. I think something horrible is going to happen tonight. Maybe right now."

She pressed END and as she did she saw the phone number for the Heavy Beans barista in her recent contacts. Her face lit up. She hit dial and a moment later, a familiar voice lilted in her ear. "Hello darling, what can I do for you?" He sounded slightly out of breath.

"Claude, it's Eve," she said.

"Eve, how is my Songbird tonight? You were marvelous yesterday."

"This is going to sound crazy," she began, "but I'm worried that Nikki is in danger. I found a note from Richard telling her to meet him in a practice room and I'm worried he might actually be the killer. I don't know what to do. What if he's choking her to death right now? I want to go over there, but I don't want to go alone. Do you think I should call the police? But what if he's innocent and nothing is going on at all? He would hate me forever."

"Oh dear," Claude said. "Richard? Do you really think so? This is a quandary. Give me a second to think...."

The line went silent for a moment. When Claude's voice returned, he again sounded winded.

"Here's what we'll do," he said. "I've actually been out for a walk and I'm just a couple blocks away from the Eyrie. Meet me in the front lobby of the practice wing, and I'll go upstairs with you to see if Richard and Nikki are there."

"Should we call the police?" Eve asked. "If I'm wrong...?"

"Yes," Claude said. "Better to be safe. I'll call them. I've got the inspector's card in my wallet. I'll let him know that this could be nothing but we'd love his help in checking it out."

"Okay, thanks," Eve said. She felt better. She wasn't in this alone. "I'll see you in a couple minutes. Thank you."

"Anything for a Songbird," Claude said.

Eve grabbed her phone and headed for the door. She hesitated a moment before opening it, but then told herself, if Richard was the killer, he was in the other tower right now, probably doing something horrible to her best friend.

That sent her barreling through the door and down the hall to the stairs.

She had to help Nikki. Hopefully it wasn't too late.

CHAPTER FORTY

The lobby of the Eyrie was still empty when Eve exited the stairwell and walked past the front desk. The glow of the television feeds behind the unoccupied chair flickered on the ceiling. As she passed the desk, they showed a series of shadowed, black and white empty hallways in the building's towers.

Nobody home. Anywhere.

But where was Mrs. Freer...or Philip? Someone should be minding the desk. The building was still open. Something felt terribly amiss.

Her heart beat harder, and Eve bit her lip. Part of her did not want to do what she knew she had to. The hallway to the other tower was a few steps away. She needed to get over there now. But she didn't want to walk down that silent, empty hall. Eve swallowed and walked in the opposite direction. It was just as fast to get to the North Tower by walking outside as through the interior. And at the moment, Eve felt safer outside this building than in. Even if she was only going to be out there for a couple minutes.

She pushed through the door and stepped out into the October chill. The breeze immediately kissed her face and she shivered slightly as she followed the cobbled path that led around the front entrance of the Eyrie to the side tower, where all the classrooms, faculty offices and practice rooms were. The trees blocked most of the starlight from the night sky, but enough got through to show the scattered leaves on the path. There were also a couple of lights on poles along the walkway which shed cones of yellow across narrow segments of the path. Eve hugged herself as she walked up to the entry to the North Tower. She had a sudden panic that the outer door would be locked and she'd have to retrace her steps, but when she reached out and gave it a tug, it opened easily. Despite the murders, the Eyrie had not broken its habits of keeping its building access open.

Eve stepped into the foyer, and the faint whispering sounds of the trees and faraway street noises disappeared. It was quiet as a crypt inside.

She walked back and forth across the wide lobby, stopping at each of the halls that led deeper into the building and turning back. She wanted to go up to the practice rooms and make sure Nikki was all right. But she didn't want to go alone. Claude had said he was just a couple blocks away, so he should have been here...or been just a few seconds behind her.

Eve pursed her lips, at a loss what to do. Every second that passed was a second that Richard could be stabbing the life out of her friend. She went back to the door and looked outside. When she didn't see anyone around, she stepped out of the door and back into the chilly night.

The leaf-strewn path and dark street beyond looked empty. Pools of light punctuated the street with occasional oases of light...but everything appeared still in both directions. Claude was nowhere to be seen. She felt horribly isolated and alone.

Eve pulled out her phone and called.

His line rang eight times until a voicemail message came up.

"Hello, you've reached Claude. Tell me what you need and I'll do my best to help."

She grimaced and decided to text him.

EVE: *Are you near? I'm worried.*

There was no reply.

"Goddamnit," she whispered.

Eve paced in the entryway for a few seconds, constantly scanning the street and sidewalk for any hint of someone walking in the distance. The area remained completely still except for the occasional falling leaf. A scream broke the silence. It was muffled, but she was sure that's what it was. Someone crying out in pain. It came from somewhere behind her. Somewhere inside the Eyrie.

That cinched her decision.

EVE: *Come find me? I'm going up to 354.*

Had that been Nikki screaming? She prayed it wasn't, but Eve's chest clenched tight as a vise. She took a deep breath and opened the door to go back inside the North Tower.

"Please be okay," she prayed. Then she sprinted down the hall for the stairs.

★   ★   ★

The third floor was as empty and quiet as the first...but darker. The 'night lights' were very low intensity, just enough so that you could see the walls and floor, but not much more. Eve left the stairs and stopped for a moment just beyond to catch her breath. The shadowed hallway to the practice rooms was to her left.
She glanced at her phone. Claude had not answered her text or call. What the hell had happened to him?

Eve stifled a tear of frustration and looked at the dark passageway beyond. She had no experience in karate or fist-fighting. She had no idea how she would stop Richard if he had Nikki pinned to the floor in a death grip. But she didn't have the option to prepare because she really didn't know what she was walking into. She didn't have a weapon, and she didn't know what she might be able to grab to use as one. This was improvisation time. She didn't even know where to start looking, but she knew she had to cover a lot of ground fast.

There was a light emanating from under the door of one of the practice rooms a few yards away on the right side of the hall. The odd numbers were on her left, so she knew that was her destination.

Her heart was beating loud enough that she feared someone could hear it up and down the dark hall. Eve was deathly scared. But she could not stop. Would not.

She grabbed the doorknob and held it for a second before making the decision to turn it. Then she flung it open and launched herself inside. Her only advantage was surprise.

There was a piano in the center of the room, and wooden floor-to-ceiling cabinets in the far wall beyond. The fluorescent lights overhead shone bright and harsh on the dark wood floor and black finish of the piano.

Eve quickly studied every corner of the room, ready to leap in and help her friend. And then she scanned the room a second time just to confirm.

While the lights were on in 354, the place where the note had said to meet, the room was empty.

"Fuck," Eve swore. It was unlike her to swear but she couldn't hold back her frustration. She had been sure thirty seconds ago that she was walking into a murder site. Instead, it was just an empty, well-lit room.

Where was Nikki?

She turned around and looked again at every corner of the small room. Nobody was there.

What if....

Eve refused to believe it was possible, but she walked forward anyway. Once she had the thought, she had to look. She opened one of the large cabinet doors that stretched five feet up the wall.

There was a tall stack of music books waiting within.

Then she opened the next one, half-fearing that Nikki's bloody body would fall out into her arms. But the result was the same. More stacks of sheet music and books.

The third one was actually completely empty. Just four wood walls.

The fourth....

Eve screamed.

Richard's eyes stared blankly back at her from the tight confines of the closet, his shoulders wedged against the wooden walls. He held his saxophone, as if he was actually playing. But there was a heavy coating of blood on the gold finish in front of his lips. And the instrument seemed a little too fat at the point that it exited his mouth.

Eve realized that the mouthpiece of the sax actually was touching the back of the closet. Someone had driven the instrument through Richard's mouth and out of the back of his head.

Blood dripped down the back of the varnished wood all around the dark wet mat of his hair. A froth of crimson oozed from his lips across the metal tube. His fingers had been propped to appear as if they were playing the keys. But Richard wasn't playing anything. Wouldn't play anything ever again.

Richard was very dead.

It took a moment for that to process. A horrible tide of guilt washed over her for her thoughts of the past two days. She'd fended him off and suspected him unfairly and probably made him wonder what he'd done to deserve it. Richard was not the killer…he had been killed. And then the guilt changed to fear. Richard was dead. Who had killed him? And was the killer still nearby?

It was only then that she noticed the thing pinned on the inside of the cabinet door.

A picture of Richard, playing on the stage of Heavy Beans. Spots of blood smeared the photo, obscuring some of the details, but it looked like their show from just the night before.

Eve undid the pin that held it in place and looked closer at the photo. Richard was soloing, the sax held out like a taunt in front of him. His eyes were half-closed as he focused on pushing the perfect notes through the metal horn. Who had taken that picture?

She stepped back from the body as the closet door swung slowly wider. Tears ran from the corners of her eyes as Eve stared at the frozen face of her boyfriend. Former boyfriend. He would never kiss her with that lopsided grin again.

After a few seconds, it occurred to her that she had come here not to find Richard, but to find Nikki. Where was her friend?

★   ★   ★

Eve backed away from the body and finally turned completely to walk out to the hallway again. There was nothing she could do for Richard. But maybe she could still help Nikki. The note had said to meet Richard here. But why? And where would the killer have taken Nikki after stuffing Richard into a closet?

All she wanted to do was run out of here, but she knew she couldn't. She had lost Richard. She couldn't abandon Nikki. She had to check the rest of the building, starting with the other practice rooms. Eve wiped the wet tears from her cheeks and left 354. The hallway was dark. A long path of shadows. The only light that allowed her to see where she was going came from the night-light on the ceiling at the far end of the hall. It gave just enough illumination that she could see the outlines of a couple of doors, and the reflection glinting off the polished wood floor.

Eve opened the door to the next room and flipped on the light. This was a practice space for winds – it had only a couple of chairs and music stands. It was empty. She flipped off the light and went to the next. And the next. She was determined to check them all. Her pulse pounded in her ears. If she took time to check every room in the building, she'd probably be too late, if she wasn't already. For all she knew, Nikki was lying in one of these dark rooms bleeding to death right now.

All she could do was move faster.

She checked three more rooms with no luck. As she exited a piano practice room, Eve froze. She'd seen something move out of the corner of her eye. Eve scanned the dark shadows of the hall and then stopped cold.

A figure was walking down the hall in her direction. A man, she guessed, from the pants and sports jacket. Something glinted off the light from the center of his chest. The lens of a camera. Why did he have a camera in the dark?

The lyric to the Cure's 'Pictures of You' sang in her head and then Eve finally made out the face.

"Professor?" she said. Her voice was tremulous. She stepped back a pace. "Is that you?"

The figure kept walking towards her, without answering.

Eve backed up another step. She could see the glint of the overhead light on his eyes. He appeared to be smiling. His hand was clenched around something. She couldn't tell what. Her mind raced. Was he holding a knife? She could only see the whites of his knuckles.

"Professor Von Klein?" she said once more. Her voice came out as a whisper. Why wasn't he answering her? He didn't stop walking. His face grew more and more clear. He was now just a few steps away. It was too late to turn and run.

"Why are you here?" she whispered. "Professor?"

CHAPTER FORTY-ONE

Prof. Von Klein stopped walking, reached up and pulled two earbuds from his ears.

"Miss Springer, what are you doing here at this hour?"

Eve let out a breath. Her heart was pumping so hard, she couldn't speak at first. "You scared me for a minute there," she finally said. "You didn't answer."

"Oh, I'm sorry," he said. "I didn't mean to startle you. I was just listening to a new recording by the Maltz Trio." He held out his hand so that she could see what he'd been clenching so hard.

An iPhone.

Eve felt foolish at the crazy thoughts she'd had just seconds ago. And then the reason she was here washed back over her like a cold wave.

"Professor, did you hear someone scream just a few minutes ago?"

His eyebrows clenched, as the professor slowly shook his head. "I did not," he said. "But I've been listening to this for a while. Are you sure it was a scream?"

"I'm sure. And...I...." Her throat began to close. She struggled to say the words. "...I just found Richard dead in one of the practice rooms. My friend Nikki was coming over here to meet him. I'm worried that she was caught by the killer too. I've been looking in each of the practice rooms to see if I can find her. What if she's lying on the floor somewhere in the dark, dying right now?"

His face grew deadly serious. "Where is Richard now?" he asked.

"In 354," she said. "It's horrible. Someone...someone drove his sax all the way through the back of his head."

The professor made a face of great distaste. "I will help you look," he said. "You've finished searching all the rooms in this hall?"

She nodded.

"Come on then," he said.

They walked to the end of the hall and were turning into an open area in the center of the building when the professor pointed at something in the distance.

"Did you see that?"

Eve tensed. "No, what did you see?"

"Somebody moving."

She peered down the hall and didn't see anything at first.

And then there was a blur.

Someone was running towards them from out of the shadows.

The professor stated the obvious. "Someone's coming."

"But who?" Eve whispered. Her whole body tensed.

A moment later, they knew.

One second, he was cloaked in shadow. The next his purple striped shirt and hunter green corduroys announced themselves before his face was clear. But just from the clothes it was unmistakably Claude.

"Oh my lord," he said as he slowed his pace and walked the last few steps to meet them. "I have been looking all over the school for you." He stared directly at Eve. "You didn't answer my texts, and I didn't see you in 354. I didn't know where to find you."

"Texts?" Eve said, and pulled out her phone. She confirmed that her account had no new messages. "I haven't received any."

Claude looked confused but then shook his head. "It doesn't matter. We have to get out of here. Now." He bent over and put his hands on his knees as he wheezed and gasped for breath.

"We can't leave," Eve asked. "We need to find Nikki."

Claude looked up at her with a look of utter horror. "We have to go. The killer is here," he said.

"Did you see him?" she asked.

"Not only did I see him," he said, still panting. "He tried to kill me! I was walking down the hall to the practice rooms, where you said you'd be, and this guy in a black mask and dark clothes suddenly came running out of one of the rooms. The only one in the hall with a light on. Where you said to meet you."

He lifted his head back and drew another deep breath before continuing.

"He came running at me with a knife in his hand. I have to tell you, I absolutely lost...my...shit when I saw the knife. I screamed like a girl and threw myself to the side of the hall. But he didn't quit. He turned right around and came after me with that blade. I don't know how I didn't lose it all at that moment, but somehow I started to run."

Claude closed his eyes and wiped the sweat from his forehead. "That's when he caught me from behind. I felt something cold on my head. I think he caught me with the edge of the blade and all of a sudden I was falling. When I hit the floor, I knew that he'd cut me, and all I could think was that I had to get away. So, the first thing I did was roll. And it was a good thing too because I saw him stab with that knife and stick it right into the wood floor. Luckily, I wasn't lying there where he stabbed it. But I'd been there just a second before."

Claude rubbed his fingers across the side of his head and came back with a touch of red on his fingertips. "Look what he did!"

"How did you get away?" Professor Von Klein asked.

Claude looked at the professor as if he were an imbecile. With eyes wide he said, "Well, I ran, silly! As fast as these legs could carry me."

"So the killer didn't chase you?"

"For a few steps, maybe," Claude said. "But then he quit. I looked behind me after a few seconds and there was nobody there at all. I don't know where he went."

"Well, I know where he's been," Eve said. "That room that he came out of? Richard is there. Richard is dead."

"Oh my God, no," Claude said.

"But I think Nikki is still here somewhere," she said. "We have to find her."

"No, we need to get *out* of here," Claude said.

"Not without Nikki," Eve said. "That's why I came here. To help her. I'm not going to chicken out now. She wasn't in the room with Richard, so she could still be alive."

"I was almost killed once already tonight," Claude complained.

"We have to look for her," Eve said. "I've already checked this hall...but there are a lot of rooms here. We have to look in each one in case she is lying somewhere bleeding."

"It won't take the three of us long to cover this floor," Prof. Von Klein said.

There were three more practice halls that emanated from the foyer.

"We have to hurry," Eve said.

"You look in that one, and I'll take this one," the professor said, pointing. "Claude, take the far one. If you see anything, anything at all, just yell and we will come. Meet here when you're finished."

"I don't want to die," Claude protested.

The professor looked at him with a harsh face. "Then run as fast as you did when you came to us, and you'll be just fine."

Claude made a face but had no response.

"Let's just go," Eve said. "Come on." With that she walked into the shadows of the hall the professor had directed her to. From the corner of her eye she saw Claude moving off to do the same.

"Don't be a hero, either of you," the professor said. "Yell if you see anything move." And then they were all in different halls, invisible to each other.

Eve opened the doors on each side of her chosen hall, flipping on the lights in each. The answer was the same each time.

Empty.

As she checked, Eve thought about the professor as much as she did Nikki. What had he been doing wandering the dark halls at this hour? And why did he have a camera? All of the distrust that she'd felt about Richard suddenly came flooding back, but this time, attached to another man.

For a couple minutes, she'd felt better about having Claude and him show up – she needed help looking for Nikki.

But...what if the professor himself was the one who had made Nikki scream? Assuming it was Nikki who had screamed. What if he had killed Richard and dragged Nikki into some other room to be tortured like Erika?

Her heart felt like an iceberg. What if the professor had intentionally sent her down a dead end?

By the time she reached the end of the hall, Eve did not trust the benevolence of Professor Von Klein at all.

There was a connecting hall that led to the faculty offices, just a few steps away.

Eve didn't even stop to think. Instead of going back to the foyer to meet the professor, she started to walk down the dark hall. She knew right where she was headed. A place she had broken into with Nikki.

The place where Isabella had been hung from a banister.

Professor Von Klein's office.

260 • JOHN EVERSON

CHAPTER FORTY-TWO

The faculty hallway was as dark as the practice rooms. But, just like the practice rooms, there was a faint light on midway down the hall. On the right.

Eve knew instantly that it was Prof. Von Klein's office. She'd been there enough. But what did it mean? She had just seen the professor; why would he have left his office light on? Unless he had taken Nikki back to the photo room?

Her footsteps echoed faintly as she hurried down the long hall past the darkened doors to reach the one that was lit. The one where something horrible was happening, she was sure.

Eve walked up to the door and her throat swelled. She felt strangled. Choked. Her hand touched the cold brass and could not move. How could she turn this handle and barge into whatever horror was inside? Wouldn't it be smarter to walk away? To board her plane home in the morning and forget she had ever come to Belgium?

She closed her eyes and shook her head. She couldn't do that. Even if it meant that she never went home again. She couldn't leave Nikki to die because she was afraid.

Eve turned the knob.

The outer office was empty. The professor's desk was to her left, the surface pristine; he was not a messy person who left papers and things scattered over his work surface when he wasn't there. There was a paperweight – some kind of insect encased in resin at the front of the wooden surface, and an ornate case that held two silver pens. Other than that, there was a computer monitor and an inbox with a few papers. The rest of the wood reflected the overhead lights.

Eve stepped inside and pulled the door shut behind her.

She looked around the room with fresh eyes, as if she'd not been there a dozen other times. The small spinet piano that she'd played the first time she'd been in this office sat with the keys hidden by the wooden cover, a batch of handwritten music propped against the wooden keyboard stand above. The walls were filled with pictures of various people; there were black and white shots of performances and faces, as well as color ones. The professor had been here a long time and his walls were completely obscured with frames and photos and small music festival posters.

As she scanned the walls, Eve's eyes lit on one particular face; she'd seen it before. It was hung next to the window that looked out onto the sidewalk outside of the Eyrie. She put her fingers on the frame and peered closer, trying to place the memory. Where had she seen this before?

And then it struck her.

This was a picture of the girl that Claude had refused to talk about when he pointed out all of the various famous people on the wall at Heavy Beans. This girl had been right in the middle of them all, and he'd glossed over her. Because, as Richard had told her, it was Claude's dead sister.

Eve lifted it from the hook on the wall. She was going to ask the professor about this girl when she found him again. Claude clearly had a grudge against the professor; she knew it from both his actions and his words. There was a story here, she was sure of it.

Holding the frame at her side, she walked over to the door that led to the inner sanctum. The photo studio behind Prof. Von Klein's desk.

Sounds came from behind the door.

Muffled cries. An extended moan. Her hand hesitated to turn the knob. She wasn't ready to face the killer. She looked around the professor's office for something she could use as a weapon, and set down the frame to grab a large metal trophy with a treble clef symbol. All she could hope to do was to clobber the attacker on the back of the head with the base.

She returned to the door and grimaced. She didn't want to do this, but she had to. Nikki might be dying right now.

When she turned the knob, it opened instantly.

Eve rushed into the room, the trophy held over her head, ready to strike.

But there was no killer to hit.

Nikki sat alone, in a chair in the middle of the room. She couldn't move. Her wrists were bound to the wooden arms with rope; a white gag covered her mouth. Her eyes bulged as Eve stepped into the room and her cries behind the gag escalated.

"Oh my God," Eve said, and ran across the room to her friend. She looked quickly around to make sure nobody else was here, but the room seemed otherwise empty.

"Who did this?" she asked as she untied the gag. "Was it the professor?"

Nikki shook her head. As soon as the gag was loosed, she said, "I don't know who it was. I was in a practice room and someone came in wearing a mask and gloves and grabbed me before I could think of what to do."

Eve knelt behind the chair and quickly unwound the ropes that tied Nikki's waist to the chair. Then she did the same for her friend's feet and hands.

"How did you end up in here?" she asked.

Nikki shrugged. "I don't know. Whoever it was hit me with something and I was pretty much dragged here. It was dark, and I was barely conscious. I didn't know where we were going until we were here."

"What happened after you got here? You're not hurt or anything?" Eve asked.

Nikki stood up and rubbed her wrists. "No, I think I'm all right. It's all a blur honestly. I remember being hit, and then blindfolded and gagged and being dragged along on the floor. I tried to get away, but...I couldn't move. I think my hands were tied before I really was back in the game."

"Did you see Richard tonight?" Eve asked.

Nikki's face twisted. Her expression was strange. "No," she said. "Why do you ask that?"

Eve wasn't sure what to make of Nikki's response. Something wasn't right.

"Because Richard was murdered in practice room 354 tonight."

Nikki's eyes shot open wider than Eve could imagine they could. "That's where I was," she said.

"That's why I asked," Eve said.

"Oh my God," Nikki whispered. "I can't believe any of this is happening."

"It is, and we're part of it," Eve said. "If we want to stay alive through it, we need to start figuring some shit out. Like...who the hell bound and gagged you?"

Nikki shook her head. "I wish I had a guess."

"Could it have been the professor?" Eve asked. "Whoever it was brought you here to his private studio."

Nikki frowned. "Maybe. I don't know," she said, standing up and rubbing her wrists where they'd been tied. She walked across the room to the locked cabinet. "Could he really have dragged me down the hall like that? But I know he's not innocent."

She tried the handle on the cabinet and it didn't budge. Then she reached into her back pocket and pulled out a pocketknife. She chose a thin file blade and jammed it into the lock.

"What are you doing?" Eve cried.

"I want to know what's in here more than ever now," Nikki said.

"You're going to get us arrested."

"I was just tied up by a murderer," Nikki said. "I am not really worried about the police right now."

She tilted her head as if listening to the cabinet and then squinted and hummed faintly as she jiggled the small blade in the lock.

"Well, hurry," Eve said. "The professor is on this floor helping me look for you. Or...at least he was a few minutes ago."

"Keep your panties on," Nikki said. "I think we've..." She gave a twist and grinned. "...got it!"

The door slid open and Nikki's eyes widened. Eve peered over her shoulder. Inside were dozens of file folders, each labeled with a girl's name. Eve saw folders for Genevieve DuPont and Isabella Neri.

Nikki reached in and pulled one out titled *Anita Strindberg*.

"Don't," Eve said. She had a horrible feeling. "I don't think you should open it."

Nikki looked at her with a troubled brow but didn't answer. Instead, she opened the folder. Anita's flirtatious 'I'm being naughty' smile was the first thing they saw. The second was her hand holding up her CBGBs shirt so that one of her nipples poked free. At the same time, her other hand was teasing down the silk triangle of a pair of black panties.

"She didn't," Nikki whispered in horror. She leafed through the next several photos, which showed her late girlfriend leering at the camera in various poses, tongue between her teeth, panties at her knees and finally, shirt completely off as she felt herself up for the camera with both hands. After the CBGBs set there were others, with her wearing chains and strips of leather, and red and black lingerie.

"All those nights I was worried she was hooking up with someone else, she was here giving the professor a free show."

Eve didn't know what to say. She reached over the files and pulled out the one labeled *Genevieve DuPont*. Her piano predecessor. She flipped it open and saw nudes of a beautiful blonde girl. Genevieve's eyes were piercing when the professor caught them looking right into the lens. In one set, she was nude but covered in red and yellow and blue paint. The colors were electric against her pale, perfect skin. She held the brush in her hand, smiling. Genevieve looked as if she were having a great time.

She pulled out Erika's folder and misted up when she saw a close-up of the Italian saxophonist's deep brown eyes and dark arched eyebrows. In the pose, she was nude, but concealing the most important things with her hands and arm. She cradled the brass mouth of her sax across the top of her thigh. The edge of a line of dark pubic hair disappeared behind it.

Eve closed the folder and put it back. As she did, she saw a name that made her take a sharp breath.

Evelyn Springer.

She pulled it out, and saw a handful of poses from the session she'd done with him for her promotional photo.

"Looks like he hoped to get a lot more than headshots in there," Nikki observed. There was a hitch in her voice as she said it.

Eve looked at her friend and was about to retort, but then she saw the tear trails down Nikki's cheeks. Instead of saying anything, she reached out to give her a hug.

But Nikki pushed her back with a shake of her head. "Don't," she said. "Just...not now, okay?" She turned away and brushed her face dry. "Let's get out of here."

Nikki shoved the photo drawer closed with a slam of her arm and walked out the door back to the professor's regular office. Anita's folder was still in her hand.

Eve thought about saying something, but refrained. Of course, Nikki wouldn't want the professor to keep those photos of Anita.

Eve followed her back to the main office. She stopped cold when she reached the door. Nikki had not made it past the desk.

Prof. Von Klein stood in the entrance, blocking their way out.

CHAPTER FORTY-THREE

"Exactly what are you doing in my office?"

Prof. Von Klein's face twisted in anger. He turned his gaze from Nikki to Eve. "How did you get into my studio?"

Eve hurried to explain. "The killer had Nikki tied up back there in a chair. I heard her crying for help, and I opened the door and found her," Eve said.

The professor's face relaxed slightly. Until Nikki held up the folder.

"Exactly what are you planning to do with these?" she asked, mimicking the professor's question as she flipped the folder open just long enough for him to see whose pictures were inside.

His eyes widened. "How did you get into my files?"

"Why do you have naked pictures of all of the girls who have been killed?" Nikki pushed back. "What did you have on them to convince them to do this? What did you promise them? And why did you murder them?"

"I did nothing at all," the professor said. "They wanted to do the pictures. I love photography, and the female form. And we have had some gorgeous Songbirds who enjoyed modeling. I just gave them some things for their portfolios." He sounded flustered.

"Anita didn't have any interest in becoming a model," Nikki said. There was a bite in her voice. "You had to have pressured her with something. Did you promise her better grades? Did you pay her?"

The professor shook his head. "She was a natural," he said. "She loved to do it for me. And yes, I paid her for her time."

Nikki launched herself at the professor at that, beating him in the chest with the folder and her fists.

Eve ran forward and grabbed her by the arms, yanking her back. "Stop," she said. "We have other problems to deal with."

She locked her arms around Nikki from behind until the girl stilled.

"Look at him again?" Eve said quietly. "His size, height. Did the professor tie you up in his back office?"

"Me? Why would I..." the professor began to protest.

"No," Nikki said. "I don't think it was him."

"Of course not," he echoed.

"Then we need to worry about who it is, because the killer is probably still in the building," Eve said. "I doubt he left you tied up without intending to come back."

"We need to call the police," the professor said. "If they trap the killer in here, we can end this thing tonight."

"They should be here any second now," Eve said. "Claude called the inspector on his way to meet me here."

"Speaking of Claude," she said, "this girl's photo is hanging up on the wall of Heavy Beans, and I noticed it on the wall here in your office." She lifted the photo from where she'd set it on the professor's desk.

"That is Vanessa Wouters," he said. "She was Claude's sister."

"But why do you have a picture of her?"

"She was an excellent musician," the professor answered. He clenched his hands as he said it. "But she died."

"What happened to her?" Eve asked.

"She committed suicide," he said. "Nobody knew that she was so unhappy."

"Was it really suicide, or was she killed?" Eve asked.

The professor looked shocked. "She took her own life. She was the first Songbird I'd ever lost." His face looked far away. As if he was reliving the death now in his mind.

"How did it happen?" Eve pressed.

The professor's face fell. "I don't like to think about it. It was terrible. So much talent gone. I had worked with her for three years and she was ready to launch. She could have been world famous. When they found her, a part of me died too."

Eve suddenly had an idea. "Professor," she said, "when did Vanessa die?"

He thought for a moment. "It was just over a year ago," he said.

Eve thought about the day she'd left New York.

"Could it have been August 21st? Do you remember?"

"That sounds right," he said. "It was just before the start of the term. I remember because she left a note that said she couldn't bear to come back here. She would rather die than start a new semester." He closed his eyes. "I had no idea," he whispered.

"So Genevieve was killed on the same date that Vanessa died."

Eve had a horrible suspicion that she knew who the killer was. If she was right, they were all in grave danger. She stepped forward, grabbed Nikki's arm and held it.

"We will call the police ourselves when we get downstairs," she said. "But we need to get out of the building. Now."

The professor frowned, but started to turn around to leave. As he did, a new figure appeared in the doorway behind him.

"Well, there you all are. I've been looking for you."

CHAPTER FORTY-FOUR

Claude stepped past the professor into the office. He pointed at Nikki and a smile broke across his entire face.

"You found her, oh, thank God! Where was she?"

"Right back there," Eve said, pointing to the back room. "I found her all tied up. We were just going to get her out of here."

He walked around Nikki, looking her over and shaking his head. "Well she looks none the worse for wear. It's good you got here in time. I didn't run into the killer again while I was walking the halls. But I did find this."

Claude held up a violin. "I found it in the first room I looked in, just hanging there on the wall. I'm kind of surprised the school would just leave one of these lying around like that."

He pulled a bow from his back pocket and ran it lightly across the strings. "It brought back so many memories," he said. Then he positioned his fingers on the neck and drew the bow again, this time, quickly moving his hand up and down the instrument to play first a simple, and then a more complex series of scales.

"Did you remember I played, professor?" Claude asked. He reached out and took the picture from Eve's hand and held it up. "Or do you only remember my sister?"

Prof. Von Klein looked faintly surprised. "Yes, you were a good student," he said. "I always wondered why you quit playing."

"Well, my sister was much better than me, as you know all too well," Claude said and slammed the violin down on the professor's desk.

He reached out and slapped the folder in Nikki's hand. "So, are you all here comparing photos? Who did the professor take the most revealing shots of? You silly lambs. Don't you realize that he is just leading you to the slaughter? He takes your nudie cutie photos and you get all hot and bothered and excited. And a little while later, he follows you down a dark hallway and throttles the life out of you." Claude looked at Eve and then Nikki. "Are you both blind? You're playing pattycake with a psychopath."

"That's enough," the professor yelled. "I would never have hurt any of them. I loved these girls."

Claude laughed. Bitterly. "I'll bet you did. I *know* you did." He grabbed at the folder of Anita and yanked it out of Nikki's hand. Photos of the dead girl in compromising poses fluttered to the floor. Claude gestured at the pictures and then looked pointedly at Nikki and Eve. "How many times has he gotten you to take your clothes off?"

"Never," Eve said. "I would never do that."

"This pervert is never going to get any of my clothes off," Nikki said. "And I may kick his ass still for getting Anita naked."

"Not if he kills you first."

Eve shook her head and stepped between Claude and Nikki.

"The professor is not the killer," she said, staring hard into the barista's eyes. "You are."

Claude's face looked as if someone had slammed it with a board. His eyes went wide. "Are you serious? You could say a thing like that after all I've done for you and your band?" He started laughing. "You know, that's the pot calling the kettle black. After you and your little Songbird friends have all been lapping up the professor here. I know what he does. He strokes your egos until you strut around like little showgirls for him. Then he takes dirty pictures of his proud little harem and makes you think you're all sultry little vixens, like you're daddy's girl... then he takes you to bed and all you can think is that the famous professor is showing you attention. Well, you know what? He shows *all* the girls that kind of attention. And then when he's done with you...."

He put his fists together as if grabbing a rope and mimed pulling it tight. "Don't you see him for what he is?" Claude backed up and pointed at the professor. "He's a predator and you girls all just let him lead you right down the path.

"How many times have you slept with him now?" he asked, looking at Eve. "Did he do it right here in his office, or did he take you to the practice room like Nikki tonight? Maybe she was still auditioning and wasn't quite ready for the office?"

"I have never slept with the professor," Eve said. "Have you lost your mind?"

"And I certainly have never done anything with this old pervert in a practice room," Nikki said. Her eyes narrowed to angry slits. "Is Eve right? Was it you who killed Anita?"

Claude put a finger in the air and shook it back and forth at Nikki. "Don't try to change the subject. Admit it," he said. "The whole reason you were up here on the third floor tonight is that you were with *him*. I saw you tonight in that practice room. I saw you with all your clothes off and your ass in the air. You weren't practicing a concerto."

Nikki's normally pale complexion turned a sudden, violent red. "I did not."

Claude put his hands on his hips. "You spread your legs in the practice room tonight, are you denying it?"

Nikki shook her head. "No," she said. "I did it. But not with the professor."

Claude's smile grew wide as a shark's. "Then tell us," he said. "Who did you do it with?"

Eve's heart froze, because she knew exactly what Nikki was going to say before the words came out.

The other girl looked down, refusing to meet Eve's wounded, expectant eyes.

"I was with Richard."

272 • JOHN EVERSON

CHAPTER FORTY-FIVE

Eve stifled a cry. She'd known what was coming but the words still felt like a punch in the stomach.

"You?" she finally whispered. "I worried that there was something between Richard and Gianna, but I never imagined you...."

Nikki swallowed hard and glared sidelong at Eve. "Why?" she said. "Because dykes don't like dick? I needed someone and he was there for me the way you wouldn't be. But I never wanted you to know. I wasn't trying to take him away from you. It would never have lasted, he just gave me what I needed right now."

Claude started slowly pacing between the girls. "Oh, what a tangled web we weave, when first we practice to deceive," he said. When he walked behind Nikki, he reached into his back pocket.

It all happened in a second.

Claude grabbed Nikki by the arm with one hand, as his other revealed a switchblade in the air. With a faint click, the knife popped up, and before anyone could move, that dangerous silver blade was lodged beneath the girl's chin.

"There's a reason she was tied up," Claude said. "You can't trust her. She may not be a Songbird, but I think she belongs with the professor anyway."

"Stop it!" Eve yelled. "Let her go."

"This has gone far enough," the professor said. "Neither of these girls have ever been models for me. So, if your issue is with me, let's talk about it."

Claude laughed. With a tug, he began to pull Nikki backwards. She grabbed at his arm, trying to pull the knife away from her throat. "Be still or be dead," he said. "I *will* cut you."

Nikki stopped struggling.

Then he looked at Eve and the professor. With a flip of his head, he gestured towards the inner photo studio door. "Get in there or I'll cut her throat right now."

They did as he said, and Claude and Nikki followed them through the doorway to the photo studio. He led Nikki to the chair and forced her to sit back down in it. Then he knelt behind her, keeping the knife at her throat, as he retrieved the rope.

"Stay still," Claude cautioned the others. "I think the time for games is done. I am not playing any longer."

Then, as he struggled to keep the knife on Nikki and deal with the rope, he changed his mind.

"Eve, come here." He tossed a rope at her. "Tie her feet to the chair. And don't screw around and make it loose so she can kick free. I'm watching."

Eve shook her head. "I won't help you," she said.

Claude pressed the knife tighter to Nikki's throat. She yelped faintly as a drop of crimson ran down her neck.

"You will help me, or I'll just take care of her right now," Claude commanded. "There is a reason I didn't kill her with Richard. She's not part of this. But I won't have her interfere. Now tie her feet up."

Eve took a breath. What choice did she have? She knelt down at Nikki's feet and pulled a circle of rope around her left foot and the left chair leg. She started to make the knot when Claude insisted, "Pull it tighter."

She grit her teeth and tightened the rope. When she finished the knot, he tossed her another length of rope and she used it to tie Nikki's other foot.

"Now her hands," Claude said. He dropped two more pieces of rope in Nikki's lap.

As he did, the professor began to move, edging towards the back of the room where his photo-developing equipment was. But Claude saw it.

"Eh-eh-eh, professor," he said. "Sit down. Right now. In the chair right there."

The professor eased himself onto another chair that sat in the middle of his photo session area, just in front of a backdrop of a beach at sunset.

"That's better," Claude said. "You just stay put there for a minute and we'll talk."

When Eve finished fastening Nikki's wrists to the chair arms, Claude shooed her away.

"Back up," he said, motioning with his hands.

She did as he asked, shuffling backwards to sit on the floor a few feet away. Claude meanwhile took the blade away from Nikki's throat and stepped around the chair to test the tightness of the bindings.

When he was satisfied, he stood next to the chair and shifted his gaze from the professor, to Eve and back again. He reached into a back pocket and pulled out a black ski mask. Claude slipped that over his head and adjusted it so that his eyes were visible through the holes. Then he pulled out a pair of black gloves from his front pockets, and slowly slipped them on.

"Is this better?" he asked. "Is this what you expected to see?"

"But why, Claude?" Eve whispered. "What did any of those girls do to you? What did Richard do to you?"

"Better you should be asking what Richard did to you," Claude said. "Sleeping with your best friend? Fucking her right out in the open in a practice room? I can't imagine what that feels like." Claude tilted his head then and put a finger up in the air. "Well, actually yes, yes I can imagine. Because I have felt worse things."

He walked over to the professor, circling the older man's chair. "Have you ever had your sister killed by a sexual predator?"

"Your sister committed suicide," Prof. Von Klein said quietly.

Claude turned on him, poking the knife in his face, holding it just an inch from the professor's mouth.

"You killed my sister," Claude said. "You used and degraded her. And the rest of your little harem taunted her and made her feel dirty and unwanted. They were all trying to be your number one girl, and they made her feel like a whore after what you did to her. She may have opened her wrists with a knife, but it was you who killed her, Professor Von Klein. The knife was you and your Songbirds."

"Vanessa was a beautiful, talented girl," Professor Von Klein said. "I only tried to help her."

"You turned her into a whore!" Claude yelled. "And when she realized what you had done, how far she had fallen, she couldn't bear to live. Her death is on your hands."

"But why kill the Songbirds?" Eve said. "Erika and Isabella and Anita and Genevieve…they had nothing to do with whatever happened between Vanessa and the professor."

"They were all the professor's whores," Claude sneered. "And they treated her like dirt. Did you know that your darling Richard slept with Vanessa after Isabella showed him the photos? He was as horrible as the whores. They all abused her."

When Eve said nothing, Claude nodded. "No, of course not. It was my arms she came home to, ashamed and embarrassed at what she had been led to do. They all made Vanessa feel like trash because of the pictures she did with Von Klein. Each of them trying to out-slut the other with more perverted pictures."

He poked the knife at Prof. Von Klein, holding the tip at the center of the man's chest.

"Do you know the day that she took that picture with the violin bow, professor? You remember, the obscene violin bow series? Playing herself for you? She came home and threw up that day, and then cried all night. It's been a perfect little setup for the old man, hasn't it? All of you Songbirds pulling off your panties and trying to give the old man a hard-on so that you could advance your careers here and beyond. Competing with each other for his camera. Well, I decided to stop it, so that it could never happen to another girl like Vanessa."

He walked over to the photo cabinet and pulled open the drawer. "You've been very busy with that camera, professor. It's a shame you didn't put that energy into music composition."

"Why all of the pictures on Facebook?" Eve asked.

Claude chuckled.

"I hoped that the police might be able to put one and one together and come up with two. But of course, they could not add. The professor was associated with all of these girls, and he was a photographer, and one of them was even killed right there outside of his studio, so the police *had* to find out while investigating that he was a photographer. I led them right to the murderer. And his photos. But was he arrested?"

"But he wasn't the murderer," Nikki pointed out. "You were."

"Shut up!" Claude yelled, brandishing the knife at her. "You were supposed to stay in that chair and go back to your life after tonight. You would never have seen my face. If Eve hadn't meddled."

"Okay, so I understand posting the pictures, but why did you keep posting the 'Pictures of You' song?" Eve asked.

"The Cure was Vanessa's favorite band," he said. "Anyone who actually knew her might have seen that as a clue. But nobody did. Why would the professor actually know anything about her other than that she had great tits? When we found her body, she had 'Pictures of You' playing on the stereo on auto-repeat. Over and over and over again."

Claude's face constricted, his eyes welling with tears.

"Please just let me go," Nikki said. "I had nothing to do with any of this."

Claude shook his head slowly. "Sometimes the innocent aren't really innocent."

He turned to Eve. "And you…you were always in my way, weren't you? The night that you were drugged? Even then you made it difficult. I took the picture of you grabbing Anita's neck while you were out of your mind…and you almost ruined everything. You saw the camera and screamed and I was petrified that someone would come running in to help."

"Why did you drug my drink that night?" Eve asked. "I had only been at the Eyrie a few days at that point."

Claude shook his head. "I didn't do that," he said. "But you gave me the chance to get Anita alone."

A quiet voice interrupted them. "That was me. I put the drug in your drink."

Eve's face twisted in surprise. "You? How could you? Why?"

"I thought Anita was falling for you, so I wanted to take you out of the running that night," Nikki said. "Eve, I'm so sorry. For everything."

Eve was overwhelmed. Tears were leaking from the corners of her eyes. She didn't know what to say. Nikki's deceit had stabbed her not once but twice. Deep.

Claude gave her a cruel smile. "Well that is karma, isn't it? She drugged you to get you away from Anita and made it possible for me to get Anita alone to punish her. Beautiful symmetry."

Prof. Von Klein chose that moment to run. He pushed up from the chair and started to dash for the door.

Claude saw the movement and didn't miss a beat. He dove for the professor like a football player, tackling him before he made it through the door into the outer office. The professor punched and struggled, but Claude subdued him easily.

Eve started to rise, intending to help the professor, but Claude pointed the knife at her even as he pinned the professor down to the floor with a hand on his throat.

"Sit down," he demanded. When she complied, he dragged the professor over to Nikki's feet. With the extra rope that dangled from the legs of the chair, he quickly tied the professor's wrists to the chair legs. Then he grabbed another length of rope from where it lay behind the chair, and tied the man's feet together.

Claude stood back from the chair and admired his work, keeping Eve in his sights.

"I didn't want to kill you," he said to the professor. "That's too easy. I wanted you to stay alive for a long time. I wanted you to suffer. I wanted the police to take you and lock you away, so that you could spend the rest of your years thinking about what you have done. But there are other ways to pay you back."

He knelt at the professor's side and took the man's middle finger in his hand. "It would be a shame if a world-class pianist were to lose the use of his fingers, wouldn't it?"

"No!" the professor cried out, and began to roll back and forth on the floor. But Nikki's weight in the chair kept him in place. Claude set the blade against the center of one of the professor's pinned hands. And then with a smile, he drew the knife towards him. Blood welled instantly from the deep cut, and streamed to drip across the professor's cheek and onto the floor.

The professor screamed.

CHAPTER FORTY-SIX

Eve dove across the room and clawed at Claude's back.

"Stop it!" she cried. "Leave him alone."

Claude swiped at her, catching her in the cheek with his knuckles. She reeled backwards with the force, falling to the floor as Claude rose from his crouch by the bloodied professor.

"I *will* leave him for a moment," he said. "Because now it's your turn."

Eve heard the tone in his voice and launched herself backwards, scrambling like a crab to get away. But there was nowhere to go. Claude was between her and the door. And now he was moving towards her, the blade held in front of him.

"This is where it all ends," Claude said. He lunged for her. The knife's edge passed an inch away from Eve's head as she rolled to the side. At the same time, she aimed a kick at the side of his knee, and Claude toppled to the ground. She came up on her hands and knees and launched herself towards the door to the theater balcony at the back of the room. With a quick turn, she opened the door handle and slipped out to the box seats. Eve slammed it behind her and then sat with her back to the door, hoping to use her weight to hold it closed. It was a temporary solution, but it was all she had.

The door crashed against her spine a second later. Eve wedged her feet against the metal base of the theater seat in front of her. She put her hand on the seat back to keep her ground. At the same time, with her other hand she tried to pull her phone out of her pocket. Could she call the police and hold off Claude long enough for it to matter?

She got the phone out and thumbed the home screen to the dial pad. The inspector was still in her recent calls list and she hit his number.

But just as the line began to ring, the door smashed with three times the force as before against her back.

As her body snapped forward, the phone shot from her hand and clattered down to disappear beneath the three rows of balcony seats.

Claude's foot had wedged itself in the gap of the door and now his hand reached through with the knife. The blade sliced into her back with a cold bite. Eve almost didn't recognize what the sensation was, and then it suddenly grew hot and she felt the wetness on her shirt. The weapon slashed again and this time she bolted forward with a scream and went down the handful of steps. As she reached the railing overlooking the theater, Claude burst through the door and came after her. There was no place to go. There were only twelve plush red velvet seats in this balcony, three rows with two chairs on either side of the center steps that led down to the rail. And it was too far to jump to the ground. She looked over at the seats below and saw a rope hanging down. It was tied to the balcony rail, and ended in a noose a few feet below.

Claude had already prepared for his final victim. Someone was going to hang tonight. She vowed that it wasn't going to be her.

Eve jumped onto the seats to her left and began to scramble over the tops, heading back towards the door to the professor's office. But she didn't make it to the top row.

Claude grabbed her ankle and yanked her backwards, banging her forearms and shins painfully against the seat tops as she struggled to get away.

"It will go faster if you stop fighting me," Claude said. "You can't escape."

Eve brought up her fist to punch him in the face. Claude countered the blow easily and then wrapped his arms around her waist and lifted her off the chairs to drop her to the carpet of the center steps.

"I hate to repeat myself," he said as he reached behind him with one hand to retrieve the end of the rope noose that hung over the balcony. "But I'm sure you know, a good coda always repeats and completes the theme. So, you will hang, just like Isabella."

"No!" Eve screamed and twisted from his grasp. For one second, she was free of his clutch as he held up the circle of the noose in the air, poised to drape it over her head. She punched him in the face and grabbed the noose with the other hand.

Claude jerked backwards for one second and then lashed out with the blade. It cut right across her shirt, leaving a long gash just below her breasts. She barely thought about the next thing she did. In that second, it seemed like the only course possible.

Eve grabbed the noose with both hands and before Claude could react, she threw herself over the side of the balcony.

CHAPTER FORTY-SEVEN

The rope held, but she almost lost her grip on it when it suddenly went taut and the slipknot contracted to squeeze her hands like a vise. In the end, that action was probably what saved her life, since the constriction of the noose stopped her from simply letting go. Her arms felt like they were yanked out of her sockets as the rope broke her fall.

"Nice try," Claude said from over the rail. "But you can't escape. You're still too far from the ground to jump."

Eve looked below and tried to gauge the distance. If she could avoid hitting the backs of the chairs and breaking a leg in the process, she thought there was a chance she could actually drop and get away. She carefully extricated her hands from the stranglehold of the noose, instead gripping the rope just above the heavy knot. Then she kicked her feet out into the open air and started to rock the rope and her body. Eve began to move in the air like a pendulum. She just needed a little arc to be able to let go and fall in the open aisle instead of in the middle of the seats. The only way out was down.

One swing. Then two. And three. Maybe one or two more, she thought.

"I don't think so," Claude said from above. She glanced up just in time to see him sawing the knife across the rope.

Shit.

Eve took a deep breath when she reached the upper arc of the parabola and released her hold on the rope, her legs pointed at the open aisle just a few yards below. She landed clean, her feet hitting the carpet first and then skidding forward as her ass slapped onto the ground with a jolt. Her body rolled, her shoulder slamming into the base of a chair. She screamed as the tumble triggered every injured nerve around her razor cuts. But other than that burning pain…Eve was all right. Nothing had snapped. She grabbed at a chair and started to pull herself up. Her butt and left leg felt almost numb. She knew she had to keep moving though. She looked up and Claude was not there. Eve limped up the steps from the front of the theater to the entry doors in the rear, grabbing at the seat backs along the way. If she could get out of the theater and back to the main lobby, she could call the police from the front desk. Maybe Philip or Mrs. Freer would be back there manning it by now.

She reached the last row of seats and started across the wide carpeted foyer to the exit doors….

The door in front of her slammed open.

"You ruined the coda, but this song is still about to end," Claude said. He held the knife in one black-gloved hand and began to advance towards her. Eve turned and moved sideways through a row of seats, angling to get back to the main aisle and run outside that way. But Claude was smarter than that. He followed her through the seats, but stayed several rows back. Pacing her. She wouldn't be able to go up the main aisle as long as he followed her like that. He was positioned to always remain between her and the exit.

Her hip still hurt from the landing but she forced herself to move faster.

Claude leapt over a row of seats and got closer to her, moving in time as she backtracked to the side aisle. There was a stairwell exit that led upstairs from backstage. That might be her only hope of getting out of the theater.

She reached the aisle and took off with a moan of pain. Her leg and cuts hurt but she refused to let it slow her. Eve made it to the stairwell on the right side of the stage and grabbed the rail to vault herself up and forward. As she darted around the corner of the proscenium, she heard the stomp of Claude's steps on the stairs she'd just left.

Backstage was dark.

There was an emergency exit light at the back near the door to the stairs which threw just enough light to see the large coils of wire, stacks of wooden crates and a ladder set off to the side. There was also a stand of costumes hung from a movable cart with hanging rails. She slipped behind that. It was close and hopefully would shield her from Claude's eyes. Maybe if he passed her, she could double back and start up the aisle to the back exit doors before he realized where she was.

Eve held her breath as she hid behind the frilly dresses and shirts and jackets on the costume rack. Through a gap in the clothes, she could just see the pale skin of Claude's face as he passed by a few feet away. She watched as he scanned the darkness, trying to find some telltale sign of where she'd gone. Eve struggled to remain silent as he turned around and around in the room, trying to see where she'd gone. The next time he faced away, she decided, she'd run towards the stage.

Claude didn't turn away. Instead, he started walking towards her. Had he seen her?

Eve's eyes widened like saucers. Did she run? Or pray that he passed by? And then she knew the game was up.

With a fast swipe, Claude pushed the clothes across the rack and opened a hole in her cover. She had just a split second to see his grin of triumph before she ran deeper into the backstage area towards the emergency exit light.

As she passed a tripod ladder standing near the back of the room, she grabbed at one side of it, and pushed it in Claude's direction. He dodged and the ladder fell to the backstage plank floor with a resounding crash.

Claude jumped over the ladder, but instead of staying behind her, he swerved to the right and went around a stand of boxes to appear in front of her.

He'd gotten between her and the stairs.

Shit.

"You're making this harder than it needs to be," he said, advancing towards her.

Eve danced back.

Claude held the switchblade out, carving slow arcing patterns in the air. From the corner of her eye, Eve saw a collection of percussion instruments just to her right. A rosewood-keyed marimba, a gong, and a half dozen different-sized bongos…. She angled towards them. She had to have something in her hands to help combat him. Anything was better than nothing. Claude continued to wave the knife around in the air menacingly. Eve kept her eyes locked on his as she paced slowly backwards. Neither wanted to tip their hand by making a run for it. And Claude could afford to take his time…she was backing herself into a wall.

At least that's what he probably thought.

In her mind, Eve counted down.

Three-two-one.

Eve bolted into the cluster of instruments and snatched up a wooden drum. She lofted it over her head and then launched it right at Claude's face as he turned to follow. The middle of the drum caught him in the forehead and Eve bent down to grab a second one. Before she could throw it, Claude barreled straight at her with the blade out. She brought the drum down hard, smashing into his knuckles. The weapon clattered to the floor and skated away into the dark.

"I don't need the knife to strangle you," Claude threatened. He grabbed and caught a handful of her shirt, but Eve threw herself as hard as she could in the opposite direction. The shirt ripped in half, separating at the seams where the blade had already slashed it and Claude found himself holding an empty handful of bloody cotton.

He dropped it to the ground and barreled after Eve, who darted around the black baby grand piano on the side of the stage. It was her piano, the instrument she used for Songbirds practice. Claude kicked the bench away and stood in front of the keys, staring her down from her spot just behind the back.

He feinted left and right and she did the same, but neither moved. Then he grabbed at the edge of the inside cabinet that held the piano's strings, and looked as if he was going to launch himself right across the guts of the piano to reach her.

Eve didn't hesitate. She sliced one hand to her left, knocking out the wooden pole that held the heavy piano lid up. The lid slammed with a crash and the theater filled with Claude's howl as the wood smashed one of his hands.

He stumbled back and fell to the ground screaming in agony at his broken fingers as Eve started to run for the door to the stairs.

The knife lay on the floor just a couple feet from where Claude fell. He scooped it up with his good hand and rolled back to his feet, still shrieking in pain. Cradling the wounded hand under his armpit, he yelled one awful cry of rage as he dashed forward, intending to skewer Eve once and for all.

She heard him coming and threw herself to the side just in time as he staggered past. One more second and she would have been dead. Eve rolled across the backstage floor. Blood from the cuts in her back and stomach coated her skin, and she felt the bare flesh where her shirt had been ripped away stick and gather the grit of the floor. Eve came up bloody and dirty, teeth bared in anger. Self-preservation and instinct had driven all fear away. Eve was determined to survive. Claude came at her fast, ready to tackle and pin her to the floor. Tears streamed down his cheeks and blood wept from the shattered bones of his hand, but his teeth were gritted in a look that said if he could get near enough to her, he would wring the life from her if it was the last thing he did.

Eve shrieked and turned to run, but too late.

The force of Claude's body smashed her to the theater floor.

"Eve, is that you?" a voice called from beyond the stage. "Are you okay back there?"

Claude's hand froze in the air as he looked to see who was out there.

A moment later, two feet walked across the front of the stage.

Eve took that moment to punch Claude in the face as hard as she could. The impact felt like she'd punched a wall.

Claude reeled back and Eve threw her body to the right, slipped out from under him. She only had a second to act before he recovered.

Eve glanced behind her. There were metal rungs in the wall that led up to the walkway above the proscenium where the stage lights were hung.

She didn't give it another thought. In three steps she reached the rungs and launched herself up the wall. Claude might be able to run after her, but with a mangled hand, he wouldn't be able to climb. Eve pulled herself up the rungs as fast as she could and just in time.

She looked back and saw Gianna walk backstage.

"Eve!" Gianna called, straining to see in the dark. "I got your voicemail."

"Get away!" Eve screamed, still climbing up the metal ladder. "He'll kill you!"

Gianna moved towards the wall. "I can't see him," she said. Her voice trembled. "It's all dark."

"And it is going to be darker," Claude's voice said quietly from the shadows. Eve could see from above that Claude was waiting just behind a box to the right of the ladder. He was readying to strike.

"Gianna, run!"

The warning was a second too late. Claude flew across the empty space and brought his knife down with a howl.

Gianna screamed and crumpled instantly to the ground.

Eve watched in horror. There was nothing she could do. She turned away from the scene and began to climb.

Claude grabbed at the rung with his good hand just a yard below her foot.

He wasn't going to let her get away that easily. He slipped the knife in his back pocket and began to haltingly climb after her. His broken hand made it difficult, but with each rung, he'd lock himself in place with the elbow of his wounded arm, then grab and pull himself up to the next rung with his remaining good hand. Eve reached the lighting platform before he was halfway up…but he kept coming. She walked carefully across the narrow catwalk. Heavy black metal lights were mounted on a steel rail all across the path. This platform was meant for a lighting technician to come up, adjust the spots, and then climb back down. There was very little room for moving. But there should be another rung ladder on the other side that she could get down. She peered down and saw the pale outline of Gianna's body on the black stage below.

"Gianna?" she called. The girl didn't move.

Eve was at the halfway point above the stage when she saw Claude grab the final rung and pull his reddened face up to look across the platform at her. He was just barely visible in a faint bit of light that hit the wall from backstage.

He didn't say a word, but pulled the switchblade back out of his pocket. He held that and also grabbed the guide rail with his good hand. Unlike Eve, he didn't move slowly and carefully across the dangerously narrow platform. Claude howled in rage and began to run across the narrow walk; the whole platform bounced. Eve grabbed on to a light to steady herself and then realized that he was going to reach her before she got to the other side. He didn't care if he fell. He was a human bullet. Nothing was going to stop him from reaching his target, and that target was her.

Eve got an idea. It was risky but...Claude didn't have both hands available to steady himself if he lost his balance.

Holding on to the rail that the lights were affixed to, she started jumping up and down on the platform. The whole bridge structure rocked and swayed and creaked. Claude staggered as the waves hit him, and instinctively grabbed for the rail to steady himself. The blade fell from his grasp to bounce off the wooden stage below.

He cursed but did not stay put.

At that moment, the stage lights snapped on. The change was blinding, and Eve grabbed harder to the rail, blinking through the glare to try to see Claude, who was down on his knees, holding the rail with his one good hand.

"Look out!" Gianna's voice called from below. "I thought you could use some light!"

When Eve's vision cleared, she looked down to see Gianna, leaning against a wall, one arm over her chest. Her arm was red with blood.

Claude cursed and threw himself forward once more, charging her. Using the pole as an anchor, Eve aimed a kick for his belly and instead caught him in the crotch. Claude grunted as her foot connected. The blow hurt. He fell face down on the walkway, legs slipping dangerously over the edge.

Claude grabbed for a metal strut with his good hand to hold himself steady, and then he looped his bad arm over the pole anchoring his body.

Eve turned to escape as he reached out once more, but a moment later, his hand grabbed her ankle. With a yell of victory and rage, he yanked as hard as he could. Eve fell to the platform with him. Claude used her body to slowly pull himself forward.

Eve kicked and tried to roll but the edge of the narrow walkway was right there at her face. She stared over it and saw how far down the hard wood stage was below. They hung over the far end of the stage now. Boxes and coils of wire and horn cases were lined there against the wall. Eve tried again and again to shake Claude loose, but he was relentless. His fingers grabbed at the waistband of her jeans and he pulled until his body was on top of her. His eyes blazed with fury. Tears and sweat dotted his forehead. In just a few precious seconds, he had managed to drag himself up and over her so the light of his manic eyes burned down on her face from just a foot above. When he spoke, drops of spit speckled her cheeks.

"It is time for your final curtain call," he growled.

Eve let go of one rail and smashed her palm into his chin. His head connected with an audible clang against the metal case of one of the stage lights.

At that moment, the front theater doors opened and a stream of people came running in. "Eve?" someone called.

Claude looked towards the seats and Eve took the opportunity. With both hands and legs, she shoved him hard. The force unbalanced him. Claude began to fall to the left as she scrabbled backwards and away. There was no place for him to land. He hung there on the edge of the platform for just a second. Just long enough for his eyes to widen and his arm to reach out with his broken hand to grab at her to stop his fall.

But the first thing his fingers touched was the edge of one of the foot-wide stage lights, which had heated up as soon as Gianna flipped it on. He yanked his hand away with a yell as the light burned him and grabbed instinctively at the pole with his broken hand instead. But as his fingers tried to clench, the pain of the bones grinding made him scream and let go. Instead of salvaging his purchase, both of Claude's hands reached into the empty open air, and he slipped through the bars to plummet away from Eve.

A second later, his body hit with a wet, solid smack that echoed off the black wooden floor below.

Eve looked over the edge of the catwalk, and saw him stretched out like a broken doll, face down on the floor, a music stand next to his head.

Inspector Martino was leading a handful of police officers down the main aisle of the theater. Eve let out a breath, and pressed her face down on the cold steel walkway to rest for a minute. Her arms were shaking as if she were bitter cold and she didn't know if she had the strength yet to get up. There were steady thuds coming from the wall at the end of the catwalk. Someone was climbing the rungs already to get to her.

"Eve, are you okay?" the inspector called from below.

"Yes, Inspector," she answered slowly. "I think I'm going to be just fine now."

She closed her eyes as a wave of complete exhaustion overwhelmed her. Eve felt her entire body go limp, but just then, hands grabbed at her arms and began to drag her towards the rungs.

"Come on," a voice said. "Let's get you someplace a little safer. This is no place for a nap."

CHAPTER FORTY-EIGHT

"Do you know who it is?" the inspector asked as one of his men helped Eve off the ladder and escorted her to the body a few yards away.

Eve nodded, just as one of the men turned the body over.

She had to look away. Claude's face looked like it had been smashed by a bat. One of the men pointed at a pyramid-shaped piece of wood that stuck out of the center of his chest. It appeared as if someone had pounded a stake into his heart.

"What is *that*?" the policeman asked. "Whatever it is, this guy took it like a bullet."

The inspector pulled a handkerchief from his pocket and put it over his fingers. Then he reached down and carefully extricated the object from the gory wound in Claude's chest. He set it down gingerly next to the body. Blood dripped from the tip of the wooden triangle point down the four flat widening sides.

"It's a metronome," Eve said. "Someone must have been using it on the floor here next to them while they were practicing."

The policeman grimaced and shook his head in disgust.

"His name was Claude," Eve said, looking away from the ragged face and into the inspector's eyes. "He ran a coffee shop nearby."

"Heavy Beans Claude?" Inspector Martino said. His face looked dumbfounded.

"Yeah," she said. "Apparently he had a grudge against Professor Von Klein." Her eyes widened as she said it and realized the professor was still likely upstairs bleeding. "Speaking of which, someone needs to go upstairs right now." She pointed at the balcony. "The professor and a girl named Nikki are both tied up in the professor's office."

The inspector motioned at two of his men and they ran back off the stage and up the aisle to exit the theater.

Eve turned then to look for Gianna. One of Martino's officers was crouched next to her where she sat, leaning with her back against the stage left proscenium.

"I'm so sorry," Eve said, and dropped to her knees in front of Gianna. "I didn't want you to get hurt."

Gianna raised an eyebrow. "I'm not too excited about it either. But when I heard your message, I knew something was really wrong. I called and called and your line was busy, so I started looking for you. I tried your room, Richard's room, and then came over here. That's when I heard you scream."

"Thanks," Eve said. "You probably saved my life. I just wish you hadn't gotten hurt doing it."

Gianna shrugged, and then moaned at the pain. "Serves me right," she said. "Karma sucks."

"What do you mean?"

"Remember that first day you joined the Songbirds?" Gianna asked. "Remember that dead canary on the piano? That was my gift."

"But why?" Eve said.

"I thought it would be funny," Gianna said. "Look, I'm a bitch, okay?"

Eve shook her head. "You're not. I always thought you hated me, but figured it was because of Richard."

"No," Gianna said. "I just couldn't see anyone filling Gen's shoes. I didn't want anyone else to." Her eyes narrowed then, and she looked hard at Eve. "You said Richard was in trouble on the phone. Where is he?"

Eve's throat constricted. She didn't want to say the words, but somehow she forced them out.

"Claude got to him before I did," Eve said. "He's…lying in a closet in practice room 354."

Tears welled up in Gianna's eyes, and she hid her face in her hand.

"I'm sorry," Eve whispered.

Inspector Martino put a hand on Eve's shoulder. "I'm sorry we didn't get here sooner," he said.

Eve turned away to give Gianna the privacy to cry. She rose slowly. "How did you find me at all?" she asked.

"You left a pretty good cry for help," Inspector Martino said.

She looked confused. "What do you mean?"

"Didn't you call me twenty or thirty minutes ago?" he asked.

"Yeah," she said. "At least I tried to. But then I dropped the phone under one of the seats up there." She pointed at the balcony.

The inspector held his phone up for her to see. It showed Eve's phone number in the window as a live call.

"Well, the call went through," he said. "And you've been broadcasting your entire ordeal this whole time. I traced the location of the phone and came as fast as I could."

EPILOGUE

"Do you think it's still appropriate to play this?" Markie asked from behind the drum kit. "I mean, with the professor kicked out of the Eyrie, should we really be celebrating one of his songs at the holiday concert?"

When the reasons for Claude's murder spree had come to light last month, the university's board of regents had made the decision to sever ties from their most famous faculty member with very little deliberation. He was 'gone' before the doors reopened to the Eyrie's dormitory and practice rooms a week after Claude's death. Philip and Mrs. Freer had also disappeared in the interim. Rumors were that Mrs. Freer's husband had come home early one day to find them both in his bed; with the school temporarily closed, they'd had no other place to carry on their unseemly affair.

Their bassist and de facto leader shook her head at Markie's question immediately.

"We're not celebrating Professor Von Klein with this piece," Susie said. "Art is a separate and distinct thing from the artist. We're paying tribute to Erika and all of the Songbirds we lost with a song that was written for them. I don't think I'll focus on where the song came from though when I introduce it at the show."

Eve swiveled on the bench from facing the piano to look at the rest of the Songbirds. It was mid-December and they were onstage in the theater prepping for an all-school concert to celebrate the holidays and the end of term. She still couldn't stop herself from looking up at the balcony that jutted out over the seats from the rear of Von Klein's former office. As always, since classes had resumed, its seats remained dark.

The complexion of the band had changed somewhat in the past few weeks. Elena had not come back to the Eyrie from Italy after her sister's funeral. Eve's roommate, Kristina, now sat in her chair instead. It had been a bit of a hard sell to convince the band to consider adding violin to the combo, but Eve had asked them to listen to Kristina play and then put it to a blind vote...and after the Brit's saucy audition, in the end, they decided almost unanimously to see what it would be like to have a violin playing some of the lead soprano saxophone lines.

Another familiar pale face topped with a crop of jagged-cut purple hair sat next to Gianna in Richard's place. It was an uneasy, fraught-with-unpleasant-meaning substitution for Eve and she still wasn't sure how she felt about having Nikki playing saxophone in the group. There were times she hated Richard for cheating on her with Nikki, and times she blamed Nikki for luring Richard to the practice rooms and ultimately, his death. There were times she wanted to forget she'd ever met either of them. But Nikki had pleaded with her, as much as a taciturn goth could, to forgive her. And she was trying.

Eve didn't take her eyes off Nikki's face as she spoke to support Susie's point.

"You can do deplorable and disgusting things in your personal life and still make beautiful music," she said. "He wrote this piece for us, and for the ones we lost. And it's an amazing tribute. I think we let the music speak for itself. It's the music that will live on after all of us."

"'Nuf said," Markie answered. "I think we play it." He looked at Susie, who readied herself at the bass.

"Once more, from the top," Susie said, and Markie counted off.

"One, two, three...."

Eve's fingers hit the keys and the reason she had come to Belgium bled from her fingers to echo throughout the empty theater. The notes ran and played, skipped and trilled, laughed and cried as she rolled and slammed and accented the honks and calls of the brass behind her. Von Klein's piece captured the chaos of storms and the brilliant beauty of a sunny morning, all in one amalgam of interwoven emotional themes. Maybe it was forbidden passions that, in the end, generated this work,

296 • JOHN EVERSON

but it was a work that even with all of the dark meanings it held for her, she believed should be played.

And played by this group in particular.

A familiar saxophone lead that had once been shepherded by Richard rose to solo with a confident sensuality above the rhythm. She still didn't know if she loved or hated Nikki, but had to concede without question that the girl could play.

And *should* play this theme.

Eve smiled through the blur of conflicting emotions and then let the song swallow her. It had always been this way for her and it was no different now. The song engulfed and transported her. It made the world, with all of its pain and uncertainty, worth living in. The past faded away.

The music was all that mattered.

FLAME TREE PRESS
FICTION WITHOUT FRONTIERS
Award-Winning Authors & Original Voices

Flame Tree Press is the trade fiction imprint of Flame Tree
Publishing, focusing on excellent writing in horror and the
supernatural, crime and mystery, science fiction and fantasy.
Our aim is to explore beyond the boundaries of the everyday,
with tales from both award-winning authors and original voices.

•

Other titles available by John Everson:
The House by the Cemetery
The Devil's Equinox
Voodoo Heart

Other horror and suspense titles available include:
Snowball by Gregory Bastianelli
Thirteen Days by Sunset Beach by Ramsey Campbell
Think Yourself Lucky by Ramsey Campbell
The Hungry Moon by Ramsey Campbell
Hellrider by JG Faherty
The Toy Thief by D.W. Gillespie
One By One by D.W. Gillespie
Black Wings by Megan Hart
The Playing Card Killer by Russell James
The Portal by Russell James
The Sorrows by Jonathan Janz
Castle of Sorrows by Jonathan Janz
The Dark Game by Jonathan Janz
Will Haunt You by Brian Kirk
We Are Monsters by Brian Kirk
Those Who Came Before by J.H. Moncrieff
Stoker's Wilde by Steven Hopstaken & Melissa Prusi
Stoker's Wilde West by Steven Hopstaken & Melissa Prusi
Creature by Hunter Shea
Ghost Mine by Hunter Shea
Slash by Hunter Shea
The Mouth of the Dark by Tim Waggoner
They Kill by Tim Waggoner

•

Join our mailing list for free short stories, new release details,
news about our authors and special promotions:

flametreepress.com